For my mother-in-law, Nan McRoberts, with love.

For my mother, Imtiaz Jafar Mohideen, with love

THE WINTER GROUND

Catriona McPherson

WINDSOR
PARAGON

First published 2008
by Hodder & Stoughton
This Large Print edition published 2009
by BBC Audiobooks Ltd
by arrangement with
Hodder & Stoughton Ltd

Hardcover ISBN: 978 1 408 42947 1
Softcover   ISBN: 978 1 408 42948 8

British Library Cataloguing in Publication Data available

Printed and bound in Great Britain by
CPI Antony Rowe, Chippenham and Eastbourne

I would like to thank:

Alex Bonham, Linda Clifford and all at Kellie Castle, Katie Davison, Louise Kelly, Antigone Konstantinidou, Catherine and Olivier Lepreux (for the man-eating tiger), Neil McRoberts, Lisa Moylett, Chris Silas Neal, Imogen Olsen and Bronwen Salter-Murison.

Prologue

Twelve black horses spanned the ring, nodding and snorting, six to either side, with their master a splash of blood red and ink black at the centre where the whip kept cracking. Just beyond its reach, the Risley man lay back on his trestle bench, knees working like pistons and satin straining across his thighs as he threw the little girls in their tutus up into the air and caught them again. The girls flashed their eyes and snapped their arms at each cymbal crash, each landing. The clowns, in their spots and stripes and checks, racing along on the ring fence, held high the paper hoops, and the grey horse cantering hard around the edge ducked its head as the girl on its back leapt clear, broke through and landed again, her powdered feet curling on to her horse's broad rump, her arms floating outwards as gently as her feathers, her smile serene. The spangled figure high in the dome swung and spun, plummeting downwards as the coils around her body unfurled, her toes pointed, the arch of her neck elegant and the tilt of her chin as delicate as a child's.

Where to look first? What to feel? Not for nothing was this called The Spectacular, where every sight and sound conspired to overwhelm the senses, excite children beyond any hope of sleep that night, pluck the grown-ups out of their slouches and back to clamorous wonder, enrapture all and keep them saucer-eyed and thrumming.

Look closer though and the bones were revealed. Nothing wasted, nothing left unseen.

1

While the spangled girl spun and every eye marvelled at her, the bare-back rider stood square and let her feathers stream. When the rider leapt, the clowns skipped along the ring fence to their spotlit marks. While the clowns tumbled and turned their clumsy cartwheels, the little girls waited, moving only to keep their balance true. When the girls rolled and flipped, the horses trotted quietly on until, at another crack of the whip, they reared up, kicking out their hooves, and every eye was drawn to them, no one looking at the spangled girl as she climbed with steady grip and slowly coiled the rope around herself again.

1

Twice a year, for a week or so, for half an hour each day, it is easy to feel glad to be in Perthshire. Between one morning and the next, when spring is unfurling, the beech walk between the edge of the park and the cottages becomes a sort of hushed nave where the sunlit green of new leaves against the filigree can lift the hearts and calm the minds of all who pass along it. And then again, when summer gives its first sigh and begins gently to sink into autumn, one day the green will turn to gold and the breeze will shake a few golden shingles free, sending them spiralling downwards and letting the sunshine dazzle through the pinprick holes in the canopy, so that one wants to stand in the dappling light and raise one's face to heaven, feeling the leaves brush past as they fall.

Today was not one of those days. A particularly gusty November had seen off the last leaf weeks ago and now the bare branches, black and slick, offered no shelter but instead only organised the raindrops into larger servings, the better to soak Bunty and me as we plodded underneath.

For all the murk and chill, though, I had been eager to set out on our walk this morning. My husband, over breakfast, had been waxing political again.

'Our days are numbered,' he had begun, from behind *The Times*, after a hefty sigh.

'Everyone's days are numbered,' I replied, hoping to offend him with my frivolity and avoid an out-and-out conversation.

3

'Well, you laugh while you can,' said Hugh, bending his newspaper down to look at me, 'but mark my words, we won't survive this, not this time. It will be upon us before we know what's hit us and we will all be swept away.' Hugh could find in the most blameless little *Times* leader sure signs of revolution blowing in like a ice-storm from the east and engulfing Perthshire. 'Lenin—' he went on, but I nipped it in the bud, for when he got as far as Lenin there was no stopping him.

'—is dead,' I said.

'—has more people coming to visit his tomb every month, it says here,' said Hugh, ignoring me.

'Why not stick to the national news at breakfast?' I suggested. 'I'm sure Russian politics can't be good for one's digestion.'

'Irish Free State.'

'Or the book pages.' I was getting desperate.

Hugh gave a bark of very dry laughter.

'The book pages!' he snorted. 'That Kafka fella has a new thing out, worse than the last. The book pages, Dandy, are far from the oasis of comfort they used to be.'

'But hasn't Mr Wodehouse just published again?' I asked.

'He has indeed,' said Hugh, with an air of triumph for which I could not account until he went on: 'and has fled our shores and gone to live in France. Must know something the rest of us haven't heard yet.'

I could not help the sudden leap of hope in my breast.

'Well, as to living in France—' I began, trying to sound casual. Once again, Hugh interrupted me.

'Never!' he thundered. 'If we are going down,

4

then down we shall go, fighting to the last.' With that, remembering that the coming revolution would provide scope for valour and glory as well as an end to life as we knew it, he took a satisfied bite of his toast and folded the newspaper to the sporting news.

Plotching rain, leaden skies and Bunty's listless snuffling in the mats of leaves (she knew that all the little creatures were burrowed away for the winter) were welcome notes of cheer after that. I trudged on, inwardly counting my blessings as Nanny Palmer's early training had left me all but unable not to do. Peace was still on the list even seven years after the armistice that put it there but it was beginning to lose its place to the everyday: stout shoes, warm clothes, a solid roof awaiting my return, hot coffee—chocolate even, if I asked for it—and health and strength and . . . I willed my thoughts towards less depressingly wholesome blessings . . . a new sable-tipped evening wrap, Christmas coming but no family visits coming with it and, next week, Rudolf Valentino at the Cinerama.

As I lifted my head, clicked my teeth at Bunty and quickened my pace for home, I caught sight of a little group of rather bedraggled strangers crossing the lane ahead of me, as though sent by Nanny Palmer's ghost to remind me that simple comforts were not to be sniffed at, not when many a decent-born family was reduced to tramping around for work and shelter. I peered after them, wondering where they had come from and where they were bound; our lane is not accustomed to much traffic. A tall thin father, a far from thin mother, a biggish child and a tiny one, I thought,

5

and then I blinked. The father had stooped to pass under the lowest branch of a beech tree, a branch to which I could not have reached my fingers if on tiptoe, the tiny child had spoken with the voice of a man, the bigger child was smoking a pipe, and the 'mother' was lumbering along with the heavy tread of a . . . *bear*? A giant, a smoking child, a midget and a *bear*? Beside me, Bunty growled. I caught her muzzle in my hand and held her head against my hip until they were gone and I could step quietly away.

My maid was still in my bedroom when I returned. I am sure she would have described herself as bent upon some essential task without whose execution my wardrobe would fall to mothy dust but really she was only cooing over my newest clothes like any miser with his gold, scattering a little lavender, pinning lace to tissue-paper, rolling a cashmere jersey around one of her little ticking bolsters as reverently as though the jersey were gold leaf and the bolster destined to lie beneath a mummy's head in a Pharaoh's tomb for all eternity. Grant really was born fifty years too late: stuffed bustles, whalebone and ten layers of starched petticoats would have soaked up a great deal more of her talent than my array.

'Filthy morning still,' I greeted her. I am quite an old hand at Scotch greetings after all these years.

'You'll not be going out again, madam,' Grant informed me, 'so I've laid out your pale blue wool and indoor shoes.' I sighed. The way she forced me into carpet slippers and whisked away my walking shoes the minute I was in the door always gave me a trapped feeling, even on a day as unappealing as this. My friend, Alec Osborne, was wont to say 'Ah, house-arrest!' whenever he put his head around my sitting-room door in the morning and saw me with my feet in little bags of felt with threaded ribbon. Besides, the blue wool get-up made me feel like an overgrown baby in a romping-suit. Thinking of which, I considered how to broach the subject in hand without sounding peculiar and making Grant stare.

'Have there been any visitors today?' I asked her. 'Downstairs, I mean. I thought I saw strangers in the lane.'

'Mr Pallister doesn't allow visitors in the morning, madam,' said Grant. 'Mrs Tilling was speaking of it only the other day again. She had the fish man in for a cup of tea and a slice of her fruitcake and Mr Pallister walked through the kitchen four and five times with a face on him like—' Grant caught herself just in time and I was sorry. She has a talent for rather cutting physical description and I had never heard her thoughts on Pallister in a temper. 'But as Mrs Tilling said, you have to keep in with the fish man or who knows what he might not palm off on us, stuck here away at the end of his round as we are, and it's not her fault he fetches up before dinnertime, is it?'

'No, quite, quite,' I agreed. I had never suspected before that the price of an occasional turbot along with the herring might be the compromising of Mrs Tilling's honour in Pallister's eyes. 'But I didn't mean visitors exactly. I suppose I meant tinkers. Knife-menders? Gypsies with pegs to sell?'

'Oh no, madam,' said Grant. 'John Bailey does all our knives every May and the gypsies—our gypsies, that is: the McRortys—are long gone back to Ireland until the spring. Mrs McRorty was expecting another baby and she's always happier if the babies are born in Ireland. Mind you, Margaret was born right here at Gilverton, two years ago at midsummer, because they could hardly interrupt themselves at their busiest time and . . .'

I marvelled to myself as she continued supplying unwanted and unheard details. To me, gypsies and tinkers are undifferentiated, welcome and useful of course, but really just part of the landscape with their ponies and wagons and black cooking pots over fires. It had never occurred to me that the camps I glimpsed now and then every summertime were *our* gypsies and that *our* gypsies had a name and a history known to all, that gypsies no less than fish men had their rounds.

'Well, I can't imagine who this was then,' I said, feeling rather chastened and thinking there were no end of people it could be, people who were woven deep into the fabric of Gilverton and about whom I would know nothing, since I seemed sometimes to know nothing at all. 'They were a funny-looking bunch, that's all.'

'Oho!' said Grant, looking up from her work and not even flicking a glance over me to see that my seams were straight. 'Well, then! It'll have been the circus.'

'The circus?' I echoed. And even though midgets and bears bore no better explanation, when I turned my eyes to my bedroom window and looked out at the grey blanket of sky, the black trees and dead bracken stretching to the brown hills in the distance, sheeted with rain and bare of a single other roof as far as the eye could see, I half suspected she was teasing me. There could no more be a circus here than a nightclub with roulette and dancing.

'At Benachally, madam,' said Grant. 'Have you not heard, then?'

I had not, but to be sure if I had to stretch my imagination around a circus without it snapping, then Castle Benachally was the only place a circus could possibly be.

'I hope they keep the bear on a thick rope,' I said. 'While they're walking around Gilverton anyway.'

It was Grant's turn to show saucer eyes to me.

'A bear?' she whispered. 'They never said there was a bear. Dogs and ponies and a black monkey in a coat, they said, but nobody breathed a word about a bear.' With that, she abandoned a lace cuff half-pinned and flitted from the room to take the dread news to the kitchens and cluck the rest of the morning away.

I did a fair imitation of flitting away myself, straight to my sitting room to the telephone to ring up Benachally and invite myself to tea. I did not try to cloak my attempt in disingenuousness; for one thing I would have been seen through and for another I, almost alone of our neighbours, had accepted all the oddnesses of the new arrivals with polite indifference, neither huffing nor interfering, and so I thought I had worked up a little credit which could perhaps be cashed in now.

'Oh yes, do come,' said the slightly husky voice of Ina Wilson, doyenne of Benachally. 'We can go over to their camp before tea and I'll introduce you. We could even walk if it ever stops raining.'

9

'But what are they doing here?' I asked her. 'Why on earth did they come?'

'I'll tell you when you arrive,' said Ina, with something between a laugh and a sigh. 'And bring Bunty,' she went on. There was a slight pause. 'Albert is at the works today.'

Ah, I thought, ringing off again. That explained the possibility of the walk too, for while Grant made life easy for herself by consigning me to my sitting room from time to time with impractical pale garments and fluffy footwear, Albert Wilson kept his wife in solitary confinement in Castle Benachally almost permanently and did it, so far as one could tell, by sheer force of personality and, one hoped, out of love.

It was impossible to say what Ina Wilson might have expected from her marriage—the alliance was a considerable leap into the unknown—but it cannot have been what she had got and I always felt rather sorry for her. Her own background was one of perfect rectitude, although not elevated socially speaking. Her father was a don at the university in Glasgow, terribly learned in one of those branches of science which the Victorians went in for, lots of cases full of samples and pieces of delicate equipment and great excitement at—it always seemed to me—the same discovery over and over again. Her mother was no less a scholar, although *her* passion was for the medieval. I never learned whether it was stained glass windows, epic poems or martyred saints which inflamed her since all I ever got were odd snippets from Ina that Mother had had a terrible crossing to Lindisfarne or had sent a postcard from Norwich where she was looking at an illuminated manuscript before it

10

got sent to its new home in a library in Boston.

It can only have been the war, surely, that put the flower of this studious little household in the way of a self-made businessman, twenty years her senior, with a red villa in the suburbs, whose very name—Albert Wilson—must have made her mother wince. (As to the nature of his business, Wilson was given to muttering vaguely about architecture if anyone tried to pin him down but in plain fact he was a brickmaker, a very successful brickmaker, with a brickworks in Paisley and another in Leith, and lately—thanks to the number of shelters, factories, hangars and warehouses thrown up for the war effort—an extremely wealthy man. Ina to her credit never tried to finesse any of this: witness her telling me that Albert was 'at the works' today, when I am sure he would have described himself as 'in town'.)

But when Ina left the West End flat full of her parents' textbooks and gave up her daily walks to chamber recitals in the winter gardens she did not settle for long in the red villa entertaining the cream of Glasgow's Rotarians. She succumbed, in the winter of 1918, to the villainous influenza which swept across what seemed like the whole world, borne home by the returning troops and wiping out great swathes of exhausted humanity as though it were swatting so many flies. Young and strong, well-nourished and comfortably tended, Ina fought it and rallied but her child, a girl of ten months old, was less fortunate and as soon as the funeral was over and Ina was well enough to be moved, her husband had sold the red villa and carried her off to a hillside far from the crowds of Glasgow to clean air, clear water and—as I could

11

attest—endless solitude.

For six years now Ina had been convalescing at Castle Benachally, drawn up in high-backed chairs in front of roaring fires, or tucked under blankets on sunny terraces, and I had watched the fleeting pallor of recent illness deepen and settle. I had watched too as Albert Wilson's concern for his wife and grief for his daughter had grown and twisted into something darker, something a great deal harder to name. Ina bore it with patience, even sometimes with cheerful patience, but others in the neighbourhood, with much less excuse since they were only visiting and did not have to live under the regime, soon became exasperated and stayed away, so Ina's isolation grew and grew.

I cannot quite say why I was not among them; I am perfectly able to summon unwarranted exasperation, but for some reason Albert Wilson's regulations did not trouble me. I accepted sitting far across the room from Ina, shouting over to her, accepted my tea being brought on a separate tray, accepted the inevitable telegram on the morning of my visit asking if anyone in the household was unwell, or had been heard sneezing, or could feel the beginnings of a cough. I even accepted the banishing of Bunty from Benachally, despite the fact that people cannot catch distemper nor dogs carry flu. Besides, today Albert was at the works and Bunty was beside me in the little Morris Cowley with her front paws on the dashboard and her tail whipping smartly back and forth, in anticipation. She has high expectations, when taken out in the motor car just after luncheon, that she will be having saucers of milk and crumbled cake for tea.

12

It was a fair drive from Gilverton to the Wilsons'—although the estates abut along our eastern boundary—and three o'clock had struck when I turned in between the gateposts with their sleeping dogs, swept past the lodge, up the avenue and over the little bridge with the gothic folly of a gatehouse built above it, and crunched to a stop on the gravel.

Bits of Castle Benachally have been standing these five hundred years and it has some Maxwells and Douglases to its name, as well as the obligatory legend about Charles Edward Stuart stopping off full of hope on his way down or washing up full of despair on his way back again, although at least there is no scrap of tapestry said to be stitched by his mother and her handmaidens while they waited there. (Really, if Mary Stuart had done even a tenth of what adorns castle walls in her name her life would have been the equal of any Huguenot tailor on piece-work rates—locked up for a week, bent over her needle night and day, then let out and on to the next job.)

Despite all this undisputed history, however, Benachally had had the misfortune to be sold to an architect in the fifties and he had spread himself with no little abandon, running up towers, throwing out turrets and tacking on widows' walks until the whole place looked like something from Grimm's Fairy Tales. Albert Wilson, I am sure, would have pitched in with fumed oak and heraldic pennants if left to himself, suits of armour at every turn on the stairs, but Ina was a calming influence upon him and the inside of Benachally was a delight. The Wilsons had been handed down no family portraits nor dubious Dutch landscapes and

13

rather than buy them up by the yard, which they might easily have afforded to do, they had left the walls almost bare: just plaster painted in cool, powdery shades like sugared almonds, against which sat oversized vases of modern design, filled with branches, looking quite Japanese in their austerity. (I had often envied Ina Wilson's vases of branches—willow, orange blossom, beech or holly in season—but when I tried the same thing at home against the wallpaper and etchings they looked very messy and made the housemaids sneer.)

Albert's one contribution to the interior was to forbid much in the way of carpets, for fear of what fusspots the world over call 'germs', and Bunty's toenails sounded like castanets on the marble floor as we approached the main sitting room, so that Ina was calling her name even before the butler swept open the door and announced me. Bunty bounded in, rushed over and subjected Ina to her usual feverish hello. The butler gave me a knowing smile and drew the door shut behind me.

'Won't he—?' I began, but I stopped myself in time. I was unsure how plainly one could talk about Albert's peculiarity without causing offence, but I suspected that one could not wonder aloud if the butler would tell tales. 'What a nice friendly butler you have,' I said in hasty substitution. 'I always think so when I come here. Mine is a fiend.'

'We're very lucky in our servants, Albert and me,' said Ina Wilson. She was tickling Bunty and so could say the next bit without quite meeting my eye. 'That is, Albert chooses them very carefully and pays them very well to follow his instructions and I am lucky that, despite all of that, they don't.'

14

This was a typical comment of hers: not quite admitting that she shared the general view of her husband and even saying as much as she did with such sweetness that the barb was lost amongst it.

'Now,' I said, once I was settled into my chair, 'please explain, because my mind is absolutely boggling. I thought I was seeing things this morning between the little man and the giant man and the bear.'

'It's not a bear,' said Ina, giggling again as she had on the telephone. I had not seen her so animated in all the time I had known her. 'It's a strongman. His name is William Wolf—Big Bad Bill Wolf, he calls himself—and he has a long beard and wears a shaggy suit. I'm sure that's who it was you saw. I almost fainted when I met him.'

'But what are they doing here?' I said. Now, when Ina smiled at me, there was the usual trace of sadness in it.

'Albert brought them,' she said. 'For me.' I awaited further explanation; for Albert Wilson, whose sole aim in life was to keep his wife from the world and the world from his wife, to bring a circus camp right into his estate grounds seemed impossible. 'It's not as ridiculous as it sounds,' she said, reading my mind. 'You see, I love the circus. I used to go every day I could get my nurse to take me when I was a child and, in Glasgow, you'd be surprised how often you could find a circus of some description somewhere. Now, I don't know if you know that I paint a little sometimes to pass the time? Well, recently I decided to paint some circus scenes—quite a compositional challenge, as you can imagine.'

'Not to mention the horses' legs,' I put in.

15

'Although, I suppose one could go in for very active scenes with a lot of sawdust kicked up.'

'Anyway,' said Ina, who was not exactly solemn but who nevertheless could sometimes make me feel, in contrast, rather flighty, 'I happened to mention to Albert how much I wished I could see a circus again and he—silly old thing that he is—he said he would learn to juggle and wear a costume if it would amuse me.' I raised an eyebrow, thinking of Hugh. 'And then I joked back that we could train up all the servants—housemaids on the trapeze, boot boys turning somersaults—and that way we could have a circus right here at home without any . . .' She stopped and I carried the thought to its conclusion for her. Without any strangers, Albert would have said. Without any danger of incomers bringing death along with them. 'And then,' Ina resumed, 'Albert had a brainwave. Instead of turning our household into a circus, why don't we turn a circus into our household? I couldn't imagine at first how he could do it. I knew that all the circuses I ever saw were in the summer, or maybe at Christmas sometimes, and I had never wondered about where they went in winter to wait for spring.'

'Nor I,' I said. 'Don't they go home?' Then I flushed. 'Oh. Of course. The caravans *are* home, aren't they?'

'They go—poor things—to what they call a winter ground. Somewhere as sheltered as they can find and as cheap as they can get it, because they won't make another penny until the spring comes and they start the show again. The Cooke circus was camped out on some horrid bit of waste ground near the brickworks in Leith—that's what

16

gave Albert the idea—and so he went and spoke to Mr Cooke and said they could have a lovely woodland site, with clean water and plenty of firewood, all free of charge so long as they stuck to—you know—Albert's rules.'

I did indeed know Albert's rules, as they applied to the servants. No popping into the village even on days off, no evenings in the pub, no visits to the cinema, no going to see their family if anyone in their family was ill or had been heard to sneeze or thought they could feel a cough coming on. The Benachally servants were handsomely paid but they certainly earned it.

'And in a week or two—for Christmas or New Year—if everyone is in good health, they're going to put on a show and I'm going to go to it.' Ina beamed at me. 'Isn't he sweet, really?'

'Except you're going to the campground this afternoon with me,' I said. 'And you've already met William Wolf.'

'Well, when Albert goes to the works, things are rather different,' she said and her smile faded. 'Don't look at me that way, Dandy,' she said. 'He really *is* very kind, but it's only the days when he's gone that have made me able to be kind back again. So don't look at me like that. Don't think ill of me.'

'My dear,' I said, 'nothing could be further from my head.' This was true. I was not sitting in private judgement on Ina or her husband; I was merely marvelling at the rich feast of strangeness in other people's lives, like looking down a microscope into a scoop of water from a pond. One hardly needed a circus at all.

Still, nothing would have kept me from going to

17

visit it and, since the rain had almost stopped, we set out on foot with me holding Bunty very firmly on a short lead wound twice around my wrist. I had no concerns about her mixing with rough company (as I always tell Hugh—a Dalmatian might be decorative but it is a real dog, not a toy) but I was sure circus dogs would be beautifully trained and would sit at their masters' sides and look down their noses while she racketed about, trampling over tents and knocking down small children, if I let her.

2

The circus folk had set up camp a ten-minute stroll from the castle, choosing an excellent spot I thought as we neared it. They were sheltered from the worst of the winter winds by a steep hill to the north and by crescent-shaped arms of pine trees spreading from the east and west and almost meeting, surely planted there to force some unnatural movement of birds (although I do not pretend fully to understand the ways of the pheasant or the wiles of their tweedy enemies, any more than I see why the grouse must have their gorse and heather in such gaudy patchwork on the hilltops, ruining the view). As well as this hill and these trees, there was a burn which gurgled down in streams and short waterfalls and ended in a pool. In other words, in summertime this would have been a sunless, boggy, midge-infested hell but in December it was an oasis, since there was no sunlight to speak of anyway and boards had been laid to the pool edge until the rain should stop, the mud dry and the ground harden with frost as it must do.

I had imagined the circus to be battened down and burrowed in, awaiting the spring, and was surprised to see the big top set up at one side of the pond, rather a small big top, frankly, but valiantly jaunty against the black pine trees, even with its wet flag wrapped around the top of the pole and the bunting on its guy ropes dripping on to the grass. It was red and white like a seaside minstrel's coat and—like a minstrel's coat—best seen from afar. Close up, the red stripes were sun-bleached here and there and the whole was rather scuffed and worn, rather muddy round the hem, and made me think of a governess between jobs and getting shabby. From inside it, as we walked by, I could hear a rhythmic thumping and grunting and although Ina had seemed very sure about the bear I quickened my footsteps.

Around the other side of the pond and quite near its edge there was a plainer but just as large a square white tent inside which, upon passing, I could see upwards of twenty horses standing, deeply strawed, in trim wooden stalls; polished black beauties and shaggy cart ponies alike, each with a stuffed hay bag hung on a nail and a water bucket hooked over the stall gate in front of its nose. There was a puff of warmth from the open entranceway and I was not surprised to glimpse three lads sitting on upturned boxes bent in concentration over a game of cards, for if one could bear the reek of horse—and some find it pleasant enough to call it, straight-faced, a scent—there would be nowhere snugger than here to pass

19

the dregs of such a miserable day.

Beyond both tents lay the camp itself, a ring of green and gold caravans with curls of wood smoke rising from their bent tin chimneys and lamplight glowing out of their lace-covered windows into the dullness of the sinking afternoon. They were set in pairs, open door facing chummily to open door, and on some of the steps women were busy peeling potatoes or mending, tiny children peeping shyly at us from behind them. In the middle of the circle a large fire was laid, ready to light, with a sheet of tin balanced over it on sticks and a collection of girded water buckets placed to catch the rainwater at the edges.

'Can you imagine living in one of those wagons?' asked Ina, waving around the campground. It was not an exclamation, but rather a question, and she studied me with some earnestness while waiting for an answer.

'Very . . . natty,' I said. 'Most . . . snug, I should imagine.'

Ina nodded, satisfied with my answer it seemed. 'We'd better call at Mrs Cooke's first,' she said. 'She's the head of the—'

'Here she is again, the pretty maid!' came a voice from the caravan nearest the big top. Bunty wagged her tail and all three of us turned towards the sound. 'What did I tell you, first time I clapped my eyes to you? A circus face. You have a circus face as sure as I ever saw one. And here you are again.'

In the doorway, stooping slightly under the bowed roof, was a dark woman of around sixty, I should have guessed, dressed in rather shiny and old-fashioned garments, with a smile splitting her

20

brown face into creases and her eyes twinkling as bright as the gold hoops through her ears. How satisfying it is when someone turns out to be exactly what one has expected and looked forward to. What a disappointment it would have been if Mrs Cooke, surely the matriarch of Cooke's Family Circus, had been an efficient little figure in serge too busy with the business accounts to pass the time of day.

Mrs Cooke stood back and let Ina and me clamber into her caravan and sit down. Luckily, she seemed very proud of her home and so I did not have to resist having a good look round; at the lace and velvet and painted enamel and brass, at the glass-fronted cupboards full of rose-patterned china and heavy crystal, at the panels which lined the walls—surely doors hiding more cupboards although I could see no handles, at the intricate moulding on every panel which was picked out in gold and blue and which, since each panel was so small that it *was* mostly moulding, made the whole of the little cave glitter with gold and blue as though we had somehow got inside a Fabergé egg and lit lamps there.

Although I am sure Mrs Cooke would not have minded, I forbore to look too closely at the box-bed beyond the draped curtains at the end, finding it odd to think that I had climbed into the woman's bedroom before she had even heard my name, but I thought I noticed a small black dog curled up on one of the many pillows and my heart warmed to her; I always let Bunty take her nap on my bed if she is not muddy.

All the time I was gazing around, Mrs Cooke was filling a kettle, opening the door of the stove to puff the fire to life, gathering cups and plates on to a tray, all without moving from her little padded stool, just reaching out to this side and that and keeping up a good-natured commentary in her nameless, but very appealing accent.

'Mrs Gilver, you say? Now, I knew some Gilvers over in Donegal, years back. Horsewomen they wurr, bred racehorses and rode them too, and they were dark like yourself there. Have you some Irish? You've a grand flat back to you, anyway. Ah well, you'll be a mixture like the rest of us and best of us. I'm mostly Russian with some Irish and French—pure circus, you might say—and Mr Cooke always says he's Scotch on account of Cooke's Original English Circus 1750 started in Scotland, but he's the same as me, and how could he not be since I'm a Cooke on both sides? Born a Cooke and married a Cooke and . . . what are you after?'

A very small child had appeared at the top of the steps and was trembling there, looking out from under a fringe of black hair.

'Come on, little Sal, speak up. They won't eat you,' said Mrs Cooke.

The child did not stop trembling but put her chin in the air.

'Is that a slanging buffer, missus, or a jugal?' she said nodding in my direction, without meeting my eye.

Mrs Cooke tutted loudly.

'Don't mind Sallie, maids,' she said. 'She's not been much around flatties and she's not five yet there. Folks that's not circus, I should say. She's just asking after the dog. Want to know if she's just a pet or if she does a turn.' Bunty, sensing that she

22

was the centre of attention, stood up and swept her tail back and forth once or twice, perilously near the crowded mantelshelf above the stove. 'Why don't you take her out and see if you can get her to slang, little maid,' said Mrs Cooke, hastily, with one eye on her brass ornaments. 'Keep you both out of mischief.'

I handed Bunty's lead over to the outstretched hand and, with one brave peek up into my face, the child turned and scampered back down the steps taking Bunty with her.

'But stay away from the tent,' Mrs Cooke shouted after them. 'You get under the feet of that prad and the rum coll'll take his hand to you.'

'I was surprised to see the big top up, Mrs Cooke,' I said, plumping for the only bit of her discourse I was sure I had understood.

'And where else would they work?' she asked. 'There's no good working an act up in a field and then asking the horse to do it in a ring, now is there? He'd knock his legs on the ring fence every step and then he'd bolt, wun't he?'

'I suppose so,' I said. 'It never occurred to me.'

'One time, when I was a girl, a chavvy—a feller, I should say—with a clever donkey act come up and joined us in the middle of the year. He'd been doing his turn on the nob there—round the streets, you know—and a fine turn it was too so my old pa took him on as a run-in to fill where a tumbler had come off with his arm broke . . . always something in this lark, and no lie there . . . but the first night in the tent, bless us if that cuddy-horse didn't stop in the middle of his turn, kick the poor chavvy's legs out from under him and take off out the door to the wide blue yonder, right across the gallery

23

packed with screaming babbies. And can you guess why?'

'Because of the tent?' suggested Ina. 'The ring?'

'No there,' said Mrs Cooke. 'My old pa was too fly not to see that. He'd had the pair of them in the ring from sun-up to early doors. No, it wurr the band. The drums and cymbals. We never saw that cuddy again, nor the rig-out and props he had on him when he scarpered. And my mother always said the chavvy did it on purpose, to land himself a new kit when his old one was wore through and then back to the street corners again.' I could not help thinking that the moral of Mrs Cooke's story was getting lost somewhere, and she seemed to agree. 'But now there,' she went on, 'Ma was a dread suspicious type, shame on me for speaking ill of my own dear mother what's gone but it's true. Nothing happened anywhere on the ground but she saw it fraying her purse string. What I'm saying is the tent's up all winter and then just you wait and see what grand acts come out of it in the spring there. Just you wait and see.'

'And will the band be playing too?' asked Ina, possibly gauging the distance from the tent to her drawing-room windows and wondering whether the drums and cymbals would carry that far.

'Time was, but no, Tam paid the band off after the last stand and we'll get another come spring again. We have one of them Panatrope machines now and them round records—does the job there.'

She had been busy plying the teapot and milk jug while she told her tale and now she watched us sipping with the delighted watchfulness of the true hostess.

'Delicious tea, Mrs Cooke,' said Ina. 'Oh, I'm so

24

glad you've come!'

'Twas a godsend to be asked, maid,' said Mrs Cooke. 'Your man has done us a favour there and no two ways, because we wurr in for a hard winter in that nasty Leith, only the shops for a bite of meat and town roughs bothering us of a Saturday night with a drink in them. When Mr Cooke told me about woods and streams and rabbits in the pot I thought *he'd* been at the bevvy.'

'I feel rather a churl for asking you to keep my little visits here a secret from him,' said Ina, but Mrs Cooke shushed her.

'Away!' she said. 'A woman needs a man and a fine strong man is the best kind, but . . .' She flicked a glance at me and, appearing to find reassurance there, she creased up into another of her grins. ' . . . but of course we have to let him think he's the king and all or he'd only think something more trouble still. Don't you fret your head, maid.'

In complete accordance about the proper disposal of our loyalties, then, the three of us drank our tea.

'I could read your leaves, Mrs Gilver,' said Mrs Cooke when we were done. I was mildly offended that I remained so called when Ina was a 'pretty maid' but then she had her circus face to recommend her and I assumed I did not.

'You tell fortunes?' I asked. I had not had my fortune told since the departure of the last nursery maid from my parents' house and my promotion to my own bedroom and lady's maid, and I cannot say that I had missed it.

'Palms and leaves,' said Mrs Cooke. 'I tell fortunes in the ticket wagon before the show,

25

Madame Polina and her crystal ball: all good news and happy futures—ah, changed days, changed days—but my real talent is palms and leaves.'

I edged forward in my seat and held my palm out to her, thinking that palms were much less mess and bother than upturned teacups and at least she could find no dark strangers or sea voyages there.

'A long lifeline,' she said, running her fingertip around the pad of my thumb. 'Very clear and sure, but your money has run out—turn your hand a little to the light—no, there it is! It's just coming from a different place now. And your heart line, let me see . . .'

'Broken?' I suggested.

'Chained,' said Mrs Cooke. 'Intertwined, doubled, and it dun't untangle any time soon there.'

I said nothing.

'And that's not all,' she went on, warming to her task now, bending close over my hand. 'What's this I'm seeing?'

'But Mrs Cooke, that's Mrs Gilver's left hand,' said Ina. 'Shouldn't it be the right?'

'Of course it should,' said Mrs Cooke, 'unless you're left-handed. Well, forget all of that and we'll start again.'

The sound of feet on the caravan steps, however, prevented it and we all turned to see a dapper little man, breathing heavily and dressed only in shirtsleeves and britches despite the cold, step through the door to join us. He was about Mrs Cooke's age but looked younger somehow, his greying curls less draining to the complexion than her blackened ones—when one looked closely one

26

could see that the black extended to her scalp and even crept across her forehead here and there. His figure was youthful too and better suited to caravan life, one imagined, than Mrs Cooke's comfortable girth.

'Here's Pa there,' she greeted him. 'Pa, here's Mrs Wilson back again, on the quiet, mind, and we han't seen her, and her friend Mrs Gilver and have we seen you or han't we now?'

'Tam Cooke,' said the man, in a voice which was of purest Edinburgh and more, like Sir Harry Lauder over-egging for Americans in the music hall. 'So you're back amongst us, Mrs Wilson. Cannot keep away.' He sat down heavily on the edge of the box-bed and wiped his brow with a large silk handkerchief pulled from his pocket.

'Is that your day done there, Pa?' said Mrs Cooke, moving the kettle forward again.

'I've done all I can,' he replied. 'The lass is that headstrong and as wick as a flea with it. Changed days, Ma, changed days.' Mrs Cooke shook her head and sucked her teeth in sympathy. 'Our newest entrée,' her husband explained to Ina and me, 'our *Anastasia*.' The word was in heavy italics. 'A fine talent for the voltige—never seen a trick rider so slick since Ma was a girl—but she's a josser all the same—not circus-born—and it shows. I'm done telling her, Ma. I'm the equestrian director, never mind the owner—Cooke's Circus, it says over the ring door, and she can read better than most.' He took a cup of tea from his wife's hand and nodded his thanks.

'Oh, Tam,' said Mrs Cooke. 'Don't you go fretting the maid there. She hasn't had her troubles to seek. Anyways, it said Cooke's *Family*

27

Circus last time I looked, and she's one of our own now, like it or not.' She spoke easily enough, but she was watching her husband closely to see how the words went with him, and the overall effect was rather pointed for the setting. Mr Cooke said nothing. Ina gazed dumbly out of the window. I cleared my throat. Mrs Cooke stepped in and ended the silence at last.

'Any sign of Topsy's swing?'

'Not a sniff of it,' said Pa, with a faint smile. 'That lass needs to learn to take more care of her props—I'm not made of money for new ropes and she should know it.' He spoke, however, with a chuckle in his voice and Mrs Cooke relaxed too and grinned back at him. 'So the Prebrezhenskys are up now.'

'Our Risley act,' said Mrs Cooke, turning to Ina and me. 'Foot jugglers—worth a look for you there.'

'For sure,' said Mr Cooke. 'They're working on the double flick-flack, and it's looking good too.'

'Tell me they've got them little maids on the mechanic,' said Mrs Cooke, pressing her hand to her heart. Mr Cooke nodded wearily and flapped a hand at her to calm her. I crossed my eyes at Ina, quite at a loss on the question of flick-flacks and how mechanics might improve them.

'Prebrezhensky!' said Mr Cooke, and his wife tutted again. 'Helps if you can even say it. I told them "Kukov" would be better for Cooke's Circus. Clever, you know? But what say do I have these days? Or Romanov, if they must. Bit of class, bit of history and it would go with our "Anastasia" at least, but they'd have none of it. "What we have lost! What have we have left but our name?" they

28

said to me. I don't know. Changed days.'

'When I did my voltige,' Mrs Cooke said, 'Mr Cooke used to ride the haute école.' She pronounced it *oaty coil*, but I had an aunt with a passion for high-school Spanish dressage and so I caught her meaning. 'And everyone in the ring was a Cooke or a Turvy or an Ilchenko on one side or both—all family.' She sighed. 'Now our boys are in America doing their act for a packet of pay and our girl's married to a tobacconist and here's me telling fortunes . . .'

'Front-of-house show,' corrected Mr Cooke, but the doldrums had conquered both of them now. 'In the old days, you never needed no fortunes told to entertain them coming in. They'd look round the menagerie and be happy as sand boys. Sometimes I think we should hang the expense and get back to it, Ma. An elephant, a camel or two, some cats, wouldn't you like that, eh? We could have a parade again—better than posting bills on lamp-posts any day.'

'And beast wagons and show wagons and tent grooms and the ticket price so high to cover it we'd show to empty galleries like as not. We're stretched flat taking on the new acts anyways. Them days is gone there, Tam. All gone.'

They sounded exactly like Hugh and me.

*   *   *

Ina and I excused ourselves shortly afterwards; Mr Cooke looked done in and I was sure he wanted to pull off his long boots and flop back on to his bed. We made our way across the ground to the big top—although I had noticed that Mrs Cooke

29

called it simply the tent—pausing only to gape, stunned, at the not inconsiderable sight of Bunty sitting up on her haunches with her front paws crossed while Sallie, the tiny child who had led her away from the caravan, waved a biscuit slowly back and forth in front of her nose. Bunty, catching sight of me, whined and lowered one paw towards the grass, but the child said 'Yat!' and clicked her fingers and Bunty turned to face the biscuit again.

'I cannot believe my eyes,' I said to Ina. 'Nothing the Bresh-whoevers might do in the way of juggling feet is going to top that.'

Of course, I spoke too soon. We pulled aside the flaps under the canopy and stepped as discreetly as possible inside, into the canvas dome, into the smell of sawdust and oiled rope, into a place even more magical in its dim emptiness than it had been filled with music, lights and laughter and the sugary tang of toffee-covered apples when I was a child.

The Prebrezhenskys turned out to be a large fair-haired man, a small dark woman like a pixie, two dark pixie girls of around eight, twins perhaps, and one of five or so with golden hair and fat pink cheeks, her father's daughter. They nodded at us in a friendly way as we entered and I attempted a nonchalant nod in return as though I found them as unremarkable as they me. In fact, all five were dressed in britches and short leather coats with fur collars and the two bigger girls had harnesses around their waists, attached to ropes slung over a pair of high beams.

'This is Mrs Gilver, a friend of mine,' said Ina. 'Now, Dandy, um . . .'

'I say for you,' the woman laughed, surveying

her family with casual pride. 'Nikolai Prebrezhensky.' Her husband clicked his heels together and gave a curt bow, no more than a nod really. 'And Rosaliya, Inessa and Akilina the baby. I am Zoya. Please to watch and please to excuse mechanic.' She gestured to the harness and rope arrangement with an air of apology.

With another bow, the man turned back to his womenfolk. He seemed to be explaining something to the girls, speaking with expansive gestures and many loud flourishes. 'Ah-Tah-Dahhh!' he boomed, spreading his arms wide. 'Bamm-Bamm!' They nodded, very serious. He dropped down on to his back on a canvas pad spread on the floor and the two girls—heavens, they were tiny!—each grasped one of his hands and hopped up until they were sitting on his feet. Their mother caught the ends of the ropes attached to her daughters' waists and began beating time against her leg with a short stick. The little girls, curled into balls, began to revolve. The baby retreated to a safe distance, clapping her hands.

'They really don't mind us watching?' I said to Ina.

'Not at all,' she replied, not shifting her gaze from the ring. 'Privilege of the tober-omey's donah, Mrs Cooke told me. The ground-owner's wife,' she explained. 'And anyway, as she said, the more distraction the better, at least as far as the animal acts are concerned.'

'Did you believe the story about the runaway donkey, then?'

'Of course,' said Ina, turning to me briefly, although her eyes soon went back to the act, where one of the girls was now balanced in a handstand on her father's feet and was repeatedly curling up into a ball and straightening out again while he bent and locked his knees in time. Her mother, who now had the rope looped firmly around herself like a belt with the end gripped in her hand, stepped close and spread her other arm wide. They must be about to attempt 'the flick-flack'. I squeezed my eyes shut and turned away. 'I mean,' said Ina, 'if you had lived all your life in a circus, with camels and elephants and Russian relations, you'd hardly need to make stories up, would you? Gosh! Oh, jolly good try! What a brave girl you are!'

I looked back to see the child swinging inelegantly on the harness, while her mother let the rope out slowly, hand over hand, and lowered her to the floor.

'That woman must have nerves of iron,' I said. 'Oh Lord, now the other one. I can't watch.'

I felt quite wrung out by the time we left them. It was perhaps only that, whenever I had watched a circus before, the acts appeared effortless, the performers boneless and weightless, the tricks just that: tricks to fool us into believing what we saw. Witnessing the Prebrezhenskys' rehearsal put the lie to that, for if practice makes perfect then necessarily anyone *at* practice is not quite perfect yet and those little girls were made of soft flesh and delicate bone, with no trick to brush simple gravity away.

Outside, Bunty was curled asleep with her lead tied to a caravan wheel and her trainer nowhere to be seen since, judging from the savoury smells wafting from several open doors, it was now

32

teatime. She rose, stretching and giving her eerie moaning yawn, what Alec calls her Baskerville yawn, and was content to leave the campground trotting at my heels on a limp lead as though she did so every day.

'Oh dear!' said Ina, her tone caught between wryness and real concern, as we neared the castle again. She pointed to one of the many turrets where a yellow duster had been hung out of a window. 'Albert's back early,' she said, pulling on her gloves and buttoning her coat to the neck. 'You know the drill, Dandy, don't you?' I nodded and veered to the other edge of the path so that I was quite eight feet from her. 'And we've been for a short turn around the grounds keeping to the gravel, not walking on the grass, and I sat for ten minutes resting before we came back again.'

'What if he's been home for ages?' I asked.

'He hasn't,' Ina said, looking sheepish. 'One duster is less than half an hour. Two is up to an hour and the plan is if it ever goes over the hour someone will slip out and come to find me. But it never has: Albert is a man of regular habits, I'm happy to say.'

He might very well have been, but he had certainly interrupted his habits that day. He had only just arrived home and was still out on the sweep when we came around the turn of the drive and into view. In fact, he almost caught the lowering of the warning flag, turning his head at the sound of the closing window as a maid drew the yellow duster in again, only missing it because he could not keep his eyes off Bunty for long enough properly to scan the entire frontage in time.

'In you go, darling,' I said in a loud voice, ushering Bunty up into the Cowley. 'You know you don't come inside here.' Bunty, still subdued by whatever circus-magic had been worked upon her, did me the credit of dropping uncomplainingly out of sight and leaving me to turn and offer my apologies to Albert Wilson. 'Do forgive me the dog,' I said. I never can bring myself to say his name. 'I've kept her well away from dear Ina and I admit I was agog for the Cookes.'

Ina cleared her throat gently, reminding me that as far as Albert was to know we had not gone within a floating germ's distance of such a thing as a newly arrived circus. It would be Christmas before she was allowed to watch the show from the back row of the big top and weeks more until it was safe for her to go hobnobbing.

'To hear about them, I mean,' I added, but Albert Wilson was too distracted by momentous news of his own to notice my blunders.

'I've brought a visitor home with me, Ina my love,' he said.

'You've brought . . .' Ina's voice trailed off in wonder. 'You've brought someone home?'

'Yes indeed,' her husband answered. His voice is normally monotonic in efforts to shake off the last droplets of Glasgow, but it swooped and fell quite extravagantly now as he delivered his news. 'We met on the train. That is, we met up on the train today, by chance; we are acquainted already, of course. As I daresay you are too, my dear Mrs . . . Dan . . . my dear.' Because I never call him anything, he has simply no idea what to call me. 'Robin Laurie,' he announced with an attempt at casualness which was spoiled by a tremor of pride.

34

A tall willow-wand of a man in exquisite town suiting and a long dove-grey overcoat of obvious Paris cut stepped out on to the step behind him like an announcing angel.

'Delighted, Mrs Wilson,' he said with a chuckle in his voice, waving but making no move to approach her. He must have been apprised already of Albert's house rules. 'Dandy,' he said to me, with a gesture somewhere between touching his absent hat and blowing a kiss; we had met many times over the years and could be classed as friends.

'Lord Robin,' said Ina and I looked at her sharply. I was used to hearing her voice sounding weary or even drained but I had never heard such coldness in it as when she spoke those two words. Indeed I have seldom heard such coldness in any voice speaking any words at all.

3

Keeping everyone six feet away from Ina at all times does tend to slow the progress of any movement in which she plays a part, the more so since I have noticed that people will carry on the six-foot rule and apply it to everyone in the party, probably to avoid the appearance that the rest are bosom pals and that she alone has been shunned. On the current occasion the four of us trooped in simply yards apart from one another, like bishops processing to an altar, and so, happily, I had a good long chance to gather my thoughts while the tail of the snake caught up with the head in the library beyond the great hall.

I could understand why Wilson had jumped at the chance to welcome Robin Laurie to Benachally although he was not at all my cup of tea. He was one of the sort who, despite advancing years, remained determinedly young in the fashion of the current day, which is to say determinedly *bright* and young; in short, a 'bad boy' and I do so prefer even boys to be good boys and vastly prefer men to be men. To an Albert Wilson, brickmaker, of Glasgow, however, who would rather have been an architect and referred to his brickworks as 'town', entertaining the younger son of a marquis, no matter what the particulars of his character, was surely a dizzy peak after years of climbing, and exactly what he had had in mind when he persuaded himself that he could afford to buy a castle and a thousand of acres of land.

What I could not understand, what I could not begin to understand, was what Lord Robin was doing here. He was a renowned snob and egotist, even amongst a set where snobs and egotists are fifteen to the pound, and had advanced from being the centre of a charmed circle at Eton, by way of a few years as a deb's delight, to his current occupation of semi-professional house guest (but only at the grandest houses with the best shooting and the most relaxed view of how to clear one's card debts), so that at the age of forty he had an unshakable view of himself as a social prize, giving meaning to the lives of lesser mortals simply by being near them, and very choosy about which lesser mortals should have their lives given meaning that way. What could have persuaded him out of his habit of stately progression around the balls and shoots of Scotland, England and Ireland and into an impromptu call on the Wilsons for tea was beyond me. Also beyond me was what it was Ina disapproved of so fiercely and with such little effort to hide it.

Albert Wilson voluntarily quarantined himself from his wife's embrace when he had been abroad rubbing shoulders with the multitude and Ina, sitting all alone and very frosty-looking with the three of us facing her across twelve feet of gleaming floor, put one firmly in mind of one of those cross Hanoverian consorts holding reluctant court. It was hard to resist the idea that Lord Robin's friendliness was designed only to annoy her even more.

'It's a joy to see you looking so well, Mrs Wilson,' he said. 'Quite an improvement.'

'I didn't know you knew one another,' I said and immediately flushed; from whichever angle one looked at this remark it was a dropped brick. First of all, it was none of my business who knew whom, especially when I was sitting in the house of one of the parties, drinking their tea, and even I—no diplomat—should know better than to chip in when a well-known rake and seducer was teasing a married woman in front of her husband with an acquaintanceship she would clearly rather ignore. And speaking of the husband it was hardly polite to draw attention to his lowly rank by wondering aloud how his wife and the exalted guest could ever have crossed paths. On this last score, however, I need not have worried. Far from being offended, Albert Wilson was pleased to have the chance to explain.

'Oh, certainly we all know each other, my dear

. . . ahem,' he said. 'I couldn't count on the fingers of my two hands the number of balls and parties we've been at with Lord Robin.'

In other words, Albert Wilson had glimpsed the back of Robin Laurie's head a few times at the kind of large public levees and garden parties out of which the one could not always wriggle and into which the other, with good works, hefty donations and sheer persistence, had somehow scrambled himself. Perhaps at one of these gatherings Robin's eye had happened to fall upon Ina and he had amused himself in the usual way. With a shudder I recalled a friend whose daughter had had her heart broken by Robin years ago chuckling most unmaternally about—as she put it—the scamp. This was far worse even than a 'bad boy'; to describe even a puppy as a 'scamp' was cloying.

'Then we found ourselves sitting in the same first-class carriage today,' Wilson went on.

'And of course Albert was in the mood for a chinwag,' said Lord Robin. He was smiling at Wilson but I could not ignore the little tickle of mischief behind his words, and Ina's face clouded more than ever. 'When he found out I was on my way home to Buckie he told me all about what kind of weather you've been having and the forecast for Christmas—it sounds shocking, I must say—and asked after my family and friends most solicitously.'

Albert Wilson beamed.

'And then of course I told our news, my love,' he said. 'I told Lord Robin we had a circus come to stay and nothing would do except he changed at Perth with me and came to see it.' So happy was he in the triumph of snagging Robin Laurie he did not seem to be troubled by how unlikely this was.

'You're a great enthusiast for the circus then?' I asked Robin.

'Well, I was changing anyway,' he said. 'But, yes, I'm a fan of the absurd.' He took care to include both Wilsons in his gaze as he spoke. 'The outlandish, the exotic, the extreme.'

'Not that Cooke's Circus is *that* kind of outfit,' said Albert Wilson. Something of Robin's tone seemed, finally, to have penetrated his happy haze. 'There are no freaks or bearded ladies.' His smile was reasserting itself again. 'No, I just told Lord Robin all about Ma and Pa and about Tiny Truman and Big Bad Bill Wolf, and the lovely little Topsy and Anastasia, of course.'

'What,' asked Laurie, 'could be more charming?'

Was it perhaps the lovely little Topsy and Anastasia, then, who were the draw? Would Robin Laurie change trains and suffer the present company (as he would see it) for the chance to meet young ladies of certain beauty and possible easy virtue who might be bored already, camped in the woods? As unlikely as that might sound, it was the most sensible thought I had had yet.

'So I think I shall saunter down there and have a peek after tea,' said Laurie, sitting back in his seat and crossing his ankles with studied languor. He drew out his case and selected a cigarette but, before he could light it, Albert Wilson spoke up. At last, the guiding principle of his existence had got out from under his awe and was back at the tiller again.

'No cigarettes in the house, Lord Robin, I implore you,' he said. 'My poor dear wife's chest

39

will not stand it, you know.'

'Albert,' said Ina mildly, although whether she was chiding him for officiousness or for dropping her chest into the conversation as though it were a blameless elbow I could not say.

'As I explained to you on the train . . .' Wilson went on, ignoring her, but Lord Robin was already snapping his case shut and sitting up straight, the picture of remorse.

'Of course, of course,' he said. 'I cannot apologise enough for my thoughtlessness.'

'I must seem a proper old fuss-budget, I know,' said Albert, wavering again now that the point was won.

'Far from it, my dear chap,' said Lord Robin, looking solemn. 'The well-being of Mrs Wilson is no less precious in my eyes than in yours. Why, if only we all had your tenderness and vigilance, think of the tragedies which might have been prevented. So, very far from it, my dear chap, not at all.'

*   *   *

Possibly, I thought to myself on the drive home, that was just more silliness and cheek, but there was a faint memory stirring somewhere. Was there some special reason that Albert Wilson had asked after Robin's family? I have no taste for gossip and can never remember it in any detail, but thankfully there was a far more reliable recorder available at home.

'Hugh,' I said, 'you'll never guess who I met up with today at the Wilsons'.' Hugh stared back at me. He never *would* guess; he would not even play

40

I-spy with the children when they were small. 'Robin Laurie of all people. On his way home.'

'Vulture,' said Hugh, which was a pretty clear indication that he must know something.

'Now tell me,' I went on, 'what was the tale? I seem to have forgotten.'

'Any number of tales,' said Hugh, 'none of them fit for your ears.' He looked mournfully at the table beside his chair where a stack of papers was sitting. He would far rather pore over them than chat to me but the tea-table had still been out when I got back and I had sat down and had a biscuit, and now—according to *our* house rules—he was stuck with it.

'No, not a conquest,' I said. 'I mean the story about his family.'

'Nothing to tell,' said Hugh. 'Absolutely impeccable pedigree—unlike those Wilsons and, I must say, your taste in companions fails to improve with age.'

'Wasn't there some illness or something?'

'Some illness?' echoed Hugh. 'My God, Dandy, one wouldn't welcome an hysteric in one's home, but sometimes your callousness knows no bounds.' I refused to rise to this and eventually he went on. 'Yes, there was "some illness". Robin is the younger son, as you know, and Buckie—the elder—married that American girl for her millions. Very practical too. She was a Ramsay but not one of *the* Ramsays and to give him his due he never pretended that she was. Anyway she, having knuckled down to filling cradles, caught influenza in '18 and died along with her children. A fair batch of them, as I recall.'

'That's right,' I said, as it came back to me. Of

41

course, if such a thing happened now, a young woman and all her issue wiped out at a stroke, it would lodge in one's mind for keeps, but in the long winter of 1918, with soldiers still dropping from cholera and typhoid fever if not from enemy fire, one had no sympathy left to lavish on the 'flu victims and could watch quite unblinking newsreels of masked men spraying the city streets with Lysol; one's sensibilities were certainly much too numb for one family's bad news to be all that shattering.

'And then blow me if the only one of the lot who hadn't got the 'flu didn't go and die anyway, hunting or boating or some such, and the upshot was that Tom Buckie himself had a heart attack, overcome by grief.' Hugh delivered this with a bit of a glare. He might have meant it to impress upon me that not everyone was lost to proper feeling, but I suspect that he was in danger of being himself overcome by the touching nature of his account and did not want me to see. 'Buckie always was rather sickly, even lankier than the brother, and he's never really got back on his feet again since. Dreadful thing.'

'He hasn't remarried yet?' I said, despising myself even as I did so, for what was running through my mind was not Lord Buckie's loneliness but, of course, the succession.

'He'll never remarry,' said Hugh. 'The marquisate and all the lolly have Robin's name chalked on the back now without a doubt and he'll run through it and sell up before his brother is cold, you mark my words.' This was the most withering insult Hugh could muster: selling up was fathoms below even brickmaking in his view. 'In fact,' he went on, 'I've heard at least one fella say' (when Hugh says he has heard something from 'at least one fella', he means from exactly one, to wit, from George, at his club, who is a worse gossip than he is) 'that Robin broke off an engagement to a very ordinary Miss once it was clear that the nieces and nephews were goners and his brother's health was shot to ribbons, and for the last seven years he's been biding his time, thinking to land himself a bit more of a whopper when he's got a coronet on.'

I usually take the wilder of George's stories with a pound bag of salt, but this one did have the merit of chiming with what I had seen earlier at Benachally. A son of the house of Buckie, who had seen so many of his family connections perish, could forgive Albert Wilson his mania for Ina's safe-keeping after the loss of *their* child that way and, on the other hand, if Ina had ever heard a whisper of what Hugh had just told me—that Robin saw the Spanish flu as a stroke of personal luck—she might well feel chilly towards him; it had not only robbed her of her only child and, apparently, the chance to have another but it had turned her life into a bore and a joke, where she had to conspire with duster-waving servants to get so much as a walk in the grounds.

'And now poor Buckie is sinking at last, I hear,' said Hugh. 'So *of course* Laurie is hot-footing it home to do the grieving brother bit. Of course he is. He's never near the place from one year's end to the next ordinarily, although I'm sure he skims off a healthy layer of the interest to fund his revelries. The old boy has a soft spot for him, so they say.'

At this point, we both heard the distant shriek of the telephone and cocked our heads for Pallister's advancing tread. I could tell the call was for me as soon as he swept in, from the flare of disdain to his nostrils and the lift of disbelief to his brows; when it is one of Hugh's cronies at the other end Pallister wears an expression of subdued pride that he has been entrusted with a part in one of the acts of decent, manly intercourse which keep the world turning and the natives from revolt.

'A Mrs Wilson for you, madam,' he said with commendable neutrality, resisting the inverted commas he must have longed to throw around the name.

I hurried to the nearest branch of our telephone line, which was in Hugh's library.

'Ina?' I said. 'Is everything all right, my dear?'

'Of course,' said Ina Wilson's voice on the other end. 'Why shouldn't it be?' There was no reason at all; only that Hugh and I had been conversing on death and heartbreak, which she was not to know. 'I'm bidden by Albert to ring up and ask you to dinner, Dandy.'

Quick work, Albert. One cup of tea with a younger son and he was suddenly equal to issuing invitations to what I am not being snobbish in calling the oldest family in the county. That, I thought, was a very sharp ascent.

'When?' I asked, with a view to pleading a prior engagement.

'Oh, eight o'clock-ish,' said Ina.

'You mean tonight?' I said, looking at my wristwatch. It was almost six now. Surely professors and bluestockings brought their daughters up with more of an idea than that, even

44

if high tea with the Wilsons had been come on in and the more merrier when Albert was a boy.

'I know, I know,' said Ina, 'but . . . Lord Robin is stopping over and Albert's in a blue funk about entertaining him, and if I hadn't rung you up he would have. And actually, I'm begging too.'

'I'd be delighted,' I said, recognising the sounds of wifely despair, 'but wouldn't it be easier just to send him packing in a car if there's no decent train now?'

'No, he *wants* to stay,' said Ina. 'I would happily send him home in a dog cart, but he's insisting.'

'Hmm,' I said. 'What's he up to?' I hoped that Ina would not be offended.

'I don't want to think about it,' she said, sounding not offended in the least, but still rather strained. 'I shall just grit my teeth and get rid of him in the morning.'

'You really aren't a fan, are you?' I said.

'No,' she said baldly. There was a long pause. 'And besides, I don't want any complications. Not right now.'

'Oh dear,' I answered. I had no idea what was afoot that would make any complications particularly unwelcome at the moment, but I knew full well that causing them was Robin Laurie's especial forte.

*   *   *

'Certainly not,' was Hugh's response to my suggestion that we cancel our own dinner, dress and drive twenty-five miles round the road to Benachally to slum it on one side and be patronised on the other. 'Ring her back and tell

45

her it's out of the question.'

'Or,' I said, considering, 'I could ask Alec to go. I'm sure Ina wouldn't mind.' Hugh looked mulish. 'Or, actually, I could go alone. That would make an even four.' The mulish look underwent a subtle change as Hugh weighed up the competing possibilities of sending me off to dine as the partner of the notorious Robin Laurie—and this in a house where, if the current invitation were anything to go by, normal standards did not apply—and handing me over to the usual thorn in his conjugal side, Alec Osborne.

'Is there anything—you know—up?' he asked, not quite looking at me. This was as close as Hugh ever got to discussing my glittering career and usually he hoped for an answer in the negative. At the current moment, however, something's being 'up' would give him the excuse he longed for to absent himself from the dinner, file Alec and me going to it together under 'work' and tuck up in his library for the evening with a pipe and a sandwich.

'Could be,' I lied.

'The Wilsons have called you in?'

'Pretty much,' I lied again.

'Well, then, you run along,' he said. 'I certainly wouldn't want to get in your way.' Hugh likes to think of himself in that light if he can, but the truth is rather plainer as his concluding remark made only too clear. 'Lord knows, Wilson can easily afford it.'

*   *   *

'And why is it we're going?' grumbled Alec as we bowled along an hour later, watching the sliver of

46

quarter-moonlight glint on the river. The rain had stopped and the temperature had plummeted, turning the weeks-old puddles into treacherous patches of ice. I crossed my fingers and hoped that we would not end up stranded at Benachally overnight, for as little as dinner had to recommend it, breakfast would surely be a great deal worse and all the more infuriating for knowing that as the crow flew one was a mere seven miles from home.

'Think of it as practice,' I told him. 'Your two hours at the barre, your daily scales in every key. We haven't had a case all year and we're getting rusty. So, here are three excellent psychological studies for the plucking, all laid on round the same table, one night only.'

'Psychological studies!' said Alec. 'What *have* you been reading?' But his voice belied his words. He really is one of the most amiable individuals I have ever been lucky enough to know. I smiled at his profile as I thought so. In the scant reflection of the headlamps, he looked rather more ordinary than by day, his curious tawny hair stripped of colour and the stippling of matching freckles invisible, the slight frown of concentration as he drove making him look nearer his true age of thirty-four than the usual tail-wagging twelve and a half he can muster when we are detecting. Or perhaps he only looks twelve and a half to me who am, as Grant described it recently, practically forty.

The bright-eyed schoolboy was much in evidence by the time we had sat down to dinner, for Ina, Albert and Robin Laurie between them surely provided all that any student of human nature could hope for and more. I had worried that Alec would get the giggles and infect me with them when he looked up to one end of the table at Ina, down to the other at Albert and across its vast expanse at Lord Robin and me, even though I had told him about Ina's delicate condition and her husband's guarding of it and Wilson himself had reiterated the main points over sherry too.

Alec had cottoned on admirably well to my run-down. When we had arrived to find Lord Robin smoking on the doorstep, he had said without prompting:

'Keeping the air clear for poor Mrs Wilson, I see. How thoughtful of you.'

'I told Wilson,' said Lord Robin, 'that just as many medicos are in favour of a bit of smoke in the lungs as against it. Protective, cleansing, and all that. Strengthening if anything. But we mustn't upset the apple-cart, must we?' He bared his teeth, threw his elegant cigarette down on the gravel to smoulder and walked inside again, letting a long curl of delicious smoke trail after him through the hallway.

'Right, first impression,' Alec had said in a low voice as we followed him, 'is that what we see here is a well-developed specimen of common "oaf".' I snorted. 'A hat stand, a coat-rack. Exists purely that clothes might be draped over it and can also be dabbed with cologne to scent a room.'

'Rather fierce,' I chided him. 'He's not that bad.'

'Women always stick up for them,' said Alec. 'Women young and old are putty in the hands of a fragrant hat stand. Tchah!'

I was startled by his vehemence, truth be told,

but I concluded that it was to be expected when one young man, blessed by nature and fortune as he was, met another much taller, a great deal richer and rather more handsome than himself. It was a zoological response, nothing more.

'Well, Mrs Wilson will be your blue-eyed girl then,' I said, mildly. 'She can't stand him.'

*   *   *

'Have you been down to the camp yet, Lord Robin?' I asked as the soup was being handed. I noticed that Ina had a maid all of her own serving her soup from her own little tureen, while the three of us shared the friendly butler, and I missed the start of Lord Robin's answer, thinking it through. Surely the servants jostled together in the kitchens and surely if I brushed against the butler and then he brushed against the maid and then the maid brushed against Ina, it was all the same as if Ina had brushed against me. There was, I considered, a goodly measure of ceremony about Albert's precautions and not a lot of common sense. I retrained my attention on the talk at the table.

'—but they clammed up rather, I'm afraid,' Lord Robin was saying. 'Perhaps I just don't have what it takes to talk to gypsies on their own level.'

The insult was subtle and Albert Wilson's smile remained undimmed.

'I don't think they're gypsies, Lord Robin, if you'll forgive me correcting you,' he said.

'The fat old woman with the ear-bobs and the crystal ball, surely,' Laurie replied.

'French, Russian and Irish, she told me,' I

49

chipped in, smarting for Mrs Cooke although his description of her was accurate enough.

'Have you met her, Dandy?' said Alec, shaking his head at me in amusement. Albert Wilson had stopped with his soup spoon halfway to his mouth.

'I did, I have,' I gabbled. 'I stopped off on the way home this afternoon. Sheer nosiness, I admit, but they didn't seem to mind. So,' I turned and looked Robin Laurie in the face, 'whatever the talent is for making friends with them, I have it too. Mrs Cooke told me an enchanting story from her childhood, without bidding, minutes after we met.' I had thought to be weighing in for Albert with this, but Lord Robin managed to turn it back on me. He gave me an impish look, as though assessing whether I was nearer in standing to Albert and the Cookes than I was to him, and then he nodded as though deciding that yes, I was.

'Quite so,' he said, grinning. 'She barely speaks to me, she shares a fond memory with you, and she gives Wilson here the life history of every last clown and tumbler in the show. Quite so.'

I suppressed a sigh. Clearly he was bored and was making fun to lift the boredom but it was getting rather blatant now. Alec's golden eyes had narrowed.

'And I'll bet their life histories are worth the telling, sir,' he said to Albert. Ina gave him a grateful look.

'Oh indeed,' came the reply. 'Take Merryman, the clown. He was the son of a gentleman and was thought by his doctors to be an idiot. Prone to fits and tongue-tied until he was ten. Then he taught himself to read and write and joined his brothers at public school.'

50

'Yes,' said Robin Laurie. 'You told me on the train.'

'Whereupon he started to grow. And grow. And *grow*,' said Albert Wilson, as though this were a fairy tale, 'so he sits himself down and thinks what will I do about this, then? And he left school and took himself a-travelling, all over Europe, all the way to St Petersburg, Constantinople and back again and taught himself everything he needed to know.'

'You've got to admire his pluck,' said Alec. 'There was a chap at my school who was ten feet tall when he was fourteen—Fanshawe—and he just had the life ragged out of him until he left.'

'And even more amazing still,' Albert Wilson continued.

'You amazed me all the way from Waverley to Rattray, changing at Perth, old man,' said Lord Robin. 'I'm not sure I can take any more amazement today.'

'Pretty good stuff of this Merryman to say instead: here I am, turning into a beanpole, now what is a beanpole good for?' said Alec, looking hard at Lord Robin who, although not quite as outlandishly tall and thin as the figure I had glimpsed in the Gilverton woods, was certainly far from stocky.

Albert Wilson, deaf to all slights directed at him by Lord Robin, was not similarly oblivious when lowly hangers-on such as Alec started taking pot-shots at his prize and, with a look at me as though asking me why on earth I had brought such a boor, he began a sustained bout of flattery which Lord Robin accepted with amused graciousness but to which I could not listen for fear of being sick.

Alec and I, instead, chatted to Ina, with Alec being quite charming, claiming common ground with her as a fellow incomer to Perthshire, as though there were no difference between his inheriting Dunelgar and Ina's husband buying up Benachally with the money from his bricks.

When the two conversations merged again, Lord Robin was saying what I knew would bring Ina great relief.

'No, I'm afraid I must be off in the morning. I can hardly forgive myself for tonight's little holiday from duty.'

'Oh, come now, Lord Robin,' said Albert Wilson, 'you'll do your brother all the more good for a night's rest and refreshment, and you know you could not have come to see us here from the sickroom. I am sorry to be so blunt but I couldn't have allowed that.'

'He's dying of heart trouble,' said Laurie. 'There's no danger of infection.'

'Your brother's dying?' said Alec, squirming a little.

'Still, once a body is weakened there's no telling,' said Wilson. He was on his home ground now.

'He is,' said Lord Robin to Alec, then he turned to Albert Wilson. 'Believe me, we are just as well versed in the knotty question of contagion at Buckie as you are here at Benachally,' he said.

'You must excuse my insisting,' said Albert, his voice rising almost to a squeak at the thought of his own temerity. 'Of course, it must seem silly to you, but we have all been through the same—'

'Hardly!' Robin said, interrupting. 'You had it easy down in Glasgow. Doctors on hand and nurses to spare. You should have tried getting a decent nurse to travel all the way out to Cullen when in town she could wait until one patient was dead and then just walk down the street to the next.'

'Robin!' I said, unable to help myself. 'Surely there's no need to go back over such things after all this—'

'What he is saying is quite true, Dandy,' said Ina, although why she should defend him was beyond me. 'I cannot imagine what it must have been like for anyone with no nurse to help.'

Robin Laurie frowned at her and then turned back to Alec.

'My sister-in-law, two nephews and two nieces died like flies all within a week,' he said.

Alec was struck dumb by this and turned to me beseechingly. Albert looked close to tears and Ina only stared into her lap.

'Too, too horrid,' I said, thinking if the conversation could not be stopped then one owed him at least a little sympathy. 'And then there was a dreadful accident too, I believe?'

Robin nodded curtly.

'The oldest,' he said. 'Drowned.' He looked at Albert Wilson as he carried on. 'And when my brother heard that, he took his weak heart and went to the sickroom and lay down beside his dead wife, holding his dead baby in his arms, and he *did not catch it*.' These last words were drilled into the air like nails being banged into oak and there was a long silence after them. Finally, Albert spoke.

'What a sad story, Lord Robin,' he said. 'I'm sure we're all very touched by it.'

'Dandy,' said Ina, rising to her feet and

53

dropping her napkin on to her chair, although we
had not yet had pudding or cheese. I stood, cast a
quick horrified glance at Alec and followed Ina to
the door. She was shaking, blundering rather than
walking, and, instinctively, I reached out towards
her.

'Careful, Mrs Gilver,' said Albert Wilson. 'Not
too close now.'

Robin Laurie behind me let out a long hooting
laugh.

4

'So I for one decided to get drunk,' said Alec on
the telephone the next morning. I was waving a
biscuit in front of Bunty's nose and she was
snapping at it and whining. 'Yat!' I said. Bunty
ignored me.

'What?' said Alec.

'You don't need to tell me you got drunk,' I
reminded him. 'I drove you home.'

'I couldn't decide which one I felt more sorry
for, you see, so I decided to give myself such a
crippling hangover that I'd only feel sorry for me.
But it was very good port and I feel fine.'

'At least I got my question answered,' I said.
'Laurie must have heard about the Wilsons and
decided to come along to tea and treat them to a
sermon. *That's* what he was doing there.'

'Pretty cruel sort, isn't he?' said Alec.

'Not usually,' I said. 'Your initial character
sketch was more on the nose—silliness rather than
cruelty, as a rule. And besides, it was in a fairly

good-hearted cause.'

'Do you think it'll make any difference? Do you think Wilson could let his poor wife live her life? Could she insist on it?'

'She's not the insisting type,' I said. 'She endures. And makes the best of it when she gets the chance.'

'Yes, but why?' said Alec. 'She can't really love the man. I could tell she was trying not to wince every time he opened his silly mouth last night. A comfortable home and respectability? But didn't you say her parents were terribly advanced? They'd surely welcome her home and tough out the divorce, wouldn't they?'

I felt rather ashamed to admit that the question had not occurred to me. One simply did endure. I did and it seemed unremarkable that Ina Wilson did too. 'Worn out by ill health?' I suggested. 'Can't summon the energy? Or maybe she does love him, deep down. Who can say?'

'No,' said Alec. 'I think you're right about the enduring, but I got the distinct impression that she has an end in sight. She's putting up with it all *until something*. Do you see?'

All of a sudden, I did. All of a sudden, Ina's kindness to Albert Wilson the evening before seemed a little like the treat one gives to an old horse while, out of sight, a groom is loading the gun.

'I suppose the obvious thing is widowhood,' I said, reluctantly.

'Not much chance of that—Wilson looks good for decades yet. I'd back him surviving her any day.'

'And she doesn't have the leisurely air one sees

when good fortune is just about to fall into someone's lap.'

'The cushioned look of sure inheritance,' said Alec. 'The one that Robin Laurie wears like a mink cloak. It's pretty sickening and, I agree, absent from young Mrs Wilson. So anyway, what did she say to you in the drawing room once you were alone?'

'Not much of import, as you can imagine,' I told him. 'She was knocked flat by that debacle at the table.'

'She must have said something,' Alec insisted. 'Tell me at least that you got to work on her and didn't just let her sit there fluttering and fainting.'

'Alec, darling,' I said, 'I couldn't truffle on just for practice. We're not on a case, if you recall.' Even as I said it, though, I could hear the approaching footsteps which would render my words untrue.

Pallister had been pushed beyond his—considerable—capacity for cold disdain and looked simply stunned.

'A visitor for you, madam,' he said and he delivered it without any editorialising at all, not so much as a meaningful hesitation; but numbly, as though in shock. He did not hold the door open but turned and walked away.

Into the doorway, with a rustle of bombazine and a flash of gold, stepped Mrs Cooke, a small black monkey in a sequined waistcoat perched on one arm.

'I'm ringing off now, Alec,' I said into the telephone, 'but I imagine we'll be speaking again very soon.'

56

*   *   *

'You'll excuse me bringing the little one, my beauty,' she said as she plumped down on to a sofa, 'only he gets so bored in the winter there and then what mischief like you wouldn't believe.' The monkey, closely watched by a very puzzled Bunty, was looking around my sitting room with bright interest and twitching fingers and I followed its gaze, taking in the Dresden clock and candlesticks on which there were porcelain petals and cherubs' wings so thin one could see the sunlight through them, and the Rockingham pottery Dalmatians, which were admittedly rather vulgar but had been presents from my sister and had terribly spindly legs. On the other hand, no one had ever called me her beauty, and as a sweetening tactic it was hard to beat.

'Would you like some coffee, Mrs Cooke?'

'Cup of tea would go down a treat there,' she answered and I pulled the bell-rope.

Pallister had clearly recovered himself enough to spread the news because the parlour maid was in the room almost before the rope had stilled again, her eyes like soup plates.

'I'll have my coffee now, Becky,' I said. 'A pot of tea too.' I glanced at the monkey. 'And some cocoa? Milk?'

'Bobbo would take a few raisins,' said Mrs Cooke. 'But he's not a lover of milk.'

I dismissed Becky with a nod and a smile and turned to business.

'Now then, Mrs Cooke,' I said, 'what can I do for you?'

'My father,' she said, apparently in reply, 'wurr a

57

lion tamer. Now, you might not think that's strange there.' She stopped and regarded me for a minute.

'It's certainly less surprising than if my father had been a lion tamer,' I said.

'Well, my beauty,' said Mrs Cooke, 'that's where you're wrong. For although there's families of balancing slangers and tumbling slangers stretching right back, for wurn't the first Tam Cooke a horse man just like Pa, the big cats is quite different, see. It's like lightning, strikes anywhere, and dun't come back.' At this moment, she unclasped a little knitted bag she had hanging from her wrist and drew out a piece of card. 'That's me,' she said, passing it to me. It was, I saw, a very old and rather yellowed photograph—a daguerreotype, probably—showing a fat baby dressed in the heavily beribboned style of the previous century, lolling amongst a set of cushions. I took a closer look and could feel my eyes widen. They were not cushions at all, but lion cubs, four of them, one of them with a big soft paw on the baby's leg.

'I loved the cats,' Mrs Cooke said. 'Watched them for hours, lions, tigers and leopards the same, watched my old pa in the cage every day, watched him break in the new stock, watched him clean their teeth and trim their claws. One time he tripped and fell over and got a bit of a biff for his trouble, because it dun't do to show a cat your belly, and that day I just watched and din't even leave off licking my lolly.

'Until this one day.' Mrs Cooke had a new note in her voice. 'It wurr a tigress. Princess Zanzi was her name and Pa had bought her from the Rosaires to make three for his second spot. Well, as soon as I saw my daddy step into that cage with Zanzi I started to scream and holler and drum my heels, just like a little flatty rakly instead of a circus girl. I got tooken out, leathered hard by my ma and put in the wagon with no dinner, tea nor supper that day. And what do you think happened, there?'

The door opened and Becky entered with the coffee tray, followed by Annie with a tray of tea and one of the housemaids carrying a plate of buns which could easily have been brought by one of the others, but I could hardly blame them.

Mrs Cooke poured herself a cup and gave Bobbo one of the buns from which he did, sure enough, begin to pick out raisins. I was mesmerised for a minute or two, watching him crouched on the arm of my sofa with his long toes curled over it, daintily transferring the little morsels to his mouth.

'Well, my beauty, what happened was this: when he'd got Princess Zanzi trained up and in the ring with the other two tigresses—and it took no time at all, for my pa worked a charm on every cat he met and she wurr a quick one to catch on—the very first show, first whip crack, she leapt off her tub and went for his throat.'

'Did he survive?'

'Oh yes,' said Mrs Cooke, 'he turned away in time and she got him in the shoulder there, but he lost his arm and near half his blood and spent the rest of the season in the hospital with doctors coming from all over to look at him, and then how many acts din't up and leave us, with the boss laid out and my mother struggling. We had a hard winter that year.' She took a swig of tea. 'Well, there's what comes of not sticking to your family

59

way, but he'd learned his lesson. When he came home at last the first thing he did wurr get a lion tamer in and himself went back to his horses.'

'And what happened to Zanzi?' I asked. 'Was she shot?'

'No, none of that,' said Mrs Cooke. 'Beast couldn't help her nature, could she? She wurr put in the menagerie and drew a fair crowd there. My ma painted up the sides of her wagon with scenes of the fight, called her Zanzi the Mankiller. Flatties couldn't get enough of her after that. And do you know, Pa ended up with a set of liberty horses as good as Tam's is now even with his one arm, so all was well and ended well there.'

I had the feeling familiar from the day before that Mrs Cooke's story had gone awry somewhere. Certainly, I could not see the moral of it.

'So,' I began, 'are you saying that lightning did strike twice in this case? That you have the gift for big cats like your father?'

'Me?' said Mrs Cooke, astonished. 'Not me. I love the beasts but I'm a Cooke through and through, horses all the way. Not but what my ma wurr pure Ilchenko and like as she had no bones the tumbles she could do. No, I've no way with the big cats much as I love them. Never even thought myself to try.' She now looked at me with as piercing a stare as two such round brown eyes could muster. 'No, it's the sight I have,' she said. 'Even from a babby. I knew trouble was coming from that Zanzi. And'—she leaned forward—'I know trouble's coming now. I'm not a maid any more and I don't scream and shout, I play clever. But I knew it, I know it and I'm not wrong.'

'What kind of trouble?' I breathed. One could

60

take or leave the second sight and one could not help thinking that the history of Zanzi and her old pa was a bit of a shunt up a narrative siding, but if Mrs Cooke had hard facts with her as well as memories, I wanted to hear them.

'Topsy,' she said and then bit her lip. 'It goes against my nap to be telling a . . . someone who's from the outside, begging your pardon. But I need help there and no other way round it. Topsy has lost her swing. Topsy Turvy, our little tumbler, my niece, more or less. Her swing what she has for the trapeze is gone.'

I had been sitting forward with my breath held, waiting, and at that I must admit I let it go and slumped back a bit again.

'And you need help to search for it?' I said. Mrs Cooke gave a short laugh, which made me blush and made Bobbo the monkey look up at us both for a moment. 'Or you need help to find out who took it?' I said; a slightly more sensible suggestion.

'I think I know who took it,' said Ma. 'I only wish I din't.'

'So,' I said slowly, but not slowly enough for what I should say next to spring to my mind. 'So . . . I'm sorry, Mrs Cooke, but how exactly *can* I help?'

'How can she help, she asks!' Mrs Cooke twinkled at me. 'Don't you come over shy with me, my beauty. I saw your hand, remember there? And I looked at your leaves once you'd gone, just to make sure. I know what you are.' I stared at her and I could feel a prickle as the hairs stood up along the back of my neck. 'Besides, it in't just Topsy. There's more going on than Pa could crack his whip at and the swing's just the tip what's broke

61

the surface like. But, one way or three, you can stop it. You know you can. You've done it before, han't you?'

'Apart from anything else,' I said, regaining some of my composure, 'it was my left hand you looked at.'

'Left hand's where some things show,' said Mrs Cooke.

I decided that a brisk air of business was the best response to such bewitchments (and I thought, not for the first time, that for a rational woman such as me, brought up to believe that miracles and wonders were the province of the vicar and he was welcome to them, I certainly seemed to be a magnet for mystic fancy).

'So who took it then?' I said.

'Ana,' answered Mrs Cooke. 'I din't see her or nothing but I'd put my toenails on it. There's no love lost 'tween her and Topsy and less every time you look there, and it's not the first time neither, although thanks be that I stopped it a-coming out or she'd have been off that ground there with a flea in her ear.'

'But if she's a thief,' I said, 'then why not?'

'Not a thief!' said Mrs Cooke, shifting and resettling herself with a great rustling of her petticoats. 'Not so bad as that. It wurr just a prank.'

'What did she do?' I asked.

'She took Tam's whip.' Mrs Cooke's voice had sunk to a whisper. 'If Tam had found out . . . it just in't circus to go meddling with props what in't yours, and the rum coll's whip in't just any old prop.'

'The who?' I asked.

62

'The boss man,' said Mrs Cooke. 'What you'd call the ringmaster.'

'You must be very fond of this Ana,' I said. 'If she's being as naughty as all that and you're still on her side . . . and against your own husband too.'

'Tin't that,' said Mrs Cooke. She looked at me for a long moment before she spoke again. 'You know our boys are away across the sea? Kushty boys, they are, both of them. Lads still, not forty, and I miss them more than I can tell you without my heart breaking in my mouth. Do you have babbies of your own?'

'I do,' I said. 'Two sons, like you. Fifteen and thirteen.' I forbore to mention that I had waved them gladly off to prep school at eight and we smiled at one another fondly.

'So there's how bad it is then,' said Mrs Cooke. 'My Tom and Joe are two of the finest horsemen I ever did see, and that's not just me what's their ma saying it. They have a voltige act for now—The Brothers Ilchenko—using their granny's name for the sound of it—a Cossack act and it's a sight to see, madam, dancing on them two ponies of theirs, fast as a blur and all the galleries clapping and stamping their feet. It wurr the top of the show.' She was getting quite misty as she recounted this, but soon gathered herself again with a sniff. 'But young Tom would have gave way in the end,' she said. 'Give over the act to young Joe and his wife— when he got one, like—and taken the whip from his pa. Tam Cooke's Circus it would be, same as ever. That's what we've thought, Pa and me, since the day he wurr born.'

'But they've gone,' I put in, hoping to keep Mrs Cooke from recounting Tom Jr's entire childhood

63

to me.

'And I thought we'd fold for sure without them,' she said. 'Till our Ana came along. Her and her golden pony.'

'She's the star of the show?' I said, guessing.

'But don't you go saying so, mind,' said Mrs Cooke. 'I mean to say, the Prebrezhenskys are a grand spot and Topsy's a pretty girl and always draws a crowd. And them two clowns was made for each other. But a circus needs animals, see? If she ups and leaves us, we won't hardly be a circus at all no more.'

'But she's trouble?'

'I wun't say that,' said Mrs Cooke. 'The poor maid's troubled in herself and who could blame her? For she's had a hard life there and come to the circus to make it better but not a scrap of luck since, none at all. Her golden pony died and Tam—I shouldn't speak ill of my own man—but Tam's that down on her and just looking for a reason to give her the ghost. Or she might just up and off by her own self, afore we have a chance to get her bound to us for keeps like. And she could have a grand life at Cooke's, if she'd just bed in. If she'd just . . . If she wurr one o' my own, I'd talk to her myself, find out what's ailing her and talk her round like. But . . .'

'She's not a relation then?'

'Josser,' said Mrs Cooke. 'Gently born like yourself there, madam. And so I thought you could mebbes talk to her in her own tongue, get close to her and get her told. Only . . . don't go talk talk talking until you know what to say there, eh? I'd talk to the rest of 'em first, find out what's what and who knows it. Them clowns is up to something

64

for starters. And not just them neither. Bill Wolf knows more than he'll tell me.'

'And I take it Mr Cooke is not to know what I'm about?' I said.

'Well, my beauty,' said Mrs Cooke, with a look of great innocence on her face that did not fool me for a minute, 'where's the use in telling a man everything, eh? He knows I think there's trouble coming, but more than that would only fret him.'

'I have had cases before where the diplomacy was as crucial as the detecting,' I assured her.

'Cases?' said Mrs Cooke, looking startled. 'Well, as to "cases", I can't be paying you, mind there. Pa and me have to pull in tight winters, but let me see now . . . We can give them two lads of yours a Christmas they'll never forget, can Cooke's Circus. And that's got be worth gold to a mother. So what d'you say?'

It did not look much, in prospect, and the briefing was far from full, but Alec and I were without a sniff of any other work and Donald and Teddy would never have forgiven me denying them circus privileges if I had such things in my gift.

No time like the present, I told myself, and twenty minutes later I had packed Mrs Cooke and Bobbo into the Cowley, although she had been more than ready to return the way she had come—on foot over the hills—and was climbing into the driver's seat to be waved away by Pallister, both footmen and the hallboy. Gilverton's servants' hall would not be lost for conversation today.

*   *   *

65

My first sight as we drew up beside the pond and stepped down again was Bill Wolf, the individual I had taken to be a bear, still wearing the shaggy suit and only marginally less alarming now that he was revealed as a man. He was sitting on an upturned barrel, beside his caravan—his living wagon, as Mrs Cooke had taught me to call it—making the most of the weak winter sunlight as he stitched at something in his lap. Mrs Cooke gave me a look and scuttled away. Ah yes, I thought, Bill Wolf is one of those who knows something. I squared my shoulders and began walking towards the giant with my chin high in the air and my teeth only chattering slightly.

They were stilled as I approached him by my noticing what I had missed before: there was a small child—next to Mr Wolf a *very* small child—tucked in between his knees, half under his beard and helping to hold taut the length of stuff he was stitching. The child watched me, warily at first, and then with frank interest as Bunty started whining and rearing up: the new little friend from the day before was beckoning from across the ground. I unhooked her lead and she went off without so much as a backward glance at her old friend of the last seven years.

'Tis a waste of a kushty beast like yon, right enough, keeping it as a pet,' Bill Wolf called to me by way of a greeting, nodding at Bunty's departing back. His voice was a guttural rumble, with the now familiar mix of Irish and Eastern, pure circus as Mrs Cooke would say. 'My Sallie there's got a way with dogs.'

'Oh, she's yours, is she?' I said.

'Aye, my little rakly, and Tom Thumb here's her

66

twin,' said Bill. He put down his sewing—it was a leather strap and he was attaching bells to it with an enormous needle threaded up with a bootlace—and ruffled the boy's hair. 'Just about five now, the two of them. Never mind autumn crocuses; more like Sarah and Abraham, eh, Ma?' He raised his voice to a boom, and a woman appeared at the window of the wagon and leaned out.

'But no Hagar!' she said, laughing so that her face creased almost as much as Mrs Cooke's and she showed every one of her dazzling china teeth. I tried not to look surprised. Why should not circus folk know their Bible, after all?

I leaned up against the side of the wagon, taking their friendliness at face value and hoping that leaning on a living wagon was not some kind of dreadful faux pas like stepping unasked aboard a yacht.

'I seen you yesterday, missus,' said Mr Wolf. 'Along with that Mrs Wilson from the house.'

'You circus-daft too, like her, then?' asked his wife. There was no insult in her words and so I did not take offence.

'It is tremendously exciting to have you here,' I answered, non-committally.

'Surely,' said Bill Wolf, not troubled by false modesty, I could see. 'If it's all new to you, it must seem so.'

'Have you always been with the circus, then?' I asked. Bill Wolf nodded.

'All our lives,' he said. 'Lally there used to have an aerial act till Tom and Sal put paid to it for her.'

'I'm not complaining,' said Mrs Wolf and with a last grin disappeared inside again.

'Then we thought to have a knife-throwing act,' Bill went on. 'Worked it up all the time Ma were carrying the nippers, should have been a treat.' I could not agree; throwing knives at one's pregnant wife seemed beyond barbarism to me. 'But Tam Cooke's no taste for it. Says it's not right circus.' Bill bent to chew off the end of a lace and then selected another bell and began stitching again. 'Not so sure myself,' he went on, spitting out some stray threads. 'Reckon it's more like he thinks it's too much of the Wild West and he can't like it, now his boys are over there without his say-so. Driv him potty, that did. Made him look bad.'

'I thought,' I began, newly careful now that it seemed there were circus acts and circus acts and the potential for offence among them, 'I thought you were a strongman, Mr Wolf.' Tom, leaning back against his father's chest, giggled softly.

'I was,' said Bill. 'I was. And now I'm a strong man for my age, maid. A strong man for sixty, but who's going to roll up to see that? And it's Bill, Pa or Wolfie. I'm no flatty, with your Mister.'

'I beg your pardon . . . Bill,' I said, smiling.

'So I do fillers,' he said. 'Run-ins. And then I've got up a one-man band for before the show. Me and Ma Cooke between us, see. A crystal ball and a one-man band and maybe they'll never notice there's no menagerie if we're lucky.'

There was something ineffably sad about all of this, I thought. Cooke's Circus shrinking as everyone in it grew old.

'And shall you retire?' I asked. 'Or shall you always stay? Until . . .'

'Until the black carriage comes for me?' said Bill. 'That I will. I must. And between you, me and who else is listening, maid'—he dropped his voice—'I've an idea for a new turn. A proper spot again. If I can get everyone as needs to be talked around to it and start the training. You'd laugh if I told you—size of me—but it's a good 'un. 'Sides,' he said in a louder voice, 'we've got to keep on till this little chavvy gets trained up, han't we? Him and his sister.' He lifted Tom right off his feet and shook him over his head, making the child squeal with delight.

'And what's he going to do?' I said. 'Train dogs?'

'Acrobat,' said Bill. 'A tumbler, like his ma. My Lally is Topsy's ma's cousin's girl and all Ilchenko on her pa's side since way back.' Bill put his son gently down on to the ground again. 'He an't no strongman, that's for sure.'

'Could be,' said Tom, getting over his shyness of me at last, and flexing his thin arms 'Might be.' His father shook his head at him, chuckling, and then all of a sudden he looked hard at me.

'And so Ma Cooke come and got you, did she? Not much gets past her.'

'Do you know something, Mr . . . Bill?' I said.

He hesitated.

'Too much,' he said, at last. 'I dunno what bee Ma's got in her hat, mind, but I know more than she does about some things. More than I want to, truth be told.'

'About Topsy?' I asked. 'About Ana?' I was feeling my way in the dark, but I thought I should keep at it while he was in a mood to talk to me.

'Ana!' he said, her name seeming to catch his interest as soon as I spoke it. 'She's a mystery to me, that one. Someone needs to have a quiet word with the maid. Tell her she wants to be a bit more careful like, keep on the right side if she knows what's good for her.'

This certainly chimed with what Mrs Cooke had told me.

'I intend to, Mr . . . Bill,' I said. 'And anything you can tell me will only help.' But I had pushed too far now; I could see it in his face.

'I've got my place here,' he said. 'And after what I've done to hang on to it I'll keep my head down.'

'After what you've done,' I repeated, careful not to make it a question. Bill Wolf's eyes showed just a dart of panic all the same.

'Making a filler of myself,' he said. 'That's what I mean. One step up from an odd-job man, that's me. But I will tell you this: that old donah loves them chavs like babbies so it's not the prads and spots that's aching her, but His Gills is just flash mad he couldn't stop them and coming down hard enough to break a king pole and if this show don't hold together there's more than me and Lall'll end up nobbing the streets with a stick and a rag.'

In other words, I thought (and getting it into other words felt more like unseen translation than anything I had tackled since my French governess had given up on me), Mrs Cooke was missing her grown-up sons as though they were children but it was Mr Cooke's pride, not his heart, which was wounded by the boys heading for Coney Island or wherever they were without his say-so and taking trained horses with them, and now Mr Cooke was stamping his authority on the rest of the outfit with such vigour that he might flatten it completely except that some of the artistes would cling on to this job with their little fingernails, ignoring any amount of trouble, if it meant they could avoid . . .

70

Madame Toulemonde herself would have forgiven me for leaving it untranslated because what could ever express abjectness better than 'nobbing the streets with a stick and a rag'? Nothing that I could think of.

I excused myself from the—unexpectedly delightful—Pa Wolf after that, mentally turning over the corner of his card to remind me to speak to him again, and wandered over to the tent.

I was hoping for twelve liberty horses or Anastasia riding the haute école, and was disappointed and not a little surprised to see, in the ring, what looked like three clowns standing smoking, with a sausage dog rolling on its back in the sawdust at their feet. It seemed unlikely that they would have to practise their funny walks and pratfalls all winter like the acrobats and high-wire walkers, but I was sure these were clowns. One was the spindly giant, one the midget, and the third was wearing a pair of long shoes and had a hoop in his trousers waist. All three had top hats on. They glanced at me as I entered and the midget nodded a greeting. The long man simply dipped his head as though too shy to meet my eyes. The third noted my presence—I should have said he knew I was coming, for he betrayed no surprise—but otherwise ignored me. He was evidently in charge and the more I watched him the more I thought I could see a resemblance to Mr Tam Cooke. His voice too as he put the others through their paces was the same.

After a few minutes, the little man took the cigarette butts from the other two and walked to the edge of the ring to stub them out and drop the butts over the side on to the grass, then he

71

waddled back at a trot and lined up. Instinctively they faced towards where I was sitting, unable to ignore an audience, even an audience of one, uninvited, to a show not yet ready to be seen.

'Akilina!' called the boss clown and at the other side of the ring the littlest Prebrezhensky girl wound up a gramophone machine and laid the arm down.

Like most people, I have not found clowns really funny since I was five but for the next ten minutes, I laughed more than I could ever remember laughing in my life. The hooped clown had a parcel to unwrap. He rolled up his sleeves and gave his hat to the tall man to hold. *He*, unthinking, made to put the new hat on his own head and finding a hat already there, removed it, bent his lanky frame completely in half and gave it to the sausage dog who ran along the line and handed it to the tiny man, who thanked the dog gravely and tried to put the hat on *his* head. Encountering his own hat, he took it off, nudged his neighbour, interrupting the unwrapping, and passed it on.

From there, the three hats were juggled round and round, faster and faster, the parcel being thrown high in the air to get it out of the way whenever a hat came the hooped clown's way. The sausage dog waited, stretched up against the leg of the tall clown, barking in time with the music, to offer his services again but the tall clown did not have a moment's attention to spare. After a furious minute the parcel was undone and what was inside but another hat, and another and another and yet another. I could not help clapping as the dog nipped the tall clown's leg and at last

72

got hold of a hat to run along with and throw up for the tiny man to catch and now the dog was part of the frenzy too, barking first in front of the tall clown, then behind him, making the poor man spin, swaying like a reed in a gale, while the hats kept coming, until, with the music building to a flourish, the tall clown spinning like a top and the parcel empty . . . they stopped.

The short clown caught all the hats one by one and the dog sat down in the sawdust again. Akilina lifted the arm of the gramophone.

'If you throw two up, Charlie, instead of giving me one,' said the tall clown to the hooped one, 'I'll spin round, Jinx'll run along with nothing and jump into Tiny's arms, Tiny'll make to throw him up in the air, I'll lean over to save Jinx and all the hats can come down into the box and you shut it.' His voice was a surprise to me. He sounded educated, no Irish or Russian about him anywhere, no circus at all.

'No, no, no,' said Charlie. 'The dog'll get the big laugh that way.'

'Well, owzabout if Andrew and me chuck all the hats on to your head and Jinx jumps into t'box, then?' said Tiny.

'And I just stand there?' said Charlie.

'Or you and I chuck all the hats on Tiny's head.'

'Won't look balanced.'

'Look pretty kushty if Tiny were in the middle,' said Andrew. The circus word sounded very odd in his accent. 'I think we always get the big laugh if Tiny and I stand next.'

'Owzabout if Charlie and me chuck all the hats on your head,' said Tiny to Andrew. He was standing with hands on hips looking up at Andrew,

73

indeed, almost falling over backwards, in fact, to look up at him. 'Or if Charlie chucks his and I try and keep missing and Jinx hands them back to me.' Charlie was shaking his head. 'Look, just look,' said Tiny. He and the tall man started the hats moving again. Not even missing the third clown they set them all spinning through the air and then, just as he had suggested, the little man started lobbing them up and the tall man started catching them on his head. Any that missed the dog caught until there was only one left. Tiny threw it up again and again and Andrew bent his long legs trying to catch it on the top of the wavering tower he was already wearing. Charlie, slowly, folded his arms, turned away and lit a cigarette, not even watching. At last, Tiny put the hat on his own head, turned the parcel box upside down and climbed onto it. He whistled the little dog up into his arms, whereupon the dog snatched the last hat off the midget's head with his teeth and flung it up on to the top of the tottering stack.

'Finished?' said Charlie, turning round again. 'Right then, here's what we'll do. I'll throw a hat up and catch it in the box, snap the lid shut. Then you'll throw them all in, one to each side, in, snap, in, snap, until there's three left and we catch those three on our heads.'

'What about Jinxie?' said Andrew.

'Four then,' said Charlie. 'Jinx gets one too.'

'Littl'un what fits or a big'un what hides him?' asked Tiny.

'Up to you,' said Charlie. 'What d'you think?'

'Big one and he trails off wearing it,' said Andrew.

'Nah,' said Charlie. 'Ends on a downbeat that

way.'

'You're the boss,' said Andrew.

Charlie's face split into a lopsided grin around his cigarette. 'Now, see, you're learning! We'll make clowns out of you two jossers yet.' With that, he strolled over to me and put one long shoe up on a section of the curved box which separated the seats from the ring. 'Charlie Cooke,' he said to me, holding out a hand. 'You're Ma's pal, aren't you? What is it—painting like the Tober-omey's missus? Writing stories?' He winked at me as he said this and I hesitated, partly because if this Mr Cooke—surely Tam Cooke's brother—was not in Ma's confidence then I should be circumspect with him too, partly because I could not interpret the wink, and partly because I was distracted by the way the hoop in his trousers waist allowed me to see right inside them, all the way down his long winter drawers to the tops of his boots.

Thankfully, he did not wait for an answer. 'What's your tuppenceworth, then?' he asked, jerking his head back to the other two who were retying the parcel behind him. It was pretty obvious that his main concern was that he, Charlie Cooke, should be the centre of the act and I half wished I could have argued with him, but I had to be honest.

'I think it's wonderful,' I said, 'and I think your ending is best.'

'There it is, lads,' he said, turning round with his arms spread wide. 'The customer is always right.' Then he shucked off the flipper-like extensions to his boots and, leaving them in the sawdust, he sauntered off out of the tent, whistling. Akilina Prebrezhensky straightened up and scampered after him.

'Sorry, chaps,' I said once he was out of earshot.

'See, Jinxie-boy,' said Tiny. The dog looked up at him out of adoring liquid brown eyes. 'Not everyone is a champion of the underdog and a friend of the little man.'

I could not help chuckling, although he was being impertinent, really.

'If you want to know the truth . . .' I said. Tiny came over to the side of the ring and hopped up to sit on the edge. 'The truth is I think the whole act would be fine with just the two of you but since he's in it it *would* be a poor show to have him just stand there for the grand finale.' I looked over to see if the tall man, Andrew, would join us too but he scraped a bow and left by the curtained exit which led to behind the scenes.

'He's shy, not rude,' said Tiny, 'is our Andrew Merryman. Not me.' He swung his short legs around until he was facing me and held out his hand to shake, sticking his arm straight out as if challenging me to grasp it. His hand was bigger than mine and his grip immensely strong; I am sure he could have pulled me off my seat if he had tried to.

'Edward Truman,' he said. 'Tiny to me friends and me enemies too, more's the pity. Big Bad Bill Wolf calls me Little Bad Ted Truman and for a time I was The Pocket Colossus, until Andrew there said it made me sound like an encyclopedia.' He hugged himself and crowed with laughter.

'Dandy Gilver,' I said. 'A neighbour. Of the Wilsons, I mean, and so of you for this winter too.'

'It's going to be a hard one,' said Tiny. 'All them girls was mumping on about the weather, mud getting inside t'wagons. Said we needed frost, cos it were cleaner.' He rubbed his big hands up and down his little arms, shivering. 'Way I see it, a bit of mud on your rug won't freeze you in your bed before the morning comes.'

'Mrs Cooke's living wagon seemed rather cosy,' I said.

'Ma Cooke's proper old circus,' said Tiny. 'Born in a wagon and lived there all her days. She keeps that stove going all night without waking. Gets up and feeds it sticks and her wagon's as warm as pies in t'morning, but see a josser like me, I fall asleep at night and wake up next day with me teeth chattering in me 'ead.'

'A josser,' I repeated. 'I'm only learning, but I believe a josser is a flatty who's trying to mend his ways.' Tiny clapped his hands, his whole body bouncing slightly with each slap of his palms. 'You're not from a circus family, then?' I said.

'Wouldn't *that* have been handy?' he replied with heavy irony. I flushed. 'No, me father had a chandlery in Scarborough. His father were a merchant seaman and *his* father, they do say, were a pirate. Well, he were hanged in Jamaica for summat or t'other. So, I suppose you could say running away is in me blood, only I reckoned I'd have more luck running away to the circus than to sea. I hooked up with me first show when I were ten and I've been atching ever since.'

'Atching?'

'Summer tenting,' said Tiny Truman. 'Travelling round.'

'Always with Cooke's?' I asked him.

'Nay, that were me first season just gone,' he answered. 'Lorra changes at Cooke's last spring.

77

Before that, I were five year with a show, name of Gregson. Lovely little show, but . . .' He stared down at his feet for a moment or two without speaking. His face with its heavy brow and flattened nose, deep lines bracketing his mouth, should have been grotesque, but there was such expression in his eyes and such humour in the wide grin that one very soon forgot to find him peculiar. He glanced up, breaking his reverie, and the grin widened. 'Old Man Gregson got past doing two shows a day, that's all. Then t'kangaroo died.'

'A kangaroo?' I could not hide my astonishment.

'That's what Gregson's were known for,' Tiny said. 'Biff the Boxing Kangaroo. As long as old Biff were still going, we was on clover, but after he'd gone . . . Ma Gregson sent him off for stuffing, but before she got him back again, the show had folded.'

'It's terribly sad,' I said, feeling the inadequacy of the words.

'Well, it is and it ain't,' said Tiny. 'Pa Cooke came to t'sale, since Cooke's and Gregson's was both in Aberdeen at the same time—and if there's anywhere more like to make a kangaroo drop dead and a show fold, I've never seen it. He were looking for working ponies, but he saw me and it just so 'appened that all season Andrew Merryman had been pestering him for a job, so he looks at Andrew and he looks at me and he puts three and a half and a little half together. He's a seeing man, Pa Cooke, knew from the off Andrew and me was made for each other.'

I nodded, thinking. In other words, both Truman and Merryman had every reason to be loyal to Cooke's Circus. If this Ana was indeed stealing props and causing trouble they would want to help. And had Mrs Cooke not said that she thought 'them clowns' knew something?

'You must,' I said, carefully, 'be wondering what I'm doing here.'

Tiny gave me a look as sharp as a little blue dagger, but before he could speak a loud dull clanging sounded from outside.

'Dinnertime,' said Tiny. He put his hands down by his sides and, lifting himself on to them, he swung his legs up behind him, clicked his heels and sprang back to land in the ring. 'Or, begging your pardon, my lady, I should say: luncheon is served.'

5

I could see that luncheon—dinner, as the circus folk called it—was delightful in its way, if one found delight in thick stew and potatoes around a campfire in the open air. I have always preferred carved slices and thin gravy eaten off a table in a dining room with the potatoes cooked in a pot out of sight in the kitchen somewhere and not plucked out of the fire on a long fork and thrown around the assembled diners with a flick of the wrist. Still, one does not like to be above one's company and so I sat down, laid my gloves in my lap and accepted a bowl of stew with gratitude, even managing to field my potato when it came.

There was a considerable crowd at the start, since the artistes and their families were joined by half a dozen others whom Mr Cooke nodded vaguely towards and identified as tent men and grooms. There was a strict order of precedence in play, however. These workers, once their plates had been filled, took themselves off to sit cross-legged on mats, at the far side of the fire, downwind of the smoke. Those remaining upwind and lording it on boxes were all Cookes, Wolfs and Prebrezhenskys as well as Tiny, Andrew and me and two equally pretty although otherwise very different young girls who I guessed were the Topsy of whom I had heard mention and Anastasia, who I only then realised must also be Ana, my prey.

There were no formal introductions and so I had to make a further guess that the diminutive little figure with the tumbling mass of golden curls falling around her shoulders and the chuckling, gurgling voice was Topsy Turvy, the acrobat, while the large, strong and utterly silent young woman with her black hair scraped back as severely as a ballerina's and her boots planted a foot apart on the grass was Ana, horsewoman and troublemaker combined.

It was not so easy to catch and name the several currents which were flowing around the company with a constant troubling hum, but it was clear that Cooke's Circus was a far from happy little band. Topsy, at first, seemed impervious to it all. She prattled on, gently teasing the Wolf children and earning their giggles. Both Tommy and Sallie Wolf, whom I had not forgotten were Ilchenkos on their mother's side, were translating into Russian for the Prebrezhensky girls whose laughter was just as loud and of an even higher pitch. Ma Cooke struck me as very composed, gossiping quietly—again in Russian, one assumed—with Mrs Prebrezhensky. This lady herself was less at ease, studiously ignoring her husband who was glowering at her from afar and kept craning in any time she spoke, as though trying to hear what she might be saying. Tam and Charlie Cooke, although they appeared calmly to be debating such mundane matters as oil lamps versus paraffin flares, 'continentals' (whatever they might be) and 'tarry tape' (apparently a scarce commodity in this part of Perthshire), kept running dry and having to clear their throats and start again.

Odd for a pair of brothers, I thought, unless it was that they were only paying heed to one another with half an ear each, both distracted by what was passing elsewhere around the fire. I was pretty sure that it was the increasingly helpless gales of laughter from the little ones which were annoying the boss, but his brother's quick glances and sudden attentive silences were all for Tiny Truman.

I could not hear what Tiny was saying from where I sat, but from the eye-rolling and occasional flourishes I could guess that he was engaged in some kind of clownish patter; in any case, it was aimed at Anastasia alone. He sat very close to her and talked incessantly, but she was a tough nut to crack and withstood quite five minutes of the little man's efforts with no more than a sleepy blinking of her dark eyes and a pointed stare at his hand whenever he emphasised a punchline by laying it on her arm. Eventually, though, at something whispered into her ear, she finally broke into laughter and her oval face lit up with a grin as wide and as wicked as Tiny's own. Immediately, he looked over to Topsy with a glint of triumph and *her* eyes, just for a moment, lost their twinkle. Perhaps making the children laugh was small beer and getting a smile from Anastasia was proof of one's brilliance as a performer.

Certainly Charlie Cooke, touchy as he was when it came to clowning prowess, was now glaring at Tiny and had stopped listening to Tam Cooke completely. Tam broke off from talking in mid-word, aware that he had lost his brother's attention again, and, in his turn, shot a look of fury at Ana, whose smile snapped off as though it had never been. Even Mrs Cooke caught some of the feeling this time and she looked up with a frown. For a moment there was silence all around and I caught Andrew Merryman staring about him at the ring of faces, smirking to himself and shaking his head slightly. Judging from his accent, I should have said he was from my world and had not long been gone from it; his memories had to be fresh still of dining rooms and of light conversations with no torrid undercurrents tugging at them and I wondered, regarding him, if he—if anyone—could really make the journey from that world to this and stay for good.

At length, Pa Cooke wiped around his bowl with a crust of bread then set it down and lit a cigarette. He offered his case politely to me, but I could see that his cigarettes were hand-rolled, their ends twisted like toffee papers, and I declined.

'Now then,' he said. 'Topsy and Ana, you're up.'

'Right, Pa,' Topsy said. 'Might as well get started.'

Anastasia's brow lowered until her dark eyes were entirely lost in shadow, not a spark showing. There was a long pause and I was aware that everyone around the fire was waiting. At last, she spoke.

'I am not a chorus girl,' she said. Charlie Cooke, I noticed, nodded slightly. 'I should appreciate not being treated like one,' she went on, looking to Charlie as though she expected more from him, but even the nodding had stopped at a quick gesture from Ma, which went unseen by her husband. Her voice was the most curious I had heard yet, with none of the lilt of Topsy and Ma, none of the colourful mix to be found in Lally Wolf and little Tommy, yet it was not the like of Tiny's or Andrew's: not, that is, an ordinary accent from somewhere or other on its way to turning circus. She spoke as though unaccustomed to English and she was expressionless to the point of sounding wooden.

'You,' said Pa Cooke, 'are an entrée artiste and every entrée artiste in this show does two spots. So unless you've got a better idea, we've an act to practise and you should think yourself lucky Topsy is letting you in.'

'Sure it's all one to me, Pa,' said Topsy. 'Until I find my blessed swing I'm stuck with the corde lisse anyway.'

Far from her cheerful assent helping matters, however, it only served to throw Anastasia into a worse light. She turned and glowered at Topsy now.

'I have two acts,' she said, and her slow, blank voice lent her words a threatening air. Ma Cooke stirred again.

'Now there, my maid,' she said. 'Let's not go back over all that again.'

'Don't you start talking comfort to her, Polly Cooke, when she's cheeking me,' said Pa. 'She needs to learn the life as well as the turns, if she's going to be circus.'

At that, Anastasia jumped up and flounced off in the direction of the horse tent. There was an uneasy silence around the fire after she had left until Mrs Cooke began to direct the collection of the plates and to issue instructions to the children about who was to wash them and who was to dry and, one by one, the others began to drift away. I lingered, having caught a look she flicked towards me.

'See there?' she said, softly. 'Don't tell me that's a happy maid.'

I could only agree and I made my way towards the tent very keen to see what act had put Anastasia in such a state of umbrage and what fountains of talent she must have to remain so precious to Ma Cooke despite having all the charm and diplomacy of a sulking mule. Except as soon as I had thought that, I came up hard against the memory of her face, breaking suddenly into smiles as though the sun had come out on a stormy day.

Inside the tent, Topsy Turvy was taking off her skirt and I hesitated in the doorway, unsure about the etiquette, but she looked over her shoulder and hailed me, quite unconcerned.

'Don't mind me,' she said. 'Looks even worse than a chorus girl, this, don't it?' Under the skirt, which she was now folding into a bundle, she wore what might have been very thick tights or very thin britches and something like a boy's bathing suit. She laid her skirt on a seat outside the ring then went over to one of the poles and began to climb it. 'Poor Ana,' she said as she ascended. 'Pa's right, so he is, but I can see both sides.'

'I can't honestly say I have a solid grasp of it yet,' I admitted. Topsy stopped and leaned out backwards from the pole looking at me upside down.

'I thought Ma had called you in to get it seen to,' she said. 'I thought you were here to talk to Ana, in her own language like, get things kushty again.'

'And what language would that be?' I asked, rather astonished. Topsy chuckled.

'Now isn't that the question?' she said. 'Isn't it just!'

'And can *you* tell me anything about what's going on?' I asked. I spoke deliberately vaguely, guessing that Mrs Cooke would not have informed Topsy of her suspicions regarding the lost swing.

'Not me,' said Topsy. 'And don't ask me what that clown's up to because there's no accounting for taste.' Her face had hardened and she glared down.

'Well, what's the problem with your double act, for instance?' I prompted her.

'Oh!' said Topsy. 'That. Well, Bisou—Ana's horse, you know—was trained up for the haute école, but he . . . well, he died, when Ana was away visiting after the last stand. And now she just has her rosy-back—her voltige pony—and only one spot, so Pa wants her and me to work up an act together for the spring.' She had reached the top of the pole now and was sauntering along a beam, high enough to make me feel dizzy just watching her.

'Do be careful,' I said.

'Now there's an idea,' said Topsy, with a grin. She had reached the middle of the roof dome, where a rope was coiled around the beam, looking like something between a wasps' nest and a Turkish basket. 'Ana thinks Pa should buy another horse for her, see, or at least advance her some of her pay so's she can buy one, but Pa says no. She could never get a new prad trained up in one winter, so she can do a second spot with me and work next season on her haute école. Makes sense anyway, because where would she be getting a horse this time of the year anyway? Needs to wait for the fairs and she knows it. But there's no telling her anything these days. She wants to watch out, madam, if you ask me.'

Her voice died away as we both heard someone come under the canopy and open the door flaps. It was Mr Cooke, still rather on his dignity, although his face softened when he looked up at Topsy high in the roof.

'There's my good lass,' he said. 'Got the circus wrote through you like Blackpool rock. Not like some we could mention, eh, Mrs Gilver? You don't catch Topsy kicking up a fuss and a bother when she turns her back and loses something.'

'Oh, Pa, come on with you,' said Topsy. She was frowning down at him from her high perch, with her hands on her hips. 'I can't just lay my hands on a prop—probably put it somewhere silly and forgot it—it's not the same. How would you feel if you went to town one day and come back to find . . . say, Sambo dead and gone, or Midnight?'

'Cheek of a monkey, you have, talking to the rum coll of the show that way,' said Pa Cooke. He shook his whip at Topsy, not too threateningly since it was trussed up like a horse bandage for safe carriage, and besides his eyes were twinkling.

Either proper circus folk had privileges of which jossers could only dream or it was just that the sweet, dimpling Topsy could wind any man around her little finger where the haughty Anastasia left them cold. As though to confirm it, his face grew stern again as he turned towards the sound of someone coming into the ring from the backstage doors. Anastasia, evidently, was not to be treated to any leftover smiles.

When the curtains were swept aside, though, it was not Anastasia and her pony who stood there. Rather stark-eyed, Mrs Prebrezhensky came falteringly into the ring.

'Mee-suss Kilvert?' she said. It took me a moment to realise that she was talking to me. 'Can I speak with you, please. It is of most important.'

'Why, certainly,' I said. 'Do excuse me, Mr Cooke.' I hurried towards the curtains, aware of his contemplative stare and a look of acute interest from the bright-eyed little figure perched above.

With the fall of the curtain behind us came a feeling that we had entered another world. We were standing in a narrow corridor whose walls were fashioned from patched and faded canvas and whose floor was made of slatted boards set on the grass below and covered with sacking. Above the archway back to the ring, the top of the tent was still visible and I could see one end of the beam where Topsy was sitting, but back here sounds were clothy and muffled and I could hear my own breathing, unnaturally loud as when one is wearing a rubber bathing cap, and could smell none of the fresh sawdust and oil of the tent, the purposeful, competent smell I had thought was the smell of the circus, but only the stale dust of the sacking under our feet and faintly from under that the cold smell of the ground, dying grass and earth turning to mud. I shivered.

Mrs Prebrezhensky laid a hand on my arm and drew me further along the corridor, past little cubby-holes full of painted barrels and harnesses, past trunks full of spangled costumes and tables covered with props. I saw the parcel of hats from the clowns' act that morning.

'I know why you are here,' she said, as she hurried me along. 'Polly told me dinnertime. It is sometimes most useful to be able speak secrets in a crowd.' She smiled at me as she held up a piece of the canvas and we stooped to pass under it, emerging from the warren of passageways into the low light of the field. 'I bring you this ways because nobody need to see we go,' she said. Sure enough, we were near the door end of a wagon and with a quick look round to see that we were unobserved, she flitted up the steps with me hurrying after.

Inside, the wagon was criss-crossed with a veritable cat's cradle of washing lines, over which were draped dozens of pairs of woollen stockings and as many again woollen vests and winter knickers. The door of the stove was open to help with the drying but it seemed to me that the washing might win and the fire lose, because the air was soft and sweet with steam and the painted walls were beaded with moisture.

'Kolya, my husband, is gone take girls to see the village,' said Mrs Prebrezhensky. Then she hesitated. 'Kolya says to me to say nothing, not to bring trouble to ourselves. He forbids me to speak. But he is wrong.'

'What is it?' I asked her. Perhaps it was her

88

accent, terribly glamorous in a sepulchral kind of way, or perhaps Mrs Prebrezhensky's flair for dramatic presentation was not reserved for showing off her girls in the ring, but I could feel my pulse quicken.

'Last evening,' she said, 'we have found Topsy's swing.' She bent down and opened one of the panelled cupboard doors. Various jars and bottles of richly coloured foods, pickles I thought, had been shoved roughly to the back and one of them had fallen over and broken, releasing a sharply pungent smell. In the space thus made was a jumble of rope with a gold lacquered stick mixed up amongst it.

'Well, that's a relief,' I said. 'Topsy will be pleased to have it returned.' I quite saw that it was not ideal to have lost property turn up in one's cupboard, but still I could not account for her sombre face, nor for the secrecy. There was no great harm done, surely.

'But look,' said Mrs Prebrezhensky, and pointed one of her long painted fingers at the bundle. I stepped closer to peer at it and could see that just where she was pointing the rope had been cut halfway through.

'It was not me,' said Mrs Prebrezhensky. 'It was not us.' In her voice there was a note of real fear, not just drama now. I stared at the rope and tried to think quickly.

'Well, of course it wasn't,' I said, after a minute or two. 'Or you'd hardly have hidden it in your own caravan, would you?' Her breath came out in a long, hissing sigh. She pressed a hand to her heart.

'Thank God,' she said. 'Thank God you are here

to help us.'

I knelt down and extracted the bundle from the cupboard, careful not to upset any more jars as I did so. Then I peered at the cut, but it told me nothing. Perhaps a sailor, or a butcher, might be able to glance at it and sketch the knife that made it, but not me.

'Nasty,' I said. I started to roll the bundle up as neatly as I could, but that was not very neatly, I suppose, and Mrs Prebrezhensky took it from me and began twisting it with practised hands. 'Who would want to do such a thing?' I asked her. 'Do you know?' I wondered how wide the suspicion of Ana might be. She shook her head. 'And why, after cutting it, would someone hide it? And hide it here? It doesn't make any sense.' I wanted to ask if Ana had any reason to do so, but did not like to drop her in it with so little ceremony, no matter what Mrs Cooke might have told me. Mrs Prebrezhensky was beaming at me.

'You good clever lady,' she said. 'You see real things. I told Kolya is very bad if we hush this, but he does not listen to me.'

'Well, he has a point,' I replied. 'Obviously, someone wanted to *make* things bad for you, Mrs Prebrez—'

'Zoya,' she said. 'I am Zoya, please.' She shook her head slowly. 'How could this make bad for us? Someone wants to make bad things for Topsy.' That was unarguable. She had finished twisting and the swing was now a tight lozenge of coiled rope with just a glint of the golden stick peeping out of each end. She handed it to me. 'And if I listen to Kolya,' she said, 'and say nothing, no one ever would know. Not clever trouble put it here in my cupboard closed for many weeks and weeks. If the jar not smash and we smell something, who knows how long a secret?'

'Unless there had been a search,' I said. 'If Pa Cooke had ordered a search and it had been found here, that would have been trouble enough.'

'But such a thing would never happen,' she said, glaring at me as though I had just suggested it. 'Never in any circus would anything so . . . what is the word? So disrespect. Never would so disrespect be from one circus man to another.'

Perhaps, I thought to myself, that began to explain what I was doing here. Perhaps it was unthinkable for Mrs Cooke herself to discover Ana's guilt officially, one circus woman to another, even if she suspected it. If so, matters might be different now: a missing prop was a prank but a prop slashed with enough venom to cut a thick rope halfway through was something else again and would surely outweigh all thought of polite convention.

'You must tell Topsy,' said Zoya, as though reading my thoughts. 'Warn her someone is make danger for her?' I hesitated. Was it dangerous, exactly? Topsy could hardly have *used* the prop; the cut was almost at the swing end, after all, and she would have seen it. It was threatening, certainly. Thoroughly nasty. But there was no real danger.

'I shall ask Mrs Cooke what she thinks best,' I said. 'In the meantime . . .' I bent and looked out of the window. Mrs Wolf was at the fire, upending washed pots on the tin roof to dry. Two of the grooms were walking four black horses towards the pool. 'Can I leave it here with you?' I said. 'It had better stay out of sight until I have a plan. Even if the damage is hidden.'

I left her busily turning summer clothes out of a deep drawer under the box-bed to put the swing at the very bottom and hurried back to the tent, keen to watch Topsy and Ana together, to see if there were signs of a deep enough hatred to explain what I had just seen.

Anastasia had arrived and was sitting astride a large and rather broad-backed dark grey pony, who stood in the middle of the ring blinking his long lashes. I glanced up and got a wave from Topsy who was perched where I had seen her last, high on the beam. In ringside seats were all of the clowns, Bill Wolf and Ma, who beckoned to me.

'Now,' said Pa Cooke, slapping his whip against his thigh to unravel it. 'I know you have your own ideas about things, Ana, but if you'll think about it for just a minute, you'll see that I, with sixty years of circus behind me and ten generations of circus in my blood, know a thing or two and this little act we're working up here is going to be a beauty. Elegant, breathtaking beauty. There won't be a sound to be heard and there won't be a dry eye in the tent. We kill the flares, we powder out Harlequin's star and socks.' He nodded to Ana's pony. 'We'll have Topsy on a black rope and the two of you girls . . . phosphorescent! You'll be like a couple of fireflies, like fairy queens. I can see you now.'

'But what do we do, Pa?' Topsy shouted down. Pa, however, had not finished setting the scene.

'Music will be clarinet and brushed snare,' he said. 'All the babbies will be off to sleep, it'll be that soothing and peaceful. And the act will be

92

called Reflection by Moonlight. You'll be the talking point of the whole show and do you know the best of it?' He paused dramatically. 'It's all the kind of lines you've been doing since you were knee-high. Well—' He broke off and spoke the next part in his normal voice. 'I mean you, Tops, but Ana will be able to do them just as well.'

He certainly knew this bit of his business, I thought. The picture he painted was irresistible.

'Moreover,' he went on, 'I am fairly sure that no such act has ever been seen before. Charlie? Bill? Am I right there?'

'I never seen it, Tam,' said Bill Wolf's rumbling voice, quick to praise the boss man. Charlie Cooke nodded rather reluctantly. Indeed, his whole demeanour was that of a sceptic, come in hopes to see the venture fail. He crossed his arms and put his tongue in his cheek. Tiny had his eyes fastened on Ana, Andrew gazed up at Topsy and Ma sat forward with such an expression of rapt attention directed at her husband that I had to bite my cheeks not to giggle.

'Now, to start with,' said Pa, 'I want just an arabesque from both of you. Start at a walk, Ana.' He clicked his teeth and Ana's pony moved forward. 'There's a good girl,' said Pa. 'Right, Topsy?'

Up on the beam Topsy had uncoiled the rope from its wasps' nest shape and let its free end drop downwards. She now turned it twice around her body and then twice around her leg. Then, somehow, and it happened so quickly that I could not see how it was done, she seemed to make some kind of a slip knot which allowed her to drop gently down until she was suspended about ten feet below the beam, caught up in the coils of rope. I took a deep breath and told myself that I was going to watch this through without squeezing my eyes shut or wincing.

'Hup,' said Pa and, in unison, Ana on the pony lifted one foot behind her and both arms to the side and struck a pose on the broad, rolling back while Topsy above pointed one leg downwards and one behind and let one arm drift dreamily free. She craned her neck to look at Ana and then set the rope spinning, trying to match the pony's gentle walking speed. There was an appreciative sigh from the ringside seats.

'Lovely,' said Ma Cooke. 'Kushty kativa, Pa!'

It was beautiful, and one could imagine that with the phosphorus and black rope it would be more beautiful still, but I could not help feeling a little sorry for Ana, because Topsy, spinning in the roof, looked the more impressive of the pair—the distance and the perspective lending her some extra magic—but I was sure that it was Ana, balanced so perfectly on Harlequin's back, who was pulling off the greater feat here.

'Both arms, Topsy,' said Pa, lost in concentration on the two girls.

'Sure if I fly with both arms,' said Topsy, and the catch in her voice came as a complete surprise to me; she looked so languid, floating around up there, one forgot that every muscle in her little body must be straining, 'then I'm going to have to wrap me rope foot and flex it. Which one's better?'

'Better match with Ana's base foot if you flex,' came Charlie Cooke's voice. I could see what he was saying. Ana was balanced on a flat foot on her pony's back, while Topsy had both feet pointed as she revolved up there.

'What do you think, Andrew?' said Topsy. Andrew Merryman started a little but did not answer.

'Try it,' said Pa, but while Topsy bent to wrap a foot in the rope to support herself, Ana suddenly rose up and stood on her tiptoe.

'That's lovely, my maid,' said Ma, 'but Topsy can't do that on a rope, now can she?' Anastasia hooked an eyebrow up as she answered.

'Can she not?' she said. 'I will keep myself to what she can manage then.'

'Here!' said Topsy. 'It's not like I'm just beginning. There's what you can and what you can't do up here, thank you very much, and you can't have a straight rope leg, a pointed toe and no hands. It's not possible. It's the laws of the rope. It's . . . Look, Pa, bent leg and I've got no problem.'

'If it's reflection you're after, Tam,' said Ma, cutting through her, 'they should be mirror image, shun't they? Someone needs to be upside down.' At this, there was an unseemly scramble while each of the girls tried to get upside down first. Inevitably Ana, with no rope to rewind, was the winner but it had to be said that her handstand on the horse, while impressive, was nothing like as pretty as Topsy's artful shape on the rope above. Tiny Truman giggled.

'Women!' he said.

'If—ahem.' I was startled to hear Andrew Merryman speak and it seemed I was not alone. All of us in the ringside seats turned to him, causing him momentarily to lose his nerve. He dipped his head and started again. 'If we're doing this by committee,' he said, 'can I s-s-stick my oar in too?'

'Course you can, lad,' said Pa. 'I'm all for listening. The rum coll's got to listen as well as shout.' He spoke very pointedly and I wondered who it was aimed at. Andrew looked uncertain at so much protesting, but Pa Cooke gestured to him to continue.

'Well, to make a reflection,' he said, 'shouldn't Harlequin be turning on the spot under the rope?' He pointed to where the bottom of Topsy's rope was swinging gently a few feet above the middle of the ring and seemed about to say more but then stopped himself and frowned. He looked up the rope towards Topsy and frowned again.

'That's a fair poi—' said Mrs Cooke, but Anastasia cut her off.

'Harlequin is a rosy-back, not a high school horse. I would need a high school horse to spin on the sp—'

'Just so, just so,' said Pa Cooke hastily. 'I thank you, Andrew lad, but we're fine as we are.'

'He is right though, Pa,' said Topsy. 'You're right, Andrew.'

'Aye, aye,' said Pa Cooke, 'but let's get on, will we?'

The work went on; halting, interrupted, slowly feeling a way towards the smooth ease Pa Cooke could see already in his mind's eye, and all we watchers fell into a kind of reverie; all, that is, except Andrew Merryman who continued to look troubled. Once or twice he half turned as though to speak to Tiny at his side, but each time he closed his mouth and turned to face the front again, still frowning. At last, with Topsy red in the

96

face and panting and Harlequin drooping a little from boredom, Pa began to scratch his head and muse about the finale.

'Shame we can't fade on you and just get you off in darkness,' he said. 'Could do if we used spots instead of phosphorus but I'd not want to give up on that just yet awhile. Trouble is it's got to be slow and it's not easy to make a slow finale. Topsy, have you ever stood up on a pony?'

'Only playing, Pa,' said Topsy.

'Voltige is not play,' Ana spat.

'I never meant it was,' said Topsy, all wide-eyed innocence. 'My stars, I just—'

'Never mind that, never mind,' said Pa. 'Here's what I'm thinking. Ana, you take Harlequin to the middle and stand straight like a little tin soldier. Topsy will come down and land on his back, then the two of you together make a line—something fancy, symmetrical, mirror-image like, and Harlequin walks off. Eh?' Topsy was already twining herself into the rope in another of the complicated slip knots, ready for her descent.

'No,' said Ana. Pa Cooke's mouth dropped open.

'Harlequin can't carry two people, Tam,' said Charlie.

'He's carried the two of us,' said Tiny. 'And I know I'm not much of a one but Andrew makes up for me.'

'It's too dangerous,' said Ana. There were jeers all around at that and I surmised that for a circus girl to dismiss an idea for that reason was a very poor show.

'I don't mind if you join me on the rope,' said Topsy, purely as Nanny Palmer used to say 'out of badness'.

'I am not a monkey to be climbing ropes,' Ana said, half under her breath. The spectators hesitated, unsure whether to affect deafness or admit that we had heard her. Topsy, unfortunately, seemed to have very sharp ears.

'Right,' she said, 'that's it. You've done it now, you stuck-up, two-faced . . .' She was wriggling around furiously as she spoke, trying to free herself to climb down. 'I've had it up to my new teeth with you,' she said. 'I'm doing you a favour, in case you didn't know. I've *got* two spots. I don't need to be working all winter to save your skin for you. So . . .' She paused and glared down at Ana, who stretched out along Harlequin's back, put her hands behind her head and crossed her legs at the ankle, looking like an odalisque on a couch. ' . . . you're going to get what's coming and don't tell me you didn't ask for it plenty.'

Those watching had not interfered up until this moment, but now Pa Cooke stepped in.

'Topsy!' he barked. 'You stay where you are. You,' he turned to Ana, 'you get that pony stalled and wiped and come to my wagon in half an hour.'

'Never you mind, Pa,' said Topsy. 'I'll sort this out right now.' She gave up trying to get free and instead wound the rope furiously around her body. 'It's been a long time coming,' she said and tugged on the knot which held her.

Andrew Merryman leapt up.

'Topsy, no!'

'Mind your business,' shouted Topsy. She tugged again.

'That's not your rope!' Merryman cried.

What happened then was both too fast to

98

understand and so slow that it was agony to watch. I saw Tiny, Charlie and Ma look at Andrew and jump to their feet, saw all except Charlie leap, in what looked like single bounds, to the middle of the ring, even Tiny covering the ground like a panther. I saw Pa, caught by surprise, look up, make a feint as if to dash off backstage, turn on his heel, and join the others, head back and arms up as Topsy plummeted towards them. Most of all what I saw was Topsy's face, her angry scowl turning to a wide-mouthed silent scream as she rushed through the air, the rope a blur around her. Ten feet from the ground, when even I had guessed what must be about to happen, right there before my eyes, Topsy turned like an eel, freed herself from the one remaining loop and, kicking out against nothing, bracing herself against empty air, leapt upwards, put out her hands like two cat's claws and grabbed for dear life on to the rope. She slid a foot or so, shrieking as the rough cords burned her hands, and then stopped.

There was a moment of total silence as she hung there and then Andrew Merryman reached up and took hold of her calves in his long, strong hands.

'Let go and sit down,' he said. 'I'll catch you on my shoulders.'

She took a while, but eventually she let go and he cradled her into his arms and sank down on to the sawdust with her. Topsy turned her head against his chest and began to weep. Ma and Pa Cooke were staring at the end of the rope swinging above the sawdust. Charlie Cooke was back in his seat, his face as white and shining as ever it could be in make-up for the ring, tears pouring down it until he wiped them roughly away with shaking hands. He was staring at Ana, who slithered off her horse as though her bones had melted and stood cowering against his flank. Tiny stood with his chin sunk on to his chest and his hands hanging at his sides.

'What went wrong?' I said at last.

Topsy looked up and sniffed deeply.

'He's right,' she said. 'That's not my rope.' She pointed past me towards it and winced as her burned palm creased, then opened her hand wide again and blew on it. As she did so, she settled more comfortably into the crook of Andrew's arm and seemed to regain a good deal of her pluck and even some of her cheer. 'Looks like I'm going to be having a holiday, Pa,' she said, showing us the red weals, 'and I won't be using it to stitch new costumes neither.' Tiny, without a word, strode off towards the backstage.

'But what's *wrong* with the rope?' I asked. I was not enjoying the sensation of being the only one who had no idea why this was happening.

'It's too long,' said Pa. 'Topsy's rope stops just here.' He held a hand above his head. 'Just right for her to touch one toe down from full stretch. If she had kept going on this one . . .' I pictured it briefly, remembering the speed she had picked up as the rope unwound from around her; she had been hurtling down like a bobbin. I could feel the peculiar prickling sensation which accompanies the departure of all blood from one's face. I had seen the cut swing; I had been warned that Ana was behind the trouble. Yet I came here and sat down to watch them practise an act together—an act bitterly resented by the one, an act where the other was hanging from a rope with no net. I could not look at either of them and turned my face away just in time to see Tiny returning with a long coil of rope across his shoulder, looking grim. He cleared his throat.

'That's my rope, is that,' he said, nodding to the one hanging from the beam. Walking over to it, he gave a little jump and caught hold of its swinging end. 'Andrew and me sometimes do a kid-on of the corde lisse. This is my one. Haven't used it for months. I'll bet if we unroll this one there'—he shrugged the coil off his shoulder—'it'll be just a bit shorter. It'll be Topsy's.'

Topsy was staring at him as he swung gently back and forward by one of his short, strong arms.

'Ted?' she said, very softly. Andrew Merryman, too, was staring hard at his friend and he tightened his grip around Topsy's shoulders.

'How could they get mixed up?' I asked.

'They couldn't,' came Pa's voice, low and terrible to hear. 'You were right then, Ma. You said there was trouble coming. I thought you were just making stories for me.'

'No, I warrn't there,' said Ma, just as quietly. 'Couldn't hardly have been more wrong.'

'What's this?' said Charlie Cooke, who had joined the others at last, still pale but no longer shaking. Andrew and Tiny had begun to uncoil the new rope, spilling in loops on to the sawdust.

'Ma knew this was going to happen,' said Mr Cooke.

'Never, never,' his wife cried.

'Knew something anyway,' Pa went on. 'Said she did and I wouldn't listen. Didn't trust her.'

'You din't have to, Tam,' said his wife. 'I went my own sweet way without you.'

101

Mr Cooke frowned at her then until she explained.

'Mrs Gilver here,' she said, 'has come to help me out. Find out what the trouble is, see?'

It took Mr Cooke a long time, with much blinking and staring, to realise what his wife was saying, and when the penny finally dropped his face darkened until it was not red but a deep and terrifying purple. Andrew and Tiny continued to examine the rope, eyes averted from Pa, but I could not help glancing at the whip he held and stepping back a pace or two.

'It wasn't your place, Poll,' he said.

'Don't you stand there and tell me about my place,' his wife said, very quietly but as firm as could be.

There was another long silence, while everyone watched, breath held, to see what he would do. At last, he stepped away from Ma, still watching her, and his shoulders dropped a little. He turned and gestured to me with one of his wide, expansive, ringmaster flourishes. 'Hear that?' he said, glaring around at everyone. 'Mrs Gilver is going to get to the bottom of this and anyone what doesn't like it and doesn't help her can walk. Right? New rule in Cooke's Circus. You keep up your own clobber, you don't drink before the show and now you help Mrs Gilver and answer anything she asks you or you answer to me.'

'Look at this here then, missus,' said Tiny, pointing at the rope on the ground. Impossible to miss, a few feet from one end, it was slashed almost all the way through.

'Ted?' said Topsy again. 'What's happening?'

'Tell me you don't know nothing about this,'

said Pa Cooke, towering over Tiny with his fists bunched. 'You swear on your life, or you'll have no life to swear on.'

'Leave the lad, Tam,' said Charlie. 'Course he don't.'

'No, sorry, course not,' said Pa, looking truly chastened. He turned and flicked a glance towards Harlequin. 'Ana!' he said, his voice angry again.

'And you can leave her out of it too,' said Charlie, even louder.

His brother ignored him.

'Get that prad stalled and come straight to my wagon,' he said to Ana. He had gathered his whip into loose coils as he spoke but leaving the tent he cracked it, just once, very hard, and left a slash in the canvas to one side of the door. Ma sighed.

'Never you mind there, Ana,' she said. 'Just you lie low till tomorrow, maid. And you can look out some fresh walling for that and get it laced on.' She nodded to the ripped canvas. Ana nodded and left the ring on rather unsteady legs, her pony close at her heels and nibbling her hair, worried about her. Charlie, with a look at Ma, followed her. Ma turned to me and drew me aside out of the others' hearing.

'You best keep out his way too, my beauty,' she said. 'Get on with your work on the quiet. He's not angry with you for helping, mind, and he's not even angry with me for being right, not really. He's angry with Tam Cooke, as usual, see?'

'But you don't need my help now,' I said. 'You said you knew it was Ana at the bottom of the trouble and now she's gone as far as this . . .'

Mrs Cooke opened her eyes very wide so that her wrinkles showed white.

'Bless us both,' she said. 'You must forget that now, my beauty. Circus folk an't what they were but no one circus would ever . . . Ana no more than me.'

'And why should Pa be angry with himself anyway?' I asked. 'What has he done?'

'Din't spot the rope end, did he?' said Mrs Cooke. She turned to Andrew Merryman and raised her voice again. 'You sure you're a josser, my fine big lad? Don't seem like one to me.'

6

Thus began my immersion in circus life, that curious winter of 1925, when rabbit stew in the open air became my accustomed luncheon, when talk of dots and batts and belly boxes grew to be second nature, when Bunty was a buffer and I was a beauty although neither of these last two developments, unhappily, was to last. It has a dreamlike quality now when I look back upon it.

At least, however, I discovered a mundane explanation for the strangest thing of all. It had not unsettled me too badly when Mrs Cooke read my palm, for I was well aware of the clever way these people phrase their tale to make one roomy size fit all, how they read one's face and tailor the talk until it really does appear that they read one's palm and one's mind, but I admit that when she arrived in my sitting room telling me that she knew what I was, I found it harder not to wonder.

It was Ina Wilson who provided the voice of reason when, the day after the incident of the long rope, she arrived rosy-cheeked and slightly breathless at the winter ground, clutching a sketchpad and a tray of watercolour paints. I prepared to offer some account of my presence, but when she saw me she only said:

'Oh! Good. You came then.'

For it transpired that Mrs Cooke had gone to Ina first, seeking help, and it had been Ina who passed her along to me, having heard of my exploits from some Fife connections of hers.

'*I* couldn't help,' she went on, wide-eyed at the very idea of it.

'No?' I asked, wondering why.

'Trouble and nastiness upset me,' Ina went on. 'I'd rather not have to know. And besides, I don't want to take sides in their wrangle and have any of them not pleased with me. Much better you, don't you think?'

When I was a child and grown-ups, Nanny usually, spoke of 'spoiling' I was hard to convince of the dangers; never could I agree that a new doll, more pudding or a carriage home from church instead of a wet walk would harm my character in any way, but listening to Ina Wilson fail to explain why she should not be troubled—fail even to comprehend that an explanation might be called for—I could not resist the thought that Albert and his devotion had—quoting Nanny at her most vituperative—ruined the girl.

'And where is your husband off to today?' I said, aware that the intention behind the question was not a kind one. Sure enough, her face clouded slightly as she answered.

'Lunching in town,' she said, 'and going on to a club for the afternoon.'

'Well, that's wonderful news,' I replied. The unkind impulse had passed and I really was pleased, for her sake. As far as I had been able to gather, Albert Wilson had not heretofore been much given to sloping off whenever he could, as normal husbands do, but if he were to begin then Ina would surely be the better for it.

'Yes,' said Ina. 'With Robin Laurie.'

'Well,' I said, 'he certainly does seem to have taken you up, doesn't he?'

Ina gave a tight smile and said nothing.

Refusing to be distracted any longer, even by such an absorbing mystery as this, I took my leave of her and squared my shoulders; I was about to conduct the interview which might bring me to the end of this rather peculiar case and I was not looking forward to it.

*   *   *

I had, the day before, had a gentle, probing little chat with Topsy in her wagon. She had been propped up in a tiny tub-like armchair near her stove with buttered muslin on her poor hands and a cup of hot broth at her elbow. Andrew was there when I arrived and left with some reluctance, unfolding himself out of the wagon like a dragonfly emerging from its nymph.

'He is a good friend to you,' I remarked once I thought he would be out of earshot.

'He's a good man,' said Topsy. She looked rather uncomfortable as she admitted it. Then she roused herself and smiled. 'A good friend, like you say. We're all good friends at Cooke's, missus— Zoya's gone to town to buy paraffin bandage for

106

me and Lally Wolf's gone along to make her get boracic lint instead.'

'Golly,' I said. 'Your hands might be soothed but you won't be able to breathe in here for fumes.'

Topsy giggled.

'Good friends for sure,' she said. 'You don't want to listen to Ma too close, you know. She's like a mother to us all and a kinder heart you couldn't wish for, but she gets run away with her stories and her "funny feelings". That rope was an accident, must have been.'

'What sort of accident?' I said.

'Tent men must have put the wrong one up at the build-up somehow,' she said.

'But wouldn't you have checked?' I said. I could not imagine climbing a rope without checking the knots and examining every inch of it for fraying.

'No need,' said Topsy. 'Tent men know their job and I got my own.'

'Are the two ropes kept in the same place?' I said. 'That seems rather reckless.'

'No, no, they're not. But it must be that.'

'But wouldn't you have noticed?' I said. 'Haven't you practised already since you got here and done a . . . one of those . . . I don't know what you call what you did at the end.'

'A rolling drop,' said Topsy, and she screwed up her face. 'I've been trying to remember and if I had to bet my wages I'd have said I did. But I can't have, can I?'

'You have a very sweet nature, my dear,' I said, 'but in this instance I think it is leading you astray. Haven't you even considered the possibility that . . .' I hesitated. ' . . . someone *changed* the rope?'

'No one would,' said Topsy. She looked away

107

from me. 'I know I had that daft idea about Ted—Tiny, you know—but just for a minute and only because I was so rattled.'

'I didn't mean Tiny, particularly,' I said.

'If one of the tent men needed a rope for something,' said Topsy, 'he'd use a spare, or he'd ask the boss if there wasn't no spare would do. No one would ever take mine. I keep my swings and rings in my prop box, but that corde lisse is up all the time and it moves with the tent rig. The tent men look after it. Tiny's long rope stays with the clowns' rig. The tent men would never go near it. And anyway, Pa has asked them already and they didn't.'

I was beginning to find her lack of suspicion exasperating.

'And the damage to Tiny's rope?'

'I don't know,' she said. 'Must be some kind of mishap.'

'Quite a string of mishaps,' I said. 'I found your swing.' I thought my voice was laden with portent, but Topsy did not notice it.

'Well, there's some good news anyway,' she said. 'Where was it I had put it in the end?'

'It was stuffed into one of the store-cupboards in the Prebrezhenskys' living wagon,' I told her. Her smile faltered slightly. 'And one of the ropes was cut halfway through.' Her smile disappeared completely now.

'Cut?' she said. 'Not frayed? Cut?'

'There was no mistaking it. Just like the other one. I did mean to tell you about it, but thought it could wait until after the rehearsal. I can only ask you to forgive me.' I closed my eyes and shuddered. I am not one of those who relishes clucking over what might have happened when nothing has, but this had been such a very near miss that I could not quite banish the thought yet.

Topsy got up from her chair and stepped over to the little window in the side of the wagon. She did not move the lace curtain aside but stood behind it, looking out at the rest of the camp, slowly letting her gaze travel all around.

'Can you think of anyone who would want to harm you?' I asked. It seemed a mere formality to me as it would to anyone who had seen the rehearsal, seen the way Ana looked at her and heard the words she spat out like venom. Topsy swung round and stared at me.

'No,' she said, but it was more as though she were forbidding me to ask than as though she were answering. 'You don't understand,' she went on. 'No one would do that.'

'Someone has,' I reminded her.

'Nobody circus would *ever* do such a thing.'

'Nobody *circus*,' I said. 'But what about someone else? Can you not think of someone else who might be angry enough to want to hurt you?'

'Who?' said Topsy, looking bewildered. 'There's nobody here.'

'There are jossers in Cooke's as well as the rest of you,' I explained, but Topsy's puzzled look dissolved and she only grinned at me.

'You're not speaking your own language, sure you're not,' she said. 'Jossers is circus, or getting there, just not proper circus. I meant flatties, roughs. There's nobody here except the folk at the house and they don't even know me.'

'Well, at least tell me when you last saw the swing in one piece,' I said. 'And let me start

109

narrowing it down.'

*   *   *

Shortly afterwards I had left, bidding her to be careful and getting the cheerful response that with no hands worth the name she hardly had scope to be otherwise. Outside, I shivered again, but this time it was only from the cold. The blink of winter sun had gone behind the pine trees already and a penetrating chill was seeping up from the ground as the light faded. I wondered where Bunty was and whether I should be able to persuade her to return to Gilverton with me that evening. Then I squared my shoulders, strode up to Ana's wagon and rapped on the door.

There was no answer from inside, but Charlie Cooke's head appeared from his own window across the way.

'She's gone for a walk,' he called over to me. 'Keeping out of Tam's way.'

I should, if I were any kind of detective at all, have been thwarted by this, but in fact a flood of relief washed over me. From what I had seen of her so far, she was a most imposing individual and I could not quash the idea that if she were beyond Mrs Cooke's powers of scolding and charming, she would make mincemeat of me.

'Are you feeling better, Mr Cooke?' I said, spurred on to friendliness by the good news of my reprieve.

'Me?' he said. 'Nowt wrong with me.'

'I couldn't help noticing that you were very upset at what happened earlier.'

Charlie gave me a long speculative look before

he answered.

'I *was* upset,' he said. 'Course I was. I'm sore fond of that little lass and I wouldn't see a hair harmed on her head.'

'How do you suppose it happened?' I asked him. This time the silence was even longer.

'I don't like what you're hinting at,' he said at last.

The next silence was all my doing. I had merely been passing the time of day. Was it possible that I had stumbled over something solid underfoot?

'I wasn't hinting at anything,' I told him. 'I know you were very shocked. I mean, you were so surprised that you stayed in your seat while everyone else rushed forw—'

'You've no business speaking to me that way,' he said, talking over me.

I was now more convinced than ever that there was something amiss here. I drew myself up.

'I beg your pardon, Mr Cooke,' I said, 'but I most certainly do. Your brother was very clear on that point.'

'My brother!' said Charlie Cooke, almost spitting. 'My brother isn't the Great Panjandrum he thinks he is, missus. I could have you off this ground before you can blink.' Then, his face thunderous, he withdrew into his wagon and slammed the window shut behind him.

He seemed very sure of himself, but I had heard enough already about the fearsome power of the rum coll to feel rather confident myself that he was wrong. For, I told myself, if circuses are full of family connections then family must abide by the hierarchy or no one would. Well, when I returned the next morning I should find out if I were the

111

honoured guest still or were to be sent packing. I would, though, leave Bunty at home for once. I told myself this was because an inglorious departure was slightly less so when there was no large spotty dog whining to stay, but it was more honest, perhaps, to say that I felt Bunty deserved a long boring day at home to remind her where her loyalties should lie.

*   *   *

I need not have worried. When Ina and I went our separate ways the next day, Ma Cooke waved to both of us alike and Pa Cooke and his horse-whip were nowhere to be seen. Nor was there any sign of Charlie. I took a deep breath, climbed the stairs to Anastasia's wagon and knocked once again.

'Enter,' she called from inside and so, feeling a little like a parlour maid, I did.

'This is insupportable,' she said when she saw who it was. 'I have nothing to say to you.'

She was still in bed, wrapped in a blanket and with a moth-eaten kind of tippet around her shoulders and drawn up over her neck. The wagon was chilly, with fogged windows and even a bloom of condensation on the paintwork here and there, and it made me begin to lose patience with her. She had at least three friends at Cooke's that I knew of so far: Charlie, always ready to champion her; Ma desperate to help; and Tiny, like a self-appointed little jester at her elbow. Besides, ponies—like rabbits and white mice and Lord knows goldfish—simply *do* die. I could not see that there was any reason for her to be in such a monumental sulk with the world at large and

112

certainly there was no call for her to be scowling so at me. On the other hand, might Charlie's frequent leaps to her defence be designed to annoy his brother? And perhaps only professional stubbornness made Tiny Truman work so hard to make her smile at him. As for Mrs Cooke's affectionate concern, Topsy had said she was a mother to all; there was no particular glory for Anastasia in it. With my spanking hand itching a little I forced myself to be gentle.

'I hope you're feeling better,' I began, sinking my chin down into my fur collar and bunching handfuls of pocket lining into my fists to warm them. 'What happened yesterday was a great shock to everyone.'

She nodded rather reluctantly.

'A very nasty accident,' I went on. 'Very unsettling.'

'It was not an accident,' said Anastasia. 'It was a warning.' She was staring straight ahead, her face a blank.

'A warning?' I echoed. Was this a confession? She shrugged. 'And what has Topsy done that she deserves such a warning?'

Now she turned to face me at last and frowned.

'Good God,' she said, 'you don't think it was *me*? Has someone said it was me?' If her astonishment was an act, then it was a splendid one. Before I could think how to continue, two great fat tears surged up in her eyes and spilled on to the tippet. 'Is that what they are saying? Haven't I suffered enough? Exile, loneliness and grief. Being treated as though I am a nothing and having to sink lower than I can bear simply to keep a roof over my head and to have a name I do not fear to speak? And now to be accused of such cold-heartedness . . .'

'Umm,' I said. 'No one has accused you of anything . . . dear. Only how do you *know* it was a warning?' The tears were falling quite freely now. 'And I certainly would not call you cold-hearted. Anyone could see how upset you were yesterday. But what do you know about it? If you can help me, tell me what you know.'

She caught her lip in her teeth and managed to stop crying with a shuddering sigh.

'Of course I was upset,' she said. 'I think that it was done purely to upset me. It is I who is being warned.'

'Well,' I countered, 'I should imagine Topsy was part of it.'

'Poor Topsy was just the pawn,' she replied, and she turned to look out of the window, although she could surely only see a patch of milky sky. 'If they have found me. I think they have. They are everywhere. And so, once again, it begins.'

She sounded, I thought, not so much an *unhappy* girl as a girl who was absolutely (as my sons would have it) barking mad.

'Who is this?' I asked, carefully.

'Before I answer,' she said, 'who are *you*? I must be careful. Trust is a luxury I cannot afford.'

Now, I try, always, to be professional when on a case, to set aside the norms of society and care only about the questions and answers, the suspects and clues, but at that moment I could feel something rearing up inside me and I was powerless to stop it. I was sitting in a damp, chilly hovel of a caravan—and Ana's living quarters were squalid indeed compared with the Cookes'—being

114

spoken to by a girl not twenty-five years old who worked in a circus, as though *I* were a girl, a girl behind the glove counter who had lost madam's order and offered madam cheek.

'Now, look here, Miss . . . What shall I call you? What is your name?'

'My name is Anastasia,' she said.

'And your surname?'

'My name is simply Anastasia,' she repeated. 'That is best for now.' I bristled. Even Mrs Cooke with her Russian blood admitted to 'Polly'.

'Well then, Anastasia,' I said, 'I am here to look into some matters which are troubling Mrs Cooke and you are one of them. She is worried about you.'

'She need not be,' said Anastasia and she smiled to herself. 'I have no choice. I have only one card left in my hand. I cannot believe that I must play it but . . . my life has been unbelievable to me for some time now. Mrs Cooke need not worry. She will triumph.'

'I am not entirely sure that I follow you,' I said. 'Mrs Cooke's concern was for your happiness not her own. She thinks you are a talented girl—she called you a star—and she does not want to lose you.'

Anastasia smiled again. 'As you say: she does not want to lose me. So it is lucky that her needs and mine march along together. She will help me.'

'Exactly,' I said. 'She will always be there to help you, but you must help yourself too. You could try to be a little more . . . Well, I noticed that you didn't seem very pleased with the new act yesterday. You could have been more . . .'

'You do not know how hard I try,' said

Anastasia. The tears were flowing again.

'I *do* understand,' I told her. 'I know nothing about circus acts and even I could see that Reflection by Moonlight is a waste of your talents. It is a hard lesson to have to learn and rather heavy-handed of Mr Cooke to force you into it, but *he's* only trying to help you too.'

Ana, at that, gave a short, dry laugh.

'Oh yes,' she said, 'everyone is only trying to help me. Everyone has wonderful ideas about how to help me. You do not know what help I must take. Just to be safe. Just to survive. But how did it help me when that man took my horse? He told me Bisou was ill and had to be shot, but I know he sold him.'

'I see,' I said, grasping on to this one little pip of possible sense in the midst of it all. 'He was your horse? The haute école pony who died? He didn't belong to the Cookes?'

'He was mine,' she said. 'I trained him as a child and no one but me ever rode him. Now he is gone, as so much that was mine is gone. But not everything. I am not without value, even brought as low as I am. I will purchase my protection, though the cost is to rip my heart out of my breast and lay it upon the altar.'

I stared at her, thinking hard. I was half convinced there was a name for what I was hearing, something which had been bandied around in the newspapers of late. Hugh had probably tutted and read out passages about it in withering tones. And stealing Pa's whip to pay him back for the death of her pony fitted all too neatly into it. No wonder Mrs Cooke was anxious about her, and one could hardly blame Mr Cooke if he

116

did feel his circus would be in calmer waters without her, talent or no. Even her denial of guilt in the matter of the rope began to lose a little of its weight when set against the fact that she sounded just as sincere talking absolute fantastical rot about nothing at all.

There was only one person I could think of who might have a different view of the unfortunate girl. After leaving her—still in bed, still under the blankets (and I felt the spirit of Nanny Palmer move within me; it was after eleven on a sunny morning) and with the temperature in her wagon dropping all the time as the stove grew cold—I sought another audience with Tiny, who certainly knew something. Ma Cooke had said so and I agreed with her. I had no more than that one look of his to go on, but it had been quite a look.

*   *   *

He was sitting peeling onions on the steps of his wagon, with the door shut behind him, and he gave a cheery wave of his knife as I approached him and winked one of his streaming eyes.

'You must be frozen,' I said, remembering what he had said about the merits of nice warm mud and the hard frost which had now descended.

'Two ticks, Mrs Gilver,' he said, 'and we'll get away inside, only I've just got me stove going strong and didn't want to let the heat out, only I can't stand t'smell of onions hanging round all day either, so here I am. Poor Cinders!' He pulled a tragic face at me and, although I had never peeled an onion in my life, I was tempted to take the knife from him and pitch in to help.

'I've just been to see Ana,' I said.

'Oh?' said Tiny, cocking an interested look at me. 'And how is she this morning?'

'Still in bed,' I said. 'Rather rattled after yesterday. She's a funny one, isn't she?'

'She's not alone round here, missus,' he said, bundling up his peelings in newspaper and hefting the pot of onions into his arms. 'Come on in. I'll make coffee.'

'Coffee?' I echoed, surprised and delighted.

'Andrew Merryman and his swanky ways rubbing off on me,' said Tiny. Inside, he set the pot on the floor, opened the stove door and pushed it inside. The stove was the same size as all the others and so Tiny did not have to bend to look into it, but the rest of the furnishings did have something of the doll's house about them—a miniature chair and table, a shaving stand not two feet tall, a ladder up to the box-bed at the end.

'Sit down,' said Tiny, nodding to a second chair. Beside his it seemed enormous, and actually when I looked closely at it, it really was enormous. 'Andrew's chair,' said Tiny, laughing at my slowness. 'I tell you when we get a good bottle down us and sit in t'wrong seats it's an uncomfortable night for both.' He closed the oven door on the pot and gave the stove a little polish before tucking the pad tidily away.

'Won't the onions make the wagon smell now anyway?' I asked him. I could remember the smell of boiled onions in milk on the nursery fire when I was tiny, never quite worth the fug no matter that they were delicious.

'No, it'll all go up the pipe now,' said Tiny. 'Oh, the winter the winter the winter ground,' he

118

moaned. 'In season, there's a big dinner twice a day. Dinnertime and again after t'show, but winters it's dinner together and shift for yourself at night, see? I'd starve if it weren't for Topsy. She feeds Andrew up and I get his leftovers.'

'She doesn't feed you?' I said.

'She's her own boss,' said Tiny. 'She does as she likes.'

'And how is she today?' I asked. 'Have you seen her?'

He nodded. 'Her hands is bad,' he said. 'Be a week before they're straight again. Lucky in a way it's winter and the start of it too. Pa Cooke would have her dropped off in t'next town and someone new in, family or no, if it were season.'

'Things are that desperate?' I said. 'Ana said something which I took to be a story, but if things are as tight as all that . . .'

'Pa Cooke stole her horse and sold it?' said Tiny. 'Who can say, who can say? Pa said the beast took a bad colic and the glue man come and shot him, but half of us was away to t'next stand and it's not like Pa to hang back at pull-down. So who can say?'

'Why on earth would he do such a thing?' I said.

'I'm not saying he did,' said Tiny, which was far from a straight answer. 'That's just Ana's story.'

'It wasn't by any means the only story she was telling,' I said.

'Oh, she's the star o' t'show and we all hate her for it?'

'She didn't touch on that particular point,' I said. 'But for some reason, she seems to think—and this in the teeth of all the evidence—that she is the target of these tricks, or whatever you want

119

to call them.'

'Wouldn't call them "tricks" now, would you?' said Tiny, his face settling in deep lines as he frowned. 'Not if this last's another one, because a missing swing's one thing, but that long rope could have killed Topsy. No, it had to be an accident. Had to be.' His voice cracked and he rubbed his hand roughly across his mouth.

'Ana called it a warning,' I said.

'Aye,' said Tiny. 'She would do. It's a little foible of Ana's, see.' He was scooping coffee into a battered tin pot, in generous quantities.

'I don't see, not really,' I said. 'When the two things that were done were specifically aimed at Topsy, I don't see at all.'

'Well, here's where I have to do my duty as a fine upstanding member of Cooke's Circus what doesn't want to get his marchers when it's so cold outside.'

'I knew you knew something,' I said.

'I knew you knew I knew,' said Tiny, then he grew serious again. 'There was more than them two things done. And the rest were nowt to do with Topsy at all. Here,' he said, 'know what just struck me? How come you're talking to me like I'm on your side, missus? How come you think whoever it were, it weren't me, when it were my rope what got used for t'swap?'

'*Because* of the swap,' I said.

'Ain't you ever heard of a double-bluff?'

I hesitated. He joked incessantly but who knew what sensitivities the jokes might hide.

'Because your rope was tied to the beam,' I said at last. 'Sorry to be so blunt.'

'You think I couldn't climb up that pole and

120

walk along that beam with a coiled rope on me?' said Tiny. He was pouring out two cups of coffee with a flourish, raising the pot as high as he could to make the tops froth. He got out of his chair and climbed on to it, pouring all the time, holding the pot high above his head and still hitting the cup with the thin stream of liquid. 'Why would that be then?' he asked me, looking straight across, at eye-level now.

'I simply assumed . . .' I began, clumsily. Tiny climbed down again and handed me one of the cups.

'Yesssss, you're right there,' he said. 'I couldn't have done it to save me life.' He paused. 'No head for heights.' I nodded. 'Never needed one. Boom-boom.' And he laughed so heartily at my discomfort that in the end I had to laugh too.

'So,' I said sternly, at last. 'The rest? That was nothing to do with Topsy?'

'But mind you, missus—Ana didn't know nowt about it. She never found out. Unless there's even more and she did spot some. Can't say for sure. First thing *I* noticed were t'balloons was swapped over. Day before yesterday, this was. The balloons Ana has for the spectacular was over with my props—mine and Andrew's—and our balloons was where Ana's should be.'

'I'm not sure I see what harm could come from the wrong balloons,' I said. 'Delicious coffee, by the way.'

'Ah well, see now, when I say balloons I don't mean balloons like you mean,' said Tiny. 'Hoops with paper in, that's a balloon to me. Me and Andrew hold them up for Ana in t'spec—for her to jump through off Harlequin's back—and then we have our own ones for one of our run-ins. Some of them is paper too, but some's rubber and I bounce right back off 'em, then there's some's solid wood. But they're identical to look at, see? That's the joke of it. First run-in, Andrew and me, we do Ana's spec turn again only with Jinxie instead of t'pony and with the trick balloons.'

'And you say they'd been swapped around? Like the rope?'

'There's no way we wouldn't have noticed, mind.'

'So it wasn't really dangerous,' I said, thinking of the cut swing, 'just threatening.'

'That's it in a nutshell where I can reach it,' said Tiny. 'Threatening.'

'And that's not all?' I prompted.

'No,' he said. 'Next thing was I noticed flour in t'resin bucket.' I waited for him to explain. 'Resin powder, see? Ana puts it on Harlequin's back to help her grip. That's how voltige ponies get their name, matter of fact: rosy-backs, they call them. Anyway, she flings on a handful every time she goes through t'ring doors, casual-like. That's what makes it seem all the worse to me somehow. Kind of more . . . sneakier than the rest. Just a bag of flour in t'resin-bucket.'

'What would it do?'

'Flour? On a pony's back what you're standing up on? Flour mixing in with sweat on a rosy-back working hard?' I could feel the now familiar shiver creeping across me again.

'It would turn to a complete lather, wouldn't it?' I said.

'Lethal,' agreed Tiny. 'Only again there's no way Ana wouldn't notice. It didn't feel nothing like resin, nor look like it, and she'd have spotted it straight off. So it was like you said, just a threat.'

'But no less nasty for that,' I said. 'And do you think there's anything else?'

'Well, let's say I was glad it were Charlie Cooke opening that there parcel of hats and not me. No, go on, I'm only joking,' he said, laughing at the look on my face. 'Andrew and me checked all Ana and Topsy's props night before last. Took us nearly the whole night. Jinxie stood guard for us. Only wish we'd thought to check our own. I just checked that my corde lisse was coiled up tidy in me prop box—and it were, as far as I could tell. Never thought no more about it.'

'But why would someone make such a good job of swapping the ropes when the swing was . . .'

'When the swing was what?' said Tiny. Then he put his head on one side. 'Hello, hello. You've found it, han't you?'

There was no point trying to dissemble since I had already betrayed myself. I admitted that I had and described the state it was in, but I insisted that its hiding place was my secret.

'Fair enough,' said Tiny. 'And has it all fell in place then? Can you hang the guilty man with a bit of rope and a gold stick?'

'To be honest, before what you told me about the flour and the balloons, I wasn't tending towards a man at all. I was tending towards Ana. She was so angry with Topsy yesterday, I could easily imagine her getting up to tricks to spite her.'

'Never,' said Tiny stoutly, and he flushed as he spoke. I looked away to let his blush fade unwitnessed. Perhaps he was not just flirting when he worked so hard to make Ana laugh with all his nonsense, perhaps he was really wooing her. I hoped not: he was a dear fellow and Ana, who would no doubt think herself far above him, did not deserve the man.

'Mrs Cooke hinted that she might have been up to some other mischief before,' I said, speaking rather carefully now that I thought he might be an interested party. 'You wouldn't know what that was, would you? You seem close to her.'

'Not me,' said Tiny, his eyes wide, although precisely which part of my suggestion he was denying was not clear. 'And anyway, it don't make no sense. How can she think it's all meant for her if it's her doing it, eh?' This was rather a good point.

'Well, the fearful act is maybe just that—an act.'

He was shaking his head again. 'No, it's real enough. Leastways she's never took a day off it since she got here.'

'And what's it all about?' I asked him.

'Oh, you'll work it out soon enough,' was all Tiny would say. 'And you'll kick yourself when you do. She's a funny one, our Ana, right enough.'

'Well, disregarding Ana for the moment,' I went on, 'the only other thought I had—and again this was before your revelations this morning—was Charlie Cooke.'

Tiny put his cup down on the stove top with great deliberation, straightened his jacket, smoothed his hair and then collapsed into rolling, rollicking gales of laughter.

'I take it you don't agree,' I said drily, 'but he was very touchy yesterday about the fact that he didn't rush forward to help. He hated me noticing that.' I was having to talk loudly above the giggles

124

and I gave up.

'Course he was,' Tiny said, wiping his eyes with a handkerchief bigger than he was. 'Charlie Cooke hurt Topsy? Never!'

'So why didn't he help?'

'He's slowing down. You've seen him, missus—you've seen Andrew and me having to take the pace off t'blessed hat juggles for him! You're right enough. We was all there under that rope before he'd even got off his seat, but there's no mystery why he didn't like you talking about it. It must be killing him now.'

'Oh, poor Charlie,' I said. 'How awful to be brought face to face with it like that, to think that he was too slow to help. If he's fond of her.'

'Oh, he's fond all right,' said Tiny. 'Hangs around her like a smell on the landing and takes care to make sure everyone sees him at it too.'

'That surprises me,' I said. I had thought that Andrew Merryman and Topsy were a pair, from the way she behaved yesterday and what Tiny had told me.

'It's true,' Tiny said. 'And he's really started in with the pomade and pressed pants lately. Coming on like love's young dream. She's had to beg Andrew not to leave her alone and give Charlie a chance to get proper stuck in, for she wouldn't want to hurt him.'

'She's a good, kind girl,' I said, thinking that actually she was a very astute young madam and playing it beautifully.

'Oh aye, she's that,' said Tiny. 'She's even had to turn to me once or twice when Andrew's been away and I'm no white knight, am I?'

'Poor old Charlie,' I said.

125

'Oh, for sure, poor Charlie,' said Tiny, sounding rather sour. 'Me heart just bleeds.'

7

Alec, to whom I reported dutifully once I was home, solved the mystery of Anastasia right away. In fact, it only took him calling it that and I had solved it too.

'Oh, come off it, darling, please,' I said. *'Anastasia?'*

'She feels herself above the rest of them, she has a very dubious accent, she believes she is in hiding and may have to fly at any moment, she has lost something pretty impressive, she thinks there are spies everywhere.'

'Yes, and admittedly Topsy was very tickled about my talking to Ana "in her own tongue". The little minx found that highly diverting.'

'That's it, Dandy, I'm sure of it.'

'But it's nonsense!' I said.

'Well, of course it's nonsense,' said Alec. 'Delusions of grandeur and a persecution complex.'

I clapped my hands. 'That was just the phrase I was trying to remember.'

'And really, when you think about it, Dan, it's exactly the sort of madness that would go along quite nicely with the kind of girl who runs away to the circus.'

'Taking her pony with her,' I said. 'Aha! Well, there's the proof that it's rubbish right there. How could she have her childhood pony with her if she had fled St Petersburg with her jewels stitched into her petticoats?'

'Dandy, let me assure you,' said Alec gravely, 'you do not need to mount arguments against it to me.'

'Although,' I added, 'if she really does think there are spies everywhere, she probably has no great love of Zoya and family and she might have cut the rope swing and put it in their wagon to make trouble for them.'

'Wouldn't she cleave to them as her country people? Subjects, I mean?'

'Well, not if they could find out that she was a fake in ten questions,' I said. 'And perhaps not anyway. Depends what kind of Russians they are, surely. What sort of name is Prebrezhensky?'

'A long and unspellable one,' said Alec, stretching out his feet towards my fire and prodding Bunty with his toe. 'Is she all right, Dan? She seems rather listless.'

'She's stupefied by an excess of effective training,' I said. 'I suppose I meant could we tell from the name whether they'd be all for the Tsar or all for the other lot. The way one would know a Cabot was a Yankee or a . . . what would a Confederate be called?'

'La Fayette,' said Alec.

'Really? How odd.'

'Besides, do you think it was the same person who cut the swing and hid it? Doesn't it seem more likely that someone who hates this Topsy did the cutting and someone who likes her hid it so she wouldn't see it and get upset? Someone who has no love for the Prebrezhenskys, presumably.'

'So Anastasia for the cutting, but not the

hiding?'

'But why, Dandy? What is it that makes you plump for her anyway?'

'Mrs Cooke said she had tampered with props before. With Mr Cooke's whip, to be precise.'

'Tampered with it how, though?' said Alec.

'Pinched it, I think. Why?'

'Well, because: slashing a prop—nasty but unmissable. Hiding it—harmless prank. Swapping the balloons—pointless silliness. The flour thingy—a bit too subtle for me but I take your word for it that the circus folk would get the gist of the threat. Then comes the long rope— underhand, subtle again but this time all too horribly effective. So until we know all the details of the whip incident I can't see the point of homing in on Ana and ignoring the rest of them. Can't see it at all.'

He gave a firm nod and sat back in his chair. I scowled at him. Alec is at his least attractive when he is magisterial and he never admits how much easier it is to make these pronouncements after my orderly reports than to come to the same conclusion when one is grubbing around in thick of it all, as I do.

'You are a wonderful sounding board, Alec,' I said, with remarkable grace. 'Thank you.'

'So, leaving aside the Tsarina, as either target or perpetrator,' he went on, 'who else is there who might be doing it?'

'No one I've come across yet,' I said. 'They all seem so lovely and so desperate to keep the circus a going concern despite their troubles. I did wonder about Charlie Cooke—actually not lovely at all, or not to me anyway—but Tiny said he was

128

besotted with Topsy and simply couldn't have done it. Pa Cooke himself has a foul temper but he's all fizz and bang—I can't see him creeping around and setting traps for people.'

'I can't see any man doing it, if I'm honest,' said Alec. 'It's all so furtive and silly.'

'Too furtive and too silly to be the work of a man?' I said.

'You sound like Mrs Pankhurst, darling,' said Alec. 'A detective, as you're always telling me, can be no respecter of persons, much less of gentle sexes. What about Topsy herself?'

'Topsy was the victim of the very worst of the pranks,' I reminded him. 'And anyway there is nothing "Pankhurst" about pointing out that when it comes to hurting young women, there is a man at the bottom of it every time.'

'So tell me about the men,' said Alec, 'and stop chirping on about the womenfolk.'

'The men,' I said, running my mind over what I knew about them. 'Bill Wolf is quite simply Father Christmas in his shirtsleeves and that's that.'

'Oh, very objective,' said Alec. 'How convincing.'

'Although he knows something he's not telling. Kolya Prebrezhensky I've yet to meet properly. Tiny Truman is perfectly friendly towards Topsy although again there's a little edge there somewhere. But he would not harm Ana, I'm sure. He's the only one I've seen being kind to her so far, more than kind; I think he might be smitten. And he doesn't have the figure for manhandling heavy ropes. Andrew Merryman . . . I can't say, but again he is a friend of Topsy's, perhaps more than a friend if Tiny's hints are reliable.'

'I don't think we can cut anyone out simply because they are friendly to one of the girls,' Alec said. 'It might be an act. And if it's more than friendship—if it's love, or passion anyway—then I should say there's more reason for suspicion not less. Jealous rages, lovers' spats, unrequited yearnings. Rich pickings, I'd say. Now is that everyone?'

'Yes, that's it,' I said. 'Except for the working men. There are five—no, six—of them. Grooms.'

'Six grooms?' said Alec. 'For thirteen horses. That seems rather lavish.'

'Well, there are as many rough ponies too,' I reminded him. 'And they're not just grooms. They're tent men. They do the heavy work. They don't seem to mix with the artistes from what I see.'

'Ah,' said Alec. 'I like the sound of them.'

'Why?' I asked. 'You've never even met them. Why on earth should the working men immediately be the suspects?'

Alec stared at me.

'Good Lord, Dandy,' he said. 'Don't let Hugh hear you. Two days' companionship with a family of Russians and you're ready to take up arms for the proletariat.'

'Nonsense,' I said, hotly. 'I'm just questioning your objectivity as you questioned mine.'

'But I'm making a serious suggestion,' Alec said. 'Anastasia, from what you tell me, is an extremely attractive and extremely haughty young woman. As likely to attract the attention of a lusty young tent man as she is unlikely to give him the time of day. And Topsy sounds an out and out flirt, who has wound at least both Mr Cookes around her little finger and has Andrew Merryman on a string too. Well, why should she not have given these working men the same treatment? And why should not these working mean, inflamed by the sight of the pair of them in their tights and costumes and yet spurned by them as honest swains, be moved to play a few tricks on them to get their own back?'

In spite of myself, I was forced to agree that this made a great deal of good sense and with even greater grace than before I congratulated him.

'And now,' I said, looking up at my clock, 'it's time to go and collect an end to tranquillity. It's waiting at the station for me.'

What I meant was that my sons were coming home from school for their Christmas holiday and I had volunteered to pick them up at Dunkeld (leaving their bags for Drysdale to collect later since I did not want the Cowley getting scratches on it). My offer sprang not, I told myself, from any wild maternal passion which could not restrain itself while they were brought the last few miles, but from a desire to hear the running jokes and slogans they had brought with them and censor them before they reached the ears of Nanny or, worse, Hugh. I was determined that this Christmas would be an harmonious one at Gilverton, without the shouting, ranting and helpless hot giggling leading to louder shouting which so often ensued when all three of my male relations were at home.

'Oh yes, Christmas,' said Alec. 'What fun.' He sounded rather doleful and I glanced at him hoping that he would not see me doing so. His mother had died since the Christmas before and his sister-in-law, or so I gathered, had quickly made the Dorset house, Alec's childhood home,

131

rather horribly her own. He must be dreading Christmas Day all alone at Dunelgar, with his staff resenting him and pitying him in equal measure.

'Come to us, of course, darling,' I said as casually as I could. 'Barrow and the rest can have a holiday.' Alec said nothing. 'Although,' I went on, 'one could kick Dickens, if he were still here to be kicked. It's his fault that the servants think they should loll around gorging on goose all day.'

'Him and Her late Majesty,' Alec said. 'It's her doing that one can't just spend December the 25th at one's chosen pursuits and have a cutlet at night without feeling tragic.'

'Well, the boys will be delighted and you can talk to Hugh about fences and make his day too.'

'Can't, I'm afraid,' said Alec, not looking at me. 'It's as I said. One is drawn in and swept along. I've been invited to Pess.'

Pess. The home of the Uvings. The home of Magnus Uving, a wonderful host with a wonderful gamekeeper whose forests and moors were jammed with plump birds, and his wife Lady Amanda Uving, a wonderful hostess with a wonderful cook, whose house rang with music and laughter all year long. No one could resist an invitation to Pess, not least for Christmas. Of course, with such delights to offer the Uvings could pick and choose their guests, and they had chosen Alec, a young bachelor of good fortune, even better breeding and the greatest of charm. For as well as Magnus and Amanda, there was it must be said Celia Uving, twenty-two, beautiful, clever and very choosy. Christmas would make Alec's fourth visit this year.

'Excellent!' I cried, hoping that my face had not

132

reddened. 'I couldn't be more pleased. I lie awake at night, you know, darling, thinking about you rattling around in that yawning great empty house all on your own. Three cheers.'

'You'll be the first to know, Dandy,' Alec said. 'But it's only Christmas for now. Let's go and fetch the boys.'

*　　　*　　　*

What unprepossessing lumps they looked trailing along the platform towards me, dragging their trunks and hatboxes—for they had been trained by their father never to wait for porters like a pair of ladies back from shopping in town. Or not lumps exactly, for they had both shot up again since the summer, but no oil paintings either of them.

'My God, two badly planted saplings after their first big storm,' said Alec, hitting the nail on the head as usual. I snorted with laughter and leaned on the horn to tell them we were there, at which they broke into an ungainly and rather wavering trot causing sweet wrappers and tattered story-papers to fall out of pockets and from under arms.

'Hello, Mother,' said Teddy, which gave me a twinge: I had still been Mummy at half-term. 'Hello, Mr Osborne.'

'Boys,' said Alec. 'I'm sorry to be so predictable, but—as I was just saying to your mother—my, haven't you both grown!'

I saved Cooke's until they had finished telling their breathless and deadly dull news of football team places and piano prizes and had asked after their dogs and ponies, been given the news that the last of the childhood rabbits had finally died alone and unmourned in its cage in the stable-yard, and been warned not to tell Hugh that they would carry out some requested task 'with a Dixie melo-deeee!' or call him Toot-toot-tootsie whenever they said goodbye (some boy in their house had got an Al Jolson gramophone record and they had been playing it all term). When they had quietened down a little at last, I dropped the news into the lull where it went off like a flour-bomb.

'Really? Really and truly? Are there tigers and elephants? Is there a strongman? Is there a flying trapeze?'

I told them that there were no tigers, elephants or even anything close and that I had no clear idea what the flying trapeze was and whether Topsy could be said to be it, but that yes, there was a strong man (for sixty, I thought but forbore to mention) and there were horses, acrobats, clowns and a monkey, and that both boys were welcome there any time to watch the performers rehearsing.

'Golly,' said Donald.

'Only it's just the circus you're to visit, mind,' I told him. 'You can't go traipsing around the castle because Mrs Wilson isn't well.'

'Mrs Wilson?' said Teddy. 'Is that the Miss Havisham lady with the mad husband?' It was rather a garbled version, but close enough and so I nodded. 'Wouldn't catch me going in there then,' he said. 'I'd get bricked up in a dungeon and fed through the keyhole.' Clearly, the Wilsons were as well known amongst the youth of the neighbourhood as amongst their elders.

'You don't get keyholes if you're bricked up, Swachekopf,' said Donald.

'Faxenmacher,' said Teddy.

134

'And don't speak German,' I said. 'Heavens! Al Jolson for Daddy rather than *that.*'

*   *   *

I had expected simply to ferry them there every morning that I was going and bring them home each afternoon again, fingers crossed that they did not in the meantime make such pests of themselves that I had to break off my work to remove them early, and I am sure that the boys harboured no hopes of any more fun than that, but on the first evening when they described the camp to Hugh over tea, almost whinnying in their excitement about the twelve liberty horses, the tin roof over the fire, the giant man, the intricacy of the rope knots in the dome—for they gave of their admiration rather indiscriminately, it seemed to me—Hugh surprised all of us by suggesting that they too might set up camp there for a day or two.

'In a tent?' I squeaked. 'It's December. It's freezing.'

'They can take my old army wool bag,' said Hugh. 'And a mackintoshed groundsheet. They'll be fine.'

'Yes! Yes! We'll be fine,' the boys chorused, unable to believe their luck.

'Absolutely not,' I said stoutly. 'They'll catch their deaths of cold and spoil Christmas.'

'Never did me any harm,' said Hugh. 'You shouldn't coddle them so.'

'The circus people are camping, Mother, and you've never seen rosier cheeks than theirs.'

'You caught pneumonia,' I reminded Hugh. 'And the circus people,' I added turning to Donald,

135

'are in wagons. Up off the ground in beds.'

'What a bore you are,' said Teddy, my wonderful gift of visits to the circus quite swept away.

'Well then,' Hugh continued, 'they can take the shepherds' hut.' At this the boys' ecstasy grew delirious and they abandoned tea to race down to the Mains to where the shepherds' hut was stored in a byre over winter. I could see that this was a much better plan since the hut, itself very like a little living wagon, had a tiny paraffin stove and walls well baffled with fleeces, and although they would have to sleep on its floor it was a lot less likely to lead to lozenges and poultices all round. The shepherds, I told myself, lived in it for weeks at lambing time every year and early spring in Perthshire is far from balmy. Still, I was puzzled; Hugh's usual role in the boys' existence leaned towards the quelling of their desires rather than the surpassing of them.

'It's an awfully long way to trundle it,' I said.

'Nonsense,' Hugh replied. 'Jimmy Purves can take it over the hills. It goes practically that far to the black-faces anyway. Much the best thing all round, I should say, Dandy.'

Which remark, I thought, began at last to shed light upon the matter; perhaps not to the casual observer, but certainly to me. Because even two individuals as fully absorbed in themselves and their own pursuits as my sons might begin to wonder at my driving them there and back every day and might begin to ask themselves what I was doing there, but the notion that I flew to them every morning to tie their scarves tighter and hold my hand to their brows would be enough to keep everyone happy and unquestioning.

For the boys knew nothing of my exploits and Hugh was very keen to keep it that way. He was not alone in this, admittedly: I had no wish to have my curious little sideline bandied about the common rooms and playing fields to be carried home and relayed to the mothers of the other boys and served up to my face with a titter at parties for evermore. (As it most certainly would be, for was I not the unwilling recipient of such choice items of news as that Tenburgh's father had written a play but could not get it performed at the local theatre in Derby even when he offered to pay or that the mother of all those endless little Sewells had been painting pictures of their aunt with no clothes on? 'In the garden too. And the garden boys were caught peeping over a wall to see and got the sack until Mr Sewell said she had no authority to sack them and anyway what did she expect and gave them their jobs back again and now, Sewell says, they haven't spoken for a month and Mrs Sewell has moved her bedroom to the far wing.' So, perhaps the supply of new little Sewells had dried up after all.)

* * *

They survived their first night well enough and were sitting on the step of the hut with tin mugs of tea and ragged slices of rather blackened toast in their hands when I arrived in the morning. Bunty, who had been left behind with them as part guard dog part hot water bottle, was tied to the spoke of a wheel just like all the other dogs around the ground, but unlike them she reared up and began to plunge about when she saw me, causing the little hut to roll and wobble and the boys to clutch the sides of the steps and slop some of their tea.

'Good girl,' I cooed, tremendously pleased at the greeting. 'Well, boys?' They needed no further encouragement to regale me with how cosy they had been, what songs they had learned from Tommy Wolf in his wagon last night and how many Russian words Inya and Alya Prebrezhensky had taught them already. With offers of a piece of toast—and assurances that it was no trouble and they had bread to spare—following on behind me, I left them to it.

My plan was to revisit the Prebrezhenskys' wagon that day. Stung by Alec's scorn, I was determined to concentrate on hard facts. I had found Zoya charming and thought her artless, but the swing was in their cupboard, they might have good reason to think little of Ana, and I had not spoken to Kolya at all yet—glowering Kolya who wanted secrets kept unspoken.

And here, I thought to myself as I crossed the ground, was another of my less known quantities. Andrew Merryman was on his way back from the stream with two pails of water and headed straight towards me. He could hardly avoid passing the time of day with me, although his blush and the dip of his head revealed his discomfort as he did so. I should, I thought to myself, hate to be shy, but perhaps if one had gone through childhood getting more and more outlandish-looking until one turned into an Andrew Merryman one would have had no choice in the matter. He really was the most peculiar figure and appeared to be practically buckling under the weight of the water pails dangling from his long arms, although that might have been shyness too.

'They m-m-might never come home again,' he said, nodding towards the boys.

'Oh, I should think I'm safe enough,' I replied, quite heartily for some reason, as though addressing him in ringing tones would buck him up a bit or at least make him stand straight; it is always wasted effort for a beanpole of a person to fold himself up trying to look shorter. 'They have absolutely no talents or skills to recommend them.'

'Neither had I,' said Andrew, and then blushed even deeper. 'Although I had an e-e-extra incentive, obviously.' I was unsure whether to pretend I did not catch his meaning or to nod sympathetically and agree. 'I f-fit right in at Cooke's Circus,' he went on. 'And I'd hate . . . I mean I couldn't bear to think . . . Tiny says you're trying to . . .'

'I am. And you can help me, Mr Merryman.'

He looked startled at that.

'Your perspective will be most helpful,' I said. 'You must be able to see them all with a clearer eye, from your position.'

'That's it, spot on,' he said and he looked around the circus as though seeing it for the first time. 'My position. All any flatty sees when he looks at me is circus. And all the proper circus see is a josser. Neither one thing nor the other, that's me.'

'Well, you are not alone,' I said. 'Ana and Tiny are jossers too.'

'So you're telling me I could be as happy and settled as Ana?' He spoke with a great air of innocence and made me laugh, even though it was

139

not funny.

'Well, Tiny, then. He seems snug enough here in the circus.'

'Tiny's a braver man than I,' said Andrew, rather cryptically. 'He's circus through and through now.'

'Don't run yourself down, Mr Merryman,' I said. 'I heard from Tiny—Mr Truman, I should say—about you checking everything over after you found the swapped balloons.'

'If only,' said Andrew. 'We didn't look at Topsy's rope.'

'But you saw the problem before anyone else,' I reminded him.

'And still I did nothing,' he said. 'I didn't want to draw attention to it. I don't like trouble.'

'You acted in time,' I said firmly. 'She was very lucky to have you there and I am sure'—here I could not resist a matronly little hint; really I cannot believe the meddlesome old matchmaker I am turning into—'that she must feel most warmly towards you because of it.' This startled him and he stood up quite straight for a moment.

'Hah!' he said, gruffly. 'Hardly!' and I made a mental note to myself to leave the prying and clucking to those many women who had a talent for it and mind my own particular business instead.

'Now, what interests me,' I said, walking along beside him, 'is the question of whether the one who cut the swing and rope put them where they were found? And if not, why was anyone rummaging around in a position to find them, already cut, and move them? And why move the swing to where I found it when the rope was so well hidden in Tiny's prop box?'

140

'Where *did* you find it?' he asked me, and then as I hesitated he dipped his head again and smiled. 'Am I a suspect then?'

'To be quite frank, Mr Merryman, everyone is a suspect right now, and no one is a suspect right now. But you can certainly help. Might I call on you later and pick your brain properly?' We had arrived at his wagon now and he set the pails down.

'I have no brain for problems,' he said, shaking his hair over his eyes and managing to make himself look more hangdog than ever. 'It reminds me of school, gives me a headache. I'd better stick to jug-juggling.' With another shy smile he opened his door and crept inside, folding himself almost in two to fit under the low ceiling. I had one glimpse of the interior—the usual box-bed missing and a long thin bunk set up against one side wall instead—before politeness demanded that I turn away.

*   *   *

My efforts with the Prebrezhenskys were not helped by the fact that only Zoya had anything like reliable English and so had to translate for the father and the girls, nor by the fact that it took me a good hour to realise that there were not, as I briefly imagined, a handful more Prebrezhenskys lurking unseen but that little Rosaliya *was* Alya, Inessa *was* Inya, Akilina *was* Ilya and 'Nikolai' was Kolya's Sunday best name. With all of that established, amid much laughter from the parents and not a few quizzical looks as though they wondered what kind of detective could have

141

trouble with it, it did not take too long to arrive at the conclusion that relations were cordial between this family and the rest of Cooke's—indeed, unsurprisingly, Zoya and Ma had quickly discovered connections, or putative connections, which suggested that this family was yet another branch of the Cooke dynasty, by marriage anyway.

As for Topsy, when I mentioned her, they all broke into smiles.

'She is like a daughter,' said Zoya.

'Gutt, gutt gorrl,' said Kolya, beaming.

It was not until I touched on 'Anastasia' that any of the smiling faces grew stern.

'What has happened in our beloved Mother Russia, it is not a joke,' said Zoya. 'It is not a . . . a silly for a silly girl to make silly fairy tale.'

'No indeed,' I agreed. One could almost become as rattled as poor Hugh if one thought about it for any length of time: to imagine our own King and Queen and all the children jostled into a basement at Sandringham as their cousins had been at Ekaterinburg and then . . . 'No, indeed,' I said again.

'My Kolya he feels it in his big heart,' Zoya went on. 'He hopes in his heart we can go home again when it is well. We speak only Russian to the little ones, against a day when once more we go back and stay.'

Kolya nodded and thumped his fist against his chest to drive the point home. I wondered if they had a source of more hopeful news than the rest of us—family letters perhaps, if these were not intercepted and expurgated on the way. Certainly, if Zoya were reading the same newspapers as Hugh over breakfast I could not account for any hope in anyone's heart. Endless, dreary, muddy gloom and lots of shooting was all there was to see.

'And have you actually ever had it out with Anastasia?' I asked. 'About this storytelling of hers.' Zoya frowned, puzzled. 'Have you quarrelled, argued?'

'No,' said Zoya. 'She is here and we are here. She is new here and we are new here. Just one season. Pa Cooke find us in Glasgow, same time as Ana, and gave us jobs.'

'Very happy,' said Kolya. 'No trouble with gorrl Ana.'

'Very commendable of you,' I said. 'It must be difficult sometimes.'

Zoya shrugged.

'We circus,' said Kolya. 'Ana circus. So. We stay'—he opened his arms wide and pointed down with both index fingers—'here and here and . . .' At this his English gave out and he rumbled a torrent of Russian to his wife.

'We keep out of her way and she keep out of our way and everyone stays happy,' Zoya said.

I nodded, thinking that for stoic endurance, Russians took the biscuit.

'To practical matters then,' I said. 'Topsy thinks she had the swing two days before her fall, at around seven in the evening. Let's try to work out when it can have been put here. What time do the little ones go to bed?'

It did not take long to establish just how endless the opportunities were. The girls were tucked up in bed long before seven but the next day the wagon had lain empty and unlocked for two hours in the morning and another hour in the afternoon while the family practised with the mechanic.

143

Someone might easily have sidled up to it with a bundle of ropes under his arm and the disarray of a pickle cupboard in his mind.

As to the deed going unwitnessed, I could only too clearly remember the way Zoya had lifted the canvas walling of the back tent and how she and I had slipped under it and into the wagon, flitting across the few feet of shadow like ghosts. Anyone could have done the same and it gave me a cold prickle of dread, as I stood on the steps minutes after having taken my leave, to think of this faceless figure moving unseen around the winter ground, with its knife and its grievances, its threats no less chilling for seeming senseless.

Something fluttered at the edge of my vision. I turned towards it and felt a cold prickle of dread, indeed, the dread of finding oneself suddenly pitched into intercourse with Albert Wilson, who was coming into the campground around the edge of the pond, almost at a trot, clearly bursting with a matter of some importance.

'My d—Mrs . . . Dan . . . Good morning,' he called to me. 'This is a surprise. A pleasant surprise, I should say.' He took a deep breath and squared his shoulders. 'This is a very pleasant surprise, finding you here, Dandy.'

My eyebrows shot up.

'I've come clucking over my chicks, I'm afraid,' I said. 'My boys. Did you know there were a couple of runaways added to the merry band?'

'Oh, don't mention it,' he replied. 'They're very welcome. Think nothing of it.'

I had not considered thinking anything of it, much less asking permission from Albert Wilson, who I always seem to forget is as much a

144

landowner as Hugh. I bristled to think I had given him the chance to forgive an impropriety. Anyway, two more and a tiny shepherds' hut were neither here nor there.

'You seem in ebullient spirits this morning,' I said, finding attack the best defence.

'Verily,' he said. 'I've come to arrange the show. Saturday night, I think. You are invited of course. You and uhhhh . . . both of you.' His high spirits, wherever they had sprung from, were not quite sufficient to let him drop Hugh's name in cold blood and broad daylight.

'This coming Saturday?' I said. 'That's rather earlier than we were expecting. I trust Ina will be coming along?'

'Oh, I should think so,' said Albert Wilson. 'She can sit quite separately from the rest of the company after all.' I had never heard such airiness from him.

'The rest of the company being . . . ?' I asked.

'Well, yourself and your menfolk.' He inclined his head as though in recognition of the honour he bestowed. 'Robin, of course, and he might bring a party. He said he might.' He gave me a smile of beatitude the like of which I had only seen rendered in marble before and, with a slight bow, he left me.

Robin, indeed! But at least I had an explanation for Wilson's new air of sublime confidence and for his dragging the show out of quarantine already. Unable to believe his luck, he was willing to risk Ina spending two hours under canvas with heaven only knew what manner of exotic germs, if he could thus snag Laurie and a party of his chums before the strange acquaintance faded away.

Ina, unsurprisingly, was livid when she telephoned to me again that evening.

'He's unmovable, Dandy,' she said, her voice coming down the line with more strength than I had ever heard in it before. 'And it's so unlike him.' I could see that while she chafed under Albert's excess of care and delighted in outwitting him when she could, she had also grown used to the idea of the caring and had to be flattered in some way. Certainly, now that concern for her welfare had been so ignominiously knocked off its spot she was far from pleased. 'And, apparently, we have a horde of hangers-on coming for dinner. He was quite adamant about that.'

'Albert?'

'Well, Lord Robin, really, but with Albert behind him all the way. So I shall have that to endure too. And after how rude he was last time.'

'Well,' I said, 'he was insufferable but I rather got the impression that you had made up your mind about him well before that, Ina. Could you not simply tell your husband whatever it is that makes you dislike the man so? Would not that nip this nonsense in the bud?' There was a long silence on the line.

'I'd rather not think about it,' she said at last. 'I shouldn't have to. And I shouldn't have to have a houseful of strangers come to stare and titter either.'

I felt a sharp retort, referencing the Queen of Sheba, rise to my lips but I managed to swallow it. Albert Wilson, with all his pandering and fuss, really had created a monster. Nanny was right, and I wondered why it had never struck me over the years before now.

146

The Cookes and what others of the circus I had a chance to speak to thought not much more of the sudden request for a show.

'It had just better not be the thin end of the wedge,' Pa Cooke said. 'A winter standing, Mr Wilson told us, a chance to rest up, make our repairs and get the new acts ready for spring.'

Bill Wolf, who was there at the time taking a glass of beer in the Cookes' wagon, thumped his fist against his knee in agreement.

'And I've got my costume all unpicked ready for making up again,' he said. 'I've got nothing to wear for my strongman run-in, and my trumpet's in fifteen bits for cleaning. I thought I had a week yet.'

'But there, he always told us there'd be a show, Pa,' said his wife. 'We knew that wurr part of the bargain.'

'Aye, one show. *One* show. For his missus, and not till Hogmanay most likely. Now here we are not even Christmas and there's a party coming. And Topsy's hands could do with more of a rest. If this is him starting to take a lend of me, now he's got me trapped here, he can think again.'

'And what would we be doing else?' said Ma. She turned to me. 'Do you know, my beauty, even Hengler's an't doing the whole season this winter, after last year nearly broke them.'

'It's them damned picture shows,' said Bill Wolf.

'I mind when Moss's Christmas Varieties was the highlight of the whole year,' said Pa. 'Even bigger than the summer tenting.'

'You're going back-aways there, Tam,' said his wife. 'Them days is gone. Let's make what we've got all it can be, eh? Let's go out with a bang.'

147

'We're not going out,' said Pa Cooke fiercely. 'It's bad luck even to talk that way.' Mrs Cooke looked uncomfortable but said nothing.

In fact, the only voices raised in hurrahs at the news were Donald's and Teddy's, for the ring boys were off on loan to Newsome's in Edinburgh for the Christmas season, Newsome's being one outfit still clinging to the old ways by its fingernails, and so the tent staff were short-handed.

'We're to wear their uniforms,' Teddy regaled me. 'Well, their coats because the trousers are rather short—perhaps Nanny might run something up instead?—and we're to do the ring fence. Andrew and Tiny are teaching us.'

'Mr Truman and Mr Merryman,' I said. 'And *what* are you to do with the ring fence?'

'Take the bit out to let the animals run in,' said Donald, 'and then put it back in sharpish so's they don't run out again.'

'Don't say sharpish,' I said. 'And don't say so's. And how on earth can you manhandle great blocks of wood?'

'Oh, Mother,' said Teddy rolling his eyes. 'It's hollow ply. Even Inya P. can throw it over her shoulder.'

'Well, don't tell Daddy,' I said, in desperation. 'At least not yet. Until I've had a chance to look at these coats and check them for . . .' I coughed diplomatically. If I said the word to them they would say it to someone at Cooke's and there would be an end to cosy cups of tea in the living wagons.

'He won't stop us,' said Donald. 'He's all for our circus adventure. You're the old stick-in-the-mud this time, Ma.'

I was less sure. Roughing it in a shepherds' hut in winter might count as building character in Hugh's book but cavorting around the ring in borrowed coats in front of society people was quite another thing; I could not guess which way Hugh would land on that question.

'Don't call me Ma,' was all I said.

8

How strange it seemed that while Pa Cooke feared exploitation at the hands of his landlord, while Bill Wolf fretted over the disarray of wardrobe and wind section, while Ina Wilson resented the deluge of unwanted guests, almost no one except me suffered any foreboding from what I thought to be the obvious quarter: almost no one in Cooke's Circus seemed at all perturbed about the prospect that the saboteur might take a hand in the show. The only other worried face was Anastasia's.

'Oh, any excuse not to work,' said Pa Cooke, as Ana stood in front of him with her hands on her hips and her feet planted, staring him down. 'Topsy's the one should worry and there's not a peep out of her.'

'Now, Tam,' said his wife. 'That's not fair. Ana's a fine hard worker and you know it.'

'Never heard the like,' said Pa. 'Not going on? I've gone on with broken limbs, 'flu so bad you could fry an egg on me. You're in the spec and you're doing one spot, my lass, and even at that you're short, so less of the nonsense from you.'

Ana smiled at that; a strange curling smile

which did not quite reach her eyes and which made Pa Cooke shift in his seat.

'Very well,' she said. 'I suppose it would be difficult to have a spectacular without me. I shall make your show for you—again.' She turned on her heel and, with a last look over her shoulder, sauntered away leaving Pa spluttering.

'You'll do what you're bid,' he shouted to her retreating back. 'The spec's about all of us, not just you.'

What he said about Topsy was true enough. She was a little hesitant about the state of her hands, but of fearfulness there was not a whisper.

'We've checked everything thoroughly now,' said Andrew Merryman, when I asked if he could account for it. 'And no one has been here to make any more mischief. We've all been keeping an eye out for "unsavoury characters hanging around".' There was a faint laugh in his voice. 'Makes a ch-change,' he explained, 'from shopkeepers and village bobbies keeping an eye on us.'

'Do they really?' I said. My short sojourn with the circus folk had already rendered them ordinary in my eyes and I could not imagine it, could barely remember that first impression: the smoking child, the giant and the bear.

'You've no idea,' he said. 'I can sometimes face them down with my best Old Harrovian'—as he spoke, the circus fell away from his voice and a haughty, icy drawl replaced it—'but I get t-t-t—' He flashed his eyes furiously and pointed to his mouth.

'Tongue-tied?'

'Thank you,' he said, letting all of his breath go in a rush. I could not decide whether, like Tiny, he

150

was teasing me. He had not seemed sufficiently at ease with himself to do such a thing but perhaps he was *perfectly* at ease with himself and now getting that way with me too. I gave him the same stern, governess-ish look that I used on his friend and returned to business.

'And are you keeping your things under lock and key?' I asked. 'Are you keeping all your ropes and poles and whatnot close by you?'

'No need,' said Andrew. 'No one in the circus would ever tamper with another man's props.'

There it was again, the wilful, blinkered and infuriating refusal to look at the plain facts and call them by their name. I heard the same thing from Topsy and Ma. No one circus would do such a thing; no one circus would even dream of it.

'But it happened, Mrs Cooke,' I said when I could not listen to it in silence any longer. 'The rope, the swing, the flour, the balloons and the whip. You told me Ana did it.'

'I said I was wrong there, didn't I?' she replied. 'She'd never have swapped that rope like that. She couldn't have. So then the whip wun't her neither.'

'Well, if no one in the circus can possibly be up to anything, then all these strange happenings have been the work of elves and pixies and I am wasting my time,' I said, not even trying to hide my exasperation.

'Oh, somebody's up to *some*thing,' she said. 'I can feel it in my . . . well, in my water there, pardon me for mentioning it in your presence. It's worrying our Ana half to death, the poor maid, and I'm vexed as a hen she won't talk to you, my beauty, no more than she'll talk to me. But all them tricks wurr a flatty what come round making

151

trouble. Must have been.'

'Somebody's up to something, but not the very things that have happened?'

'Never, not no way,' she said.

'And the rope switch was hardly a trick,' I said. 'I'd have called that attempted murder.'

'That's what I'm saying,' said Mrs Cooke. 'That proves it. 'Nobody cir—'

I held up my hand; if I heard it again I should scream.

'You know your business, my beauty, but I know mine,' said Mrs Cooke and she sat back in her chair, folded her arms under her considerable bosom and began nodding, very slowly, as though she would never stop.

I gave a sigh and left her. All I could say was that I was glad *I* was not dangling from the rafters, or galloping around on a bare-back pony jumping through hoops. I was glad that Donald and Teddy were signed up for no greater a commission than to lift a section of ring fence up and slot it back into place again, and even at that I told them to stay well back when the horses were passing and not to stand under anything tied to a beam.

*   *   *

Dinner with the Wilsons before the show was every bit as excruciating as might be expected. Hugh declined to attend and not even the clamour of the boys as they told him in shrill and outraged detail what he was missing could sway him, but Alec was there looking almost as stony as Hugh might have as the rest of the assemblage was introduced to him.

Gathered in the hall of the castle, where two sumptuous fires of apple wood crackled and flickered in the grates and the shadows of holly branches danced on the plaster walls, were every raffish younger son, every disgraced wife and discarded husband, every overly merry widow which Perthshire and points north could muster. The hall, usually as calm as a chapel, rang with laughter and glittered with jewels—they had all opted for a fair amount of finery this evening, even to go and sit on wooden benches in a tent—and the smell was an ever thickening fug of French scent, hair oil and that new top note at all the parties just then: the smell, unidentifiable at first whiff but unmistakable ever after, of feathers and metal threads warming as the women in the fringed dresses grew hot and raucous, cocktails in hand.

In the middle of it all sat Robin Laurie, lolling on a sofa like a leopard in a tree, his own cocktail barely tasted and pushed away from him and his hip flask unstoppered and constantly at his lips.

Margot Stirling had even had the nerve to bring along the boy, a chauffeur to my recollection or a gardener perhaps, for whose sake she had given up her name and her reputation and with whom she was now ensconced in a tiny cottage on her brother's estate. I was very glad that Hugh was not here to see her, and even more glad that he was not here to see the way she glanced at Alec and then winked at me. The boy himself looked perfectly at his ease in his surroundings, gulping his drink and affecting an insolent sneer, and the others for the most part ignored him—Margot was a chum and therefore a given, but there were limits—and shrieked across the room at one another.

'But darling, that's what I told you. I don't think I ever did go to one when I was tiny. I think this is my very first time.'

'Such a thrill! I'm much too excited to eat any boring old dinner first.'

'But I don't want to sit near the front under the thundering hooves, for I shall scream.'

Albert Wilson bustled and scurried, nagging the sweet butler about drinks and practically bouncing on the balls of his feet with glee to be hosting such a party. At least, I noted, the guests were not laughing at him or teasing him into greater vulgarities than he might naturally display, although their wholesale disregard was just as rude in its own way. They acted as though he were another butler, and one with no tray and therefore nothing to offer them that they could possibly want.

When Ina arrived in the hall, Albert made extra efforts to gain their attention and actually managed to get through about a third of his prepared talk about her health and the guarding of it before the shrieking began again and his audience was lost to him.

'Now, really, I must just tell you,' he said, his voice rising. The chattering voices only rose still higher and drowned him. 'And please, ladies, no cigarettes, I implore you.'

'Don't trouble yourself, Albert dear,' said Ina, 'I shall go into the dining room and take my seat. Please, dear, please.'

Robin Laurie, hearing this exchange, making quite sure that he did hear it, I thought, from the

154

way he leaned forward and stared at Ina as she was talking, spoke up at once.

'Splendid idea, Mrs Wilson,' he said, his eyes dancing, 'let's go to the dining room and wait for dinner there.'

The shriekers turned to face him as one and there was a moment of quiet, before the first of them answered.

'What a naughty Robin,' she said. 'Why on earth?'

'We can't let our hostess sit all alone,' said Laurie, 'and you have spread yourselves all over the place in here and left her nowhere safe to perch. I told you all about Mrs Wilson, didn't I?'

'Such fun,' said another of the women, this one a rather raddled forty-year-old got up like a girl in pink frills and white satin shoes. 'I haven't gone in to wait since nursery tea. Do let's.'

So, to Albert Wilson's bewilderment and his wife's silent fury, the shrieking women and drawling men put down their cocktail glasses and trooped along after Ina into the dining room, where obeying the name cards set out at each place they sat around the table in a horseshoe all staring at her alone on the fourth side.

After a long and rather hollow silence, someone giggled, and one of the parlour maids poked her head in at the door, her eyes round with surprise to see us all there.

'Perhaps we could have a glass of wine while we wait?' said Laurie. Albert Wilson leapt to his feet.

'Oh yes, splendid, an excellent idea. I believe there was going to be sherry with the soup so maybe we could have that now and then if I can just . . .' He drew the butler off into a corner of the room, but still his hissed questions about the sherry and the temperature of those bottles of good Sauternes were clearly audible. The giggles began to grow.

'What the bloody hell is he playing at?' said Alec to me under his breath.

'He's just a wrecker,' I said, not caring that Laurie must guess we were discussing him, for we were both staring right at him as we murmured to one another. 'Just a silly little wrecker. And the rest of them!' I glanced around at the faces, some still sparkling with the enjoyment of the moment, some bored again already. 'My God,' I said, 'it's like the fall of Rome in here.'

At that, even Alec giggled a little and I almost joined him, although I was quite serious really in my way and I did not dare look at Ina. Fortunately the kitchen staff came up trumps; perhaps they had been well beforehand as my own dear Mrs Tilling always prefers to be, or perhaps there was a gas ring which could be pressed into service to speed things up. One way or another, the soup began to arrive before the vexed question of the sherry could be settled and while it was handed and drunk things became slightly more normal again.

Alec, bless him for it, dug deep within himself, all the way to prep school tea with the housemaster's wife and after-church chats with ladies from the village, and kept the table afloat through soup, fish, venison and spiced steamed pudding, valiantly quizzing Albert on the broad sweep and the nitty-gritty of the common house brick far beyond anything I could have imagined possible. Of course, the topic rendered the rest of

156

the company helpless with silent amusement and one or two of Wilson's earnest answers even brought gales of quite loud laughter. Meanwhile, I did what I could with Ina, reminding myself more than a little of a governess taking a child for a long walk in a high wind, one part exhortation and three parts dragging. By the time the meal was over I was exhausted.

Thankfully, there was no time for coffee in the drawing room and port around the table, just some hot cocoa to help the spiced pudding do its work and then we were off to bundle ourselves into furs and make our way through the icy night to the circus.

And what a very different prospect it presented, with the great white stable tent glowing like a full moon come to earth and the performing tent starry with lanterns. There were no tickets to be sold but there Ma Cooke was in the little ticket wagon anyway, with her black hair piled on top of her head and festooned with gold-coloured beads as bright as the rings in her ears.

'Roll up, roll up, roll up there, my fine ladies and gents,' she said. 'Madame Polina welcomes you to Cooke's Family Circus, the oldest circus as ever was in all this scepter'd isle and still the finest.' Of course there were giggles at that, but they seemed less harsh than they had before, less braying, with a little real pleasure at the magic, even the tawdry magic, of it all.

At the door of the tent, where the canvas flaps were covered with sleeves of red tonight and looped back with gold braid ropes, stood Donald and Teddy. They looked rather splendid in their blue satin coats and pillbox hats (all well-doused with Keating's powder) and with red ribbon hastily tacked down the sides of their old school trousers by Nanny that afternoon—proper circus, as Ma Cooke would say—and none of the guests gave them a second glance, except Alec who pressed ten-shilling notes into their hands as he passed, with a wink. They winked back, but scrupulously ignored me.

Inside, Albert Wilson ushered Ina into a seat in the back row to the left of the door and stood guard on the end to stop anyone joining her there, before taking his place a couple of rows in front. He need not have worried. In the manner of the bright young things they were hoping to be taken for (and might, in fact, be) all of the ladies raced to the front and packed themselves in like children on a school treat, jostling and giggling, and pleading with the men to sit in the row behind to protect them. The men, for the most part, filed into the row with good grace, only Robin Laurie himself standing aloof and amused in the doorway, finishing his cigarette, before sidling into the back row across the aisle from Ina, where he leaned against a pole and stretched his long legs out in front of him. Ina, looking straight ahead, nevertheless scowled and shifted slightly in her seat until she was turned far enough away from him that even his shoes must be out of sight to her.

I sighed and led Alec to a seat midway between the pack of giggling idiots at the front and whatever nonsense was passing between Laurie and Ina at the back.

'And remember,' I said to him in a low voice, 'we're not here to amuse ourselves. We're here to watch. Watch their faces, watch for hints of dark passion, watch for glares of hatred, watch for . . . anything really.'

But there was nothing to see; there was no hint at all of what would happen until the very moment it did.

Sallie Wolf, who was huddled beside the gramophone close against the ring fence behind one of the king poles, now grasped the handle in both hands and cranked it furiously, looking like Buster Keaton on one of those frantic handcart journeys along desolate railway tracks (a journey which he takes inexplicably often to my mind; I have never known anyone in real life who did so). When the contraption was well wound, the child set the arm down with a slight screech and the tent began to fill with a rather reedy oompah-oompah, which Sallie augmented with a little drum of her own, and soon there was enough noise to make one feel a thrill of anticipation.

The chatter of the crowd subsided until only one or two giggles were breaking out intermittently from the front row and then Donald and Teddy, to my astonishment, swept the ring door flaps aside and strode confidently inside holding them open. Through the opening Pa Cooke appeared, swaggering in gleaming boots and britches and a tailcoat, his hair glittering with brilliantine and his moustache waxed to needle points. Donald and Teddy sprang forward and lifted out a section of the ring fence to allow him to pass through on to the sawdust, into the lights. Behind him came one, two, three and then too many to count snorting black horses, their coats shimmering like pools of ink. They lifted their hooves high, knocking foot against hock, foot against hock, as though they were dancing and all the time their beautiful necks arched to one side and then the other nodding their heads in time to the music. They fanned out on either side of Pa Cooke and at a crack of his whip they began to canter. The show had begun.

It opened with The Spectacular, in which everyone crams into the ring at once and performs edited highlights of their acts, not the highest of the highlights, for those are saved for the act finales with drum rolls and spotlights, but some of the tricks which are impressive enough to whet the appetites for more. So, Pa's horses stepped in time, rearing up and bowing down; beyond their reach, Anastasia circled the ring on Harlequin's broad back, jumping down to one side and the other and leaping back up again to stand with her arms spread behind her, her face a picture of joy; Topsy, her hands strapped up in what looked like strips of leather, wheeled and spun on her corde lisse, matching each flourish to a bang on the drum; Charlie Cooke juggled and danced; Andrew and Tiny, when they were not holding up streamers and balloons for Ana, tumbled and turned cartwheels, perfectly in time with one another, perfectly in tune, the little man ducking in and out of Andrew's flailing limbs like a pilot fish.

Presently the black horses stopped wheeling and began to weave chains instead. Into the open space they had made, the Prebrezhenskys bounded as though on springs and, once Kolya had thrown himself down, the girls leapt up on to his waiting feet and began spinning. Zoya walked around, beaming, showing off her girls with a flourish of her arms, inviting us to marvel. At least that was what we were supposed to think, I realised. In fact, she was watching them closely, moving in whenever they attempted a high somersault, and stepping back, her face filled with relief, when they had landed again.

Down by the king pole, Sallie was cranking the gramophone handle as though her little life depended upon it; the clowns' somersaults grew faster until they were flashing past one another like a kaleidoscope and then with a final spring and bound they were gone. The horses reared steeper and paddled their hooves, Alya and Inya, with their mother standing rigid, one hand up towards each, flew up in the air, higher, higher, twisting like bobbins. Topsy held on to the rope with one foot and her teeth, or so it looked to me, and spun so fast she was almost a blur, Ana flashed by on Harlequin, now on her hands, now on her feet, tumbling over and over, faster and faster. She passed behind the line of weaving horses towards the back of the ring and . . .

Nothing stopped, but everything, somehow, slowed and there were no more flourishes, nothing to make one gasp, as though everyone was marking time, waiting. Ana had left the ring. Pa Cooke kept his whip cracking, kept his horses dancing, but glanced over his shoulder. Zoya signalled to her husband with a downward pressing movement of her hand and the swift shuffling movements of his feet grew calmer, the girls making easy little spins. It was Topsy who took matters into her own hands and she had no choice: she could not keep spinning for ever for once the coiled power in the rope was spent, it was spent and besides she was panting hard, her ribs under

161

their spangles heaving and her arms beginning to show the strain, juddering and twitching as she held her line.

In the end, she had to do what she did, which was let herself down hand over hand to the floor with her legs kicking out like the sails of a windmill around her. She bowed as soon as she touched her feet to the sawdust and she was off. Then the Prebrezhensky girls jumped clear and landed with their arms spread wide, Kolya leapt up and all four of them bowed low and bounded from the ring. Pa Cooke shouted some swift command to his horses and they formed a ring again. I could see Donald and Teddy lifting the piece of fence and as soon as the first horse reached the ring door it led the procession out.

'Ladies and Ah-gentlemen,' bellowed Mr Cooke, for the applause was clamorous, 'thank you thank you thank you. I thank you.' At last the audience stilled but his voice remained as loud as ever. The gramophone record had wound down; he was shouting not to be heard above it, but to drown out the sound of commotion from backstage. 'And first, for your delectation and delight, may I present The Troupe Prebrezhensky.' He swept away backwards, his movements as sure and as firm as ever, only a slight frown twitching at his face showing that the raised voices from behind the ring doors were angering him. He bowed deeply and left the ring empty. We waited. Donald and Teddy shifted their feet a little, shooting panicked looks around them. The silence lengthened and the guests in the front row began to glance about themselves too and whisper. I looked behind me and saw Albert Wilson, sitting up very straight, frowning. I could just see Robin out of the corner of my eye but of Ina there was no sign.

'What do you think—' Alec began, but he did not get a chance to finish it. From behind the ring doors, slightly muffled by the canvas but piercing enough at that, there came a thin, high scream.

I leapt the ring fence, in step with Alec, and raced across towards the door, turning halfway to shout behind me: 'Keep to your seats, ladies and gentlemen. Keep to your seats.' The last thing we needed was the bright young things surging through into the warren of the backstage when heaven knew what was going on. The two rows of guests stared owlishly back at me. Albert Wilson was wringing his hands. Robin Laurie was on the edge of his seat, his head cocked up in alertness. Ina, I noticed, was still nowhere to be seen.

As we burst through the doorway, I could hear the sound of someone weeping but whoever it was was a long way along the winding passageways; we were almost at the back flaps before we saw them all. Both Prebrezhensky girls were wailing and in one voice I thought I could hear the shrill note which had produced that scream. Topsy and Tiny stood, arms around one another, their chests still heaving from their exertions in the ring, but their faces stricken behind the paint. Mrs Wolf was standing staring at the ground, little Tommy's face buried in her skirts. Charlie Cooke was sitting on a barrel with his head in his hands, still wearing his wig, the red woolly tendrils sticking out between his fingers.

'Get out the back and find Harlequin,' said Pa Cooke's voice, sounding ragged. As Kolya stepped

163

away to obey him and Zoya followed, shepherding the little girls, I saw what they had been hiding. Ma Cooke was sitting on the ground halfway out into the open, plumped down with her Madame Polina skirts spread around, her shoulders shaking and her head bowed low. In front of her lay Anastasia. She was on her side with her legs bent beneath her, her hands flung wide, her hair covering her face. I stepped off the board on to the worn grass in the doorway and crouched down beside Ma, putting out a hand to feel Ana's wrist. It was limp and still. I gathered up a handful of her hair and swept it back from her face. Her eyes were half-open, staring. From the side of her head where it lay on the ground a dark stain was spreading. I let her hair fall again and sat back on my heels. Mrs Cooke gathered one of Ana's hands under her chin with both of her own and began rocking, mumbling a quiet prayer.

'I found Harlequin,' said Andrew Merryman's voice. He was panting and when I looked up I saw his thin chest heaving hard. 'He's fine. Rattled but fine.'

'Get a board,' said Mr Cooke to Bill Wolf, who was standing in the shadows with tears rolling down his cheeks and into his beard. 'Ma, go and see that her bed's made up nice and let's get her shifted.'

'Wait!' I said. 'You can't move her.'

'What?' said Mr Cooke. 'Of course we're moving her. We're not shy of life here, missus. We don't leave the work for some undertaker. It's not our way.'

'The men carry her home to her bed and the women sit with her is the circus way, my love,' said

Mrs Cooke.

'But the police . . .' said Alec. 'They'll need to see her where she lies. Where she fell.'

Mr Cooke set his jaw so firmly that a small muscle danced in his cheek.

'A doctor,' he said. 'A doctor, I'll give you. But there's no need for anything else. The poor lass fell off her horse—there's no need for any of that.'

A long silence met his words.

'F-fell off her horse?' said Andrew Merryman at last. He was still holding Harlequin by the bridle, just outside the entranceway, and both his and the horse's breath were pluming in the cold.

'And hit her head on the ground,' said Pa Cooke. 'It's like iron, cold snap we've had. Even this close in to the tent, it's frozen solid, see?' He grasped the handle of his whip like a staff and banged down hard with it, the knock of stiff leather against the stony ground almost ringing out, thrumming into us through the soles of our shoes.

'Even if Ana . . .' said Tiny. Pa Cooke swung around to look at him and he faltered. 'Even if she fell, she'd never let her head hit the ground. She fell out of a handstand last month and just rolled and got up again.'

Ma Cooke spoke up then. Her voice was low, deadened, painful to listen to, but everyone turned to hear her.

'They're a pair of jossers, Tam, and the fright's driven the circus-sense clean out of them there, but Mrs Gilver is right. If nobody saw it happen we need the police. Just to give the maid her due we need to do that much.'

Slowly, the fire in Pa Cooke's eye faded and his

shoulders drooped.

'Aye, right,' he said. 'I know it. I know, I know. But this'll be the end of Cooke's Circus. You just see if it's not.' Without warning, he rounded on Ma and brandished his whip at her. 'You and your feelings,' he said. I took a step back and I was not the only one. Harlequin shied away and Andrew had to grapple with him to bring him to a standstill again. 'Strangers here, seeing it all. We could have . . .' He threw me a disgusted look and pushed his way out into the darkness, shoving Harlequin viciously aside with an elbow.

'Don't you mind Tam there,' said Ma Cooke. 'He's just upset. Takes it all on himself, does Tam.' She smiled, rather a sad smile, looked down at Anastasia again and then put her hand to her mouth, her eyes filling.

'Mrs Cooke,' I said, 'you mustn't wait here until the police arrive. It's bitterly cold already. Everyone, please. Do go back to your wagons and make yourselves comfortable. You've all had the most dreadful shock.'

I expected a fight, at least from some of them, but they nodded glumly one by one and filed out. Charlie was the last to go, heaving himself to his feet and standing staring at Ma and at Anastasia on the ground for a long time before he moved away.

'I'll wait here with poor Ana,' said Alec. 'Until the police come.'

'No,' I said. 'Leave that to me, Alec. Perhaps you could go with Mr Cooke. He looks as though he needs some brandy.'

'But I'll stay too, though,' said Ma in a tone that brooked no argument. Groaning a little, she sat

166

back down on the ground and took one of Ana's hands again.

Out in the tent, the audience had passed beyond being restive and had begun to break up into little groups as though at a party, standing around smoking and sipping from flasks. Ina was back in her seat again, breathing hard, looking feverish, flushed, as though she had guessed there was trouble. I felt a faint fizz as I watched her but then my attention twitched away again as my eye landed on the two forlorn figures huddled in their borrowed coats on the ring fence.

'What's happened, Mummy?' said Teddy, reverting to the comfort of childhood. 'Mr Cooke won't tell us a thing.'

I started to sit down, thinking to put my arms around them. That 'Mummy' had worked its spell on me. Then I stopped.

'Mr Cooke?' I said. 'Has he been round to speak to you?'

They nodded.

'And what could you tell him?' I asked them. Clever old Pa; they were the only ones who could have seen what happened here at the back of the ring, behind the horses.

'What do you mean?' asked Donald. 'What's wrong? Who screamed?'

'Miss . . . Anastasia has fallen off her pony,' I said.

'Is she hurt?'

'Yes,' I said, bluntly.

'Is she going to be all right?'

'No,' I told them. There was no way to keep the news from them for long and perhaps it was best not to fudge it, for I have had occasion to note that

167

the imagination supplies grisly details usually far in excess of reality if allowed to. 'What did you see? Why did she suddenly rush out of the ring?'

They looked at one another, under their lashes. Was it a sly look or were they simply bewildered to have their mother fire such questions at them? I knew, in either case, that now was not the moment for a grilling.

'Wait here,' I told them, and walked over to address the company on the far side of the ring. 'I'm afraid there has been an accident,' I said. 'There is not going to be a show after all.' Albert Wilson was bustling forward, his face puckered with concern at the wreckage of his party. 'Ina, my dear,' I said, before he could reach me, 'I think it would be best to lead everyone back to the castle.' It worked; Albert Wilson swung around like a tram at the end of its route and forged back towards his wife. The very thought of her being swept up in a crowd of careless strangers wiped every other consideration clean away from him.

'And perhaps you could telephone to the police station at Blairgowrie?' I called to his back. He gave me one fearful glance over his shoulder and nodded, but kept going.

9

The police, as might be expected given the lateness of the hour, the treacherous icy cold of the night and the miles of twisting road between Blairgowrie town and Benachally, took an age to arrive. By the time the rather creaky old Belsize came rumbling into the clearing, Ma Cooke and I were frozen to our marrow by that slow, creeping chill which only comes from standing about in cheerless surroundings for purposes drear. I have most often felt it when following guns, tramping over wintry moors and standing statue-still pretending to watch Hugh blast away at grouse for hours on end, but the longest, darkest, dullest day of shooting in my memory or imagining could not produce even a fraction of the hopeless cold which engulfed me, engulfed both of us, in the dim corner by the doorway of the tent that dreadful night.

Of course, it was not only the cold that was the trouble. On the ground between us, although the light was low and the huddled shape quite small so that one should have been able to overlook it lying there, Anastasia seemed to glow and even glitter as though with movement and one had to make efforts, over and over again, to look away. Perhaps there *was* movement; there must have been—her hair bright and soft in the lamplight might have settled gradually against the ground; certainly from the way her costume winked the sequins must have been shifting somehow although there was no breeze. And there were sounds, which was worst of all. Once, a sigh, unmistakable, and other sounds too, infrequent and faint, but they kept us silent, catching at our breaths and straining to hear any more.

At each soft terrible sound, each hint of settling movements, impossible, unbearable, Ma Cooke moaned gently to herself and once I heard her whisper, 'I'm sorry, I'm sorry,' almost too quiet to be heard.

It was my first experience of spending this

169

time—this slow and gradual dying time—with someone who, as Mrs Cooke put it, is leaving; my first lesson that we do leave gradually, the body rather more reluctantly letting go than the soul. I had seen people die before that night, several times in the officers' convalescent home in the war when it turned out that some young man was not convalescing at all, but was dying of something so swift and inevitable that there was no reason, sometimes no time, to move him. I had even seen violent death before—twice since taking up this new occupation of mine—and it had its horrors, but I had never stood sentinel like this while the coil was left to its slow unwinding.

No particular wonder, then, that the arrival of the police, far from striking the final note of despondency one might have expected, seemed rather more a welcome relief. Certainly the two large constables and the sharp-eyed sergeant did well to avoid having me fall upon their necks when they lumbered in.

Inspector Hutchinson did not inspire anything like such confidence at first glance. His hair was rather long for a policeman and a kind of defeated grey in colour. His moustache was grey too and drooped down low on either side of his long mouth. Brows high in the middle and low at the ends and heavy pouches under his eyes only added to the impression, and the bluish mottled cheeks hinted not even just at weariness but positively at drink.

Sergeant McClennan took care of the first formalities. Ma identified herself as Polina Ilchenko Cooke and Sergeant McClennan extracted a full measure of sighing and rubbing out before he had got it down, working off the frustrations of his own pointlessly elaborate name, I thought, which must have given him a lifetime of mishearings and misspellings even in his native land. (I have often wondered why anyone perseveres with the endless MacLellands and McLennans and MacClements, when they are obviously exactly the same thing, appearing distinct only because of the early—and let us face it, not so early—illiteracy of the Highland clans.)

'And this?' said the sergeant, pointing to Ana with the end of his pencil, once he had got Polina Ilchenko Cooke and Dandelion Dahlia Gilver printed out in neat letters and had got his eyebrows down again.

'Anastasia,' said Ma.

'Oh aye?' said the sergeant.

'I can't tell you her surname, for I never knew it myself,' Ma went on, 'but it'll be with her papers in her wagon there and someone'll find it for you.'

'Aye, right,' said the sergeant.

'What my sergeant means is we'll take care of that, Mrs Cooke,' said Inspector Hutchinson rather more diplomatically. He stepped forward and crouched beside Ana, lifting her hair and shining his electric torch into her eyes. I looked away.

'Poor lass,' he said. 'Just a girl, isn't she? Twenty? Twenty-five?'

'Couldn't have been much more, if that even,' said Ma, and her voice was tremulous. The inspector stood up again.

'Well, how about we away somewhere into the warm and let my lads take over watching her?' he said gently. 'I think you could do with a cup of tea,

Mrs Cooke, at least. Let's away and you tell me all about it, eh?'

*   *   *

In the Cookes' wagon, over strong, sweet tea laced with whisky, which made me retch and shudder but certainly warmed me, Inspector Hutchinson drew the story of the evening out of Ma, Pa, Alec and me. Sergeant McClennan sat with his notebook in one hand, pencil in the other, looking like nothing so much as a small boy with a net and jar waiting for butterflies to flutter into range, but the inspector's questions were quite benign.

'Mr Truman, Mr Merryman and a Mr Cooke,' he said. 'A relation?'

'My brother,' said Pa, 'but you must understand, just because they were behind the doors, that doesn't mean they saw her. They'd just as easy have been in their wee place, getting propped for the first spot, and Ana—well, she'll have gone straight through most like. There's a horse tent by the back doors. Not the proper stalls, they're down away separate, but a strawed tent where the prads go between spots, and Ana will have trotted Harlequin straight there, straight past the clowns. They'll not have seen nothing.'

'I'm sure you're right,' said the inspector. 'I'll have a word with them anyway, though. Anyone else?'

'I was back there,' said Ma. 'And Bill Wolf too. He wun't in the spec tonight, but he was running on and he was waiting ready. Lally Wolf too, getting little Tommy togged to run on with his pa.'

'And what did you see?' said the inspector.

172

'What can you tell me?'

Ma Cooke looked at him for a long time before she spoke, and the hesitation was so out of character for her, the slow careful look so unlike her, that I found myself watching her closely. I saw her considering her answer, screwing herself up towards courage and then, at the last chance, with her breath already gathered in to begin speaking, subsiding again, sinking back into her chair, shaking her head a little even.

'Nothing,' she said. 'I was in by Zoya's trunks there, getting the shawls ready for them little maids. Cold as it was, I'd thought to put them round hot bricks and so I was unwinding them again ready for the spec coming off. I din't see nothing.'

'Did you hear anything?' said the inspector.

'Heard the clowns come off,' Ma said.

'Anything else, Mrs Cooke?'

Once again, Ma Cooke took her time to answer.

'You must understand,' she said at last, 'that it was noisy from the ring all this while, see? I can't be sure, but I think—think, mind—I think Tiny and Andrew went straight to their table and so they wun't have seen nothing. That right, Pa? They take care of the props, most usually, 'count of Charlie is the boss, see?'

'Boss of the clowns, she means,' said Pa. 'I'm the boss of the circus.'

'Well, I beg your pardon, Mrs Cooke,' said Inspector Hutchinson, 'but it's no use telling me what should have happened, according to the rules. I really need to know what you heard. What you actually heard, see?'

'And in't that what I'm saying?' said Ma. 'I heard

173

two of them go to the props table. Two sets of boots on the boards. All I'm telling you there is what two it was, most likely.'

'And the third?'

'Charlie? I can't say where he was. I din't hear him passing and he din't call out to anyone. Most likely,' she held up her hand as if to acknowledge the inspector's objection before he raised it, 'I wun't put my hand to a bible on it, you're right there, but most likely he'd go to the back door and have his smoke.'

'And when you say the back door, you mean the door where she fell?'

Ma opened her eyes very wide and put her hand to her mouth.

'Here,' she said. 'I din't mean nothing by it. I din't see him nor hear him. I shun't of spoke up at all there, really.'

What was she playing at? I was not fooled for a moment by the hand clapped to the mouth and the look of surprise. She had deliberately dropped Charlie Cooke right in it. I was not alone in being troubled. Pa's chest was rising and falling rather rapidly, the spangles on his lapels winking in the lamplight, and he chewed on the ends of his moustache as he watched her.

'I'll start with Mr Cooke then,' said the inspector. 'He might be able to clear all of this up and let us away to our beds, eh?'

'He never said a word, Poll,' said Pa, unable to keep quiet any longer. 'When we were all together with the poor lass. He said not a word.'

'Aye, but still,' said Mrs Cooke, 'he wurr shaken up bad, wun't he? He might have been too upset by it all to speak. Mind you,' she went on, 'if it

174

wurr me I'd start by asking myself why she come off when she did. I'd start by asking them ring lads and little Sal on the Panatrope what they saw, cos of no one else could see what happened behind them liberty horses, could they?'

Now it was my turn to catch my lip. What was she doing? She had set the inspector on to Charlie Cooke as surely as pointing her finger and crying '*J'accuse*' and now my poor boys were to be tossed into the fray too.

'And where might I find those three?' said the inspector.

'Little Sallie Wolf's in the second wagon before the pond over the ways there,' said Ma, 'and . . .' She looked over at me, rather belatedly it seemed to me.

'Yes,' I said, for there was no use trying to avoid it. 'The ring boys. My sons, as a matter of fact. I'll show you their wagon, Inspector, and I shall stay while you question them too, if you don't mind.' I am not proud to admit that as well as a deal of confusion, shock, a little cold still and more motherly concern than is my usual measure, I was feeling a surge of angry delight that, when one got right down to it, my boys being woken in the night to answer police questions could be laid fairly at Hugh's door. I was almost looking forward to telling him about it.

'Your sons,' said the inspector in a carefully blank voice. Sergeant McClennan had looked up from his notebook too. 'I see. Yes, I had been wondering how you fitted in exactly, Mrs Gilver. Your sons, yes, I see.'

I attempted an explanation as we crossed the ground, Alec hindering rather than helping with his tuppenceworth, and Inspector Hutchinson could hardly be blamed if he formed the opinion that Donald and Teddy were spoiled brats, I was a clinging fusspot, Hugh was indifferent to all three of us, and Alec was so lost to decency that he not only trailed around the countryside after me to dinner parties, married woman or no, but did not trouble to keep away from my impressionably aged sons, who thought of him as a kind of uncle. Actually, the last of these points was not too far from the truth, but it is always a bother to have such people as the inspector cast an eye over one's perfectly blameless existence and draw their own thrilling conclusions, for the shopkeeper class—being by far the most rigidly proper and as a result the most filthy-minded—do tend to gasp and fan themselves at the very ideas they alone are entertaining. As Grant says about the seamstress in Gilverton village who makes her frocks: shocked to the core, tell me more.

The touch of Alec's hand to my arm as we neared the shepherds' hut was especially unwelcome, then, but when I ignored him he tugged quite urgently and I could see his eyes flash. He jerked his head backwards the way we had come and I turned just in time to see a shape moving along behind the wagons on the far side of the ground. It was a shortish, roundish shape, moving swiftly. At a guess, I should have said it was Ma Cooke and the steps she slipped silently up and the door she eased silently open were Charlie's.

'Now then, Mrs Gilver,' said the inspector, stopping at the shepherds' hut. 'You had best go in first and wake them. We don't want them

176

alarmed.' The alarm, though, was all mine for the little hut was empty, the stove cold, the bedrolls nowhere to be seen.

At least that should convince the inspector that I was not the clinging type, I thought to myself, but I did feel a growing sense of something or other. Had I even given them a glance as I made my way back to Ana earlier? Had I simply swept past? Was it possible that hours later they were still sitting there on the ring fence as I had told them to? Words cannot express the surge of relief I felt at the sound of a door latch lifting and Zoya's voice calling gently from the nearest wagon pair.

'They are here, Mee-zuss Kilvert,' she said. 'Asleep like babies. All good, all well.'

We trooped over to the Prebrezhenskys' wagon and crowded around the door. Zoya and Kolya were sitting wrapped in dressing gowns with glasses of tea and Donald and Teddy were indeed fast asleep, top to tail, in a little wheeled cot which had been trundled out from under the box-bed. Inya and Alya were sleeping cheek to cheek in another and little Ilya waved drowsily at us from a canvas hammock strung above them. Bunty was in front of the stove, on her back with all four paws in the air waggling gently at each breath.

'Well, who would have the heart?' said the inspector, his face softening as he gazed at them. 'The morning will do, I'm thinking.' With a nod at the adults he stepped away and closed the door softly.

'A very touching little scene,' he said, standing and rubbing his hands together, looking around at the ring of wagons. 'A . . . taking . . . kind of a place, isn't it, a circus? The more for being so precarious, these days. I can see how a body could be quite swept away with it all. I can quite see how a body could get to thinking what a shame it would be if anything came along to spoil it. They're lost for ever once they're gone.'

He turned, rather abruptly, to face Alec and me and switched on his torch. Of course, he did nothing so boorish as shine it in our faces—he was very careful not to—and so we did not screw up our eyes, but treated him to a clear display of expressions in which guilt, surprise and sheepishness were chasing one another around like horrid little olives being swirled in the dregs of a particularly nasty cocktail.

'Here's another view of it,' he said, and for the first time there was not a trace of warmth in his voice. 'A girl is dead. A bunch of circus folk—understandably—have got the willies from her dying and don't much want the police about the place, and a pair of . . . I'd put a tanner on self-styled detectives . . . who should know better are playing silly beggars instead of doing their duty. Mrs Cooke has fed me her brother-in-law like a sweetie for a bairn and now she's taken off on tiptoe to tell him what to say when I get there. Will I carry on?'

'I can only apologise, sir,' said Alec, who had reddened, as he has a tendency to do—such a trial for a gentleman, who has no recourse to powder. 'It's exactly as you said. We simply got caught up in the . . . Gosh, in the conspiracy to cover up a murder, I suppose you would say. I for one feel utterly—'

'Don't bother about all that,' said Inspector Hutchinson. 'This isn't the officers' mess and I don't have time for speeches.' Alec blushed even deeper and although I gobbled for a retort—such rudeness!—he had a point and there was no answer. 'What I would like to know is why you are here.'

We told him. Pacing around the edges of the pond by torchlight, the frost crackling under our boots, we told him all about Ma's premonition of doom, about the tricks played on the hapless Topsy and the tricks planned, although scuppered, for poor Anastasia.

'This Topsy needs to be careful now,' said the inspector. 'She could be next, wouldn't you say?'

'I can see the sense in that,' I said, 'but I have to tell you, Inspector, our suspicions were tending in quite another direction before tonight.'

'That Topsy did all the mischief, you mean?' said Hutchinson. 'That she played tricks on herself to cover her tracks? And were you alone in thinking it or was that the general view? And what might she have rigged tonight? Because she was still in the ring when it happened, wasn't she?'

'No, no, no,' said Alec, with an agitated note in his voice. Stopping the inspector's stream of ideas was a little like trying to catch up with a runaway train. 'We didn't mean Topsy . . . Quite the rev—' His voice faded and he stood blinking. 'But Topsy does make just as much sense, actually, Dandy. A lot more sense now, when one thinks about it.'

'Alec, you weren't there the day of the rope,' I said. 'Topsy positively hurled herself at the ground, Inspector. No one could have done that if she had known what was waiting at the bottom. I can't think of it now without blanching.'

'What was waiting at the bottom was a leap

179

upwards and a bit of a sore hand,' said the inspector. 'And leaping around on ropes is Miss Turvy's idea of a quiet day at home, is it not now?' I shook my head again. 'And if she really did "hurl" herself as you say, Mrs Gilver,' went on the inspector, 'she must have quite a temper.' I fought hard against the feeling of being scooped up and swept along.

'On the contrary, Inspector,' I said. 'We think, that is, Mrs Cooke voiced a suspicion to me, that it was Anastasia behind all the trouble.'

'And so who more likely than this Topsy to pay her back, eh? Still, I need to speak to these clowns, this Bill Wolf, Topsy, your boys—with your permission, of course—and the rest of them. Any point trying to track down all the guests from the big house, do you think? Could you give me their names?'

'Ahhh, most, I think,' I said, checking with Alec. He nodded.

'I should say so,' he said with one eyebrow hooked up. 'I've only been in these parts a year or two, Inspector, but even I've heard most of the names who were here tonight.' He rattled off a few and Hutchinson's eyebrows lifted too, until they were almost vertical.

'Phew!' he said. 'Lady Maude MacAlpine? Really? The Stirling woman? I thought these Wilsons were the sober, respectable type, from all I've ever heard of them. A businessman and a schoolteacher's daughter, aren't they? Made their fortune and came to the hills for fresh air and views to sketch. But should I be having a look at *them*?'

Now, at this point, my duty was clear; at least

the inspector would have said so. While assuring him that the Wilsons were the very souls of propriety, although a little odd each in his own way, and that this evening's party was quite out of character for Benachally, I should certainly have passed on the interesting fact that when Anastasia upset the smooth running of the spectacular with her early exit, Ina Wilson was not in her seat where she should have been, but was back, breathing heavily and trying to hide it, by the time I addressed the gathering and bid them all return to the castle, their motor cars and home.

Yet all I did was shake my head. Ina Wilson? Preposterous! I looked forward to asking her just where she had been, of course, but I thought I could shield her from the inspector's rather scorching attentions, in the meantime anyway. My conscience demanded it, for what would the man who had so efficiently cut Alec down to size make of the Wilsons if he got them in his view? After the mortifications of the early evening and the eventual travesty that the circus treat became I did not want to heap insult on them, the poor silly pair.

*   *   *

Watching him at work on Charlie Cooke made me very glad that my conscience had a greater measure of compassion than scruple. The inspector and his sergeant trundled into the ground the next morning in a BSA and sidecar which made even the Belsize tourer of the previous evening look sleek by comparison. Sergeant McClennan hopped off the motorcycle spryly enough, but to see the inspector unbuttoning himself from the covers and struggling out of the contraption like an overturned tortoise trying to shed its shell was a sight to be savoured.

'Blasted thing,' he said, tugging and twitching at his overcoat, once he was finally upright. 'Well I remember my cosy wee perambulator when I was a bairn, and I had a sleigh ride once that was like sitting in an armchair, but that thing? Pure torture.' He gave it a swift kick. 'Now, Mr Charles Cooke Esquire, for you and me, madam.'

I raised my eyebrows in surprise.

'For he won't know what to make of you,' Hutchinson explained to me.

'So then won't taking me along make him more careful than ever?'

'Not a bit of it,' said Hutchinson. 'He's been well coached by that sister-in-law, but he knows she's had her claws into you too and he won't know which way to play it if we face him together. He won't know if you're there for Ma Cooke or for me. He'll be tossing like a cork on the tide.' The inspector beamed at me.

'You are very happy in your work,' I remarked drily.

'Well, Mrs Gilver, it's not a mile off your work,' he replied, 'and I'm assuming you weren't conscripted.' Once again, I was left like a trout on a bank, my mouth opening and shutting but to no purpose. It was a feeling with which I was to become familiar while Inspector Hutchinson's path marched along with mine.

'Mr Cooke,' he said in the same ringing tones, when Charlie answered his knock. 'I think you are

182

the man I need.' He ushered me into the wagon and followed me. 'Mrs Gilver needs no introduction, I know,' he went on, settling himself down with great rearrangings of the skirts to his tweed coat. As the inspector had predicted, Charlie Cooke glanced rapidly between the two of us and a frown spread over his face. I felt a little pity for the man; he could not have slept a wink in the night if his pale cheeks and red-rimmed eyes were to be believed.

'A very sad day for you, Mr Cooke,' said the inspector.

Charlie nodded and there was a fresh welling of tears which he scrubbed at roughly. Then he looked up at Hutchinson and frowned.

'What do you mean "for me"?' he said.

'What is there for me to mean?' Hutchinson shot back.

Then Charlie seemed to realise, rather late, what the inspector was at and he countered it.

'It's a sad day for all of us. Me no more and no less than anyone,' he said.

'Quite so, exactly,' the inspector said. 'Now then.' He opened a notebook and snapped the band smartly into place, then held up a slim silver propelling pencil and twisted it vigorously until a good half-inch of lead protruded. I wondered if he knew that he looked exactly like a doctor rather too enthusiastically preparing his smallpox vaccine while a toddler trembled before him. I rather thought he did. 'Start from when you and the other clowns came out of the ring,' he said, and although Charlie Cooke *was* a clown and so there was no insult in saying so, still I got the impression that the inspector had prepared the line in advance and

183

greatly relished delivering it.

'Aye, well,' said Charlie, struggling to regain composure. 'Yes, well, off we came, as you say. Tiny and Andrew went to our stall.'

'Your stall?' said Hutchinson.

'Our table and boxes—our props like.'

'And where exactly is that?'

'Second one along from the ring doors, flush against the walling. Equestrian director's table is first, only proper, and then the clowns', always, on account of all the quick changes and all the multitude of props we have to take on and off. Then it's the strongman and the others have their stalls wherever they can fit them in.'

'Wherever they can fit them in,' the inspector said slowly as he wrote it down. 'I was going to ask about the layout of your backstage. It's a gey queer set-up, is it not? Are all circuses that much of a rabbit warren?'

'That's Tam's idea,' said Charlie Cooke. 'My brother. Says it calms the animals to have a passageway straight to their stall and not just have them milling.'

'Makes sense,' said Hutchinson, with real appreciation in his voice. 'But tell me,' he went on, and then stopped. Charlie Cooke was shifting around on his perch on the edge of the box-bed. (It appeared that every living wagon came with exactly two chairs, no more and no fewer, no matter the size of the household, the way that every kitchen I have ever seen has had a single Windsor armchair (and what feuds betwixt cook and housekeeper could be laid to rest if the mistress just delivered one more).)

'Is something troubling you, Mr Cooke?' the

184

inspector asked, his voice bland and his eyes round and blinking. Charlie Cooke could hardly answer. What was troubling him was plain to see: he was distressed and exhausted but he had a job to do, a tale to tell, and could not be easy until he had told it, but here was the policeman chit-chatting away about the backstage and thwarting him. My pity flared again and perhaps not mine alone this time, for Hutchinson relented.

'So you came off,' he said. 'Then what?'

'As I say, Tiny and Andrew went to our stall and I carried on round the passage to the back door to have my smoke, like I usually do.' Charlie was looking over our heads at the wall behind us as though his words were written there.

'You didn't help with the props?' said the inspector.

'I leave that to the youngsters,' said Charlie. 'On account of how I'm the boss.'

'Ah yes,' said Hutchinson. 'Do you know, your sister-in-law said almost the same thing last night. Almost exactly the same words. I should have taken more notice of that.'

Charlie Cooke tensed his jaw a little but carried on.

'Well, I was there at the back door, as I say, and I heard the pony coming. That's funny, I thought to myself, for it wasn't nearly time for anyone else to be off yet. I drew in to the side of the door out of the way, thinking Harlequin would go straight through and then she . . . she come round the corner and he went over. He just went over and she come off and there she lay, never moved, not a sound out of her. There she lay.' His voice cracked and he stopped talking.

'You're telling me you saw the whole thing?' Inspector Hutchinson said. Charlie Cooke swallowed hard and brought his eyes down to meet the inspector's. He nodded.

'But why—' I began before I could stop myself.

'Then what happened?' said Hutchinson.

Charlie Cooke looked down at the floor as though working to remember.

'Andrew and Tiny went rushing up to where she was lying. Andrew took off after Harlequin. Tiny made as if to follow but by then Topsy was off and she cried out when she saw what had happened so then Tiny wheeled round and came back, sort of as if to comfort her. Then the Russians come off and Tam's prads. My God, the time we had! Trying to get they twelve horses past her and not have her trampled. For they were straight to their stalls no stopping them. A brick wall couldn't have stopped them. What a to-do. And then when the prads were away one of they wee Russian raklies seen Ana and screamed like a train. That's when you showed up, missus, you'll be able to tell him all about it from there.'

'And where was Mrs Cooke all this time?' said the inspector.

'I can't say,' said Charlie. 'I don't right know. All the confusion.'

'Now ask your question, Mrs Gilver,' said Hutchinson. 'I'd like to hear the answer too.'

'Mr Cooke,' I said, trying to be gentle, to balance the hard note in Hutchinson's voice, 'why on earth didn't you say any of this last night? Right at the start. If what you say is . . . Well, what I mean is that we really didn't need to call in the police at all, did we?'

'I was too shaken up,' Charlie said. 'I don't think I could have said a word.'

'Ah yes,' said Hutchinson. 'That's what your sister-in-law thought it must be. That's almost exactly how she explained it to me.'

I was trying to remember whether Charlie had indeed spoken while we were all gathered in the tent. I could not say with any certainty. It was Ma who said most, Pa who did the shouting, and to my best recall Tiny and Andrew were the only others who had had a view to share.

'He *was* very upset, Inspector,' I said, remembering the way he had sat with his head in his hands.

'Can you understand,' said Charlie, 'wishing so hard that it wasn't happening, you could make yourself believe that if you just keep quiet, it wouldn't be?'

Both the inspector and I were silenced by that. The pain in his voice could not be other than real. When Hutchinson spoke again, his voice was softer.

'You were particularly close to her then? Miss . . . Tchah!' He had clearly not found out Ana's surname yet and it was troubling him.

Charlie roused himself.

'No,' he said, carefully. 'Where did you hear that?'

'You've never seen an accident before, then?' the inspector went on. 'Is that it? Lucky, surely? How long have you been a circus man?'

'Born and bred and ten generations before me,' said Charlie, stung by the implication. 'And sure I've seen plenty mishaps in my time. When we had the big cats I saw things that would lay you out, I'd wager.'

'So . . . ?' said Hutchinson.

Charlie shook his head a few times and began to speak almost to himself. Both the inspector and I keened forward to listen.

'I'm getting old,' he said. 'I was an aerial acrobat, you know. Trapeze, tight rope, slack rope, perch and pole. I used to play a fiddle, standing on a chair on a rope, pretending to be drunk, brought the house down. And now? I can see a young lass heading straight for trouble and I'm too slow to do a thing about it. I just stood there and watched it. It was all over before I knew it had begun. I just stood there. So no, Mr Policeman, you're right. I wasn't too upset to talk, I was too ashamed. There. You happy now?'

This, I thought, had the unmistakable ring of truth about it, except that he was speaking of Topsy, not Ana, and of a rope instead of a pony.

*   *   *

Inspector Hutchinson puffed out his cheeks and rolled his eyes when we left Charlie's wagon a few minutes later, but he did not speak until we were well away from it and could be sure that no one was listening.

'Not a great liar,' he said, 'but I've heard worse. Could you tell where the join was, Mrs Gilver?'

'I think so,' I said. 'All the stuff about the liberty horses and the Prebrezhensky girls was true enough—it was so detailed and it tripped off his tongue. But he wasn't at the back door having his gasper, was he? He didn't actually see a thing.'

'No, that was all Ma Cooke's doing,' said

188

Hutchinson, 'and he made one big blunder that clinched it.' I waited. 'He said he was by the doors near Ana and when she fell and Andrew and Tiny "went" rushing up to her. See?'

'No.'

'Here's Ana,' said the inspector, marking the ground with the heel of his boot. 'And here's Charlie.' Another mark. 'Here's the other clowns. Now when she fell . . .'

'Oh, I see. He should have said they "came" rushing up, shouldn't he? Very subtle, Inspector.'

'It's the kind of thing you should look out for,' said Hutchinson modestly.

'Are you sure you want to be encouraging me?' I asked him, matching his tone if not his mood exactly. 'Shouldn't you be rather down on me and my like?'

'Not me!' said Inspector Hutchinson. 'I'm hoping you'll keep at it and fill me in as you go. The more the merrier, keep them all on their toes.'

'And will you return the favour?' I said. 'If I'm to be much use, it would help me to know what's happening.' I half expected a ticking-off for cheek and a swift end to our collaboration, but the inspector surprised me.

'Of course,' he said. 'And the first thing I must tell you is what the doctor said. First impression only, you understand, for he will not be doing the post-mortem examination until later on today, but as far as he can gather she really did die from hitting her head on the ground. The injury is quite clear, he says. One blow to the side of her face, bruising from jaw to temple, shattering her cheekbone and fracturing her skull.'

189

I swallowed and nodded.

'If she had been bashed on the head and then arranged on the ground, the injury would be quite different. As would the bloodstain. He was as sure as he could be that she hadn't moved after she started bleeding.'

I could believe it. I remembered from the night before how, until one moved her hair and saw the spreading stain, one could tell oneself she was just resting there.

'And there is a slight swell on the ground just where she came down,' said the inspector. 'Just a bump—you'd never notice it under the grass but it was enough to make the difference.'

'So she really might just have fallen off her horse?'

'I doubt it,' said the inspector. 'But what I do say is that whoever pushed her or pulled her off or set a trip to throw her off, maybe he didn't mean to kill her. Maybe that was just bad luck.'

'Can I tell Mrs Cooke you think that?' I asked him. He considered me for a moment before he answered, looking as weary as ever again.

'Aye, why not?' he said. 'I've no time to be bothering with charging her and all that palaver, mind. So I don't want to see her or Charlie down at the station confessing to false evidence. But if you can get her to stop making my job harder for me, you feel free.'

Not, I thought to myself as he strode away from me, one of those policemen who thrive on dotted 'i's and crossed 't's, and I wondered what his Chief Constable would say if he heard the half of it. I had once been landed with the Chief Constable of Perthshire at a Hunt Ball dinner and I knew that there was not an undotted 'i' or crossless 't' anywhere about him.

10

Mrs Cooke, however, was not to be swayed.

'Poor Charlie,' she said, when I waylaid her in her wagon. 'He saw the whole thing?'

'Yes, and told the inspector about it in more or less identical words to your own,' I said. She looked back at me blankly. 'Inspector Hutchinson is not the kind of man to be fooled,' I insisted. 'And anyway, what I'm telling you is that the surgeon thinks she fell off her horse and hit her head on the ground. Do you see? If only you would leave things be and let the police draw their own conclusions, the chances are they would call it an accident. The chances are it *was* an accident. Oh, don't you see?'

'Of course it wurr,' said Ma. 'If it wun't, you think I'd have asked Charlie to—'

'Aha!' I said, making her put her hand to her mouth as she had the previous evening but in earnest this time.

'All right there,' she said. 'I got Charlie to say he'd seen it. So run me in. Tell your inspector to get his handcuffs ready.'

'I shan't,' I said, very glad that Inspector Hutchinson had as good as told me not to. 'But what you're doing, you and Charlie, is only raising suspicion instead of quelling it.'

'I'm not one for the police,' said Ma. 'Too many's the times they've listened to the flatties calling us thieves and tinkers. Too many's the times they've run us off grounds what we've every right to be stopping on. I'm glad they've the sense to see it wurr no murder, but I'd still rather have you tell me what happened than them. You'll puzzle it out for me, won't you, my beauty?'

'I shall try,' I said, feeling far from certain on the point. 'And you can help me out with some practical details. For instance, we know that Ana left too early and spoiled the spec, but what was supposed to happen? How should it have gone?'

'Well,' said Ma. 'We've got two specs. In one, the Russians goes off first, then Topsy, then the liberty prads, clowns next and Ana last, but Pa always said it wurr wrong to have the ring so empty at the end.' I must have looked sceptical, because she nodded as though agreeing with me. 'I know,' she said, 'but he's always been a proud man and it's getting worse the less he has to be proud of. Breaks my heart sometimes. Anyways, it wun't do me no good to stickle over the likes of that so we changed it. And in the new spec Pa's prads wurr the last to go. Just like last night—except for Bill being in it too. The clowns off first, then Ana, Topsy, the Russians, the prads and Pa at the finish.'

'Just as they did, in fact?'

'Only a bit later. It was Ana going off four swings quick what threw Topsy and knocked the timing.'

'And was it supposed to be bang, bang, bang one after the other?'

'Never, no,' said Ma, her enthusiasm for the spectacular growing in her voice as she recounted it. 'Ana did her best stuff once the clowns went off,

192

most usually, even if she had less time in this spec than the other. The little maids had their finale next and they went off to leave Topsy space for a few lines on the floor—beautiful floor-work she does, seems a shame sometimes she's always up on a line. If we could get a base man she could work up an adagio before dinnertime. My own ma had an adagio spot—mind you, them days the roughs would cheer to see a lass in tights whether she was any good or no, but my ma was—' I cleared my throat, and Ma brought herself back to the matter in hand. 'Then the liberty prads did their last show, all up on their back legs—lovely—and that was that. A good spec, even if I'm saying it myself.'

'Very interesting,' I said. 'That was tremendously helpful—thank you.'

'What is it you're thinking?' asked Ma.

I shook my head at her. 'I don't want to get your hopes up,' I said. 'It's just something the inspector mentioned that I think is worth checking. But I have to be frank with you, Mrs Cooke. If no one did this, if Ana simply fell, I may never find out why. There may not be anything to be found out.'

Ma shook her head, setting her curlpapers bobbing, and retied her dressing-gown cord a little tighter around her middle, as if girding herself for battle with me.

'She'd no more do such a thing than you would pitch yourself out of that chair right now and smack your face on the rug there,' she said. 'Than you would put your hand in the fire reaching out to lift your cuppa, than you would drive yonder little car of yours face first into a brick wall trying to turn a corner.'

'But if you don't believe she was killed and you

193

can't believe it was an accident, what else is there?'
I said. 'And I must say, since I've been here I've
heard of nothing else but broken legs and lost
arms.'

'You dun't understand,' said Ma. 'How do you
think Ana learned to stand on Harlequin's back?
And the arabesques? Handstands? Flick-flacks?
How do you suppose she learned it all?'

'On the mechanic,' I said, 'like Inya and Alya?'

'No, none of that,' said Ma. 'Ana's not proper
circus. She's a josser. She taught herself, from a
little maid. And how she learned was by falling off,
on to the grass of a paddock, every blessed time
until she din't fall off no more.'

I was still confused but I was intrigued by the
glimpse of Ana's past, the first I had heard so far.

'What do you know about her?' I said. 'About
when she was a little . . . maid, I mean.'

Ma laughed softly but her eyes glistened with
sudden tears.

'Well, she wun't no Russian princess, that's for
sure,' she said. 'She wurr a lady, though, no doubt
about that much. Beautiful things, she had.'

'What kind of things?' I asked. I had only seen
Ana in her ring costume and in the same rough
practice clothes as all the others.

'Her nightgowns and her chimmies,' said Ma.
'Pure silk like spiders' webs, they wurr. And a
writing case all set with mother-of-pearl and pens
to match. But there's more to life than silk and
pearls and she had a hard start. You could see it in
her eyes even if she never let me read her palm
and so I reckon whatever she wanted to forget, she
was welcome to forget it and tell her own tale.'

'It didn't endear her all round,' I said. 'Not

everyone has your sympathetic spirit, Ma.' I flushed, for the name had slipped out unbidden, but she only smiled at me and inclined her head as though acknowledging a compliment, which I suppose it was in its way.

'I'd have got round them all in the end,' she said. 'I told Topsy many's a time she din't know how lucky she wurr, big band of Turvys and Cookes all about her all the time, so's she was born knowing who she wurr and how come. Family's the thing, see, but try telling that to young ones. Topsy wun't know what it felt like to be a lost soul and she'd no call to be laughing at Ana for the pain of it. Same as Tiny and Andrew, I used to tell her. Ana din't fit any better into where she come from than them two. Except as her not fitting was all on the inside. Like that Tober-omey's missus. Her spirit's dying in her breast, you ask me. She don't fit where she's landed, not nearly.'

Now that was very interesting, I thought to myself later. I had simply hinted that someone—no one in particular—might feel rather less than sympathetic in regards to Ana's nonsense and Topsy's name had come up without my giving it the slightest nudge. Could it be that Inspector Hutchinson was right after all? And did Ma actually know something or had she simply divined it? I had no high opinion of Madame Polina with her palms and leaves but there was no denying that Polly Cooke had a feeling for people.

First stop the shepherds' hut, I thought, where Donald and Teddy were looking rather tidier than the previous morning; perhaps Zoya had more interest in brushed hair and scrubbed necks than me, who had been planning rather vaguely to drag them back to Nanny in a day or two and hand them over for sluicing

'We had cheese sandwiches for breakfast, Mother,' said Donald. 'And cocoa.'

I suppressed a shudder.

'Well, good then,' I said, trying to sound brisk since I was sure that briskness was the usual sound of their mother and would put them at their ease. 'Now, tell me, boys. What happened last night at the back of the ring?'

At that, the simple internal comforts of the sandwiches and cocoa seemed to recede a little; both of them looked instantly less rosy, less replete. Teddy visibly shrank into his chair, shook his hair down over his forehead and then looked up at me from under it in that way which was intermittently endearing a few years ago but had long since palled.

'What do you mean?' Donald said.

'Why did Anastasia leave?' I asked. 'She wasn't due to, you know. Did you see anything? Did she say why she was going?'

'Is she dead?' said Teddy. 'Mrs P said she was gone, but we couldn't be exactly sure what that meant, could we?'

'She is,' I said. 'She fell off. Like Perdita's uncle. Cousin Bellamy, remember?' I had clear memories of their re-enacting the grisly end of distant Cousin Bellamy all over the nursery, gardens and especially banisters since he had come off at the top of a steep stretch of scree and had tumbled backwards under the hooves of the following hunters, coming to rest face down in a streambed or, in Donald and Teddy's version, a heap of coats and dog blankets thrown down at the foot of the stairs.

'You mean she got squashed by the liberty prads?' said Donald.

'No, no, simply that she—'

'What did she fall down? Did the pony hare off up the path beside the waterfall?'

'No—'

'Only we thought she was in the back tent, didn't we?'

'Or else what was the scream? We thought that was Inya, didn't we?'

'Blimey, Ma, don't tell me that scream was Anastasia. Did she see someone back there and scream and rush off up the hill and tumble down into the pool? Did she drown?'

'No—'

'Only Anya said last night she had hit her head.'

'Did she hit her head and pass out and *then* drown?'

'And get dragged back to the tent by one mangled foot stuck in a stirrup, all wet and dead?'

'Will you stop it?' I managed to get out at last. 'Yes, she is dead. Do you hear me? Anastasia died last night. Will you stop being such . . .' I could not finish the thought, since what I was asking, in essence, was that they stop being such *boys*. 'All I need to hear from you is what happened when she left the ring.'

'Nothing,' said Teddy. 'Nothing at all. She went cantering round and round and then . . . why does it matter anyway, Mother?'

Donald kicked him.

'Nothing happened,' he said.

'She just left?'

They nodded.

197

'Did she look at all perturbed or anxious?'

This they considered for a moment before answering, but very soon Donald began to shake his head and Teddy joined in.

'And did it seem to you as though Anastasia was still in charge of her pony?' I asked. This was something which had only occurred to me in the night: had the placid rosy-back had some kind of fit? He had seemed as calm as could have been reasonably expected when Andrew Merryman brought him back to the tent doors and had accepted Pa Cooke digging him in his heaving ribs really quite stoically, but it was one possible explanation and I had dispatched Alec this morning first to the stable tent to commune with Harlequin himself—Alec has an excellent sense for horses—and then to track down Andrew and quiz him about the pony's state of mind.

Donald and Teddy glanced at one another again.

'Hard to say,' was what Donald plumped for at last. 'Was it Ana or Harlequin bolting? What did you think, Ted?'

'It could have been him,' said Teddy, thoughtfully. 'That would make most sense, wouldn't it? If Harlequin had a sort of a brainstorm and he just leapt the ring fence and galloped off through the ring doors into the night. That would make sense of everything.'

'But it's a clear case of an improbable possibility,' I said, more to myself than to them, 'and so not to be preferred.'

'Says you,' said Alec Osborne a little later when we had rendezvoused in my motor car over a flask. 'You might be impressed by that particular little

198

riddle, Dan, but I've always found it to reveal itself as clever tosh if one wheels around suddenly and snaps one's fingers.'

I unstoppered the flask and poured out a measure of steaming, rum-scented coffee into my silver cup. Mrs Tilling's tender feelings towards me were never more evident than in her preparation of warming drinks on cold mornings.

'What did you mean anyway?' Alec said.

'Just that while an ordinary pony might be prone to fits of temperament, bucking, bolting and what have you, surely such a pony could never do what Harlequin does every day of the week.'

'That's a probable impossibility, though, isn't it?' said Alec, squinting with the effort of concentration.

'Yes, but what do you think of the idea itself?'

'I'll have some of that coffee, if you can spare it. The idea that . . . ?'

'That Harlequin—his years of excellent behaviour in the ring and out of it serving as his character witness—simply could not have had what my sons called "a brainstorm" and bolted, so Ana must have taken off deliberately, and so must have done it for a reason, and so it is worth our trying to find out what that reason was.'

Alec nodded but was prevented from answering immediately since he had just swallowed his first draught. Mrs Tilling's idea of rum coffee was not a cup of coffee with a splash of rum in it, but a cup of rum with just enough coffee to warm it through.

'Whewf!' Alec said, after a couple of gulps. 'Yes, I agree. I can't believe that pony has a temperamental bone in his body. I've never seen a bigger eye nor a softer lip and I ran my hands right up and down all four legs—and this on first acquaintance and after his upsets yesterday evening—without him so much as flinching.'

'You sound worse than Ma and her tea leaves,' I told him.

'And while he was most certainly frightened last night—plunging around in the dark—I hear he wasn't the least bit angry and came over for kind words and strokes without even being called.'

'This from Andrew Merryman?' I guessed. Alec nodded. 'And do we trust his judgement? Do we trust his *word*, come to that?'

'I do,' said Alec. 'Because you'll never guess what, Dan.' I waited. 'Andrew Merryman is the name of a circus clown.' I waited again. 'I mean to say, "Andrew Merryman" is a clown's name. Like "Jack Pudding".'

'Who?'

'Or Charlie. That's not his real name, you know.'

'Charlie Cooke?'

'No, it's Thomas.'

'It can't be. His brother's name is Thomas.'

'No, his brother's name is William. He's the younger one. He took on the name of Thomas because Tam Cooke is always the ringmaster of Cooke's Circus. And Charlie is Charlie because he's a clown.'

'But he's only been a clown since he gave up the trapeze,' I said. 'And everyone calls him Charlie all the time.'

'Oh, Dandy, he's always been a clown. I bet it was he himself who told you about the trapeze, wasn't it? He used to do some wire work—a little—but he's always only ever been just the clown. His brother was the boss from the beginning. Their father handed the circus on that way, cut out the older son.'

'Poor Charlie,' I said. 'No wonder he's so touchy about it all.'

'But really, when you think about the way Ma clicked her fingers and got him to lie to the inspector about seeing Ana fall, you can see he's not the commanding type.'

'How did *you* know he lied? Where are you getting all of this?'

'Miles Fanshawe told me,' said Alec, enjoying the bewildered look on my face. Fanshawe was ringing a faint bell. 'Remember, Dandy? Fanshawe from school, who growed and growed? It's him.' Illumination shone on me at last.

'Andrew Merryman?'

'And you have to admit that he was right to go for the change of name, wasn't he? Tumbling Miles Fanshawe would be too silly for words.'

'Amazing!' I said. 'My goodness, you must have been thunderstruck to see him.'

'Didn't recognise him,' said Alec. 'Believe it or not he's filled out since schooldays and Fanshawe would never have had that look of . . . what would you call it? Quiet confidence? Manly competence? Fanshawe was a bit of a ninny, truth be told.'

I was having trouble reconciling any kind of confidence or competence with the wavering, blushing Andrew Merryman and my doubt must have shown.

'Ah,' said Alec, 'no less hopeless in the presence of girls, eh? He spent one Easter with a pal we shared and hardly came out of his bedroom on account of an overdose of giggling sisters. Still, I think we can safely accept his word and his judgement, don't you?'

I suppressed a snort of laughter.

'Certainly not!' I said. 'Because he's an old Harrovian? Because he's "people like us, darling"? Of course not.'

Alec was staring at me, rather red, and he is always at his most endearingly peculiar-looking when he has turned red. It clashes so dreadfully with his tawny hair and makes his freckles look yellow.

'Well, I think that's a bit much,' he said. 'Miles—Fanshawe—Merryman,' he announced this last with an air of finality, 'Merryman wasn't on our list of suspects for anything at all yesterday. And we already knew he was "people like us" as you so revoltingly put it—what a snob you are, Dandy—so the only thing we've found out really is that yes, he went to my school, and was in my house, and now all of a sudden he's more suspicious than before? All of a sudden, he's the one we need to keep our eye on? I just think that's a bit much.'

I sensed that it was best to move to other matters. 'And what about Topsy Turvy?' I said. 'Has one been insulting her dignity calling her that all this time?'

'Strange to tell,' said Alec, 'Turvy is her family name and she was christened Topsy. One of a long line of Topsies, if you can credit it.'

'I can. The circus is wrote through her like Blackpool through rock,' I said. 'And such sound knowledge of where one belongs is not be sniffed at, Alec dear. Ma is all too convincing on that score.'

'Well, in any case,' said Alec, uninterested in my quoting new friends if I would not listen to what he had got from his old ones, 'whether Harlequin took it upon himself to leap the ring fence or Ana made him leave, it brings us back to the idea of an accident.'

'Why?'

'Because how could anyone know that she was going to be backstage when she shouldn't have been?'

'But darling, that's the thing,' I said. 'She should have been. She was a tiny little bit early but she was just about to go off anyway and everyone in the circus knew it. Come with me.' I stepped down from the motor car and made my way to the back door of the tent.

'I'm not sure I see the import of that,' Alec said, following me.

'It was the inspector's idea—one of the many, just mentioned in passing. A booby trap. A trip wire.'

'When could it have been done?' Alec asked. 'It would have to be after the animals came in or they'd have broken it going the other way.'

'But they came in first. There would have been heaps of time for anyone to stretch a rope across the passageway afterwards. And I just wondered . . . wouldn't it leave a trace, a mark of some kind?' We had arrived. I could not help a shiver as I looked around, for that drab little corner was so familiar to me after the long wait for the police with Ma that I was sure I should never forget an inch of the canvas, a plank of its gangway or a single blade of the trodden, deadening grass.

'This is the spot here, isn't it?' said Alec,

nudging with his toe a place where the grass had been killed, scoured away, by—one guessed—a scrubbing brush and some fearsome caustic solution.

'So if that's where she fell,' I said, 'where would she have come off? Where would Harlequin have had to stumble for Ana to end up there? Would she fall forward, Alec, or backwards? How far?'

'Forward,' he said. 'Just like a refusal.'

'Of course.' My first ever experience of carrying on without a pony who had decided to stop was over thirty years ago now, but I still remembered the sudden weightlessness, the seemingly endless flight over the spurned hedge and the sharp drop into the nettles beyond. 'So let's say between here and there,' I said, pointing. Alec did a couple of knee-bends as though warming up for a PT display and then crouched down at one side of the passageway. I turned my attention to the other.

'If we do find something,' I said, presently, 'let's say a pair of stout nails with shreds of rope still clinging to them, we mustn't touch anything. We must hand it straight over to the police.'

'Who have probably already checked,' said Alec. 'And wouldn't whoever put the rope across have made sure to come back and remove the nails afterwards?'

I sat back on my heels and looked over at him.

'Would you? If you had got away with it, would you risk being seen tidying things away?'

'Excellent point, Dan,' said Alec and bent his head again.

The canvas walling of the tent was tacked every five feet or so to a thick post and while these posts bore all the marks of a long hard life, the only nails

I could find were ancient, rusted and hammered in hard to the wood out of harm's way.

'I don't think much of the tent men,' said Alec. 'Leaving so many good nails behind them instead of prying them out and keeping them in a jar for next time.'

I had never been convinced of the moral necessity to gather jars of old nails about one, even if one did not have to cart them around the country between standings, so I said nothing.

When we had worked our way back farther than remotely plausible, I stood up at last. There had not been a single new bruise showing white on the dirty wood, not a single new nail hole and not even any suspiciously soiled patches where someone might have ground in mud to hide them. I looked up, wondering if anything could have been rigged from above. Alec's eyes followed mine. The roof of the tent was dizzyingly high and my shoulders and spirits slumped at the thought of clambering up somehow and inching around up there, fruitlessly searching.

'It would have been nice to find something,' said Alec, 'but the absence of physical clues doesn't prove that you're wrong. You've always scoffed at the idea of them before.'

'I've scoffed at inch-square swatches of unusual tweed smelling of unusual tobacco,' I said, 'but I think if there had been a trap rigged here we would have found something.'

'Not if the cord or whatever was tied to a stake that was banged in and then pulled out again.' Alec looked about as enthusiastic as I felt about the idea of crawling around the grass looking for holes or plugs of mud where holes had been and gone. 'I'll ask the tent men if they saw anything odd. It'll give me an excuse to get talking to them—most welcome. What a great pity Donald and Teddy couldn't be more firm about what they saw. But they hadn't been briefed, had they?'

'Alec, please,' I said. 'Of course they hadn't been briefed. They are only here to lend my presence a respectable justification in the eyes of Hugh and the world at large. I'm hardly going to draft them on to my staff like . . .'

'Special constables?'

'Quite.'

'Has Inspector Hutchinson grilled them yet? Lord—*grilled*? Skinned, filleted, diced and fried: I felt five years old last night when he started in on us, didn't you?'

'They are certainly in his sights,' I said. 'He's already made short work of Charlie.'

'And who's next on *your* list?' Alec asked.

'I'm going to tackle Ina,' I said, 'which is a job best done by me alone, I'm sure you'll agree.'

'Tackle her about what?'

'She wasn't in her seat last night when Inya screamed, when you and I raced across the ring. I need to know where she had got to.'

Alec whistled and raised his eyebrows.

'Ina Wilson?' he said.

'Well, no, not really, not for any reason that I can imagine. Apart from anything else she couldn't possibly have known when Ana was going to leave the ring. But I need to check, don't you agree?'

We parted company at that, Alec leaving by the back doors for the stable tent and I making my way to the front doors to begin my walk to the castle. It was rather a splendid winter's day, half past eleven the very peak of it. The worst of the overnight chill was gone and the low sun was doing its best, dazzling through the tree branches and melting a little of the frost off the grass here and there. In another two hours it would give up the fight again, of course, and the cold would creep back across the lawns from where the shadows had hoarded it all day, but now was the moment to be out in it if one had to be out at all.

The sweet butler looked troubled when he answered the door and I suppose the very fact that he was on duty there instead of one of the maids, like a bear in the mouth of his cave ready to repel all invaders, was more evidence of the mood in the house.

'How is Mrs Wilson this morning?' I said as I followed him up the short half flight of marble steps to the level of the great hall.

'She's fine, thank you, madam,' he said with just a touch of emphasis on the first word.

In the hall, Ina did indeed look fine, the chalky pallor of the previous evening quite driven away and replaced not by the flush which might be expected (for the hall was still rather stuffy from the evening before and both fires were once again burning high up into the chimneys) but by rosy cheeks and clear, sparkling eyes, and to see such a marked change, given my current mission, made me rather uneasy. If one comes delicately to enquire where a friend was when death was being dealt, one does not welcome the sight of that friend transformed. I told myself sternly that the transformation—if indeed one should call it that and might it not be less fancifully described as a good mood?—could easily arise from a certainty that the travesty of the circus party would have seen off Robin Laurie from their door for ever, or could even be owing to the nasty events of the evening before making Ina, not to mention Albert, forget about her years-old and let us face it rather distant brush with death and just think about something else for a change.

Albert was certainly distracted, I could be sure. He was pacing up and down in front of the nearer of the two fireplaces, with his hands laced together behind him under his coat flaps, staring at the rug as he crossed it. Ina sat at the piano against the far wall. There was a great jumbled heap of sheet music on top of it and spilling on to the floor as though she had spent hours searching for just the right piece to suit the occasion. Since what she was still fingering away at in a desultory fashion was a Strauss polka, however, one could only conclude that she had given up.

'Ah, Mrs Gilver,' said Albert. 'I'm so glad you're here.' He had clearly suffered a great downturn in his view of himself since yesterday and there was to be no more 'Dear Dandy'. On the other hand, he was too preoccupied to simper and the result, overall, was the most sensible speech I had ever heard fall from his lips. True, it was nothing of any import and could have been replaced by a smile and a wave but it was a refreshing change not to be tired of him already. 'Have you come from the winter ground?' he went on. 'We have just had a visit from that dreadful man, Sergeant McClennan, and he said the circus folk are being questioned.'

Ina stopped playing and looked up.

'You didn't tell me that, Albert,' she said. 'Sergeant McClennan didn't mention it either.'

'You didn't speak to the sergeant together?' I asked, thinking it a very bad thing for the Wilsons if McClennan had deliberately separated them to go through his questions. That fate had befallen Alec and me once, in the past, and nothing I could imagine was more designed to make one feel shifty. Of course, when Alec and I had spent our uncomfortable spells in separate back rooms of an Edinburgh police station we had rather better reasons for feeling shifty than the policemen's caution. I hoped that the same was not true of the Wilsons today.

'If I had had my way my dear wife would not have had to speak to the man at all,' said Wilson. 'But he insisted she join us and give her impressions. I congratulate myself on keeping her away from the worst of it, though. Yes, I congratulate myself heartily on that.' Then came the customary pause, presumably so that I could congratulate him too. Albert Wilson's short leave from duty as an oddity was over.

'Well, my dear,' said Ina, 'no one could say you haven't taken excellent care of me throughout the whole sorry episode and since Mrs Gilver is here now—if you'll stay and have some coffee with me, Dandy?—I think you would be more than justified if you returned to your own concerns.'

'I have nothing pressing on me, my love,' said Albert.

'And would not tell me if you did,' said Ina, bestowing a sweet smile on him.

'That I should not.'

'So, you see, I cannot help but worry that you are neglecting it all,' Ina said, and she knitted her brow and pouted like a child in a soapflakes advertisement. It was sickening to see. 'And then I worry that when it does catch up with you, you will be so busy that you'll tire yourself and become ill and then I shall have to do without you more than I could bear or can bear even to imagine.'

Albert Wilson, as might be expected unless one knew in advance that he was a very unusual type of man, lapped all of this up and then trotted out of the room like a well-schooled pony. Ina and I listened to his footsteps crossing the dining room and then pattering away up a distant flight of stone steps—Benachally is one of those fearfully inconvenient houses with a spiral staircase at every corner and every bedroom leading out of another one. Eventually the sound reached us of a far-off door slamming shut and we both sat back, I against the plump velvet cushion at my back—and it always amazes me how the Wilsons' cushions are never damp or musty despite that barn of a hall— and Ina against the open piano, her elbows crashing a jagged chord out of the keys.

'Have you come from the circus now?' she asked me. 'This minute? Have you seen them this morning? How are they all?'

I nodded. This was heartening: if she had quizzed me on what the police were up to and what the gossip was, I should have worried even more than I was worrying, but a sweet concern for how her circus friends were bearing up under their misfortune was a relief to behold.

'I've seen Ma Cooke and Charlie,' I told her.

'No one else?'

'Alec managed a quick word with . . . one of the clowns.' I was not about to get embroiled in Miles Fanshawe's rebirth as Merryman. 'And he went to

210

visit Harlequin too. There at least the news is all good—calm as a millpond and full of breakfast, apparently.'

'And what are the police making of it?' Ina asked. 'Sergeant McClennan wouldn't tell us a thing, no matter what Albert says about having to shield me.'

'Inspector Hutchinson is making plenty of it,' I said and she sat forward, jangling the piano keys again. 'That grey hair and grey face are a brilliant disguise. He's actually a remarkable man, rather terrifyingly so, spouting new suspects and new theories like mushrooms—one shrinks from mentioning a name to him.'

'But whose name have you mentioned?' said Ina, looking alarmed. 'Dandy, what have you done?'

'Oh well, Topsy's—inadvertently—and my sons are in for a roasting too, I rather think.' I was looking around the room as I spoke, very airy, but I did manage to see Ina sit back, just a little.

'Well,' she said. 'That's all right then. I mean, Topsy and your two were in the ring when it happened, weren't they?'

'Yes,' I said, 'and speaking of who was where . . .'

'If only it had happened earlier,' said Ina, speaking over me. 'While everyone was still in the ring, then there would be no suspicion at all and the police wouldn't even *be* here. It's so horrid to know that they're all being pestered by that nasty sergeant and if Inspector Hutchinson really is as fanciful as you say then goodness knows what he'll come up with and how they'll suffer.'

I felt myself forming the words to ask her who would suffer more than Anastasia had, but they

211

sounded waspish even in the planning and I felt sure that waspishness was not the best tone to adopt since I had questions needing answers.

'Hmm,' I contented myself with saying and when I continued I tried very hard to speak gently. 'Anyway, Ma and the Wolfs were back there throughout, so there would always have been someone under suspicion. And besides, nasty as it is—and I quite agree about the sergeant, what a terror—one can hardly let it pass unchallenged. Ana died, my dear Ina, a young girl died.'

'Don't,' said Ina, her eyes filling. 'It was a horrid accident. Let's not think about it. Don't make me.'

'How can you be so sure it was?' I asked. 'Did you see something?'

'What do you mean?' she said, stopping with her handkerchief up to her eyes and staring past it at me. 'I saw what you saw. Less, even. I thank the Lord I did not see what happened . . . behind . . . afterwards. I couldn't bear to see the things you have to look at, Dandy. I do think you're wonderful for being able to face it.'

I felt myself rise up from in my middle and sit six inches straighter in my seat, as though Nanny Palmer had just—as once she used to, twenty years ago—put her knee in the small of my back and pulled hard on my stays. It might work on Albert Wilson, I thought, but it would never work on me.

'I am glad, for your sake, that you didn't go around and see anything horrid,' I said. 'Where *did* you go?'

Now Ina rose and straightened.

'I beg your pardon?' she said.

'When you left your seat,' I reminded her. 'Where did you go?'

'Oh, you mean earlier!' she exclaimed. 'Yes, I did slip out a little earlier, just for a moment.'

'Well, I don't like to argue with you, my dear,' I said, not meaning a word of it, 'but you weren't back when Inya screamed, were you? You might have left earlier, but it can't have been for a moment, because you weren't there. When she screamed.'

'Dandy!' said Ina, laughing and shaking her head. 'Can you really be saying this? Can you seriously be saying these things to me?' She was an excellent actress, having had to learn the skill to survive her marriage and not run mad, but it was only acting.

'Of course not, you goose,' I cooed back, no mean actress myself and trained at the same school, 'what an idea! But I just wanted to know if you *saw* anything or anyone—anything out of place or anyone creeping around . . . or anything really. Where were you? Where did you go?'

'It's going to sound so silly,' Ina said, dipping her head and looking up at me shyly, 'but I went out and came back in, that's all. Went outside and stood in the dark, looking at the stars, and then came back in again.'

'Why?'

'Well, that will sound even sillier.' I noticed, however, that she did not redden as she spoke.

'Please don't worry about looking silly in front of me,' I assured her. 'I look silly at least once every time I leave the house.'

'Well, those awful people had ruined it for me, rather,' she said. 'Robin Laurie and the rest of them, and then Albert was fussing as usual and I thought if I went outside into the dark and then

213

stole back in on tiptoe, I should be able to feel the magic of it—properly—the way I was so looking forward to. See? Silly.'

Indisputably, I thought, and all the more plausible for it, but not actually true.

'I looked around and couldn't see you,' I said. 'And then when Inya screamed, Alec Osborne and I rushed across the ring and went out through the curtains—the ring doors—to the backstage. Halfway across, I turned around and called to everyone to stay put. You would know I did, my dear, if you had been there, which you weren't, as I know, because I didn't see you.'

I was rather proud of this, but it cut no ice at all with Ina.

'I know what you did and what you said,' she told me. 'You shouted "Keep to your seats" and I remember thinking what a very forthright way it was of speaking. I wondered if it came from the army or something.'

I could not bring to mind exactly what I said the previous evening. 'Keep to your seats' did not strike me as something too alien ever to have fallen from my lips although I agreed with Ina that it was brusque and none too feminine an expression. Had she accused me of saying 'Don't move or else' I should have known she was lying, but this was either a lucky guess or it was true.

'But I couldn't see you,' I said.

'I told you,' said Ina, 'I could never do what you do. I thought I was going to faint, even without seeing a thing, even without knowing what was there to be seen. I felt my eyes begin to roll up and so I . . .' I knew what she was going to say before she said it. ' . . . I put my head down, in between

214

my knees.' She did it again, there on the piano stool, folding herself flat and letting her arms brush against the tops of her shoes. Rather spry for an invalid, I thought.

'Ah well, that explains it,' I said, once she had sat up again. 'I do apologise. But I really was only trying to pump you for clues about the others, you know. I didn't imagine that you harboured murderous thoughts of Ana.'

'Well, you were pretty fierce then,' said Ina. 'I'd hate to see you when you *were* suspicious. You could give Sergeant McClennan a run for his money, any day.'

I laughed along with her, feeling sheepish.

'It would have been a foolish story to tell anyway,' I said. 'Robin Laurie was right there— you were in plain sight of him—and I don't think he'd have been overcome by chivalry, do you?'

Ina Wilson's smile left her face at that. It would not be true to say that it faded or even that it died upon her lips; it went like a lizard's tongue, or a bullfrog's wattle—snap!

'Why do you loathe him so?' I asked her. 'He's a bit of a blister, I grant you, and I don't imagine that his suddenly chumming up with your husband springs from any well of brotherly friendship, but he's . . . Oh, how does one put it? He's not a serious individual, do you see? Like a little boy, really, and—like a little boy—the best thing to do is to ignore him, no matter how much one's hand itches to give him a sound spanking.'

'I agree,' said Ina. 'I'd rather never think about him.' She spoke so vehemently that I blinked.

'Forgive me,' I said, 'I had no idea that you really knew him.'

'We shared a nurse,' said Ina, startling me. I had shared a nurse, in a way, as a tiny child. That is to say, one had been poached from a neighbour, enticed into my parents' house and up the nursery staircase with promises of undreamed-of freedom—bottles of stout after lights out every evening and my mother encouraging all the maids to throw away their corsets and take up cycling. The trouble was that Henry Elder, the smallest son of the neighbour, had been inconsolable with grief at the loss of this nurse—she was a darling—and had practically moved in with us for a whole summer until he was sent away to school.

'You shared a nurse?' I echoed, trying to imagine how the nursery wing of the seat of the Marquis of Buckie could have shared its staff with the West End flat of a minor Glasgow don.

'A hospital nurse,' said Ina, 'when I was ill. He spoke of it the other week, don't you remember? At least, he alluded to it. My nurse came to us from Buckie, came back to town after nursing the Laurie children and their mother.'

'I see,' I said. 'Oh, I see! And Robin knew that? He blames this nurse leaving for . . . Oh, and Albert *doesn't* know, does he? Gosh, what a tangle. How very uncomfortable for you.'

'Yes,' said Ina. 'It is. It's horrid.'

'Only,' I said, my thoughts catching up with me at last, 'doesn't that episode reflect rather better on him than almost anything else one has ever heard? Why exactly would this shared nurse make you revile him? I mean, if he was incensed by the nurse leaving his poor brother's family in the lurch, then he can't be as mercenary as all that. At least he didn't throw up his hands and shout hurrah at the thought that they might succumb from lack of expert care. Because one of the worst things I ever heard about the man—and there is plenty to choose from—is that he stood idly by rubbing his hands and counting his gold while they all went down. That *would* have been shocking.'

Ina was shaking her head.

'Susan Currie is an excellent nurse,' she said, 'but discretion is not her strong suit, at least it wasn't then. She should never have come prattling to me about her last case. She shouldn't have burdened me with it. It wasn't fair.'

'I can see that,' I said. 'But did she actually tell you anything about Robin himself—anything that's worse than we all know?'

But Ina only shook her head again; clearly, while Nurse Currie might be a bristling switchboard of sickroom gossip she—Ina Wilson— was a dead line.

11

Back at the ground, it might only have been my fancy but there seemed to be an atmosphere hanging over the place as palpable as a low fog, at least as far as the adults were concerned: no one in her doorway; no one mending his props by the big fire; all the wagons closed tight against the roaming inquisitors in a way they were never closed against simple cold. The children on the other hand had bounced back like rubber balls let go at the bottom of a pond. Tommy Wolf and Little Sal were juggling what I shuddered to notice

217

were glass beer bottles to one another, with Bunty wheeling between them, but not wheeling in her usual fashion, whining with excitement and snapping her teeth; wheeling in perfect figures of eight with her nose and tail high, and snootily ignoring the flashing bottles above her. The Prebrezhensky girls were there too, wrapped up in their thick jerkins and leggings and looking infinitely snugger than the others (I supposed they were prepared for Russian winters and so did not have to make do with an extra jersey and two pairs of mittens during a cold snap in Perthshire), and had taken on a far greater task than the training into submission of my beloved Dalmatian: amid great gales and shrieks, they were teaching my sons to cartwheel.

I drew back into the shade of the trees to watch them for a while. Of course, Donald and Teddy had precisely five days of circus under their belts compared with the others' years, but I fancied I could discern something slightly more foursquare about them as they smacked their leather-gloved hands together and launched themselves at the frozen ground. In the execution, though, they looked pitiful and it was a lesson to me to compare their helpless flailing legs and clumsy landings with the appearance of helpless flailing that Andrew Merryman put on. I could see, all of a sudden, that the cringing and buckling he had shown to me might have been the act, the skill and precision he used to produce it being the real Andrew, the real Miles, the man himself.

'I wouldn't tip them, would you?' said Alec's voice at my shoulder, making me jump.

'What?'

'If I saw them on a street corner. I'd keep my change in my pocket.'

'Oh, I don't know,' I said. 'Pity opens more purses than pride.'

'Dear God, Dandy.'

'I know,' I said. 'But I can't seem to get Nanny Palmer out of my head this morning, and she was right. I can sweep past any number of fiddlers dancing a jig on street corners but there's an old soldier with no legs and a black spaniel who sits at the Waverley steps and I simply pour my wallet into his cup every time I see him.'

'Him!' said Alec. 'Yes, me too. I've started going up the other way out of the station to avoid him.'

'How were the tent men?' I asked him.

'Oh, all together before the show started and for its short duration,' said Alec. 'So either they're lying for one another or they're out of the running. And they were in the strawed tent—the animal tent at the back doors. They didn't see a thing.'

'Are you sure?' I said. 'I can understand the grooms being there, but why the tent men? Shouldn't they have been in the tent?'

Alec gave me a little smile, one which I have come to know as the accompaniment to his beckoning me after him along the path of greater knowledge where he precedes me. I loathe those little smiles.

'It's an obvious mistake,' he said, 'to imagine that a tent man is a kind of stage manager and will be hanging around to help with the running of the show. In fact, they have very little to do with that side of things. They are more like handymen. They erect the tent and set the larger props, that's all. For instance, they attached Topsy's rope as soon as

219

Cooke's arrived here.'

'And there's no chance that the rope met with a mishap and they helped themselves from the clowns' props?'

'None,' Alec said. 'That would be far too lackadaisical. What you don't seem to appreciate, Dandy,' and there was that smile again, 'is how expensive rope is. How closely guarded and well maintained.'

'How about motives then?' I said. 'Any rumblings of unrequited love for Ana or Topsy, as you suggested? You seemed pretty sure on absolutely no evidence.'

'There's no need to be quite so scathing,' Alec replied, which I took to be a no. 'How did you get on with Ina? Doing anything there?'

'I'm not sure,' I answered. I had been musing on Ina's story all the way back from the castle and I was far from certain what I thought of it. 'She had an answer for everything I threw at her, but the timing didn't seem quite right. I tell you what would help—let's go into the ring and walk it through.'

We were in the performing tent before I had finished explaining it, and Alec was nodding.

'Sounds rather fishy,' he said. 'You looked around before the scream and couldn't see her.'

'And she can't have had her head down then because it was supposedly the scream that made her feel woozy.'

'But she'd hardly have slipped out to stoke up on all the moonlight and magic after things had started to go awry. Very well, you sit and I look, or I sit and you look?'

'Well, it was me looking before, but then you're

rather bulkier than Ina. Let's try both.'

I could certainly see Alec bent double in Ina Wilson's seat, even when I ran much faster over the ring than I had before; the sawdust had been swept away this morning and there was no chance of slipping if one put on a good pace. So, we swapped roles and that was how Inspector Hutchinson and Pa Cooke came upon us—me going up and down like a jack-in-the-box and Alec lolloping backwards across the ring, shouting that I stuck out like a sore thumb and a blind man could have seen me.

'What's this, what's this?' said the inspector. I took a deep breath, sent a silent apology to Ina Wilson, for whatever she was up to I was sure it was not knocking Anastasia off her pony, and told him. Pa Cooke looked as delighted as might be expected to have someone who was nothing to do with Cooke's suddenly dragged on to audition for first murderer, but to my surprise, the inspector shook his head.

'I'm going to forgive you for not telling me, madam,' he said, 'and here's why. You weren't looking for her last night, were you? You were just looking around.'

'Yes, but I very clearly remember not seeing her,' I insisted. 'As evidenced by my going to her today to ask where she was.'

'I always said she was a funny one,' said Pa. 'Very keen on hanging around us, she was, Mr Hutchinson. Right from day one.'

The inspector waved him into silence.

'Yes, but looking and not seeing someone bent down and practically out of sight is completely different from looking to see if you can spot someone you *know* is bent down out of sight, and seeing a bent-over figure who's the only buddy in the place is quite different from noticing someone all crouched over when there are forty other people to be looking at. The difference, my dear Mrs Gilver, between "can you see this, that or the other" and a plain "what can you see" is not a small one.'

Alec looked ready to argue, but Inspector Hutchinson put his thumbs in his waistcoat pockets and began to pace up and down as though he were a professor on a podium settling into a long lecture. I hoped not.

'Similarly,' he began, which was a heart-sinkingly professorial opening, 'when I spoke to your sons just now'—I felt a slight flush creep over my cheeks, for I had had good intentions of being there when Teddy and Donald were ground through the inspector's mill and I had quite forgotten—'I was very careful not to ask if they saw such and such or did such and such, but merely asked them what happened last night, what they could tell me.'

'And what did they tell you?' I said.

'That something happened to the pony,' said the inspector. Alec, Pa Cooke and I all shared one ricocheting look amongst us, which I was almost sure the inspector missed. 'They're very bright young lads, Mrs Gilver. You must be proud of them.' I nodded and managed to hoist a smile to my lips, briefly. I was sure that what the inspector described so diplomatically as Donald and Teddy's 'brightness' was the same facet of their personalities which made me want, sometimes, to roll them up in a thick carpet and lie on top of it.

222

'They said exactly what they thought I wanted to hear, assuming that I wanted to hear what you did. And you too, sir.' He gave first me and then Pa Cooke one of his most paint-stripping stares. Then he turned to the doorway. 'Boys!' he shouted, and Donald and Teddy appeared, still slightly red in the face from their cartwheels and still in the leather gloves which made them look like dockers.

'Now, lads,' said the inspector. 'Tell me again what you told me earlier on.'

'Certainly, sir,' said Donald in a voice clear but rather high. 'We were watching the show, as we said. We couldn't see the acrobats and the light was a bit dazzling to see much of Miss Turvy, but the liberty horses were absolutely thrilling and even though Anastasia did all her best stuff at the front of the ring, it was still jolly exciting every time she came whipping round past us.'

'And then,' said Teddy, taking over very smoothly, 'this one time, round she came and the pony's ears were flat back and his eyes were rolling and he was showing all his teeth—trying to get behind the bit, you know—and with Ana clinging on to his—would you call it a bridle, Mr Cooke? That fancy thing Harlequin wears?—well, anyway, with Ana clinging on for dear life he just kind of scissored over the ring fence and shot away out of sight.'

Pa Cooke was by now staring at the boys out of narrowed eyes and one could almost hear the cogs turning. Cogs were turning in me too but I am sure my eyes were as round as eggs, my mouth hanging open. I could not help shaking my head a little: this was nothing like the version they had given me.

'Now, sir,' said Hutchinson, putting out an arm towards Pa Cooke as though ushering him to centre stage to start an aria. 'What exactly did you say to this pair? Hmm? Can you remember how you put it?'

'Say to them?' said Pa Cooke. 'When? What are you getting at, man?'

'On the way out of the ring last night, of course,' said Inspector Hutchinson. 'I'd like confirmation of what it was you said, and the more accurate the better.'

'Confirmation,' Alec murmured at my side. 'Oh, very clever.'

And indeed the hint that the inspector knew everything already and that denials would be useless and make Pa look a fool did the trick rather neatly.

'I asked them if they'd lifted the box,' he said.

'I know you did,' said the inspector. 'Little Sallie heard you. She's a delightful unspoiled little lass, isn't she? And what about you, Mother dear? Can you bring to mind what you said to your lads in preparation for them speaking to me?'

'Now, come, please, Inspector,' I said. 'Yes, I spoke to them but I will not agree to "preparation".'

'My apologies,' said Hutchinson. 'I'm afraid in my line of work I do get in the habit of talking very plainly and I forget what's expected in polite company sometimes.' This, of course, was no apology at all but I settled for it.

'I asked them whether they thought Anastasia had decided to leave the ring or whether her pony had run off with her,' I said, which was true, to the best of my memory.

'And they told you what they've just told all of us here now?' said the inspector. 'Ears back, eyes rolling, bit between the teeth.' One knew he was talking about the pony but one had to marvel.

'More or less,' I said, but then something got the better of me. I like to think it was sheer selfless integrity and honour. 'Less,' I said. 'Much, much less. They did think, on reflection, that Harlequin was the one who decided to leave, not Ana, but there was none of the . . .'

'Incidental colour,' finished the inspector. 'I thought as much.'

Donald and Teddy did not quite seem to be following all of this, but they understood enough to know they were in trouble and they each pulled their trick of choice. Teddy looked younger in that way he still can; a remarkably effective talent which stays Hugh's hand and Nanny's tongue. Donald, years past such ploys, put all his efforts into such a look of cow-eyed innocence that he took on the appearance of a halfwit.

'Now, listen to me and listen well,' Inspector Hutchinson said to them, 'I'm going to forget everything you've told me and we'll start on a fresh page. Agreed?'

The boys nodded, looks of youth and innocence going strong.

'Very good. Did the pony run off with that poor girl last night or not?' said the inspector, breaking his own rule of how to ask questions.

'Yes,' said my sons, in unison.

'Just as well for you,' thundered Hutchinson; the fresh sheet had clearly been a ploy.

Before he could continue, although he looked as though he would have had plenty more to say to fill a silence if he had to, we were all distracted by the sound of a motor car approaching and drawing up outside.

'Reinforcements, Inspector?' Alec said, but it sounded to me like a far more expensive engine than that of the policemen's Belsize, sounded rather horribly familiar in fact. I excused myself to the others and made my way to the door.

Hugh was standing with one foot still inside the Rolls, but with his arms crossed, which made him look rather insecurely balanced, like one of those rugby football players posing with a ball, except that they are usually flanked by supporting team mates and so less likely to topple.

'Hugh!' I said. 'What brings—'

'Is it true?' he said.

'I'm sorry, Hugh, is what true?' I answered, but a sickly feeling was beginning to grow in me, starting in the middle and spreading rapidly outwards.

'Was someone really murdered here last night?'

'The police are tending towards an acci—' I bit my lip. 'I mean, yes. Possibly. At least, she did die.'

'And the boys?' said Hugh, his voice cold enough to freeze the rum coffee in the flask in my pocket at ten paces.

'Are quite well,' I replied. 'They've been jolly helpful, actually. They saw something useful and have told the inspector all about it.'

'They *saw* it?' It might have been my imagination but I thought he swayed slightly.

'No, of course not! Honestly, Hugh. The girl died in the backstage area and the boys were in the ring.' Too late, I remembered that I had not, in the end, told him this. ' . . . side seats, watching the

226

show,' I added, and it would have been unconvincing even if I had been able to meet his eye while I said it.

'I cannot believe it of you,' Hugh said, shaking his head slowly. 'That you would come home alone and leave them here in this den of—'

'Den of nothing,' I said, hotly. 'Den of perfectly charming people who happen not to be lairds of estates but clowns and acrobats instead.'

'Den of tricksters and sharpers,' continued Hugh, 'and at least one out and out rogue, one murderer, Dandy, for God's sake, and you left them absolutely unprotected in a flimsy little shepherds' hut.'

'It was robust enough when you suggested it,' I reminded him. 'And they weren't unprotected— they had Bunty—and besides, they weren't in the shepherds' hut last night anyway. They were with the Prebrezhenskys.'

'The *who*?' squeaked Hugh. I felt I had landed what I believe is known in sporting circles as a knock-out punch and I sailed on.

'Zoya and Kolya Prebrezhensky. The Russian foot-jugglers. They were well looked after and breakfasted off . . . Oh God.' I may even have take a step backwards.

'Russians?' said Hugh. He uncrossed his arms at last and gripped the top of the motor-car door for support. 'Russians?'

'I'll just fetch the boys,' I said. 'And you can run them home.'

Surprisingly to me, they were only too willing to comply, almost eager to be gone actually. Perhaps the gravity of what had passed here had finally struck them, nailed home by the inspector.

227

I tried to encourage Bunty into the motor car after them, meaning it as a gesture of affection and generosity. Hugh, of course, took it as an impudent assumption that I could offload my dog on him without even asking and shot me a glare.

'I'll follow on as soon as I can,' I said as the boys were shutting themselves in.

'No rush,' said Hugh.

'Now look,' I began, for out and out rudeness in the boys' hearing was stepping beyond our unwritten rule. Hugh slammed the door shut and walked around to stand beside me. I stretched up and pecked him on the cheek—for the benefit of the many eyes I felt sure were watching from behind lace curtains—and he managed not to recoil although his face darkened. 'Look,' I repeated, 'I can see where your feelings have sprung from.' Hugh dislikes accusations of emotion almost as much as he dislikes implications that he is an open book to me, and I knew it. 'I admit, I did feel a twinge of something much the same.' Shared feelings now; he would not stand for much of this. 'But the very fact I could forget the boys last night means that deep down I knew they were fine. If I hadn't known the circus folk were all good eggs, bricks and fine fellows, I daresay I should have been as rattled as you.'

There were so very many sources of offence in this short speech that Hugh was still working his mouth silently, trying to choose an opener, when Inspector Hutchinson drew up beside us.

'That you off, sir?' he said, affably. 'Fair enough, I know where they are if I need them. And I'll try not to keep your good lady from you any longer than I have to. I'm just grateful you're not

228

whisking her home right now. Thank you.'

'You're very welcome,' said Hugh, and his meaning was clear.

'Ah well,' said the inspector, as we stood watching the Rolls pull away. 'Understandable, eh? It must have sounded bad repeated at third hand from the back of the butcher's van or whatever.'

'I wonder how he did hear?' I said, this thought occurring to me for the first time.

'Well, however it was, you can be sure it got embellished in the telling. She'll have had a dagger through her heart by teatime. And I'll not get my quiet pint of stout tonight.'

'I'm sorry?'

'You can be sure every roofer and carter in the Royal will have a better idea than me of what's happened and they won't stand for "an accident", by Jove they won't. See, if it was the superintendent who had to listen to all the experts in the public bar he'd not be so quick to haul me back to the station and get me on to the next thing, would he? But he's a teetotaller, and you just don't get the same dedication to gossip in a church choir. And he's not married either, so he won't be hearing about it when he gets home.'

'*Has* your superintendent hauled you?' I said. 'When? Has he telephoned to the castle?'

'Not him,' said Hutchinson. 'He'd never pester the big house. But I can feel it coming like thunder.'

'How could he?'

'Surgeon's report,' said Inspector Hutchinson. 'That and the fact that it's circus folk, I'm sorry to say. Different if it was locals, respectable types, with their birth and marriage lines and all their school reports tied up in a bow. We can't even get a name for this poor girl.'

'Really? Nothing amongst her things?'

'Not a sausage. Not so much as a letter from an old chum to be found and it's bothering my super's tidy mind. He'll be glad to close the door on the whole thing.'

'Do you think he's right?'

'No fear,' said the inspector with a dry bark of a laugh. 'I can feel that too, more like an earthquake than thunder—rumbling away underneath us. Not that I've ever felt an earthquake, mind, but you know what I mean. You'll not give up, madam, will you?'

'I certainly will not,' I assured him.

'But for all the underground turmoil,' the inspector went on, 'I can't believe it was any of them that was off when it happened.'

'Did you look for a trip or trap of any kind?' I asked.

'Sergeant McClellan did,' Hutchinson said. 'He couldn't find a sniff of one and sniffing things out's his party turn.'

'If you could be said to have a party turn,' I replied, 'although it's rather disrespectful to put it that way, I should have said it was . . . intuiting with such perspicacity as to appear psychic.'

'Some parties you must go to, madam,' the inspector said. 'Aye well, there's not much springs to my mind out of the spirit world or anywhere else. Except for this: Topsy's stuff was slashed and then hidden or swapped. Ana's stuff was swapped only—no damage done. That seems significant to me. And I'd like to know why old Ma Cooke and

Charlie are in cahoots, wouldn't you? The boss man has got wind of it, if you ask me, whatever it is. He's a wee thundercloud all of his own.'

'Thank you, Inspector,' I said. 'That gives me something to start on.'

'That's my—' He broke off, but I should not have been offended to have been called his girl. Very far from it. I felt my chest swell.

'And I assume that if I uncover anything incontrovertible, you'll be ready to rejoin the fray.'

'Just whistle,' he said.

'I'm surprised, though, Inspector Hutchinson, that you can't talk your boss round. I should have said—and I mean this most admiringly, I assure you—that you could talk him off the edge of a cliff if need be.'

'Oh, I could, I could,' said Hutchinson. 'Of course. Only I like to play my cards a wee bit closer. If I told him everything, the jail would be full and the caravans empty and I don't want that.'

I nodded.

'That's exactly what I was just trying to tell my husband,' I said. 'As bad as it looks, these circus folk are decent, honest—well, honest-ish and if not then it's for noble reasons—and don't deserve any of this really. They don't even suspect one another. They can't quite believe she fell either, mind you. It's left them utterly bewildered.'

'Aye, either that or we're a pair of fools,' Inspector Hutchinson said and, tipping his hat, he left me.

I told myself that, while no one would ever find the notion outlandish when applied to me, Inspector Hutchinson was so very far from being a fool on his own that even with me beside him we

231

did not add up to a pair and so I managed a very confident smile with which to greet Alec as he joined me.

'Thought it best to lie low during the touching family reunion,' he murmured. 'Is he in a complete rage then?'

'Pretty much,' I said.

'He does have a point, you know,' Alec reasoned. It is one of the more annoying of his habits to champion Hugh to me at odd moments. I briefly considered trying to construct a defence but there were far more serious matters at hand.

'So where are we?' I said. 'What do we think about Ina after what the inspector told us? Are you persuaded?'

'Not entirely,' Alec said.

'Me too. Neither, I mean. Except that she did seem to know what it was that I shouted out while I was crossing the ring.'

'I was puzzling about that,' said Alec, 'then I realised that she would still have heard you from outside the tent or round the back somewhere. Canvas, darling, you see? Anyway, we can check.'

'How?'

'Well, that's the bad news—Robin Laurie, I'm afraid. He must have seen her leave and return. He'd be able to pin it down for us. And he could confirm whether she really did put her head down. But you'll have to get off after him as soon as you possibly can because the memory won't be a significant one and it will start to fade very quickly.'

'I?' I said, crossing my arms. '*I'll* have to go running after him? Why not you?'

'Because I'm going to stay here and use my old

chumship with Miles Fanshawe to get closer than ever to the rest of them.' This was unanswerable and Alec, knowing as much, gave me a rather sly grin. 'I'm pretty sure I can reignite the old school spirit and turn it to good use.'

'What is the old school spirit?' I asked. 'What's the battle cry of the Harrovian?'

'Let fortune attend those who dwell here,' cried Alec, brandishing an imaginary and rather inapposite sword.

'Hmph,' I said. 'Not exactly to the current point, is it?'

'More impressive in Latin too,' said Alec, putting the sword away. 'But still, Miles for me and Robin Laurie for you.'

'If I can even find him,' I said. 'He gets about, you know.'

'He's at Buckie,' said Alec. 'At the deathbed. And you'd better hurry, because as bad as it's going to be for you to roll up now, crashing the funeral would be in very poor taste, don't you agree?'

12

I still felt most acutely that I was being shunted offstage and leaving Alec in the thick of the action when I set out on the long drive north the next day. His central point could not be argued—I could certainly confirm Ina's story by asking Robin Laurie—but, suspicious as her behaviour and her explanation for it were, I did not seriously entertain any idea that she was bound up in Ana's death. Even if there had been time, there was no motive, and even if there were some motive I could not imagine, the act itself—the only act Ina could have performed—was so unlikely to have had the outcome it did that surely she would not have risked it: a circus girl shoved off her pony should have, would have in nine cases out of ten, simply rolled over and leapt to her feet, blazing angry and shouting the name of her attacker to the top of the king pole. If the act had been more than that, if Anastasia had been grabbed off her pony and her poor head deliberately struck against that cold, hard ground (I shrank from the very thought of it), then I was far from sure that it could have been the wan and willowy Mrs Wilson behind it.

All in all, then, a day's drive and my uncomfortable insinuation of myself into a house of illness gearing up to be a house of mourning appeared to be taking diligence to its farthest point, and I was sulking. To be sure, I relished the prospect of keeping out of Hugh's way for another day; I had stayed out late the night before, scratching supper with Alec at Dunelgar, and had risen long before dawn to get away before the household was stirring. I was mildly interested, too, to have another crack at the puzzle of Robin Laurie and Ina Wilson, for the animosity of the one made no more sense than the leering familiarity of the other. Still, I could not help but feel that Alec had kept the plum for himself and was worming his way into it in rather a selfish way, while I was being sent packing with a pat and a sandwich like an unwelcome child, not to return before bedtime.

I had forewarned them of my visit, stopping just

short of actually asking permission to arrive (in case I was refused), and since this necessitated a telephone call it was hard to resist the temptation to let the telephone call take care of the entire business.

'Be my guest,' Alec had said—had drawled, in fact—lying back in his chair and stretching his legs out in front of him. He applied a match to his pipe and disappeared behind belching plumes of smoke, looking quite diabolical. 'If you can work a telephone call around to the point and get the matter tied up neatly then three hurrahs for you. I shall listen and learn.'

Of course, he was right. I ascertained from the butler that there was no blanket ban on visitors and when Robin was summoned to the telephone I delivered the little speech Alec and I had concocted about my passing Cullen on my way to a visit at Cairnbulg and my wondering if I might stop in.

'But of course,' said Robin Laurie. 'Of course.' He spoke with such an air of understanding and with so little surprise that one could not miss the implication: that of course *I* wanted to see *him*; that ladies begging to see him was a cross which manfully he bore. On the other hand the implication was so subtly laid down that one could not counter it—to deny it would be to confirm it.

'Latish on tomorrow then,' I said. 'I shan't want dinner,' and, blushing, I rang off. 'Oh, shut up,' I said to Alec, who had not spoken.

Cullen, the estate of the lords of Banff and Buckie, unrivalled bosses of this particular corner of the eastern Highlands, at least since the MacDuff family, earls of Fife, had turned up their

235

toes centuries before (for reasons never quite clear to me despite Hugh's retellings, although I could not help slightly blaming Shakespeare), was a large square block of uninspiring scrub farmland bound on the north by battered coast, where grey villages alternated with grey cliffs, and unleavened by anything so dashing as a glen, a forest or even a heathery moor. (And when one finds oneself regretting the absence of a heathery moor, one knows one has arrived somewhere one should not linger.) The first time I had ever endured the endless slog up the side of the Spey and the even more endless chug along the coast road eastwards to Cairnbulg—for the friends were true, except in that they were Hugh's friends and I would not voluntarily have paid them a visit if they had been giving away mink coats and diamonds—I had remarked aloud that the north coast was not actually that much worse than Perthshire. This was in the early years of my marriage before, by a combination of my learning some tact and Hugh's stopping listening, I ceased giving daily affront. Hugh, who had not yet given up trying to educate me, informed me in clipped tones that we were not currently *on* the north coast, that the north coast was a hundred miles further up and was perfectly charming although not quite as lush as this, the Grampian coast. I had looked around at the dried-out grass, the sheep—who seemed, even for sheep, quite remarkably forlorn—and the few stunted trees, leafless already in September and bent over like crones by the ceaseless howling winds, and had said nothing.

Cullen Place itself, when I arrived there, came as rather a relief. I knew that there was a Castle

Cullen, brooding on a headland somewhere hereabouts, but a practically minded Georgian had turned his back on the salt spray and had erected, in a sheltered dip a mile inland, a comfortable little mansion house after the style of John Nash—or it might even have been with the help of John Nash, I supposed, if the Buckies had been in funds at the time. It was, I could see as I swept up the drive and puttered around wondering where to leave my motor car, a cosy kind of overgrown cottage, facing south and catching the last fiery rays of the winter sun in its pink-washed plasterwork and in the bays and french windows it sported here and there wherever some Victorian inhabitant had felt they should like a better view or an easy stroll out to the gardens; a house made for the comfort of a family, one where the servants' wing took up more space than the whole suite of formal apartments, and that is always a very good sign. I have spent far too many visits, cold, starved and wretched, amongst the marbles and Fragonards of the other kind of house ever to sniff at one which makes do with just two drawing rooms and concentrates itself instead on dairies, smokeries, fish stores, laundries, and above all a boiler house, reeking of coke and pumping delicious warmth around the place with the zeal of a speeding steam engine. I was sorry, as I walked up to the front door, that I had been so unequivocal about not staying for dinner or even stopping the night.

A parlour maid showed me into a ground-floor room at the back of the house before going to announce my arrival to 'master's brother' and, thinking I should look less like a lamb on an altar if I were not seated when he entered, I wandered around while I waited, slapping out a little tune with my gloves. Oddly, the room had an air of disuse despite being decorated as a family apartment with its plump, mismatched cushions and its footstools worked in the drab and lumpy tapestry covers so redolent of captive girlhood. Well I remembered the lumpy tapestry covers I produced myself, with many a droplet of blood from my pricked fingers, in the empty years between dolls and cocktails (although the covers themselves were not around to remind me since my mother had been something of an aesthete and she had tended to beam at my footstools and send them straight to Granny).

The chimneypiece and tabletops hinted at an explanation: they were crowded with photographs, the silver frames gleaming, the glass twinkling and smelling faintly of lemon from a recent wash. There in the biggest and grandest frame of all was the wedding photograph of Lord and the new Lady Buckie, looking young, scared and rather strangled, he in his high collar and she in a hideous wedding dress which topped off its leg-of-mutton sleeves and pouter-pigeon bodice with a kind of surgical neck-brace in ivory brocade with a row of pearls under the chin. All around this one were gathered smaller photographs of the ensuing progeny: the christening portraits showing the same girl, less frightened now, clasping armfuls of frothing ruffles from which, in some of the pictures at least, a fat arm or sturdy booteed leg was waving in blurred abandon; later pictures of the children too, taken in this very room against the french windows, where they sulked in ribbons and buttoned boots, staring down the photographer and hating every minute of it. There were a few happier moments: a boy on a riverbank holding up an enormous perch and beaming; a big girl leaning forward on a black pony, hugging its neck; a row of small children on the same black pony with their sister proudly holding its nose; two small boys, one just a baby, got up as pixies in acorn-shaped caps and pointed slippers with shining buckles. It was hard to tell how many children there had been for the crowded frames might have easily held a multitude of different babies, toddlers and growing girls and boys snapped just once each and, before the younger ones had begun to take on the finished look of grown people with the same recognisable features every time, the pictures stopped. That must be it. Small wonder that the room was not the first choice of retreat for the widowed and now childless man who lived alone here. I turned away, heaving a sigh which I hoped would take such thoughts away with it when it left me, and jumped to see a figure in the doorway.

'Dandy,' said Robin. For once, he was not smirking and both of his eyebrows kept their line. If I had not known the circumstances, I should have said he was cross about something, but perhaps this was only another morsel of evidence that there was a tender heart beating underneath the elegant waistcoat and the teasing. He must have thought I was being a perfect ghoul, peering at the photographs of the dead babies; perhaps I was—not a pleasant notion and one which I batted firmly away, telling myself that if they did not want people to look at the pictures they could pack them away or show guests into another room. I refused to hang my head about it.

Sticking my chin resolutely in the air, then, I walked over and shook hands.

'Robin, thank you for letting me stop off. It's much appreciated. How is your brother, if you don't mind my asking?'

Robin frowned, no more than a twitch, but I could not miss it.

'He's much iller than he or anyone else in this place will admit,' he said.

I made a few inadequate sorry-noises.

'Now, then,' he went on, sitting opposite me and slinging one long leg over the other with a gay unconcern for his trouser creases. 'Something to ask or something to tell?'

'Neither,' I said, possibly too stoutly to be quite plausible, but it had rattled me to have him cut to the heart of the visit that way. 'I just can't resist the chance to chew it all over again with one who was there. Most excitement there's ever been within a day's drive of Gilverton, and I'm utterly thwarted. The police are being the expected plods and the circus folk have turned Trappist to a man.'

'Closed ranks, eh?' he said. 'Hardly surprising.'

'Yes,' I replied slowly. 'Of course, one cannot help the thought that it was one of them, but it does occur to me'—I tried to sound as though as I were only just realising this as I spoke—'it does occur to me that everyone in the crowd really should have been interviewed too. Plods, you see? Plods. They haven't even asked for anyone's addresses, Ina tells me, and now the case is all but wound up.'

'And you said you had nothing to tell!' Robin cried, flapping a hand at me in a gesture

240

reminiscent of an elderly woman gossiping in the street. I had the uncomfortable feeling that he saw straight through my careful show of thinking aloud and was laughing at me. Still, what could I do but plough on?

'I suppose that is news,' I said, attempting a look of innocent surprise. 'Yes, they think it was an accident. They think the pony bolted and Anastasia was just dreadfully unlucky.'

'Anastasia?' he said. 'That was the girl?'

'I nodded.

'So why the desperate urge to "chew it over"?' said Robin. 'If it's all done and dusted, as you say. You are confirming a view of your sex that ladies more often seek to overturn.' He flicked a glance at the silver-framed photographs again as he spoke but he was twinkling at me, the frowns quite vanished. I flushed and decided that I would have to take a more purposeful tack.

'To be perfectly frank,' I said, 'I'm feeling rather uneasy about something. My conscience is pricking me.'

Robin opened his eyes very wide, looking thrilled and horrified in equal measure.

'She was an unappealing girl, to be sure,' I went on.

'I shouldn't have said so,' said Robin. 'I'd have taken the little one on the rope if given a choice but . . . Oh dear, now I've shocked you.'

'Not at all,' I retorted, although he had. 'Her character, I mean. Terribly difficult for the Cookes to manage—disruptive, eccentric—but if it wasn't an accident, then no matter what her shortcomings, she deserves more than to be tidied away and forgotten. Do you see?'

241

'And are you going to tell the police about this pricked conscience? This unease? Whatever it is,' said Robin.

'Possibly,' I replied. 'Except that it's more than likely nothing to do with Anastasia at all and one doesn't like to cause mischief willy-nilly.' Of course, causing mischief willy-nilly was one of Robin Laurie's favourite pastimes and so I hurried on. 'It's about when Mrs Wilson slipped out, during the show. She can't give me any very plausible account of where she went or why or even when.'

'And should she?' said Robin. 'Give you an account of herself, I mean.'

'Not—no—not in the ordinary way of things, of course. Why would she? But only just because I knew she'd gone and I asked her about it instead of telling the inspector and so I thought she should come clean, to repay the favour. To set my mind at ease.'

'And how did you come to know that she had slipped out?' said Robin.

'I happened to turn around and I saw that she wasn't there.'

'Really? You do surprise me. You turned around, turned away from the spectacle?'

'Just briefly.'

Normally, one would say that Robin Laurie's gaze was all show, his eyes flashing a message of mischief out to the world, but just then he was also gazing to *see*, taking everything in that he could, drinking it in. After a moment, he seemed to come to a conclusion.

'Am I to understand, Dandy, that you think dear Ina might have bashed the circus girl on the head and you would like me to be her character witness and alibi?'

I would far rather it had not come to this, for Robin Laurie was the last man on earth to be trusted with a woman's reputation; I could just hear him pointing her out to his chums and telling them that she owed him her freedom—nay, her neck!

'Let's say I should feel a little more comfortable about not telling the police if . . . if it were on your head as well as mine.'

There was another long pause and then he grinned at me, a fresh, uncomplicated grin like a schoolboy's.

'Yes, she slipped out,' he said. 'She didn't catch my eye or wave or anything. She's not my biggest fan, you know, although she hides it marvellously. I'd have said she was going for a quiet smoke if she'd been anyone else. And it was ages before all the fun began.'

'I see,' I said, shuddering a little at the word he chose. 'Yes, that's exactly what she told me.'

His shoulders dropped a little as though from a small tension let go. 'Did she tell you what she was doing?' he asked.

'She did, but . . .'

'Of course, of course,' he said. 'I wouldn't have you betray a confidence for the world.'

'Oh, bother it! There's no "confidence" to betray,' I said, once again finding myself hooked by an unspoken implication, this time that Ina was up to something not to be mentioned in the hearing of men. 'I must say, you have an uncanny knack for—' He bent his head in eagerness to hear the end of this and I bit it off. 'She went out to the moonlight, to regroup.'

'Regroup?' said Robin. 'And it wasn't moonlight that night, by the way.'

'Well, the starlight, then. Yes, to regroup. To reignite her innocent excitement about the circus show, which had been driven off by the crowds and ... very well you know this ... by you!'

He nodded sagely and explored the inside of one cheek with his tongue.

'And you believe that, eh?'

'Stop it,' I said. 'Behave.' I had finally been provoked into treating him as though he were a child. He sat back, triumphant, counting this a victory. 'So,' I continued, trying not to look or sound stern, 'in summary, she slipped out, just for a minute or two, and back in again, and this quite early on.'

'More than a minute or two, I'd have said,' Robin replied. 'Long enough to subject these "stars" to a thorough inspection, but otherwise that's about it.'

'And later?'

'Later?'

'When I turned around and couldn't see her, it was actually later than this starlight trip we've been discussing. It was just as we were realising something was wrong.'

'She went out twice?' said Robin. 'Is that what she said?'

'Is that what you say?' I asked him. It was one of the first rules of detecting not to provide the witness with a story to confirm or deny, but instead to coax the story out of his own mouth, from his own memory, but my word it was an odd way to carry on with someone who did not know what one was up to. Robin Laurie was staring at me in a most squirm-inducing way.

'I'm not saying what she did,' I said, trying to help him along, 'only that I couldn't see her. She wasn't visible.'

He looked more perplexed than ever. 'She was invisible?'

I could feel a flush beginning to spread up from my collar, but just then he smacked his hands together and laughed the boyish laugh again.

'Oh, I get it!' he said. 'You couldn't see her! Yes, of course, she put her head down on her lap, didn't she?'

'Thank you!' I exclaimed, flooding with relief. 'That's what I meant. She said she was bent over in her seat, feeling faint and doing what one is supposed to do to get the blood flowing.'

'I thought at the time she was having some difficulty with her stocking,' Robin said. 'I almost offered to help.'

Ordinarily, I should have frowned at this, but I was so grateful to have got around the awkward corner that I smiled at him. This time we both sat back in our seats and let huge breaths go.

'Now,' said Robin, presently, rummaging in his waistcoat pocket and then flipping open his watch with an extravagant gesture. 'Tea? Or a drink perhaps? I took you at your word about dinner, I'm afraid, but if you didn't mind taking pot luck . . .'

'No! Heavens no,' I said, making those vague and meaningless patting gestures at my hair and clothes which, who knows how, have come to betoken imminent departure.

'My brother . . . I don't ask the kitchen to put

245

four courses in the dining room for me every night
... but you're very welcome.'

'I shouldn't dream of it,' I said, standing, having
an abhorrence of being that most burdensome of
all burdens: the unexpected guest.

With nothing to look forward to except the
Brodies of Cairnbulg, then, I took my leave.
Dinner, two hours of cards, bed, breakfast and off
again, I told myself, and it was in a good cause. I
stepped into my motor car and slammed the door.
Hours and hours of driving, a disgusting dinner,
two hours of cards played geologically slowly and
with much discussion—Ernest and Daphne were
well known for their habit, when a rubber had got
away from them, of requiring their guests to lay all
hands on the table for a post-mortem. How the
sister-in-law who made her home there stood it, I
cannot imagine, except to say that she was always
drunk by tea. After the card lesson, nothing but a
hard bed in a cold room, porridge of the stiffest
order and the same hours of driving all over again.
All to find out that Ina Wilson had been telling me
the truth about her short trip out to the starlight
that night and why I could not see her when I
looked.

Yet it was not just the prospect of the Brodies
that kept me sitting there on the gravel at Cullen
instead of dragging myself off down the drive
(although they helped). A far weightier anchor was
the niggling little voice in my head telling me that
it did not add up, and that even if it was a tiny
question, invisible to the naked eye, and even if
marching back in there and asking about it would
destroy any shreds of the cloak of casual interest
under which I had hoped to hide and would reveal

246

my mission to *be* a mission, it would still be there like a pea under twenty feather beds every night, and that sooner or later I would be on the telephone anyway, shredding my casual cloak the finer.

Quite simply, if Ina Wilson, as Robin had just confirmed, really did have her head in her lap fighting faintness when I looked round, then she had put her head there before the scream, and that might have been because she knew the scream was coming, because she knew what was happening, because—taking the argument to its conclusion—she had somehow made it happen and was sickened by remembering it.

The sun had gone completely now and the house looked tired suddenly, the pink plaster cold and the windows dark and blank. I crossed the porch and opened the inner doors to the hall. (My return would be less peculiar, I thought, if I treated it as a second thought and did not summon a servant with the bell.) Almost at the same time, a door opposite me opened, spilling lamplight into the dimness. A tall figure stepped slowly into the square of light and stood there silhouetted, looking back at me.

'Ah good,' I said, 'sorry to disturb you again, but there's something troubling me.'

'I'm sorry?' came the voice, and I started. What could possibly have befallen Robin in the time it took me to go out to the drive and come back again that could have taken the drawl out of his voice and left that weariness in place of it? I moved forward.

'I'm sure it's nothing,' I said, 'but I've got a bee in my bonnet for some reason.'

'Who are you?' the voice said.

I was only steps away from him now and yet still, as I gazed up at his face, I could not make sense of it. Not until I looked downwards and saw the cardigan jersey, the bagged corduroys and the carpet slippers, did I realise my blunder.

'Lord Buckie?'

'Who are *you*?' he said again, and I could hear a very faint echo of his brother's voice as his surprise gave way to a natural amusement.

'I—Oh my goodness, I do apologise. Yes. My name is Gilver—Dandy . . . lion. I dropped in to see Robin and I just . . . I haven't come for the silver. Don't worry.'

'Well, I'm afraid he has gone out,' he said. 'Might I relay a message from you?'

'Not really,' I said, feathers of panic begin to tickle at me. I did not want to have to tell this man about Anastasia's death. 'I could leave a note, perhaps. Will he be gone long?' Not having heard a motor car, I suppose I imagined that he had taken a dog for a walk or something.

'He could be.' Lord Buckie—it was a struggle not to think of him as 'the old man' and yet I knew he was barely fifty—treated me to a considering look, deciding whether to go on. 'I expect he has gone visiting. Of course, you are very welcome to wait.' He bowed slightly and ushered me towards the open door behind him. I made a slight bow in return and trooped wordlessly to where he was pointing. It was only after I got there that I regretted it.

It was his library, and quite clearly his bolthole, one comfortable chair drawn up by the fire and a table littered with books, pipes and spectacle cases. There were not, as far as I could see, any of the expected accoutrements of serious illness, no bath chair or chaise, not even any medicine bottles or so much as a blanket, nothing but the thinness of his legs under their corduroy trousers and the bony chest above the cardigan buttons to speak of his frailty. His skin too, I saw as I came into the light, was stretched pale and papery over his cheekbones. Only in silhouette could he ever be mistaken for his brother, one of them as lithe as a green willow-wand and the other as dry and hollow as a reed. He settled back down into his chair and waved me into a seat on a hard sofa against the wall.

'Now then,' he said. 'Are you sure there's nothing I can do to help?'

'Quite sure,' I said.

'Then might I offer a little advice?' he went on.

I nodded, rather puzzled.

'I am very fond of my brother,' he said, 'but I have no illusions about him. If I were you, Miss Gilver, I should count myself lucky that he was not here today and I should give it up now. I mean no disrespect to you in saying so, my dear, quite the reverse and I hope I haven't shocked you.'

He had, of course, *horrified* me and at the same time had flattered me more than I had ever been flattered in my life.

'Lord Buckie, we seem to be at cross-purposes. I'm Mrs Gilver. From Gilverton.'

'Hugh Gilver's wife?' said Lord Buckie. 'Hugh Gilver's wife, here to see Robin?' Now I was in even greater danger of collapsing into giggles; of course, he must have some experience of the odd Mrs coming mooning around after Robin as well

249

as the hopeful Misses, tails wagging and hearts about to break.

'I'm on my way to Cairnbulg,' I said, and I had never been more grateful to know the stainless Brodies, all but pasteurised in their rectitude. 'I just dropped in in passing, truly, and am in no need of your protection.'

At last, the earnest look fell away from him and he sat back and gave a short laugh.

'But why did you drop in to see Robin alone and not me too?' he said. 'I'm always happy to have some company. Really, you can hardly blame me for thinking it a tryst.'

'I had heard you were ill,' I said. 'I had got the idea that you were . . .'

'At death's door?' said Lord Buckie, baldly. 'Or halfway up the drive? Unfortunately not.'

'Hardly unfortunately,' I said, very uncomfortable. 'Thankfully, mercifully.' I should have kept quiet, for the discomfort only grew.

'Oh no, you mustn't say that, my dear,' he said. 'Whatever fleeting moment of sorrow you would feel to read over breakfast one morning that Old Buckie had popped off at last, it cannot count against my claims.' I frowned and shook my head slightly, not following him. 'My life has long been a burden to me,' he explained. 'Its loss would be a release.'

'I'm so sorry,' I said, cursing myself for being drawn into this. No wonder he did not get many visitors if this was how he entertained them.

'Please don't be,' he replied, and went on: 'Eternal rest and an end to cares. What reason is there to be sorry?' Well, I thought, I was sorry I had come and sat down in this library for a start.

250

With dismay, I realised that the question was not a rhetorical one; he was looking at me, expecting an answer.

'You said you were fond of your brother,' I blurted out. 'And from hearing him speak I know how much he cares for you too. That's something worth living for.'

'I have lost more than a brother can ever make up for,' he answered. 'I wish I could believe that I shall see them all again—my housekeeper never tires of trying to convince me—but at least I shall stop missing them. I could give up twenty brothers—even twenty Robins—to stop missing them.' At the close of this speech, quite the most doleful I think I had ever heard in the whole course of my life, he finally took pity on me and rallied a little. 'But how cheering to hear that Robin speaks kindly of me in my absence. I never imagine the parties he attends to be places where relatives are asked after.'

'It was not a typical gathering,' I admitted. 'But he did seem—and it was remarkable to me too—to be a very family-minded young man.' It was with some surprise that I realised this was true: all of the poison regarding Robin's cold-hearted desire for his inheritance had come from the gossip of others and the only words I had heard from the horse's mouth spoke of warm feelings and a heart which could grieve with the best of them. 'He does hide his finest qualities very skilfully, doesn't he?'

'Good God, no!' said Lord Buckie, near laughter again. 'That's exactly how he does it, my dear. He doesn't hide his tender heart. Not at all! He offers tantalising glimpses of it in between the roguery and every woman between twenty and fifty

251

decides that she can save him.'

Not every woman, I thought to myself. Ina Wilson, for one, was having none of it.

'But I love him dearly,' Lord Buckie went on. 'He has such claims on my heart that I forgive him anything.'

'I have a brother myself,' I said, 'and a sister, and you make me ashamed, Lord Buckie, for I am not sure I would ever describe my own family feeling in quite that way.'

'It's more than family feeling,' he replied. Then he gave me a shrewd look. 'Forgive me, I can see how uncomfortable I'm making you.' He paused while I mumbled a pointless denial. 'But I rarely get the chance to speak of them . . .' A pause and a sigh. 'When my dear wife died'—I could not help a sinking feeling, seeing that our excursion away from doom was over—'all but one of my children were already gone. And that one, my oldest, wasn't even sick. She didn't have it.'

'I know,' I said gently.

'She drowned.' He looked up at me. 'And Robin almost drowned trying to save her. Did you know that?' I shook my head. 'I have never forgiven myself.'

'For what?' I asked him.

'When her mother died, I meant to rouse her, to stop her sinking into the kind of grief I feared she was too young to bear, but instead I only added to it and . . .'

'I am sure you could not have done that, Lord Buckie,' I said.

'I told her she was more than enough for me, that we would be everything to one another now. It must have seemed that I was asking her for strength she did not possess, that I was asking her not to mourn. So she went to the cliffs and threw herself into the sea.'

I gasped.

'I—I—thought it was an accident,' I said.

'We managed to keep it very quiet,' he said. 'Or rather Robin managed. Out of kindness to me. And so I could forgive him pretty well anything. Even his afternoons of visiting.'

'Ah,' I said, 'visiting! A young widow? I hope not the wife or daughter of one of your men.' I was trying desperately to lighten the mood. 'Very bad for the estate, that kind of thing.'

'A retired piano teacher,' said Lord Buckie, himself making a brave effort to sound cheerful. 'But between you and me, my dear, she still sees one pupil. Robin is always to be found there whenever he's feeling ruffled. She lives in the head groom's cottage as was and pays her rent on time.'

'A retired *piano* teacher?' I was trying and failing to picture Robin Laurie drinking tea in a cottage with my first piano teacher, Miss Cribb— moon-faced Miss Cribb with her slightly crossed eyes and her bun so tightly scraped back. I always wondered that it had not managed to uncross them.

'Well, my housekeeper maintains that she might well know how to *dance* on a piano but nothing more.' He was almost animated as he spoke, and I considered, quietly to myself, the growing puzzle of Robin Laurie. A scamp? A blister? Could any man who lit his ailing brother's final hours this way be all that bad? Could anyone who jumped into the sea to save his niece be a cad at heart? Could anyone who kept up something as cosy as this

253

afternoon arrangement with the piano teacher really be the kind of wrecker who deserved all of Ina Wilson's disdain?

In fact, I told myself later as I drove away, Ina Wilson's view of Laurie was getting curiouser all the time. For it seemed to me that the shared influenza nurse must have seen Robin the brother and Robin the uncle at his most impressive and endearing and could only have praised him to the heavens to her next patient. Well, perhaps the nurse was pretty and Robin had seduced her or perhaps—this was much more likely—Ina, knowing that he was a poppet underneath, found his veneer all the more tiresome and did not trouble to hide it. Perhaps she was one of the many who had tried to save him, got stung and retired, smarting.

13

Determined to show Hugh that his capacity to do without me was more than matched by my utter indifference as to whether he were a feature of my day, I went straight back to the winter ground from Cairnbulg on Tuesday morning and arrived to find the circus in a state of some uproar. There were raised voices in the stable tent, sounds of childish weeping from the Prebrezhenskys' living wagon and the unexpected sight of Bill Wolf stamping up and down in front of the performing tent, his brows thunderous and his boots making the very earth shake beneath them. Mrs Wolf could just be seen watching from behind the lace in her wagon window, a pained expression upon her broad face, and Tommy and Little Sal were sitting on the steps gazing at their father with a mixture of curiosity, trepidation and awe.

Ma Cooke popped her head out at the sound of my motor car and came over to meet me, moving at a trot, wiping her hands dry on her skirt as though upon an apron which her evident agitation had made her forget she was not wearing.

'So, here you are back again and where were you when we needed you so?' she scolded me as she arrived at my side.

'What's happened?' I said.

'The police have gone. Accident, they said. Only to be expected, they said. What were we doing wasting their time a-calling it anything else?'

'But you didn't want them to stay,' I said. 'So what's wrong?'

Ma's eyes flashed to Bill Wolf before she said anything. He had ceased his stamping up and down and was now stamping over towards us.

'Fie, fi, fo, fum,' I said under my breath. 'What on earth's up with Bill?'

'The good Lord knows and He won't tell the likes of me,' said Ma. 'I don't know what we're at, my beauty. I've known that man there fifty years and more and been in the wagon with thon forty-five and this is the first time either of them's puzzled me in all my days.'

' "Thon" would be Pa?' I hazarded.

'He's gone too far now,' said Bill as he drew close to us. It was a considerable effort not at least to take a step back from him. With his shoulders thrust forward, his fists bunched and his voice an angry rumble he made one think of those thrilling

255

gods from *Norse Stories Retold*; thrilling, that is, when presented in the form of a little woodcut showing how Thor got his hammer, but rather terrifying when standing right before one, larger than life, clearly fuming. 'What's he playing at, eh? He's overstepped the mark and no mistake about it.'

'Isn't that what I'm telling Mrs Gilver? I don't *know* what he's at. I can't work it out for my life. And there's Inya, Alya and Ilya breaking their little hearts.' Ma sounded almost ready to join the Prebrezhensky girls with some weeping of her own.

'But what's happening?' I insisted, hoping that I did not sound as shrill as I felt inside.

'He's lost his senses,' said Ma. 'Lost his circus sense anyways. He's said he's going to shoot the pony and won't hear a word against it. As soon as the police told him what they'd made of it, he decided. I tried to change his mind and Charlie tried, then we both tried together and he just got madder and madder and he won't listen to anyone.'

'But I won't stand for it,' said Bill, his temper rising again on the swell of his booming voice. 'I won't be made a fool.'

'Shoot Harlequin?' I said. 'Kill him?'

Ma nodded miserably.

'But . . . but what about Princess Zanzi?'

'Who?' said Bill.

'Tigress what bit my pa when I wurr a little maid,' Ma told him.

This was very troubling news. The hasty shooting of hapless little ponies was common enough in my world, of course, where fond fathers of suddenly crippled daughters were wont to reach for their guns, but Pa Cooke killing off a highly trained and surely valuable rosy-back prad, at a time when Cooke's Circus was far from thriving, and when the lost girl had been such a thorn in the collective Cookes' side? The only explanation I could see for that was not one I welcomed: the police had chalked up Ana's death as an accident and happily wiped the chalk dust from their hands and Pa was falling over himself to boost the official version. Surely, he would only do that if . . .

'Oh no,' said Ma. 'No, no, no, don't be thinking that there. Pa would never.'

'You give me goose pimples sometimes, Ma,' I said. 'How did you know what I was thinking?'

''Twas wrote on your face like love and hate,' said Ma, and for once I should rather have thought her psychic, since to have his every thought 'wrote on his face' is as unhelpful to a detective as to a card player.

'And you, Bill,' I said, mustering my courage and turning to look up at him. 'What think you? And why are you so angry?'

'I think no harm of Tam Cooke,' said Bill, rather unconvincingly to my mind. 'And don't you go twisting up my words on me. I just want what's best for us all. All I ever did. And killing Harlequin is just burning pound notes, to my mind. I won't stand for it.'

'I'm not sure I shall either,' I said. 'Where is he, Ma?'

*   *   *

Pa Cooke, as Ma indicated with a jerk of her head, was in the performing tent so squaring my

257

shoulders I strode off to have it out with him. He was standing in the middle of the ring in what I had come to think of as his rehearsal dress, long boots and flashing whip but coatless and with his sleeves rolled to the elbow, shirt buttons open piratically low upon his chest, giving an effect close to pantomime. Certainly his audience seemed not far from booing and hissing. Topsy, arms folded very tightly across her chest, was looking stonily ahead without a trace of her usual twinkles. Zoya and Kolya, just behind her, were slumped forward, elbows on knees, staring coldly at Pa and muttering now and then to one another in their guttural Russian, a language so suited to gloomy muttering that one does wonder how Russians do anything else, such as telling jokes or wooing maidens, and surely a Russian wedding with the vows repeated in those doleful lumps of sound could not be festive.

Pa saw me enter, but only cracked his whip and turned his back. I slipped into Alec's row of seats and shuffled along until I was sitting beside him.

'You're back,' he said. 'Have you heard what's happening?'

'Ma just told me. Do you have any idea why?'

Alec gave a short laugh. 'I'm up to my eyebrows in artistic temperament and haven't the faintest of clues about anyone. Even Miles is beginning to seem a bit odd, frankly.'

'Quiet,' barked Pa, from the middle of the ring. 'Quiet when we're working.'

'News to me,' said Topsy and Pa treated her to a glare. Then he whistled earsplittingly shrilly through his teeth and Tiny and Andrew came bowling into the ring on two unicycles, with

Charlie Cooke trotting after them pushing a wheelbarrow. Jinx, in the barrow, looked his usual irrepressible self but Charlie's face was mutinous and a moment's viewing told me why.

'This is instead of Ana and Harlequin,' Alec whispered, as Tiny and Andrew sped around the edge of the ring, juggling coloured balls, while Charlie and Jinx chased after them, never catching them up.

'Charlie won't think much of being the chump,' I said. 'I take it he can't ride a unicycle himself, then?'

'I suppose not,' said Alec. 'But look at Bill Wolf: packed up his medicine balls and crossbows and took to the accordion with never a grumble.'

'He's grumbling plenty today,' I pointed out. 'Stalking up and down like a thundercloud out there.'

'That's because Pa chucked him out of the tent. For lip.'

'Can he do that?' I was amazed. I had grown used to the idea that the circus folk were as civilised as Alec and me, only sprinkled with a little strangeness, as a kind of garnish.

'Apparently,' said Alec. 'Because he only had to say it once and off Bill went. It seems the boss can do whatever he likes.'

'Even as far as killing ponies,' I agreed. Most unfortunately, there had happened to be a moment's silence just then while Tiny and Andrew balanced, arm in arm and wheels still, and so my words reached Pa Cooke's ears.

'Right,' he yelled, 'that's it. Clear the tent. Everybody out.'

'I'm not presenting to an empty tent, Tam,' said

Charlie. 'You clear them out and I go too.'

'That's right,' said Topsy. 'You always said an act needed eyes and ears right through from first reckoning, Pa. Like you always say an act needs noise to rise above if it's any good.'

'You stick to what you know, lass,' said Pa. 'It's only an animal act that needs to practise noisy.' Then he seemed to realise what he had said and shut his mouth firmly, glaring round, daring anyone to make something of it. Andrew Merryman, of all people, took the dare.

'I can only offer again,' he said. 'If you would let me go and get Harlequin and show you what Tiny can do . . .'

'Arabesques as elegant as I can make them,' said Tiny, jumping down from his cycle and striking a pose on the sawdust, with one short leg stuck up in the air, foot daintily pointed. 'I'll even wear a tutu and tights. Owt for a laugh, me.'

'Because it's like you always said, Pa,' Andrew went on, 'bringing the cycles out in the spec is going to kill our first spot.'

'Enough,' said Pa. 'Out with the lot of you. You'—he jabbed a finger at Tiny—'and you'— another jab in Andrew's direction—'two spots and the spec from everyone and don't tell me I didn't say that up front. The spec's my worry and the spots are yours.' Now he turned and scowled at Topsy. 'I'll not be bending over to help anyone with a second spot ever again.' He wheeled back again. 'And Charlie? Brother or none—I'm the boss of Cooke's Circus and nobody talks to me that way.'

With one last poisonous look around the tent he marched away to the ring doors and disappeared through them.

'Golly,' said Andrew, which made Topsy laugh and eased some of the tension.

'Only don't you think his exit would be stronger wi' a puff of smoke?' said Tiny. 'I'll suggest it later, maybe.'

'This is no time for jokes,' Charlie snapped at them. 'That lass is still in not in the ground.'

The other clowns and Topsy looked at their feet.

'That is not the only why is no time for laughing,' Zoya said. Kolya nodded gravely and turned to me.

'Mee-zuss Kilvert,' he said. 'You talk to him, heh? One more act go pfft! and we all gone.'

Between the beseeching look on his face and the knowledge that he would not understand my excuses anyway, he was hard to refuse. So, reminding myself firmly of what Ma had told me— that Pa Cooke's bark was all and that his bite was toothless and hardly deserved the name—I hopped over the ring fence and followed him.

'Mr Cooke?' I called, scurrying through the backstage warren. 'Mr Cooke? Wait, please. I need to talk to you.' I caught up with him, rather unfortunately, just at the back doors, almost at the precise spot where Anastasia had lain. 'Mr Cooke,' I said, panting slightly. 'Ma told me about Harlequin, but I could scarcely believe it. Why would you do such a thing?'

'I've no call to be giving you an account of myself,' he said. His tone was lofty, but the anguish upon his face belied it.

'I'm not sure I can agree,' I told him. 'I am engaged to make all well at Cooke's Circus and

261

you said that I was to expect cooperation from everyone. Are you exempting yourself from the requirement?' It was hardly unexpected that his eyes widened at that; my own heart was thumping at my temerity and I was not unconscious of the whip coiled in his hand. Did I only imagine it twitching?

'I never knew what nonsense Ma was at getting you in here anyways,' he said. 'She gets these feelings of hers most days and twice on Sundays.'

'But this time she was right,' I said. 'The rope and the swing and . . .'

'Aye, this time,' said Pa. 'So I thought it'd do no harm to let them know you were here watching and reporting back, let them know who's boss, in case they were forgetting.'

'But don't you see? The police might be wrong. Whoever played the tricks might have killed Ana.'

'Never, never, no,' said Pa, contradicting himself rather. 'Your own babbies saw what happened, didn't they? And a pony that can't be trusted in the ring is no good to anyone and I can't afford to keep him in hay, not with things the way they are.'

We had arrived at his wagon and since he did not say goodbye to me, but only mounted the steps and opened the door, I took it upon myself to follow him. Inside Ma was perched on one of the armchairs and Ina Wilson was ensconced in the other. Ma's face was drawn with worry, but Ina greeted us with a smile and continued stroking Bobbo and feeding him raisins with a great show of cheerful nonchalance.

'Missus,' said Pa Cooke politely when he saw her.

'Well?' said Ma to me. I shrugged. She turned to

262

Pa. 'And didn't Old Nellie once crush a lad in her trunk when my pa took her calf off her too quick and she was broken-hearted there? And didn't she turn out to be the best elephant as ever was in the ring and out of it? Flatties could ride her, little chavs and raklies could run under her belly and she never turned a hair.'

'Have the clowns finished?' said Ina.

'Aye, they're off,' Pa replied, 'if you could call them clowns. If you could even call them circus. And my own brother too. I never thought I'd see the day when being the boss meant less than that.' He snapped his fingers. 'When my old granddad was the rum coll at Cooke's his word was law, and the whole place run a sight better for it.'

'Your Grandpappy Cooke bought a unlucky white dog what Old Man Chipperfield himself couldn't do nothing with, Tam,' said Ma. 'And he finished up in the ring, in a silver halter pulling a little carriage full of doves. My Auntie Magda told me. I think I might have a photograph of him somewhere in my cupboards there.' She looked about at the panelled walls of her home as if about to leap up and begin rummaging for it. 'Snowball. Swiss mountain dog, he was. You must remember him yourself.'

'You've no need to be telling me all this like I don't know,' said Pa. 'I've never been hard on any beast in my life, or that wee soul wouldn't be sitting there, would he?' He pointed at the monkey, who stopped with a raisin halfway to his open mouth and gazed back at Pa.

'What's Bobbo been up to?' I asked.

'Oh, he's always been a cheeky one,' said Ma.

'He took Ma's sewing scissors to my whip, is

263

what he did,' said Pa. 'My whip! She found him sitting on the box-bed, tail end of last season, snipping it up into scraps, din't you, Poll, eh? When I was a lad you could get the ghost just for touching the rum coll's whip. It was the crown jewels and the true cross. I never laid a finger on my old pa's whip till he was laying dead in his coffin and even then my hands were shaking.'

'If the clowns are off,' said Ina, just as though they had not spoken, 'I think I'll go and see if I can catch them.' No one answered her. Pa was gazing fondly at Bobbo and Ma and I were trying not to catch one another's eye. So Ana, if indeed it were she, had not only stolen the whip, but had cut it too, as she had cut the swing and the corde lisse. And Pa had forgiven Bobbo a deed much graver than Harlequin's lapse. 'They said they might put on their make-up to let me try a portrait,' Ina went on. 'Thank you for the tea, Ma. Goodbye, Pa. Dandy.' She fished her pad of paper and her paint box out from under her chair and skipped off down the steps with an air of girlish innocence which would have been hard to take in a twelve-year-old and was sickening for a woman in her twenties. I could not help but stare after her.

'Aye, the head empties when the heart fills,' said Ma.

'Is her heart full then?' I said.

'For sure. There's a change coming there, you mark me.' She reached over and picked up Ina's teacup, turned it over on the saucer and twisted it three times then peered into its depths as though she were looking down a well. 'Aye, a change coming, no mistake about it.'

I played down the mystical element somewhat

264

when I spoke to Alec and did not mention the teacup at all.

'You yourself said, darling, that Ina Wilson was biding her time, remember? Well, now she's jumping up and down with glee.'

'Very suspicious to have her in such tremendous spirits all of a sudden,' said Alec. 'Did what you found out from Laurie put her in the clear or in the soup, Dan?'

I had to think about this for a moment or two before I answered, for the whole of the interlude at Cullen was rather confused in my memory. I was driving us back to Gilverton, where Alec was to act as a buffer between Hugh and me while I got to work on the boys. It had occurred to me that while they had been leaned on good and hard about Ana's exit from the ring, any other impressions and overhearings they might have come by had been left untapped. I steered the Cowley around the curves of the lane, planning just how I should attack them, with fired questions and threats like the good inspector, or with cakes and cuddles and warm maternal urgings to get all the nasty memories off their precious chests.

'Dandy?' Alec prompted. 'Is she in the clear?'

'Almost,' I said at last. 'I mean, probably. Oh, for goodness' sake yes. Of course. I mean to say, she really did just pop out and then pop back in and she really did put her head down. It's just that I know for a fact that her head was down before the screaming started.'

'She would have to be very sensitive to atmospheres to come over faint because the spec went off its timing,' said Alec.

'But never mind that,' I said. 'What we should

265

be concentrating upon is Pa getting rid of the pony. That's far more suspicious if you ask me.'

'Especially given the lingering question about the other one who supposedly dropped dead,' Alec agreed. 'What was his name?'

'Bisou,' I said. 'Exactly. Pa says he can't trust Harlequin and can't afford to keep him as a pet, but there must be more to it than that. Circus people, Alec, keep the tigers who eat their fathers and boast of the fact on the sides of the cage. If some moth-eaten kangaroo dies of old age, they stuff it. Pa himself—and wait for this, for it will knock you flat—still gazes fondly upon Bobbo even though Mrs Cooke told her husband that Bobbo had cut up his whip. Pa's whip, I mean.'

'So Ana cut it, didn't just steal it?' Alec said. 'But why would Ma cover that up for her?'

'I don't know, and apparently the rum coll's whip—'

'Quite,' said Alec. 'I've been steeping myself in circus ways, Dan, you don't have to tell me. It's sacrilege.'

'You know, Inspector Hutchinson told me just before he left that he found it significant the way some props were slashed and some just moved around.'

We drove in silence for a while.

'And maybe to Inspector Hutchinson it was,' Alec said at last. 'What else did he tell you?'

'He said he'd like to know what kind of understanding there was between Charlie and Ma. And actually, Ma did just tell me that when she and Charlie tried together to change Pa's mind about Harlequin, he got angrier than ever.'

'She seems ready to side with anyone except her

own husband,' Alec said. 'For all her talk of "family" all the time.'

'Don't be harsh,' I said. 'I agree that she's up to something—up to plenty, probably—but disloyal she's not. Her devotion to her sons puts me to shame, I can tell you.' I am sorry to admit that I left a small pause here, in case Alec should want to contradict me. 'Anyway, what about your discoveries?' I asked him, after it. 'What did you find out in all your steeping?'

'There's something up with Andrew,' Alec began. 'Not just the upset over Ana and disgust about Harlequin.'

'What then?'

'He just seems to be dancing to a different tune, if you see what I mean. In a bit of a . . . what's that wonderful Scotch word, Dandy, that sounds like a Hindu prayer?'

'A dwam?' I suggested.

'That's it,' said Alec, chuckling. 'A bit of a dwam.'

'How on earth did you hear that?' I asked him.

'I came upon a housemaid standing on the front stairs staring out of the window across the lawns, steaming up the glass with her breath, no less, and instead of blushing to her roots and scurrying off she just said, "Michty me, surrrr, I'm aff in a dwam."'

'How charming,' I said, without any enthusiasm, for Scotch phrases leave me quite cold and it is irritating to see Alec's servants—so new and full of promise—begin to flex their brawny muscles and take over the house as mine did long ago. I was sure if he had started out with a little austerity and a few judicious sackings he could have stopped it.

267

'You're sure this . . . daydreaming, this wool-gathering, isn't Andrew's natural way?'

'Hard to say. He was never exactly hearty but I haven't seen him for years and I can't tell what he's like as a rule these days.'

'Well, I must say, Alec my darling, that doesn't seem to me to be enough to have justified your staying behind; I could have told you that everyone was in a bit of a state, which is all your discoveries amount to.'

'Moving on from my valuable impressions, then,' said Alec, 'to my more practical discoveries, I've also established the alibis once and for all. Tiny and Andrew vouch for one another and for Charlie Cooke too. All three were in mutual sight at the props table when Anastasia went thundering by and they saw nothing. Ma and Bill Wolf likewise. The tent men as we know were playing cards in the animal tent with the stable lads. Actually two of the stable lads were mucking out while they had the chance, since all the prads were in the ring, but they are all accounted for one way or another. Saw nothing, know nothing, saying nothing.'

'What about Mrs Wolf?'

'She and Tommy had been out front watching the spec and came round when they heard the commotion. She says you saw her.'

'Of course,' I said. 'Yes, that's right, I did. She helped Zoya take the children away. Is that everyone then?'

'Every last soul. It was surprisingly easy to tick them off the list too. All cosy together like little animals in their burrow.'

'Suspiciously so, do we think? Are you saying

268

they were each careful to provide themselves with alibis?'

'Good God, of course not. What a nasty mind you have these days, Dan. I was only saying that if this were mid-season, there'd be bandmen and their families, countless more workers and grooms, and they'd be spread over the land in the summer sunshine. I was just saying we were lucky to have them huddled together for warmth.'

Stung by the accusation of nasty-mindedness, I forbore from voicing any further opinions but looked forward to getting something a little more concrete out of Donald and Teddy, if the gods were smiling on me.

The gods were not, or at least not entirely, for the boys had gone stalking up on the moor and so, as always when they are stalking or hunting, they would fall to Nanny upon their return, for blistering hot baths and bread soup in front of the nursery fire before an early bed. The boys' nanny, Nanny Younger, was very far from being the presence in the house that my nanny, Nanny Palmer, had been but on stalking days she was not to be crossed lightly. I had seen her stare down Hugh—even Hugh!—and I certainly could not summon the boys to my sitting room and interrogate them there.

However, since they were on the moor, the silver lining was that Hugh was up there too and would stay up there until night fell then hang about the yard with the ghillies until the last dog was fed and every carcass—assuming success—was hung and dripping, then would feel justified in demanding a mustard bath, a rug and a toddy—his own bread soup by the nursery fire, in effect—and

I should not see him until the morning.

Alec stopped long enough to drink a cup of tea with me and then took himself off; he has a nice sense of how to play our friendship in my house when Hugh is absent, I must say, and he was, besides that, reluctant to find himself included in the outing in prospect that evening. For I was Cinerama-bound, as would be many of my staff too, I expected. Hugh is wont to curl his lip and think it a victory when he hears that a pair of housemaids and I have converged at the box office in pursuit of Mr Fairbanks or, as in this case, Mr Valentino, but I do not care. It might not be true of Hollywood that all of life is there, but more of life is there than one can ever find in Perthshire.

Before that, though, there was an onslaught to be borne, one to which Alec's departure on top of Hugh's absence had left me wide open. I had been days and days at the circus, tramping around in the damp, and then two days of driving in a leather bonnet and an overnight stop in a house too cold to permit any kind of ablutions.

'Right, madam,' said Grant, closing my bedroom door firmly at her back and advancing. 'Let's see what's happened under that hat.'

Nothing tremendously out of the ordinary, was the judgement, but the sight of my nails had Grant fanning herself and calling for salts.

'What have you been at?' she squeaked, turning my hands over and back in her own and shaking her head. 'What have you been doing?'

'I hardly know,' I answered, a little nonplussed, if I am honest, at how blackened and grimy they were and sheepishly hoping that the sparse, smoky candles in the dining hall at Cairnbulg had hidden them from the two sober Brodies the evening before. The third, less sober Brodie would not have noticed, I am sure. 'I've hardly touched the monkey and I haven't unwrapped a hot potato straight from the fire ash since last Friday. I can't think how I've got so filthy.' I stopped shy of an out and out apology, which might in ordinary circumstances have put Grant out of humor, but she was very keen, I think, to hear about the monkey (and the potatoes) so she contented herself with a fond shake of her head and went to get two bowls of hot lemon for me to plonk my arms in while I bathed.

'And the caravans themselves are quite spotless,' I told her, once I was back and at my table wrapped in a dressing gown. This was one of Grant's own favourite terms of praise. 'Very neatly organised inside, like those wonderful old steamer trunks. I miss those.'

'You and me both,' said Grant. 'Madam. I loved filling your trunks for a voyage in the good old days. It was the nearest thing I've ever had to a doll's house. A place for everything and everything in its place.'

Well I remembered it; when such divertissements were part of my life in my early married years Grant used to plan my wardrobe down to the last boot button and prided herself on packing more completely different ensembles—costumes, she called them, harking back to her theatrical days—than any other woman on board could believe or live up to. Most gratifying of all to her, I always suspected, was the fact that she could swat away any of my puny attempts to have a say in matters. If I suggested some frock other than she had laid out for me, her face would close up as though on a drawstring and she would say: 'Can't, madam, I didn't pack it,' or 'No, madam, we're saving that for Saturday night and if we wear it now, we'll have to go to the ball in the figured silk with the wrong shoes.'

'They sound civilised enough, anyway, circus or no,' said Grant. 'When we heard about the poor girl, we did wonder.'

'What *did* you hear?' I asked, not expecting much, for if there were a single grain of truth amongst the cloud of gossipy chaff that must have been carried over the hills to Gilverton, I should be surprised to hear it.

'That the poor love fell to her death and the elephant took to the woods and the heartless so-and-sos just kept right on with the show, juggling and tumbling and what have you except for one clown ran after the elephant because it was worth more to the ringmaster than what the poor girl was, and her his own flesh and blood. And that they only called the police to get their names in the papers for a bit of free advertising of how dangerous the acts are, otherwise they'd just have buried her in the woods like all the others and say no more about it. But if they keep their houses clean, they can't be all bad.'

My head was reeling, but I made an effort to be fair.

'She did fall and hit her head as far as we know,' I said. 'But it was a pony, not an elephant, and they only kept going until someone found her and they hated the police being there. As far from enjoying the drama as could ever be imagined. And as for heartless, the circus boss has said the pony is to be

272

shot, although the girl who died *isn't* one of the family and wasn't even much of a favourite with the rest of them.'

Grant turned on a sixpence.

'What? They can't even bite their tongues and say they liked her now she's dead and gone? Oh, that's cold, madam, isn't it? And the poor pony! Still, I daresay there's a lot of eating in it and they're all foreigners, aren't they?'

*   *   *

I was in bed that night, still reliving the last thrilling moments of *The Eagle*, when I heard a scuffling and whispering outside my door. Bunty wrinkled her brow at me, wondering whether to bark, and I shushed her, put a marker in my book and waited, hoping that whoever it was would fail to summon the courage and creep off again. I often wish we had a housekeeper at Gilverton, for maids in torment have woken me in the night fairly regularly over the years having run through their other options and found them wanting. I was led by my own mother, upon my marriage, in supposing a cook and butler quite sufficient for the household's needs, but I overlooked the role of the housekeeper as a kind of matron to the lower servants; a service my own very motherly mother never minded taking upon herself but one which chafes at me like horsehair.

This evening, I was not to be lucky and at length there came a timorous knocking. Bunty sat up, towering over me on the bed, and wriggled her rear end against the blankets in anticipation.

'Come in,' I called. 'If you must,' I added under

my breath, and I turned up the gas and laid my
book aside.

It was not however a stricken girl and her
quaking companion who stole inside, white-faced
and knees knocking, but my own two sons, whose
knees under the striped flannel might be still but
who were certainly white-faced enough, with
invisible lips and purple smudges under their eyes,
although whether from trepidation or from killing
deer was not immediately clear. I should like to
think that the sight of their prey crumpling to the
heathery ground could turn them pale, somehow. I
do not mind the stag shoots in summer but I loathe
it when my menfolk go off to shoot does and come
back grinning.

'What is it?' I asked them. 'Where's Nanny?'

'We wanted to ask you something, Mother,'
Donald said.

'Can't it wait till morning?'

'Not really,' said Teddy. 'Maureen said that
Nanny told her that Mrs Tilling said at supper that
Grant told everyone at tea that you said to her that
. . . is it true, Mother? Has Harlequin been shot?'

'Is this what can't wait until tomorrow?' I asked
them.

'You must tell us, Mother,' said Donald. 'We
can't sleep until we know.'

'And probably not after either or ever again.'

'Now, don't be silly,' I said. 'If there is one thing
I cannot abide it's sentimentality about animals.
It's one thing that Daddy and . . . that is, Daddy
and I are in complete agreement there.' Donald
and Teddy were not bold enough to glance at
Bunty, asleep again now, with her head on my
knees, but I could tell that they wanted to. 'Yes,

Harlequin is to be shot,' I went on rather more brusquely than otherwise I might have, 'although he hadn't been when I was at the circus earlier—but there is no call for you two to moon about it.'

'We're not mooning,' said Donald, and he did sound genuinely stricken, I must say. 'Is he . . . Are they shooting him because of his funny turn? Because he ran off?'

'You must understand, boys,' I said, rather more gently, 'that a circus pony has to be as solid as rock, it's not like a naughty pony that you or I might put up with because we love him and just make sure to wear a hat and keep off the hard roads. If one is standing on his back on one tiptoe and cantering round and round one must be able to trust him with one's life. Literally, with one's life. The one you should be sorry for is poor Ana. Think of that.'

Both boys bowed their heads, letting their long forelocks hang in front of them. Donald nudged Teddy and Teddy nudged Donald back. In the end they both looked up again together.

'But he might not be shot yet?' Teddy said.

'*I* don't know,' I said, losing patience. 'I shall find out for you tomorrow.'

'Because he didn't,' Donald said, suddenly rushing forward and putting both hands flat on the bed. Bunty rolled over to look at him. 'He didn't have a brainstorm or even anything. He didn't take off, Mother.'

'And we don't want him to die.'

I stared at them for a moment before speaking again.

'Are you telling me that you lied?'

'Well, you've always taught us not to say that

someone lied, Mother. You always taught us to say that they "told an untruth".'

'Yes, Donald my dear, thank you for the lecture,' I said, 'but I've also always taught you not to tell untruths, haven't I? You'd better explain exactly what happened.'

'It was Mr Cooke,' said Teddy. 'After everything went wrong that night. After Inya screamed and everyone left and you told us to stay put, remember? Well, we stayed put and Mr Cooke came back, snorting like a dragon and glaring, thrashing his whip and he saw us and asked us what had happened.'

'Well, he asked us if we lifted the box,' said Donald. 'Except he called it the dash box.'

'Do you mean that he swore at you?'

'Like anything. He was beside himself. Worse than Rumpelstiltskin.'

'Don't try to be to be sweet, Teddy. This is hardly the time. What letter did it start with?'

'B,' said Teddy.

'All right, so he asked you if you had lifted the bloody box, then. Don't be prim, boys—it's most unappealing.'

'Yes, he asked us that and honestly, Mother, if you could have seen him. He was towering over us, smacking his whip against his legs and gnashing his teeth. He looked ready to kill us if we admitted that we had.'

'So you lied. You said you hadn't.'

There was a long, confirming silence.

'And then you lied to me.'

Another silence.

'And then—good Lord—you lied to the police and when Inspector Hutchinson saw through it and tried to penetrate those bed knobs you have on top of your necks instead of heads, you toned down the nonsense but stuck with the lie.'

Great fat tears of shame were wobbling on Teddy's lower lashes by now and Donald's shoulders had slumped so far that I wondered his dressing gown didn't slip off them and land on the floor.

'I shall have to tell Daddy.' Four beseeching eyes met mine. 'At least. And Inspector Hutchinson. If not your housemaster too. I am thoroughly disgusted with the pair of you.' The tears spilled at last and splashed down Teddy's pyjama front. Donald screwed up his eyes and scrubbed his nose with the heel of his hand.

'Will we go to jail?' said Teddy. Donald, with a faint return of spirit, told him to shut up but looked at me for corroboration.

'Of course not,' I said. 'But your names will copied down in a . . . in a big ledger at the police station and kept there, on file, in case you ever do anything so naughty ever again.' I was only trying to frighten them but as I spoke I began to wonder whether it might not be true and I hoped that I should be able, in conscience, to keep it from Inspector Hutchinson after all. 'Now, without embellishments or omissions, if you please, will you tell me what really happened?'

'Of course,' said Donald. 'We're really very sorry, Mother. What actually happened is that Anastasia came past and gave us the nod.'

'Meaning we had to lift the box for her to go out next time round, you know.'

'So we did and off she went and we put it back again.'

'And how did she look? When she nodded to you?'

They considered this for a moment and it was a relief to me to see that they really were trying to remember and not just deciding what to say.

'She looked a bit alarmed, didn't she, Ted?'

'Well, I'd say surprised, rather than alarmed. Alarmed is too dramatic-sounding. I'd say she was unpleasantly surprised.'

'I agree,' said Donald.

'Honestly? She'd had some kind of nasty surprise? You're not just—'

'No, Mother, we're not just anything. We've learned our lesson, really.'

'Hmm,' I said. 'It's Harlequin who's learned your lesson, poor thing.'

At this they drooped again and I packed them off to bed, hoping that they would toss and turn all night thinking about him.

I myself spent a good hour, turning this way and that and punching my pillows until Bunty gave a long protesting moan and persuaded me to lie at peace. What a pair of goops I seemed to have introduced into the world, a world already well served with them and in no need of two more. A pair of what the army calls yes-men with withering disdain (even though it produces most of them), kowtowing to Pa Cooke, making up fluffy stories for me, not having the courage to come clean to Hutchinson and only being stopped in their tricks by soppiness about the damned pony. Well, I was jolly well going to let them sweat for a few days before I told them it would be our secret. I did not care to hear Hugh's views on the matter and of course, the police and housemaster had only ever been a little—warranted—bluster of my own.

14

All the same, I set off rather earlier than usual the next morning and felt a great weight lift off my chest when I tiptoed into the stable tent and saw Harlequin tugging at his hay.

'Oh, good boy,' I told him and rubbed the stiff nap on his nose. He gazed at me from melted-chocolate eyes and chewed calmly. I patted a few of the liberty horses too, having been brought up not to have stable favourites, but they were not much interested in the giving and receiving of affection—typical beauties, who often do prefer to be admired from afar—and, although they submitted, their black eyes flashed and they paddled the ground with impatience until I gave up and returned to Harlequin.

'What a lovely boy,' I told him. 'Best of the bunch.'

'He is that,' came a voice from inside the stall, making me jump. Groaning, Pa Cooke rose from the straw and brushed himself down.

'Have you been here all night?' I asked him.

'Not the first time,' he said. 'Least I could do.' He stroked Harlequin firmly and I thought I could see the sheen of a tear in his eye. 'And I'll not have been missed in the wagon, anyway.'

'Well, I have very good news for you,' I said. Quickly, I brought him up to date with the true history of Anastasia's last exit and my offspring's failings. 'The question is: do we need to tell

Inspector Hutchinson?' Pa Cooke watched me with held breath. 'Would he begin to doubt his conclusion if he knew that Anastasia was not out of control of her horse at all but had decided to leave the ring of her own accord? We already thought it unlikely that she would fall so badly, but if Harlequin was in his usual gentle frame of mind ... do you see?'

'I do, I do,' said Pa. 'Aye. If she was in control of her pony. I do see.'

'But on another point,' I said. 'At least this chap is reprieved.' There was a silence at that. 'Isn't he? I mean, there's no need to do away with him now.' Still Pa said nothing. He opened the stall gate and stepped out to stand beside me.

'Time was a boss-man could do what he liked and never dream of ocht but the respect that's due him,' he said, which was cryptic enough to puzzle me, but he went on and things became clear. 'Times being what they are, though, if I go back on my word now there'll be nothing but smirks and whispers all winter, and all of them saying I'm an old man and needing my leisure.'

'I had no idea circuses were such hotbeds of mutiny,' I said.

'No more had I, lass,' said Pa.

Thus, somehow, Pa Cooke wrung out of me an agreement that he would spare Harlequin but that, to safeguard his standing amongst his rebellious crew, it would all be done on the quiet-like.

'And speaking of which,' he concluded, with a great air of magnanimity, 'I don't see no need to go blabbing on to the police. Your secret—your lads' secret, I should say—is safe with me.'

'I'm not at all sure I *want* their grubby little

280

secret kept safe,' I said. 'They have a lesson to learn, after all. And besides . . .' I wound down into silence; what I was thinking was that the very fact of Pa's eagerness to sweep the new-found facts back under the carpet was a sign that he should not be allowed to. 'But very well,' I concluded at last, 'for the time being. But on one condition only. That I continue, that is to say *redouble*, my efforts. And that if I make any material discoveries, any discoveries *ad hominem*, we dissolve our pact.' Mr Cooke stared at me so I paraphrased. 'If we find out who done it I shop him.' My sons—or their reading tastes, at least—were good for something.

'See this though, missus?' said Pa, rubbing his face roughly. 'What worries me is that, if you go lifting stones, you're going to find a sight more than you're looking for, you know that?'

'And so I put the stones gently back down again,' I said.

*   *   *

'Shall I give the view halloo?' said Alec, who was waiting for me outside, propped against the wing of the Cowley, filling his pipe.

'A cautious tally-ho, anyway,' I said, 'although I'm annoyed to hear that I hide it so badly. Come with me.'

As I led him to the performing tent, I regaled him with the overnight news. He murmured, 'Oh, jolly good, Dan,' to hear of Harlequin's ensured survival and gave a restrained 'Dear me' in reference to my sons, but otherwise bore the revelations so calmly that I wondered if he had missed the point of them.

'You should give bulletins on ticker-tape, really,' was his overall pronouncement once I was done.

'You do see, don't you,' I demanded, 'the implications of Ana deciding to dash out of the ring? She must have seen something which frightened her.'

'Or offended her or angered her, yes.'

'Oh. You do see.' I am grateful, as a rule, that Alec is so swift on the uptake. 'So we must ask ourselves *what* she saw.'

'The fastest set in all of Perthshire, the Wilsons, you and me,' said Alec.

I sat down on the bench where I had been on the night of the show and looked around me. The tent was as dankly cold as a dungeon today, impossible to believe that it was wood and canvas and that it had ever dazzled and resounded with lights and song. Alec sat down and leaned back against the bench in the tier behind him.

'She had seen me before,' I said. 'So I'm in the clear and I'll do you the honour of assuming it wasn't you who put the willies up her. But it could have been anyone else.'

'Unlikely. They're an unprepossessing lot but it's hard to see why any of them should cause panic.'

'If she knew the person and didn't want to be recognised.'

'Who, though?'

'Someone from her mysterious past, I suppose. An old enemy? A wronged lover? Someone she had harmed in some way?'

'Seems pretty thin,' said Alec. 'But if you're right, we'd be down to three possibilities.'

'Would we?' I said. 'That's quick work. There

were dozens of us.'

'But only Robin Laurie, Albert Wilson or Ina Wilson could have slipped out without being seen. All the others were in front of you and me.'

'But then she knew the Wilsons already—or at least had met them, had seen them.'

'Had she? Are you sure?'

I thought about it briefly and the possibilities were most appealing. 'Gosh,' I said. 'Maybe not, because *something's* up with Ina. This different mood she's been in ever since the murder, if murder it is, is bothering me. If she had spotted her old enemy Anastasia around the camp but hadn't been spotted back, and had planned to bump her off . . . and actually it makes one wonder about Mr too. About the whole set-up, I mean. It's always seemed odd that he'd dragged a circus all the way up here and marooned them. What if he did it to get Anastasia into his clutches?'

'Albert Wilson?' said Alec, grinning. 'A ravager of maidens and a murderer of them? Come off it, darling. Robin Laurie, perhaps, but not little Mr Wilson.'

'But it can't have been Robin,' I said, 'because even though Ina slipped out for a moment she would have seen him either going or coming back again, wouldn't she? And actually, she'd have seen Albert too. And anyway, why would Robin Laurie kill a circus rider?'

'Why would anyone? Why would Ina Wilson? Or Albert? But there at least your point about his wife seeing him can be batted away. Wouldn't she lie for him? If Albert Wilson enticed the circus here to bump off Anastasia—another fragrant expression, Dandy; I do cherish them—perhaps his wife knew and approved the plan.'

'But why on earth would they let Robin Laurie fill the place with guests? And why would Albert pick such a moment to do it? And such an unlikely way too.'

Alec lifted his hand and shushed me, frowning as he does to let me know that he is thinking.

'Perhaps,' he said at last, 'Albert Wilson planned to kill Anastasia. Ina knew and approved. Albert saw Laurie and Co. as just what they were—distractions, camouflage—and that's why Ina was so livid to have Laurie arrive! But it worked and Ana is dead and that's why Ina is full of the joys.'

'But Robin Laurie would have seen Albert leave the tent. And anyway, no one in his right mind would hatch a plan to kill someone bare-handed by bashing her head against the frozen ground.'

'Perhaps he didn't,' said Alec. 'Perhaps he had a knife or a rope but he didn't need to use them. Perhaps he is hugging himself in delight at his luck.'

'Revolting!' I said. 'And why exactly would Robin keep quiet?'

'No reason at all that I can imagine,' said Alec. 'But we're going round in circles, Dandy. Let's at least find out if the Wilsons had met her. And she them.'

'Yes,' I agreed. 'I need to go to the castle anyway. I want to borrow their telephone and ring home.'

Alec looked enquiringly at me.

'I need to speak to . . . Oh Lord, a groom, really. But how could one engineer that? I suppose it'll have to be Grant, sworn to secrecy. As though she needed another stick to beat me with.'

284

'What are you talking about?' Alec said.

'Harlequin is coming to stay with us until all of this is over,' I explained. 'But to spare Pa's blushes, he's being removed from Benachally in the knacker's van.'

'Is there such a thing?' said Alec.

'A splendid one,' I told him. 'Peter McTurk—a black van with gold writing. You must have seen it. He ranges the length and breadth of the county but he lives in Bridge of Cally not five miles away. So I need to warn the head groom and beg him to keep quiet for me.'

'I should say you do,' said Alec, wide-eyed, highly diverted. 'A pony being delivered out of the knacker's van and into the stables at Gilverton? Hugh would explode, darling. Literally explode. You'd be a widow by tea.'

*   *   *

Albert was at home and so Ina, inevitably, was in her chair, under her rug, with her shawl about her shoulders and her feet up on a stool. Even still, how could Albert Wilson fail to see the change in her? Not only were her cheeks still blooming, her movements had an animation about them I had never seen; she plaited the fringes of her rug and polished the gilt studs on the scrolls of her chair arm with a restless fingertip and was altogether quite unlike the girl who always before had lain on her chaise like a length of dough in its tin, her hands in her lap as dead as a pair of empty gloves forgotten there.

Albert smiled cautiously at Alec and me but, for a wriggling, awkward moment, no one spoke.

285

'Any news of a funeral?' said Alec at last. As an opener in the general sense it was a bit of a brick, but for our purposes I thought it an excellent one.

'Poor girl,' said Albert. 'Thursday. Christmas Eve. Of course, I'm going to foot the bill and she will be buried here.'

'That's extraordinarily generous of you,' I said, grasping the opportunity to get straight to the point. 'You had got to know her well, then?'

'No,' said Albert Wilson. 'Not at all.'

'You mean you'd never seen her before the show that night?'

'Oh, I'd seen her. I had a short conversation with her one day. I asked about her horse and she was quite rude in reply. Really most impolite which . . . why?' he finished abruptly, staring at me. It was quite a convincing tack: if guilty, surely he would either have refused to answer or have demanded an explanation for the question right away. This had the air of him thinking on his feet and voicing his thoughts innocently as they came.

I wished I had had the chance to mull over my next move with Alec in private, but I was almost sure I was right. I saw no reason that an innocent Wilson should not hear the truth and, on the other hand, if he did have something to hide his reaction would be worth getting. So I cleared my throat and spoke up.

'I'm investigating the murder,' I said. 'For the Cookes.' And I let it settle, watching Albert very closely, before going on. 'I was engaged to investigate another, although possibly related matter, but then the murder happened and I . . . folded it into my brief.'

'You're invest . . .' said Wilson. He was gaping

286

like a cod. 'Murder? But it was an accident. The police have gone. We're having the funeral and Mr Cooke has even said that he'll put on another show. How can you be speaking of murder and why would you . . . even if . . . what . . . ?' He ran out of breath or ideas, or perhaps both.

'I think the police have got it wrong,' I told him cheerfully. 'And if I find any solid evidence I shall go and tell them so.'

'You astonish me,' Wilson said. 'I can hardly credit it.' He stared and blinked for a bit, but went on at last: 'As I'm sure you will appreciate, I sincerely hope the police are right and you are mistaken, but I shall give you every assistance.' There was something almost noble about the way he said it. 'Now, why did you want to know if I was acquainted with—Oh, my!' Albert Wilson rose to his feet as the penny dropped as though he and it were on a see-saw. 'Oh, dear! Oh, my!'

'Just to strike you off the list of suspects, naturally,' said Alec, which only upset Wilson even more.

'List of suspects?' he wailed and sank back down. It was quite some time before he roused himself, but when he did the noble note was back mixed with just a pinch of petulance. 'I cannot tell you anything about the unfortunate girl. I didn't know her at all, only spoke to her that once. I don't remember anything else. Mrs Cooke told me about the artistes—she's a prodigious talker—but there were no introductions.'

'As we thought,' I said, still very brisk. 'Well, thank you, Mr Wilson. That's no end of help.' I had been hoping that my tone of dismissal would see him off even though I was the guest in his

287

house and indeed he rose to his feet again and, bowing slightly, took off at a trot to where the spiral staircase led to the sanctuary of his business room. I caught Alec's eye as he left and we exchanged an agreement. That, we were both assured, had been completely genuine. Albert Wilson was not our man.

'Poor Albert,' said Ina, when he was gone. 'You have a mischievous streak, Dandy, don't you.'

'And now, for the sake of completeness, you understand,' said Alec, 'how about you, Mrs Wilson, if you don't mind? What can you tell us about Anastasia?'

'I adored her,' said Ina. 'I adore all of them.'

'You did know her then? You had talked to her and she to you?'

'Of course,' Ina said, looking rather puzzled at the question. 'I had become very close to her, as a matter of fact. She and I could have been great friends.'

'Really?' I said. 'I found her difficult the only time I spoke to her at length.'

'She was circus,' said Ina. 'No less part of it for not being born there. More so, if anything. It takes a splendid kind of girl to do what she did, wouldn't you say?'

*　　*　　*

'So,' said Alec, when we were alone again. 'We believe Albert.'

'Oh, Albert!' I said, unable not to laugh at the memory.

'Do we believe Ina?'

'I'm less sure,' I admitted. 'There was something

288

very odd about what she said, or at least about the way she said it, and I never saw any sign of this bosom friendship. Over-egging the pudding, if you ask me, and only making herself look more suspicious in the end.'

'It's easy enough to check,' said Alec. 'Someone must have seen them if they had been together enough to get as chummy as all that.'

*   *   *

I could hardly remember the time when I had looked around the little ring of wagons and found it so cosy and charming. Now, they pressed inwards, each little window like a single eye watching the others. The circus people were going about their business with their heads bent and their mouths drawn down and every door was closed tight. My hand shook as I knocked at the Wolfs' wagon, the nearest to Ana's and the obvious place to start.

Lally Wolf was sitting on her heels in the middle of the floor rummaging in a small trunk and sending wafts of camphor into the air.

'Here they are,' she said, dragging out a pair of enormous black trousers and holding them up. 'I'll get a suit for Tom out of these no trouble. Funeral's tomorrow and my babbies haven't a stitch of black to their names.'

'I'm sorry to be disturbing you, Mrs Wolf.'

'No, you're fine there,' she said. 'Life goes on. We've a show to do right after we lay her, you know. Life goes on with the good and the bad all mixed in together.'

'A show?'

'Our show,' said Mrs Wolf. 'For them Wilsons. Like what we was always meant to.'

'Actually, it was the Wilsons I wanted to ask you about. Well, Mrs Wilson, anyway. About her friendship with Anastasia.'

'What friendship's that?' said Mrs Wolf. 'My wagon looks right over at Ana's and I never saw that Wilson donah going round there, and no more did Bill neither, because he'd of said—gossip that he is and he took an interest in the lass. Too much of a one, if anyone's asking me.'

*　　　*　　　*

Bill Wolf treated me to a long and speculative look, when I approached him.

'The Tober-omey's donah?' he said. 'What's got you on to that?'

'Do you know anything?' I asked him. 'If you really know something for sure, Bill, you must tell me. In all conscience, you must.'

He shook his head.

'I know plenty and I say nothing,' he rumbled. 'I've learned my lesson. You stick your neck out and it gets you that.' He snapped his fingers in my face, turned on his heel and left me. 'Anyway,' he said, over his shoulder, 'Charlie Cooke's the one to ask about Ana. Not me.'

*　　　*　　　*

'Oh, can you not just leave us be?' said Charlie. 'Let us lay her to her rest. It's bad enough having to go straight from the graveside to do a show.'

'It does seem callous of Mr Wilson to ask you,' I

290

said. 'And if Mrs Wilson was fond of Ana I can't understand her letting it happen.'

'Never you mind about Wilson,' said Charlie. 'It'll not be him making us all jump.'

'Your brother?' I guessed.

'He thinks he's showing himself strong,' said Charlie. 'Same as with those lads of his—down on them so hard, he lost them. And that prad. The whole show.'

'Yet each man kills the thing he loves,' I said half to myself.

'That's it exactly, missus,' said Charlie, and his eyes filled with tears.

'Mr Cooke,' I said. 'If you know something definite, you can tell me in the strictest confidence, but you must tell me. I can tell Inspector Hutchinson and we can stop the funeral.'

That made him look up at me. His eyes were still shining but he smiled.

'That's right,' he said. 'That's your way, isn't it? Killing each other for a sideways look. But it's not circus.'

'Well, to be fair,' I said, 'it's not *anyone*.'

'What? I read the papers, you know. Affairs, inheritance, insurance, blackmail. Never a Sunday goes by but there's not some babby killing its own pa for money or some chav squeezing the life out of his lady love for dancing with a sailor. But it's not the circus way.'

With some difficulty, I swallowed my affront.

'So what *did* you mean?' I said.

'I'm a disappointed man, missus,' he said, 'never married and never will now, and I'm old enough to know that life isn't a fairy tale. Or I should be anyway. My brother's the boss of this show and if I

291

can't give him all the loyalty and buttoned lips he deserves then who can, eh? I'm old enough to know better.'

'Rather older than him, in fact,' I said as gently as I could. 'Actually the head of the family, isn't that so?'

'Oh, you heard that, did you?' said Charlie Cooke. 'Well, it's no secret. Aye, and I thought as late as this it might all come good for me.'

'How's that, Mr Cooke?' I asked him, but he only shook his head and sighed.

'No fool like an old fool,' he said.

*   *   *

At first I could not see Topsy; the ring was empty, the air still, and then I jumped at the sound of her voice floating down from the dome of the roof.

'Are you after me, madam?' She was knotting ropes on to the beam.

'A brief word,' I said. My voice sounded strange from the way my head was thrown back, very deep and threatening, not at all conducive to a fruitful interview. 'Are you up there for the duration?' I said. 'Or can you come down?'

'If only,' said Topsy. 'Way things are these days I wish I *could* just stay up here out of it all. Mind out there, madam, a minute.'

I stepped back towards the ring fence and Topsy sent two ropes tumbling down to hang with their looped ends dancing above the ring. Then she shuffled along the beam and grasped the pole to climb down to me.

'Trouble is,' she went on, joining me on the ground and going to tug on the ropes, 'you still see

292

it all even if you're up and away. See even more of it from up there sometimes.'

She spoke carelessly enough, but her words struck me.

'You don't mean . . . ? You didn't see what happened to Ana that night, did you?'

'No,' said Topsy. 'Don't know whether to say "worse luck" or "thank God", mind. If I'd have turned me round I could have seen it, but I was facing out. Never saw a thing. And I was down before anyone knew what had happened.'

'A pity,' I said. 'Anyway, what I wanted to ask you, Topsy, was something else you might have seen, actually. Mrs Wilson and Anastasia. Did you ever see them together?'

'Mrs Wilson?' said Topsy. She had been tying wooden rings to the ends of her ropes with a series of complicated knots, but she stopped now and stared at me. 'Sure it makes more sense than any of us, but why?'

'I'm only asking if they knew one another,' I insisted, but there was no fooling Topsy.

'I'm keeping out of it,' she said. 'I don't know what happened or what's happening now or what's going to, but I've done enough.'

'What have you done?'

She shook her head until her curls bounced.

'I thought I was so smart and I've just made a mess of everything.' She was beginning to sound ragged and looked as though she might cry. 'I can't help you, madam. I never saw a thing.'

*   *   *

I was getting precisely nowhere and was stirring up

not even hornets' nests, for at least hornets come right out and sting one in an honest fashion, but rather wisps of ghosts of hornets which threatened to sting but disappeared when one swatted at them. So I rapped rather more sharply than was warranted on Andrew Merryman's door and could hardly blame him for opening the top half and peering out rather than calling a welcome. When he saw who it was, though, he unfastened the bottom and waved me inside where, sitting down again, he looked like some kind of giant insect, his knees around his ears and his elbows out to the sides, while he stitched at an enormous patchwork garment with a tiny needle. There seemed to be much more sewing involved in a circus life than I could easily manage, even if I ever got used to the box-beds and ashy potatoes.

'A quick question, Mr Merryman,' I said. 'It's about Mrs Wilson and Anastasia, and how well they knew one another.'

'Hardly at all,' he said. 'Why?'

'You know that for a fact?'

'Yes. Why? Do you think Mrs Wilson would be in danger if Ana had confided something to her before she died?'

'Confided what?' I asked, astonished.

'I've no idea but why else would you be asking?'

I had to disagree with Alec; this was no dwam and the briskness seemed to strike up an answering briskness in me.

'I'm asking because despite the fact that the police have given up on Ana and she is to be buried and forgotten and all as you were, I'm still trying to solve a murder.'

'No one would have murdered her,' he said. 'It's

294

not circus.'

'Good Lord, not you too!' I cried.

'It's a hard thing to explain to an outsider,' he began.

'Oh, come now, Mr *Fanshawe*,' I said. 'If I am an outsider then so are you. And, more to the point, so is Mrs Wilson.'

'Mrs Wilson?' he said, looking puzzled. Then his mouth dropped open. 'Is that why you're asking about her? What on earth would make you think that Mrs Wilson had anything to do with it?'

'Honestly?' I asked. 'It's a straw and I'm clutching at it. Mrs Wilson . . . is not being herself. But then, no one is. You're not, Bill, Topsy, Pa, Charlie—everyone is hiding something.'

'How true,' said Andrew. 'And you missed out Tiny.'

*   *   *

'You've come from Andrew's, han't you?' said Tiny, crinkling his eyes at me. 'I can always tell. We've got a trick we play in t'big towns, sometimes. We put on our checked suits and yellow bowlers and do quick swaps in café windows. Get it? Some flatty looks over, sees Andrew, looks away and back, sees me, goes to get his mates and we swaps again. Nearabout caused a tram crash one time.'

'Wicked man,' I said, and Tiny gave a very convincing diabolical laugh and hugged himself.

'What can I do for you?' he asked presently.

'Confirm what is becoming very clear,' I replied. 'Anastasia was not a chum of Ina Wilson's, was she?'

295

Tiny shook his head as I had expected.

'No, but her man's laying on the funeral anyway,' he said. 'Did you know that? Should have been Cooke's that paid for it, like, but we're not in a way to insist. Coming to something, in't it, missus, when her nearest and dearest can't give her a proper goodbye. That's the least we should do.'

'You are very kind,' I said. 'But surely you—you, personally, I mean—are not scratching around for "the least you should do"?'

'Am I not?' he said, his face falling, deep lines forming on either side of his mouth. 'You're being too kind to me,' he said. 'Dazzled by my mesmerising looks and my charisma. But there I go again, see? I wasn't kind to that poor girl. Not at all. She needed to be took serious, to be cared for gentle, and I just joked and teased and used her lightly same as I do everyone. I'd have been better just to keep right out of her way, like the Russians did, and there was no love lost there. At least t'rest can make theirselves feel better by carrying her coffin tomorrow, but I'm not cut out for a pall-bearer, me.'

* * *

Zoya was alone in her wagon with Akilina, her youngest child. The little girl was sitting very still while her mother snipped with scissors at her wetted fringe.

'Forgive me stay busy,' said Zoya.

'While you work,' I said, settling myself down in the other chair, 'might I ask a few questions?'

'Of course,' Zoya said.

'I shan't say anything that might upset the little one,' I assured her, but she shrugged off my concern.

'Ilya has got not much of English,' she said. 'Kolya is so sure we will go home and our girls need to be Russian girls for then.'

'Very well,' I said. I was sorry that her mind was tending towards her 'beloved Mother Russia' given what I was planning to ask her, but I smiled encouragingly and pitched in.

'It's about Ana,' I began. Zoya interrupted me.

'I am patient woman,' she said. 'Everyone circus must be very patient, very steady, or never learn anything, see?' I nodded. 'But that one, "Anastasia", she make my blood to boil like black sugar spilled over.' It was a horribly apt phrase, even coming from this calm, pale woman bending over with her face so close to that of her daughter.

'I can see that she must have annoyed you.' I said. Zoya looked up at the inadequate word. 'Incensed you, I mean.' She looked down again and smiled at Akilina. 'What I need to ask is this. I'm just about sure of what the answer will be, but tell me: did you ever see any sign that Mrs Wilson was a friend of Anastasia?'

'Mrs Wilson? The lady from the castle? You think she killed Ana?'

'No, no,' I said. 'I just want to know if you ever saw them together. Or if Ana ever mentioned her.'

'Anastasia never spoke to me of anything,' said Zoya. 'She had too much pride and too much fear to speak to me.'

'Of course,' I said. 'You could have been her undoing in an instant.'

'Until very soon ago,' Zoya said, sitting back

297

and thinking about it. 'Some weeks, a month. Before we come here. Then she said to me one day: "I will reign over you, Madame Prebrezhensky. You shall see. You shall be sorry you ever to laughed at me, when I reign over you." That is what she said.'

'You must have been very angry,' I said.

'What, you think maybe I kill her?' said Zoya. 'You think all Russian just go kill everyone, hey?'

I began to clamour, shouting her down, but she was smiling at me.

'How?' she cried. 'How? Magic? Send a spell?' She closed her eyes and chanted a strange incantation in her sepulchral voice then opened her eyes wide and threw her arms up in the air like a falconer letting his hawk go. Akilina giggled.

'Of course not,' I said, thinking to myself that there was never a set of people in the world less prone to taking offence than these circus folk. Who else could one rather doggedly accuse of murder day after day only to have it brushed off with smiles.

Outside, I was looking around the ring of wagons wondering where to turn next, when I became aware that Akilina Prebrezhensky was standing at my side, looking up at me intently, her gaze all the more piercing given the severity of her mother's trimming. She licked her lips and spoke in a tiny, peeping voice.

'Missus,' she said. Her hand curled into mine as small and soft as a rabbit's paw and she pulled me backwards, pulled me outside the ring of wagons altogether, into the shadows where we would not be seen.

'Missus,' she said again. 'Me seed.'

'You seed?' I echoed. I did not want to be discouraging, but I could make nothing of that. Akilina pointed back over her shoulder towards her wagon and mimed to me, making heads of her hands and snapping her fingers and thumbs together rapidly like talking mouths. She pointed at me and made the mime again. It began to make sense.

'You understood what we were saying?' I said. 'In there?' She nodded hard.

'Me seed,' she said again. With the kind of prickling sensation one sometimes gets from large gulps of overly fizzy champagne, I felt illumination spread through me.

'You saw?' I whispered. She nodded again. She pointed at her own living wagon and mimed crouching at the window, her hands up under her chin as though grasping the windowsill over which she was peeping.

'What did you see, Akilina my darling?' I asked her. 'What did you see?' Akilina licked her lips again and took a couple of deep breaths, scraping for the words to tell me.

'Missus Lady . . . tchah!' she said, then she pointed frantically over her shoulder. I turned round.

'What? The stream? The water?' I was miming too now.

Akilina shook her head, stood high on her tiptoes and heaved her pointing hand over her head as though trying to throw a heavy object a long way. I thought about what was beyond the stream and the trees.

'The castle!' I said. 'You mean the lady from the castle? Mrs Wilson.'

Akilina clapped her hands and nodded, jumping up and down. She pointed to the performing tent and then walked her fingers away from it. And it was then that I realised, with a thump of excitement, that Alec, checking off his list of witnesses from the night of the show, had missed someone out after all.

'Yes, yes, you're quite right. Oh, you clever little girl. She left the tent.'

Then Akilina pointed at Ana's wagon and shook her head hard, her mouth pushed out in a pout and her brows low and angry.

'No!' she said. 'Not Ana! Lady no!'

That could hardly be clearer.

'She didn't hurt Ana?' I said, just to check. Akilina shook her head so hard that the rats' tails of her still-wet fringe banged against her head. Then her expression changed. She put her arms out and circled them as though embracing someone, closed her eyes and made loud kissing noises, swaying dreamily like Mary Pickford and Douglas Fairbanks. She was an accomplished little actress and it should have been squirm-inducing to watch, but just then I did not care.

'Who?' I asked. 'Who was she kissing?'

But Akilina was lost in her performance now and could not be halted. She mimed writing, sealing the letter with a kiss and blowing it into the air, where it became a bird and fluttered away, coming to earth a long way off, piercing the lover in the heart and making him swoon.

'All right,' I said, 'not just kissing, eh? Love?'

'Love,' she said and then began a new bout of really rather excellent silent acting. She breathed out hard four times, moving her head a little between breaths, and then she polished the four spots she had breathed upon. She swept the ground with a broom, shook out and laid a cloth upon a table, lovingly smoothing it, and set down upon it a lamp, also burnished in passing, which she then lit. Her meaning was clear.

'Love and marriage,' I concluded. 'I see. But who is it, darling? Who is it she loves? Who?'

Here, maddeningly, she stopped miming, stopped even pointing and spoke a stream of Russian, higher-pitched than one would have imagined Russian could be and at breakneck speed.

'What? Who? Slow down,' I said. 'In fact, no. Point. Where is he? What does he look like?' With my hands, I sketched a beard and a fat middle, spectacles and a long nose. Akilina gave me a pitying look—clearly unimpressed—and then set to herself. She held her hand up high above her head, as high as she could reach, then she smoothed back imaginary hair, plucked at a bow tie, twirled a walking stick and sauntered back and forth in front of me like Burlington Bertie from Bow.

'The tall gentleman in the beautiful suiting,' I said. 'Robin. Of course.'

*   *   *

My head was popping like fireworks with new ideas, zapping with every new connection like low branches touching a tram wire in a thunderstorm, but one thing was very clear. I squatted down, ignoring the sound of my skirt seam straining and splitting, and looked hard into Akilina's grey eyes.

I needed all my tiny store of miming talent now for, if Ina Wilson were out of the picture, there was no other possibility except that one of the circus folk was guilty after all. And that meant that this little girl, with what she knew, might be in danger.

I pointed at my chest and at Akilina's, put my finger to my lips and let out a long, very quiet, Sssssh!

Akilina turned a key in the middle of her mouth, took the key out and handed it to me. I put it in my pocket. We nodded again, and sealed the bargain by shaking hands. Then she stole away round the outside of the wagons to her own and I sidled off in the opposite direction feeling like a spy.

*   *   *

I found Alec without delay, but it was a considerable challenge to keep from blurting until we were right away from the tents and from all the wagons. I took him up to the pool at the foot of the waterfall where our voices would be drowned by the crashing of the water and where we could easily see anyone approaching.

'Earth-shattering news, darling,' I said, 'and yet, and yet, you're going to kick yourself when you hear it, because in the five minutes that I've known all kinds of odd puzzles have been fitting together.'

'Shall I go and get a snare drum from Mr Wolf?' said Alec and, although I had been all ready simply to tell him, his disdain in the face of my excitement turned me mulish and made me want to give him, as Nanny Palmer always used to say, 'a spoonful of porridge from yesterday's pan'. Unfortunately, Alec saw this plan forming and treated me to a withering look. 'Oh, all right then,' I said, 'and don't ever tell me I'm not an angel, because I'm far more of one than you deserve, frankly.'

'Get on with it, Dandy. It's freezing.'

'If Ina Wilson,' I began, 'is indeed looking forward to an imminent change in her life, the way you thought she was, I know what it is. She is, I should imagine, hoping to leave Albert to join her lover as soon as his circumstances resolve themselves.' I paused to allow the excitement to mount even further. 'I should imagine that she hopes to become, after her divorce and remarriage, and the death of her brother-in-law-to-be, the Marchioness of Buckie.'

Alec, who really is quite good value sometimes, gave a long low whistle with his eyebrows lost somewhere in his hair.

'How did you find out?' he said.

'They were seen. By Akilina Prebrezhensky, kneeling up in her bed looking out of her window at the stars on the night of the show.'

'Peeping through the banisters,' said Alec. 'A thing that all children do and all adults forget they do. Is she sure?'

'Absolutely, and she's a remarkably stout-hearted little person—I have not a shadow of a doubt on the matter. Ina and Robin crept out to a short tryst in the moonlight while no one was looking. And that was the reason he was so utterly pole-axed by me going and telling him I turned around and asking him about Ina leaving and what he saw!'

'He must have thought you were threatening

him with exposure,' said Alec, beginning to smile about it.

'And that's why he was so unsure of what to tell me and why he suddenly turned on the charm—unable to believe his luck that I didn't know and trying to stop me thinking about it any more.'

'They were taking a bit of a risk, weren't they? Albert was right there in the tent. What if he had turned around?'

'Well, maybe it wasn't a tryst exactly,' I said. 'Maybe Ina dragged Robin out to scold him about turning up there. It was her only chance to get him on his own. And she *was* furious with him, livid.'

'Which all of a sudden begins to make sense, doesn't it?' said Alec, nodding. 'We never could get to the bottom of why she loathed him—the hints about the sickroom gossip never convinced me—but, of course, she was angry!'

'Besides, she does have a heart,' I said. 'She does care for Albert a little and even if she's leaving him she wasn't happy to see him be made such a fool of.'

'Not that he knew.'

'Yes, but he will, afterwards. He'll know then and he'll spend the rest of his life wincing about it.'

'He only has himself to blame,' said Alec, sounding rather heartless. 'He was never going to make her happy and as for all this nonsense since the 'flu—he's had a longer run with her than he deserved to, if you ask me.'

'I suppose so,' I said. 'And I suppose one can understand the attraction of Robin—when one has Albert Wilson to set him against, I mean.'

'I wonder how they met,' said Alec. 'And when.'

I gasped.

'I've just realised something,' I said. 'Hugh told me that Robin Laurie was engaged once to what Hugh described as "a very ordinary Miss"—I remember the phrase he used most particularly because I thought it was beyond vulgar—and that he broke it off hoping for better things. But perhaps it wasn't that.'

'You mean perhaps he broke it off in case his brother disinherited him on account of Ina's inferiority?'

'Exactly. Were the shades of Cullen to be thus polluted and all that.'

'*Could* he disinherit him?'

'Very possibly,' I said. 'I don't go as far as to say I listen when Hugh regales me with thrilling tales of Scotch succession but some of it has seeped in over the years. You wouldn't believe the shenanigans, if I told you.'

'And so the lovers parted to wait for the old boy to die.'

'Only Ina was offended and married Albert Wilson just to anger Robin. Or because she knew he would be running fast and loose with every chorus girl he could lay his hands on and this was the only way she could pay him back for it.'

'Hang on, though,' said Alec. 'The Buckie wife and children died of influenza and Ina was already married by then.'

'A divorcee!' I cried. 'Even better.'

'And so Ina Wilson is crossed off our list of suspects once and for all,' Alec said. He sounded exceedingly gloomy about it. 'And it's back to the circus folk.' He sighed. 'Are we still thinking it was a booby trap set by someone who was in the ring when she fell? Or do we think it was someone backstage and someone else is lying for him?'

'I don't know,' I said, 'but they are tremendously loyal to one another and surely *would* lie. And as for getting her off her horse or setting a trap and then spiriting it away . . . when one thinks about what that would need, doesn't it come down to things like split-second timing, sleight-of-hand, physical strength . . .'

'Misdirection of the eye,' added Alec miserably. 'Tiny and Andrew have promised to teach me some of the basic stuff if I'll stay on after tea. They've been delighting to show me what they can do in plain view without being seen, just by making everyone look elsewhere. Oh, Dandy, don't you just hate this sometimes?'

15

There was rather a difficult telephone call to be made when I got home, and however I rehearsed it while ringing up and waiting for the butler to fetch his mistress, I could not make it sound any less of a humiliation.

'Ina?' I said, when at last she came on. 'It's Dandy. Darling, I'm sorry, but I must beg a favour of you. Could you send someone down to the circus and see if Alec Osborne is still there and if he is could he please bring Bunty home? I've left her. Yes, I know. I know. I can't imagine, except that I was terribly distracted.'

I was desperate to ring off, not only so that she could dispatch the message, but out of embarrassment to be talking to her, knowing what

I knew and knowing, moreover, what I had so recently suspected, but Ina was in a chattering mood and short of blatant rudeness I could not get rid of her.

'You've heard about tomorrow night, I suppose?' she said. 'The show?'

'I did,' I said. 'Can't you persuade Albert that it's too cruel to put them through it?'

'Albert? He would happily never go near the place again. It was Pa's idea—meant to rally them all after their loss. We're not invited to the funeral—circus only, apparently, and I don't count after only this much time and not actually living there. So the least we can do is go along and cheer them afterwards. You must come. I won't accept a refusal.'

I was not sure how to respond to this new, strikingly different Ina, unable as I was to forget its source, but I think she had a moment's clarity of her own just then and gave a small self-deprecating laugh.

'You must be wondering what's going on with me, Dandy,' she said.

'Not at all,' I said. 'It's good to hear you in such . . . fettle.'

'Fettle!' crowed Ina. 'Well, I haven't lost my mind in case you're worried. I've found it. I've . . . the truth is . . . and you mustn't tell a soul, just yet . . .'

'I know, dear,' I said. 'I guessed. I am a detective after all.'

There was a short silence during which I could hear Ina breathing rather hard.

'Well?' she replied at last. 'What do you think?'

'It's a big change,' I said, feeling the inadequacy

of the words most acutely. 'And you must be ready for some opprobrium. The world is not a kind place, as I'm sure you know.'

'I don't care,' said Ina. 'I love him and, besides, I'm dying here.'

I am no admirer of such penny-paper outpourings and had had more than enough of them at Buckie on Monday afternoon, so I should gladly have let the matter drop, but Ina pressed me.

'Do you think I'm a fool, Dandy?'

I was about to deliver a little vague wittering, but then the question struck me as one deserving of an answer. Did I think she was foolish, to leave the blameless but soul-destroying Albert for the much more dashing but horribly unsteady Robin? To leave the joke of her life at Benachally for the scandal of her life at Cullen? What would I do in her shoes? The plain fact was that I should never have stepped into her shoes: I should never have married Wilson and no matter how neatly he could turn on the charm like a gas lamp when its light was needed I should not choose to be Robin Laurie's consort either. For a moment I felt—and it was a very odd feeling—rather grateful for Hugh.

'I think life is always a matter of considerable compromise,' I said, 'no matter where our lot falls. You will have a great deal to put up with—I hope I don't speak too frankly?'

'Not at all.'

'But you have obviously decided you can take all that in your stride and no one can deny that there are going to be enormous . . .' I wanted to say rewards, but it sounded too baldly financial for

308

words. ' . . . silver linings,' I concluded at last.

'Yes,' said Ina, dreamily. 'He's not . . . or rather the situation is not . . . what I ever foresaw, but I really do love him.'

With an inward hurrah I saw my sitting-room door handle turn and the door begin to open.

'Ina, so sorry, must dash, till tomorrow, lots of love, bye,' I said in one breath and put the receiver down on her gushing with a shudder and, if I am to be honest, a small wriggling thing in my breast which felt suspiciously like envy.

'One abandoned dog,' said Alec, standing in the doorway. Bunty moped into the room, gave me a withering look and curled up on the blue chair. 'I suppose it's not as bad as the time you left the children, but don't tell Hugh in case it sets him off again.'

'Hugh would be delighted if I left her there for ever,' I said. 'You never do believe what a churl he can be when no one else is listening. And don't be fooled by that.' I pointed at Bunty. 'She's just worn out from all the good behaviour. Now thank you for returning her and please stay for a drink, because I need at least one extra brain to help me with all of this.'

We had two drinks in all, enormous ones, but as Alec drained the last of his second one and chewed a thoughtful olive, we concluded together that while our martini cocktails might be clear and sparkling, our conclusions were mud.

'The thing is, of course,' I said, 'if someone did it then they are no doubt lying and so any part of what anyone told me today might be utter eyewash.'

Alec nodded.

'There's certainly plenty going on,' he said. 'I'd be happier, though, if amongst the "goings-on" there was something that looked like a motive.'

'But there is,' I insisted. 'They all so desperately want the circus to survive and Ana was just no end of trouble. She infuriated Pa, sent the Prebrezhenskys into a patriotic huff; she even seems to have got under Bill Wolf's skin somehow. There's three possible suspects. And she might have been playing a lot of very nasty tricks on Topsy. So Topsy or anyone who cares for Topsy might have done it. One way and another, between circus loyalty, revenge and sheer loathing, it really could have been any of them. And the way they keep insisting that it couldn't have been just makes me suspect them all the more.'

'Even Andrew's at it now,' Alec said. 'Nay, mister, murder just in't the Harrow way. Maddening.'

'All that said though,' I went on, 'I really do think we must give them peace tomorrow to take care of the funeral. Let's drive over together just in time for the show.'

Alec cleared his throat and shifted his feet before he answered.

'Actually, you'll have to do without me for the next day or two, Dan. Christmas, you know.'

I had forgotten—absolutely forgotten—and now began to gibber like a squirrel.

'Of course, how silly. Heavens, yes. You should start early. It's a terrible road. And how long are you staying? I'll catch up with you after New Year, I suppose.'

'Just until Boxing Day,' Alec said, 'then I'll be home again.' He grinned at me. 'And actually, since the show is practically a matinée and my invitation is for dinner, perhaps I *can* come along. And then set off to Pess straight from Benachally when the curtain comes down.'

I shrugged rather than jumping up and down in a display of girlish delight. If Alec was to pursue this Pess connection as far as bringing Celia home to Dunelgar and installing her there, then many adjustments might have to be made and it was not too soon to start them.

* * *

Practically a matinée was not how I should have described the timing of the show although it was not an evening gala either; curtain up in fact at the highly inconvenient hour of half-past four and so I decided that we were entitled to present ourselves at Benachally beforehand for tea. Thus it was that we happened to see the sorry end of the funeral procession straggling its way home as we traversed the park towards the castle. The undertaker was clopping along on his horse at the head of the rest, was in fact beginning to pull away from them as we passed. He nodded curtly, his many chins disappearing into the knot of his black scarf, and then looked quickly away, rather less sorrowful and more irritated than was strictly proper, as though he begrudged the service to the circus folk and was chagrined to have been seen by members of the county, carrying it out.

After him came the entirety of Cooke's, artistes, tent men, wives and children, in deepest black— albeit rather showy, shiny black in most cases as though a selection of ring costumes had been

311

turned to account as mourning. Ma Cooke in her bombazine and velvet trim, with black berries on her hat and jet droplets dancing at her ears, was as festive as could be and all the little Prebrezhensky girls, their heads covered with black lace tied under the chin and enormous silver buckles on their black patent shoes, had stepped straight from a fairy tale. Only Andrew Merryman looked like an ordinary gentleman dressed for sombre duty and this was almost as great a surprise; to see him in a dark suit, stiff collar and black tie, without any of the trappings of the circus, not so much as a spotted handkerchief around his neck or a flash of satin down his trousers seam, was to remind oneself of his beginnings and of the extraordinary course of the life which had brought him here today. His allegiance was clear; he ignored Alec and me completely, as did the others as they paced by.

Up at the castle, Ina was one rosy, happy day nearer to the fulfilment of her dreams and Albert, looking on bewildered, was tense and miserable, all his bustle quite gone. He could not even summon his usual lecture when Ina patted the sofa beside her and bid me come and sit near the fire.

'Oh, oh,' he moaned, but Ina only rolled her eyes at him—or rather not at him but at me, about him, which was schoolgirlish and nasty and set an answering nastiness going in me.

'My dear,' I said in a low voice, once Alec and Albert were safely talking and could not overhear, 'I've been unable to stop thinking about you and I hope you don't mind me butting in, but it just occurs to me—the more since I see you are burning your boats here—I suppose you have had a definite proposal, haven't you? A definite offer of marriage?'

Finally, Ina's happy bubble was pricked and it vanished. She glared at me but I was unabashed for it was not sheer cruelty that made me say it, not just a quick desire to see her chastened as she sneered at her poor silly husband; the possibility really had begun to press upon me overnight as I thought things through. I was sure that Robin Laurie was equal to seducing Mrs Wilson away from her respectable home for a short dalliance and a swift drop, and I was a great deal less sure that sweet Ina would think of it.

'Thank you for your concern,' she said, 'but I know what I'm doing.'

With a sinking inside, I took that to be a no.

'Oh, dear,' I said, far from diplomatically. 'Are you sure?'

'We'll get around to it, but we are both a lot less bothered about such things than you are, or Albert is,' she said, and I am sure that linking my name with his was designed to annoy me. 'We have both thrown off the shackles. There really is more to life than that, Dandy.'

I could not have been more convinced that she was wrong; Robin Laurie keeping her in the background all these years while his brother held the reins showed a great deal of concern for the mundane matters of wealth, name and property, and although it was true that his set was a rackety one I wondered if Ina realised how much more the lapsed ladies in it were made to suffer than the rakes. Well, I had voiced my worries and I was not so keen to be lectured any further about the great wondrous expanse of life beyond my tawdry

313

reckoning that I was going to press the matter.

'And what are your plans for tomorrow?' I said in a more normal, carrying voice. 'Do you have guests for Christmas Day?'

'We *never* have guests,' she replied and a dip in the conversation of the men told me that she had been overheard. 'I'm going down to the winter ground,' she went on. 'They're having a roasted pig and fireworks.'

'My love, my love,' said Albert Wilson, 'I implore you. You are not yourself, dearest, please let me call for the doctor.'

'I have never been so well in years, Albert,' said Ina. 'I have never been so well in my life before.'

Alec got to his feet and cleared his throat.

'Dr Walker can perhaps prescribe you something calming,' said Albert. 'Just until after the New Year and then maybe a little holiday? The seaside?'

'In January?' said Ina.

I too stood up then and began to rebutton my coat, which I had not the chance to remove.

'Perhaps we'll just go straight on down to the ground,' I said.

'Yes!' Alec exclaimed. 'Splendid idea, Dandy.' We both began to move, with a show of casualness that we did not feel, towards the door.

'Unless by "seaside" you mean that sanatorium again,' Ina was saying.

'Redroofs is a rest-hotel,' Albert answered, 'and it's always done you such good before. Your nerves, dear . . .'

We closed the door behind us and crept away down the marble stairs to the front door and the peace of the circus instead.

314

*　　　*　　　*

We were not, however, in luck; very far from it. Pa Cooke, evidently having heard the motor car, came striding out of the performing tent in his ringmaster's coat and britches.

'Looking forward to the show?' he asked, slapping his whip against his boots. All around the ground, heads were popping out of doors and faces appearing at windows. Tiny and Andrew were the first to emerge fully, coming out of their wagons in their bright suits and red shoes, already with their faces white and with the gaily checked bowlers on their heads above the red wool of their wigs. Behind them from her wagon came Topsy, in criss-crossed tights and with her hair piled high on her head and stuck with feathers, but wrapped in a wool cloak and with galoshes on over her slippers.

'Should be a good one,' said Pa. 'Greatest show on earth, as they say.'

Now Ma Cooke descended the steps of her wagon and came over to us, satin skirts swishing and gold earrings glinting and jouncing at every step.

'Cooke's Family Circus bouncing back bigger and better than ever,' said Pa with his arms spread wide.

Charlie, he too in his wig and make-up, had come out and was staring at his brother, his expression impossible to read behind the enormous painted grin and red-circled cheeks.

'So come on with you,' cried Pa. He wheeled round and glared at them all. 'Look lively.'

Zoya and Kolya Prebrezhensky were here now,

wrapped in cloaks like Topsy and looking strange and startled with their black and white make-up gleaming in the darkness.

'The show goes on,' Pa Cooke shouted, whirling his whip around himself.

Bill Wolf joined us, standing in his leopard print costume and his long leather boots. He looked a perfect savage with his hair deliberately knotted and teased until it stood out from his head in a tangle.

It was Andrew Merryman, of all people, who spoke up at last.

'No thanks to you,' he said.

There was a moment of silence while everyone stared at Pa, waiting.

'What's that, boy?' Pa's voice was light and easy, more terrible than if he had bellowed it. No one said a word. 'Speak up,' said Pa again, and now his voice was shaking. 'I said, *speak*!' He cracked his whip and it sounded like a gunshot. I flinched and Alec did but the others stood their ground.

'You're killing this circus off, one act at a time,' Andrew said softly.

I grasped Alec's arm but said nothing.

'That's right,' said Bill. 'Like my adagio. Where was the harm in that and you put your foot down and said no.'

'Who wurr you going to work up an adagio with?' Ma asked. I stared at her. Why was she making this chit-chat after what we had just heard?

'With Anastasia,' said Bill. 'But *he* said no, like the fool he's turned into.'

'Now here,' Ma scolded him. 'I won't have him spoken to like that.'

'I don't need your pity, Poll Cooke,' said Pa.

316

'You save it for them as wants it.'

'You tell him he don't need an act?' said Zoya, to Pa. 'How is this fair? And you.' She turned to Bill. 'Should be a good example to your children, like Kolya and me. Should work, should show them what circus is.'

'No, you're missing the point, Zoy,' said Tiny. 'Bill works for his place, don't you? He sits up for Pa like a little dog begging scraps. Keeps his nose clean.' He was mocking Bill now, his hands held like paws under his chin and his tongue out as he panted and wagged his behind. Bill took a step towards the little man.

'Don't you dare!' said Topsy, stepping between them. 'Size of you, you big bully.'

'I can fight my own damn battles,' said Tiny, shoving her aside. 'I'm a man, not a pet lamb.'

'Man?' said Topsy. 'You're worse than a schoolboy with all your games.'

'Is that where *you* learned them?' said Andrew. 'Helps a man to be treated like one, you know.'

Topsy rounded on him.

'Oh, you're so good at telling us all how to behave, ain't you, *Andrew Merryman*. Seems to me you need to decide whether you're one of us or not before you start throwing your mouth around.'

Andrew's face fell and he turned to Tiny.

'What have you been saying?' he demanded.

'Don't start on him,' Topsy said. 'I see plenty for myself. I see you sneaking around like we're not good enough for you. I see plenty of sneaking around folks might wish I didn't.'

'You mind your mouth, Topsy,' Charlie said.

'Scared she's seen you where you shouldn't have been, eh?' said Pa. 'My own brother!'

317

'*You* can talk about sneaking around,' said Bill to Tam.

'What?' said Ma. 'What do you mean?'

'I mean the horses,' said Bill. 'No, I've had it, Tam. I'm done with it. Ana was right. He sold Bisou. Roped me in to stand there and look threatening and get him a good price. And I couldn't refuse, could I? It's like Tiny says. A dog begging for scraps.'

'But why?' said Ma, looking at her husband. 'Why would you do that?'

'To keep Ana down of course,' said Charlie. 'To stop her looking like what she was. The star of the show. He hasn't got the sense he was born with.'

'Don't you talk to me like that,' Pa shouted at him.

'But why you shoot Harlequin then?' said Zoya. She had been gabbling furiously to her husband, relaying the words as fast as they came.

'Aye, the poor maid was dead by then,' said Bill. 'What was that about?'

'He didn't,' I said.

'Hold your tongue!' thundered Pa, but I went on just as loud if a little less steadily.

'He's at my house. Pa just wanted him out of the way.'

'What you up to?' said Ma, staring at him hard.

'Don't you see?' Andrew gave a heartless laugh. 'Can't you see it? A circus isn't a circus without animals and look around . . . what are the only animals left? Pa's prads.'

'Tint just the beasts,' said Tiny. 'He's holding us back, holding us down. Me, Andrew, Bill and Ana. Topsy's the only one he's any time for and only because she won't say boo.'

318

'Keep your nose out of my business,' said Topsy. 'It's none of yours. You've made that quite clear.'

'Quiet,' Pa shouted at the top of his voice. 'Quiet, the lot of you or you'll all be out on your backsides.' He looked around them. 'Every. Last. One. I'm the boss of this circus.'

'And the mess you're making of it now,' said Charlie, 'the things that are coming out now, I think it's time for a change.'

'Aye,' said Ma. 'Me too.'

'Don't you dare,' said Pa, wheeling round to face her. 'Don't you dare stand there and say that.'

'You never had a hope!' Charlie shouted at him. 'You couldn't have beaten her. You couldn't keep her down. She would have been the boss of you all, in't that right, Ma?'

'You!' said Kolya in a thunderous voice, making us all jump. He was glowering at Charlie. 'You trick us. You make fool.' Zoya was nodding feverishly fast at his side and she began to shout too.

'You tell that bad, evil girl she going to be the queen of me?' she said, jabbing her finger at Ma.

'But that's the last thing she should have heard, Charlie, you old fool,' said Andrew. 'Her fantasies were bad enough without you giving her more.'

'Don't speak like that about her and her not cold,' bellowed Charlie, wheeling round on him. 'Show some respect.'

'You dare to talk about respect,' Pa shouted, rushing at him. 'My own brother.' He took hold of Charlie by his lapel and shook him. 'After what you've done,' he spat. He swung his fist back and Charlie braced himself for the blow, staring Pa down, fearless.

Just then we heard the noise of the Wilsons' motor car rumbling down the track towards the ground. Pa dropped his hand to his side.

'Time for the show,' he said.

Charlie left first, Zoya and Kolya each giving him a look of venom as he passed them. Then they followed. Topsy watched them leave with tears standing in her eyes and then turned to Tiny and stared hard at him. He spat on the ground, not at Topsy exactly but too near her for politeness, and went trotting after Andrew who, for once, did not check his stride to match his friend's at all. Bill stood looking at Pa for a long time, both with their chests heaving, then he gave a scornful laugh and turned on his heel, Lally scurrying after him. Pa's face was bleak, his eyes dead, not even flickering as I crossed in front of him.

*   *   *

Alec and I took our seats in stunned silence.

'What was all that about?' he asked me. 'Do you know?'

'Not all of it,' I said. 'I don't know what's wrong between Ma and Pa and where Charlie comes into it.'

'It's pretty serious whatever it is,' said Alec, 'to fire up such passion. *What?*'

I had grabbed his arm. An idea had struck me, as irresistible as it was unbelievable.

'Passion!' I said. 'Exactly! We wondered what manner of cahoots Ma and Charlie were in. We wondered why Pa was so worried about being shoved out of his place. And Charlie's so-called wooing of Topsy was, as Tiny suspected, just a blind. Well, there it is.'

'There what is?' Alec said.

'Ma and Charlie Cooke,' I told him.

'You're joking!' said Alec. 'She's married. She's sixty. You think Pa's jealous of his own brother and his own wife?'

I was married and almost forty and Hugh was not a man to stride about with a whip and I should rather have died than point any of that out, but I still thought I had hit on something.

'And what does it have to do with Anastasia?' said Alec.

'I don't know,' I admitted. 'Oh, God. Speaking of love's young dream.'

Alec looked behind himself and groaned. Ina Wilson was picking her way along the row to sit beside us.

'Albert isn't coming,' she said, 'what with one thing and another he's not in a very festive mood.'

I rather thought it would not be a very festive show and Albert Wilson could have joined us without any threat to his low spirits.

At the side of the ring, Sallie Wolf wound up the Panatrope, Inya and Alya popped out in their spangled suits and opened up the ring doors, Pa strode into the middle and cracked his whip, then with a cacophony of stamping and snorting the black liberty horses began to fill the ring.

Strangely, Ana and her rosy-back were hardly missed at all; the ring was as dazzling and bursting with action as ever. Andrew, not needed to hold hoops and garters now, was weaving amongst the horses on his unicycle. Bill Wolf was carrying Tiny, who leapt around until it seemed the giant man was almost juggling the little one. Every so often

321

the dwarf would fall, timing each drop with a cymbal crash, and would tumble around amongst the horses' hooves until Andrew, weaving on his cycle, scooped him to safety again. Kolya was tossing Alya high in the air and catching her on his feet, while she rolled like an otter. Meanwhile Inya and Tommy Wolf cartwheeled around the edge of the ring and Charlie juggled enormous silver hoops, Topsy catching them and setting them spinning around her sinuous body until she had seven, from her neck to her knees, so fast they began to blur.

I had been gripping my hands so tightly against the edge of the ring fence that my arms were aching. Who was going to crack first? Who was going to look into the eyes of another and remember the angry words so recently spoken? Pa had Andrew and Tiny in amongst his horses' hooves and at a whistle from him those huge hooves would rise up and come crashing down again. Charlie sent his hoops spinning inches past Kolya's flashing legs; Kolya who had shouted at him as though he were a naughty child. Poor Bill had in his arms the little man who had trampled over his pride for all to see. And there was Tommy, Bill's only son, the apple of his father's eye, walking on his hands around the ring with only Zoya Prebrezhensky at his side, one hand out to save him if he fell.

I let go of the fence and sat back, blinking, watching the concentration behind the beaming smiles, watching the deft hands and steady feet, watching the great beast of the circus grip and release, flex and turn, all of its arms and legs and bodies working, and suddenly I could see what it

322

was they had been telling me, every chance they got, from the very first day.

'They would never have killed her,' I said, out loud. 'It's not the circus way.'

'What?' said Alec, and Ina too turned towards me.

'They might have hated her,' I said. 'She infuriated them, exasperated them, but she was one of them. They would never have hurt her. They would never have dreamed of it. They were telling me the truth all along.'

Alec turned uncertainly back to face the ring again but Ina Wilson remained looking at me.

'You see?' she said. 'They are wonderful people, no matter what you say. They truly love one another.'

I nodded absently and then stopped nodding and frowned at her.

'I never said they *weren't* wonderful. And I should say it was something deeper than love of the individual which stopped them; I think they loathed Ana personally.' Ina, silly romantic girl that she was, looked troubled at my cynicism and so I relented. 'Very well then, they loved her. But Ina, my dear, you of all people should understand that one can love and hate at the same time.'

Ina turned her head away from me again and went back to watching the show.

'I suppose you mean Albert,' she said, 'but I never loved Albert and I don't hate him even now.'

'Actually, I meant Robin,' I said. 'You have not chosen calm waters there, you know.'

'Robin?' said Ina, glancing at me again. 'Robin Laurie? What?'

The spectacular had ended; the artistes were

bounding out of the ring; Pa's horses were bending their pretty hocks and bowing.

'I thought . . .' I began. Alec was staring at me again now. 'You said you loved him. You were leaving Albert for him. Akilina Prebrezhensky *saw* you and him together.'

'Robin Laurie?' said Ina again. 'She said she saw Robin Laurie and me?'

I thought back, trying to remember. 'She said—well, she indicated that is, that she saw you together that night, the night of the show. The lady from the castle and the tall gentleman.'

In the ring Tiny was running up and down with Jinxie. The ring doors opened and into the doorway came Andrew Merryman, his hat tipped over one eye and his cane twirling so fast I could hear it whistle. Ina's face broke into a great beaming grin when she saw him, and Alec and I gazed at each other with mouths open wide.

'I think the little Prebrezhensky girl did see us once,' Ina said. 'In the woods. One of the first times we met by design. But she can't have seen us that night. Andrew was in the ring. I crept out and went to leave a letter in his wagon. I had just decided to take the plunge. I was almost sure already but that dreadful dinner party made my mind up for me. I went to leave a letter for him and to look around—at my new home.'

'But Robin seemed so keen to back up your word,' I said. 'Why would he? And how could you think it was wise to creep out when he was right there watching you? He could have followed you, or even drawn everyone's attention to it.'

'He did follow me out, but he won't make trouble,' said Ina, 'because I could make even

324

more for him. I wouldn't, but he doesn't know that.'

'Robin followed you out?' said Alec.

'Oh!' said Ina. 'Do you suppose that's where Akilina got the idea that we were meeting up?'

'Did he speak to you?' said Alec. 'What did he say?'

'No, no, no,' said Ina. She was still gazing at Andrew. 'I say he followed me, but really he just left after I did and he was back before me too.'

'How long were you gone for?' I said.

'Five minutes perhaps,' said Ina.

'Where did he go?' Alec said.

'I've no idea,' said Ina. 'For a smoke? I tried not to think about it. It was most unfortunate that I saw him at all. I wish I hadn't done. It almost spoiled the precious moment completely.'

Alec was staring at her as though she had grown horns. I did my best to talk calmly.

'Spoiled the . . . You didn't think of telling the police?'

'I don't like thinking about Robin Laurie,' she said. 'I don't like him. I could have made lots of trouble, but I just wanted him to go away and if the police had suspected him he might have had to stay longer. I'm very glad I'm leaving his sort behind.'

'What trouble could you have made?'

'I could have told the world what Nurse Currie told me,' Ina said. 'She made me promise not to, before I knew what it was, and that was most unfair of her. Telling me and making me have to think about it. It would serve her right.'

'But what was it that she told you?'

'I'll say it once, but you mustn't ask me

questions and make me keep on about it,' said Ina. Alec and I nodded impatiently. She took a deep breath. 'Robin Laurie killed one of his brother's children.'

'What?' We spoke in a chorus.

'He tried to *save* one of his brother's children,' I said. 'The last surviving one who jumped into the sea. Are you telling me he killed one of the others?'

'No, no, that's the one,' said Ina. 'He didn't try to save her from drowning. He drowned her. Nurse Currie told me all about it, seven years ago. Which was very unkind of her.'

The clowns were finished now and left the ring, rather puzzled I think at our indifference to their antics. They were replaced by the four Prebrezhenskys, beaming and clapping their hands. I stood up and dragged Ina to her feet, hustling her out of her seat and away from the ring to the doorway where we would not be seen. Alec came after us, taking long angry strides.

'Do you mean to tell me,' I said, 'that you saw Robin Laurie—a man you knew to have killed before—killed a young girl before—sneaking around the night another young girl was killed and you said nothing?'

'I told you,' said Ina, her voice high with wonder as though Alec and I were being unkind to her, 'I don't like him and I don't like thinking about him. And anyway, why on earth would he kill Anastasia?'

'What were you thinking of?' I wanted to shake her.

Unbelievably I heard a sound halfway between a chuckle and a happy little sigh.

'Andrew,' she said. 'Our future.'

Alec—quite without brusqueness (for he is the sweetest of men), but really rather firmly—pushed me aside and stood in front of Ina, actually taking her arms in her hands.

'I have known Andrew Merryman for twenty years,' he said, 'and I shall do everything in my power to make sure he wakes up and sees you for the fool you are before you get your nasty little claws anywhere near him.'

Ina's smile was replaced by a pout and she looked up at Alec from under her brows.

'How horrid you are,' she said. 'How dare you speak to me that way.'

'That's nothing,' I said to her. 'Because circus or no, Christmas Eve or no, you are coming to Blairgowrie with us and I shall have the greatest satisfaction in seeing what Inspector Hutchinson makes of you.'

16

We were given the inspector's address by a startled constable who came to the door of the police house in Blairgowrie in shirtsleeves and braces. Behind him a lively pack of small children in nightgowns were scampering up and down the stairs and his attempts to shush them only turned the row they were making from cheerful shouts into loud whispers and explosive giggling.

'Begging your pardon, sir, madam,' said the constable, 'but there's no settling them tonight.' He gestured along the garden to the police station proper, its blue lamp gleaming out. 'I can easy open the office for you.'

We assured him once again that it was his superior upon whom we had our sights and I—after a brainwave—added a firm promise that any possible repercussions arising from the inspector being disturbed on this of all evenings would lie with us alone. I had guessed correctly and, thus mollified, the constable wished us the compliments of the season and bade us goodnight.

'You can drop us off and then get on your way, Alec,' I said, as we hurried back to the motor car. 'What time are you expected at Pess?'

'Oh, I'll telephone to them and apologise for dinner,' Alec said, glancing distractedly at his watch. 'There's a crowd tonight, I shan't be missed.'

Hutchinson, thankfully, seemed not at all disturbed by our sudden intrusion into his evening. He lived in a neat little stone villa on the Perth Road, two bay windows with a lit porch between, where the door was opened by an equally neat little wife, swathed in a white apron and smelling of spices.

'You'll be after Maynard,' she said and, with a quick downward look which told us more clearly than a command that we should wipe our feet before entering, she led us into a sitting room.

'Maynard,' I mouthed to Alec as we followed her.

'Now you'll have to excuse me,' said Mrs Hutchinson when she had installed us and turned up the gas, 'but I'm cooking for the morn's morn as you can imagine and my daughter will be here any minute with the bairns, so I'd best get on.'

Alec, Ina and I waited like schoolchildren in the headmaster's study, glancing around ourselves at the lace cover on the piano, the shining leaves of the potted palms and the brush marks on the thick carpet, evidence of a recent fierce sweeping. I wondered how Inspector Hutchinson managed to maintain his dishevelment in a household where not a single palm frond nor tassel was out of place, or alternatively how the housewife who had scoured those ridges into the nap of her good carpet could bear the dull shoes and crumpled trousers of her mate.

'Well, well, well,' said Hutchinson, bursting in on my thoughts. He stood in the doorway exuding welcome, pipe tobacco and whisky, and a close look at him showed that his face, always mottled, was this evening as decorative as some kind of rare orchid, in purple and yellow patches. I began to wish we at least had been a little more temperate, perhaps telephoning to Hutchinson after Boxing Day; suddenly the great rush of discovery was looking a little threadbare as I gathered myself for my report.

I should not have worried. Inspector Hutchinson listened with as much avidity as I had ever seen in him, sitting forward and fastening his gaze upon me as I spoke. Of course, if it had been Sergeant McClennan the avid effect would have been the more impressive (Hutchinson's keenest look was still more reminiscent of an elderly bloodhound waiting for table scraps than of a terrier snapping and raring to go).

'No whiff of a motive,' he said, sitting back once I had finished, which was a quelling start, 'but opportunity and something of a track record.' He clapped his hands together and then smacked them down on to his knees, making his feet jump. 'With opportunity and a history of mischief, I think even my super is going to have to listen to me.'

'And don't forget the witness,' Ina said, simpering. Inspector Hutchinson turned his pouchy eyes upon her, and Alec and I, who had seen the like of what was coming once before, drew back to remove ourselves from the line of fire.

'A witness?' he said. 'Now, you see, madam, a witness—to my way of thinking—is not just "a buddy that saw what happened". No, a witness is a person of sound understanding and good character who can come through cross-examination making sense and looking as pure as the driven snow. What we have in this case is an informant, a very useful type of creature, of course, but we have no witness. Ah well, we'll manage without one.'

Ina took at least half of this speech to begin to comprehend it, for the inspector's avuncular look and respectful tone were most misleading, but when she did she sat back reddening and with her mouth slightly open.

'In fact, I'll not keep you hanging about much longer, Mrs Wilson,' said Hutchinson, 'but I wonder if you can inform me on one last point? Would you have an address for this nurse?'

Ina shook her head.

'Aye well, I suppose she could hardly keep up a correspondence with every Tom, Dick and Harry,' he said. 'We'll find her. Now, I'm going to ring up my sergeant to get you a lift home and you can wait for him in the wee room across the way. You'll not be in anyone's road there.'

'You could surely have taken her, Alec,' I said, when they had left the room. 'It would get you started on your way. You're going to be terribly late as it is.'

'I rather think that Pess will have to do without me after all,' said Alec. 'It would take more than the delights it has on offer to tear me away from this now.'

'They'll never forgive you,' I said. 'You're burning your boats.'

How perverse that just when he was turning from the prospect I finally began to urge him towards it.

'Some boats are best burnt,' Alec said.

The inspector returned to us within minutes and Mrs Hutchinson, her cooking evidently in hand, unbent enough to bring a tray of cocoa and biscuits although she gave a marked look at both the biscuits and her carpet and left me in no doubt that food in the parlour was a great concession and I should be very careful (as Nanny used to say at nursery suppers) to eat over my plate.

'Now, it would take more of a man than me to knock up the super tonight,' said the inspector. 'He'll be at the kirk till gone twelve—it's a big night for the choir—and he'll be there all day tomorrow, of course. Anyway, I need to speak to the brother first to firm up this earlier crime—there's no motive there either when you look at it front on, since it was a lass he's done away with and not a son and heir—but I'm not for bothering him on Christmas Day, are you, madam? No, Boxing Day's a good day for visiting. So you and me and your man there can just bide our time—have a wee dram and a good chow at the plum pudding—and day after tomorrow I'll hitch a lift north with you.'

'It's going to be a delicate matter,' I said. 'Lord Buckie lives in his grief, Inspector, to an extent that is hard to explain.'

'Wears it like winter drawers, eh?'

The phrase had some aptness if no poetry.

'And he is far from well. Dying, in fact. Hearing this about his brother might be the end of him.'

'I'm sure you'll do a grand job of softening the blow,' said the inspector. 'And I'll be right there to help if you need me.' I was about to argue with this proposed division of labour, but the memory of Lord Buckie in his library, in his cardigan, and the thought of him wilting under the action of the inspector's caustic tongue swayed me. I have never thought of myself as having a particular way with words but at least what talents I had did not run to scorching epigrams and unanswerable put-downs of the sort Hutchinson scattered about him; I would make the best of it that I could.

First, though, I had the cosy family Christmas to which I had been looking forward with such simple joy and the prospect was almost enough to make me regret those hordes of relations who were not, by lucky chance, converging upon Gilverton this year. As well as the lingering sulks the circus had engendered—by its withdrawal in the case of the boys and by its development into mayhem as far as Hugh was concerned—all three were feeling bitter about the loss of a day on the hills.

'Not much of a holiday, Mother,' said Teddy. 'Church!'

'And nothing but stodge to eat all day,' said Donald.

Indeed, Mrs Tilling always made three kinds of potato to accompany the goose as well as strengthening her bread sauce with barley until it stood up in the sauceboat with a spoon in it like a flagpole on a hilltop, and then there was nothing at tea which had not had the benefit of a little suet somewhere in its gestation, and neither Hugh nor Nanny would countenance a winter morning which did not open with porridge; by suppertime on the typical Christmas Day a steam engine, ploughing into any one of us, would not have knocked us off beam.

My day was brightened, although Hugh's was not, by the late addition to our party (for I could not in all conscience ignore Alec's plight, no matter what he had said about a quiet day at home and a cutlet). He arrived, just after breakfast, bearing gifts of such finely judged propriety that they made me smile: a box of excellent cigars for Hugh, lavish heaps of silly games and sickly chocolates for the boys and, for me, a rare lily bulb wrapped in instructions for its successful growth and a hideous little enamelled watering can with which I was supposed to hover over it until it honoured me with a bloom.

Hugh was delighted, no less by the lily bulb than the cigars, I thought, and the day plodded on in its suety way harmlessly enough until just after tea, when we were all gathered in front of the library fire, faced with the big decision of the season: to veto charades and feel oneself a churl or to play charades and half die from embarrassment and boredom. Every year one hopes that the boys will have outgrown the desire and every year one's hopes are dashed again.

'Oh, come on, Mother,' said Donald. 'One hour of fun, one day a year.'

'I cannot agree with your summary of your woes,' I told him. 'When you are grown up you will look back and see that your lives have been nothing but fun since the day you were born. You are as spoiled as any two children ever were.'

'I'm not spoiled,' said Teddy. 'Gosh, Mother, if you saw the prep we do and how hard we work all term, you wouldn't begrudge us one measly little game of charades at Christmas.'

'And anyway,' said Donald, 'when I'm grown up, I'll be doing what Daddy is doing now. Shooting and mucking about and fishing and what have you.'

This was said with such innocence that I could not help laughing even though Hugh's brows lowered.

'I have some telephone calls I need to . . .' said Alec, fleeing the room and the need to keep his face straight.

'When I'm grown up I'll play charades with my children every day after tea,' said Teddy, as dogged as ever.

'You'll be stuck in a law office or stuck in the army, Ted,' said his brother. 'I'll be here playing charades with my children but there'll be none of that for you.'

Teddy's face clouded and Donald gave him a look of pure glee.

'Hugh,' I said. 'What have you been—' I managed to bite my lip, but I had gone too far already. Hugh's face was stony.

'No, no, no,' said Teddy, just as he had ever since he was a tiny boy, always trying to out-argue his brother and never quite making it. 'Because maybe Mr Osborne will leave me Dunelgar, so there! Because he's got no wife and children and we're practically his family anyway, so there! And Dunelgar is bigger than Gilverton and it's got better—'

'Go to your rooms, now, both of you,' said Hugh. If he had had a whip he might have cracked it.

'Hugh,' I said. 'Christmas Day, dear.'

Donald and Teddy, possibly reading his face more accurately than I, got to their feet and scurried out.

Hugh and I were silent for a minute after they had gone. Then, unwisely, I spoke.

'What have you been saying?' I asked again.

'This place *will* be Donald's and that's that,' he replied. 'No point in pussy-footing around the plain facts.' He paused. 'But there are rather uglier facts I should rather my sons did not have forced down their throats, Dandy.'

'Their mother having a job of work to do and having a little help with it is not an ugly fact,' I said. 'And it's hardly shoved down their throats— they know nothing about it.'

The ensuing stubborn silence was still going strong when Alec joined us again. He congratulated us on heading off the charades. He got no answer from either of his hosts. And so another merry Christmas danced to its close. Even Bunty was dejected, missing the circus girls greatly and shooed out of the kitchen by a harassed cook and maids while the unwanted feast was prepared and the even more unwanted leftovers dealt with afterwards.

By ten o'clock on Boxing Day morning, the spirits of all were on the rise again. The staff were having their party, Hugh, Donald and Teddy were back amongst the gorse and bracken with another poor doe in prospect, and Alec, Hutchinson and I were bowling north in the Vauxhall tourer which had been Alec's Christmas present to himself.

'Much more economical than the Bentley,' he said, when I raised my eyebrows at the sight of it. I was familiar with the undentable male philosophy that the purchase of a new motor car can save pots of money, and so I said nothing.

Bunty, full of cold potato and therefore good cheer, was standing on the back seat with Alec's spaniel, Milly, their two heads stuck out into the wind, eyes streaming and teeth snapping at gusts, while Inspector Hutchinson gathered his coat round him and assured us that the fresh air would do him the world of good. (He did look rather grey after his 'wee dram', and Alec's driving, with or without a new engine to run in, is never quite like a nursemaid rocking a cradle.)

'And at least we know Robin Laurie is not going to be there,' Alec said as he swung sharply on to a bridge, bounced over its summit and hooked his way back out on to the road again (why the bridge makers and road makers of this land could not have sat down together over a can of tea in their bothy and organised the join between their two enterprises, I have never been able to see, but any road with a goodly share of bridges upon it always gives a slight feeling of going in and out of the dusky bluebells; on the current occasion, Inspector Hutchinson gave a soft moan).

'Do we?'

'I rang round,' Alec said. 'Caught as many of the Benachally dinner gang as I could put a telephone number to. I'm going to have to have them all at Dunelgar for a party—that was my pretext—but I managed to work Robin in a few times and apparently he's in town.'

'Odd,' I said. 'His brother's last Christmas by all reckoning and whether Robin is the paragon of fraternal affection Lord Buckie thinks him, or a vulture ravening after the spoils to come—the more likely alternative, given what we know now, don't you think?—I'd have bet high stakes he'd be up there.'

The winter weather—most disobligingly given the expectations one has inherited from so many Christmas cards—had abandoned the tingling crispness of recent weeks in favour of fog and drizzle and the morning had seen Perthshire at its most unutterably grim, when the stink of winter fodder and the soft oppressiveness of a thousand damp pine trees seep in at the edges of the window frames and take over the house. But there must be some point on the globe where latitude begins to trump meteorological pressure, where the weather simply gives up and hands responsibility over to the Gods of the North. If so, then somewhere between Perth and Banff we reached it and came out into glittering brittle sunshine. To inhale the air was like plunging into a mountain stream and the inspector breathed it in deeply and began to grow some pink and purple patches again.

'Nice spot,' he said. 'I've never been much of a one for coming up north. No need for any more of what we get plenty of in Blairgowrie to my mind— I'd rather get the train to the wife's sister in the

Lakes, except for the beer—but this'll do.'

Lord Buckie, we heard with some surprise upon presenting ourselves at Cullen, was in the garden, taking his morning constitutional, but a hallboy would be dispatched to fetch him in if we would care to step into the library and wait.

I put a hand on the arm of the maid to stop her (for it is often surprisingly hard to stay a well-trained servant in her tracks and certainly they can ignore any amount of verbal persuasion), saying that the gentlemen would go to the library but, if she would direct me to the gardens, I should go to Lord Buckie myself.

The maid seemed to catch the scent of trouble we could not help having brought with us.

'Nothing wrong is there, madam?' she said, looking warily at Alec and the inspector. A town maid would surely have identified Hutchinson straight away even with Alec's complicating presence at his side, but this girl might never have seen a specimen of the type before and so although his air, his notebook, his very winter coat and brown boots, screamed 'police' as clearly as would his whistle, she abandoned her short attempt to place the unlikely trio and merely curtsied.

As I let myself through the garden door, I was still wondering about the oddness of a dying man tramping around bare paths in the depths of December but, given the southerly slope of the ground, the high surrounding wall clothed with the delicate skeletons of fanned fruit trees, and the bright mossy green of the winter lawns, dotted with balls of box and with peacocks fashioned from golden-leaved yew, it was very far from being the desolate wasteland of the Gilverton gardens at this time of year, was almost pleasant on such a sunny day.

'Mrs Gilver?' Lord Buckie had seen me before I him. He was standing at the end of a long arbour, bare now and very bright with new paint, looking up along a grass path towards me. 'You creep in and out like a house mouse, my dear,' he said, 'but very welcome, always welcome. I am delighted to see you.'

He would not be if he could divine my purpose and I should not, for kindness' sake, postpone setting it out before him.

'Lord Buckie,' I said, 'I am charged with a very difficult task this morning.'

'Not bad news?' he said. 'Oh my, not Robin!'

'Not . . . I have no news of him,' I said, shrinking from actual reassurance, 'but I do need to talk to you and I am going to be asking you to revisit very painful memories.'

'On what . . . Pardon me, my dear Mrs Gilver, but on what authority? On what grounds?'

I stared unhappily at him. Ought I to tell him that there was a police inspector in his house? That *was* my authority, after all.

'I am trying to help someone,' I said, which sounded feeble even to me, but he was a shrewd as well as a kind old thing, and I fancy he saw that only some urgent purpose could overcome my clear distaste for the task before me. He tucked my hand under his arm and began to walk again, leading me around the paths, among the trees, passing frozen ponds, catching occasional drenches of impossible sweetness from the tiny waxen flowers of some bare-branched shrub which lined the walkways.

'It's about your daughter,' I said.

'Ambrosine,' said Lord Buckie, knowing immediately which daughter I meant.

'And how she died,' I went on. 'Did you— forgive me—but did you see it?'

'I am not sure whether to be glad or sorry, but I did not. Why do you ask?'

'Did anyone?'

'Anyone besides Robin, you mean?'

'Yes. Anyone else.'

'No,' said Lord Buckie, 'he was quite alone, otherwise there might have been a happier outcome. I was here when he came back, soaked to the skin, shivering. Of course I was sure he would be next for the wretched influenza and then I should have no one. But he and I were both spared it.'

'And was Robin . . . I do not know how to say this . . . Was he a fond uncle? Was he a favourite amongst your children?' Lord Buckie gave a short and rather dry laugh.

'He was young and full of his own concerns,' he said. 'Rather wild, as a matter of fact. Rather wilder even, in his youth, than he is today.'

'But Ambrosine,' I persisted, 'he must have been terribly fond of her to risk his own life that way. Or would you say he is just one of those men who would act without thinking, for anyone?'

'I couldn't say,' said Lord Buckie. 'He was decorated—he's no coward. Perhaps it was unthinking or perhaps he did it for me but it was an unselfish act, of that we can be sure.'

'Of course, of course,' I said absently, quaking at the thought of taking his cherished memory and

340

twisting it into a blackened travesty of itself, telling him that Robin had killed, not saved, had hated or at least had felt a cold nothingness, had certainly felt no love.

'No, I mean a really truly unselfish act,' Lord Buckie said, and he shook my arm slightly to emphasise his words. 'My boys went first, you know, in that terrible plague. Two strong lusty boys, snuffed out like candles. And then my two little girls. But I still had my oldest. My heiress. I am a marquis, you see. This is a Scottish marquisate, my dear, not an English earldom.' He must have seen my look of puzzlement. 'I inherited my title from my mother. The Marchioness of Banff and Buckie. My grandparents' only child and what is called these days a game old bird. She laid out these gardens and put in all the heating, you know. Drew up plans herself and fired five builders before she was satisfied. Ah, Mother! But the point is—I am an old man, and I'm beginning to ramble—that any of my five children could have been my heir. The girls as well as the boys.'

'I see,' I said. 'I had no idea there was such provision.'

He laughed his dry laugh again. 'Such provision! You make it sound so cobbled together. I have come across the view before amongst you Southerners'—here he squeezed me to take the sting from the insult—'that there is something illicit in our ways. But Amber would have been a worthy successor. She was my mother all over again and of the five . . . of the five . . . well, I loved each of them and I shall not say it aloud. But she was the healthiest, finest, strongest girl ever born. Full of mischief, fearless, a rascal when she was a

341

child. The stories and nonsense she used to tell us all. She made me weep with laughter. "Where did you come from?" I'd ask her. "Did the pixies leave you? What did I do to offend the pixies that they left me you?" And she'd laugh back in my face.' He sighed. 'It was only poor Ambrosine's drowning that put Robin in the way of all this.' He stopped and waved his hand around at the castle and gardens, even waving it at himself, at—one supposed—the marquisate incarnate. 'So, you see, it was a *most* unselfish act to have tried to save her. No mistaking that, and I love him for it.'

I said nothing. Here was a motive indeed. Here was a sack of lead to heap on the scales of justice against Robin Laurie. I considered and rejected half a dozen and more ways to tell him, and was silent so long that he turned a querying look upon me.

'Does any of that help?'

'Thank you, it does,' I said. I had decided to say none of it. 'Now surely you have walked long enough in this cold air. You are not taking very good care of yourself, I must say, although I feel very matronly to be saying so.'

'You are a child,' said Lord Buckie, and for the first time I could discern a glimmer of the same charm that Robin could summon with a whistle. 'And I am fine. I do not know why everyone around me always treats me as though I were dying. I have never been strong, but I am quite well, really.'

I had no reason at all to tamper with *this* delusion, and I would not have dreamed of being so matronly as all that, so I contented myself with telling him that I and the two friends who had accompanied me would be leaving him in peace again, but first, might I have a word with his cook.

'My cook?' He was astonished.

'I have a piece of business to put through,' I said. 'A very delicate piece of business. The trading of a recipe for the honour of another recipe. My Mrs Tilling would not rest when she heard where I was bound.'

'And what speciality of Cullen is it you are bidding for?' he said.

I gulped. It had occurred to me while we were talking that the second of my two questions should not be put to him at all—he would have no idea where to find the nurse from all those years ago; he might not even remember the woman's name—but to the upper servants instead. No one on earth, in my experience, keeps up a correspondence like that of a cook.

'Mrs Tilling said your cook would know,' I said, thinking it a great brainwave.

'Ah, the almond tart!' said Lord Buckie.

'Indeed.'

*   *   *

Nurse Currie, I learned in the kitchen, had left Glasgow after 'thon dreadful winter' and, unable to face again the kind of emptiness she had found on the Grampian shores, had plumped for a happy medium and was now settled in Stirlingshire, working—so Mrs Mallen told me—in a 'very nice' mother and baby nursing home and walking out with a builder.

'Not, you understand, m'lady, a home for mothers, dear me no'—Mrs Mallen lowered her voice even at that to prevent the scullery maid, a girl of very tender years, from hearing—'but a lying-in hospital for ladies. Happier work she said in her letter to me when she took up the position there, much happier work bringing babies into the world than easing souls out of it. She was shaken to her marrow that terrible Christmas time she was here with us, m'lady.'

I had encountered Mrs Mallens and their m'ladying before in my time and they always amused me. The idea was—in so far as I had ever been able to pin it down firmly—that they had spent so long so deeply embedded in such an exalted household that they had quite forgotten there were such things as commoners in the world and every female guest was an automatic m'lady. Of course, the expectation was that one would correct them and then endure the look of surprised pity as they adjusted one in their view. If, as I did now, one let the matter hang, one put the poor fools in a state of impotent torment from which there was no escape.

'And so you have her address, Mrs Mallen?' I said.

She did and, with a great show of effort and much stertorous breathing, she removed her apron and cuffs, washed her hands under the cold tap and stumped off upstairs to her bedroom to copy it out for me. This took an unconscionable length of time but eventually I rejoined Alec and the inspector on the drive and there had been time for the interior of the motor car to heat through beautifully and for Bunty and Milly to recover from the excitement of the reunion and fall back to sleep.

344

'Well, he certainly had a motive for that one,' said the inspector, when I had relayed my discoveries. 'It beggars belief, this nurse keeping her lip buttoned. Wonder if she's on the take? Or I tell you what—you said this Laurie character has women stashed here, there and yonder. She might be another of them.'

'What I said was that he has an understanding with a piano teacher who lives on the estate,' I reminded him.

'And there was the low-born woman he ditched years back, when the title bobbed to the surface.'

'Perhaps it's Miss Currie who is to be elevated when Lord Buckie pops off,' said Alec. 'Perhaps she's waiting in Stirlingshire like a princess in a tower for her prince to come.'

'Perhaps she killed the lot of them.'

'Perhaps she was never a nurse and Laurie brought her in to see if she could polish them all off for him.'

It was rather like listening to my sons.

'I have a serious point to make,' I said, and then I regretted the way they instantly sobered, with twitching lips and brows pulled ostentatiously downwards—why does any pair of male creatures always gang up on and make ridiculous a solitary female who comes to join them? 'This low-born female. The ordinary Miss as Hugh called her: what if it were Anastasia? What if Robin recognised her and she recognised him and that's why she left the ring and that's why he killed her?'

'Why, exactly?' said Alec. 'I agree about the recognising. But why would she have to die?'

'And didn't she leave the ring because her pony threw a wobbler?' said Hutchinson. I looked away from him. I had not, as yet, come clean about Donald and Teddy.

'His "wobbler", Inspector,' said Alec valiantly, 'could have been caused by her reaction to seeing Laurie. I mean surely he must have been even more attuned than an ordinary pony to her every twitch and shudder, and I remember being thrown off a very well-schooled mount once, just for sneezing.'

Inspector Hutchinson answered Alec although his eyes were trained on me.

'Very nicely argued, sir,' he said.

'My sons were fibbing,' I said, glad to have got it off my chest at long last. 'Pa Cooke terrified them and they panicked.'

There was a long silence, during which the picture of Donald and Teddy in arrow-patterned suits, familiar from the Cinerama, pressed in on me.

'Well, I did say I wasn't in the business of collecting scalps,' said the inspector at long last. 'Good to have it straight in the end, though.' I was blushing furiously and I busied myself with a non-existent problem in the area of my glove-buttons until the blush subsided. 'But we all agree,' he went on, 'that it's a country mile more likely he'd kill someone he knew than a complete stranger?'

'Of course,' I said, 'but we need something more than his knowing the girl to serve as a motive proper.'

'Well, having knowledge of women is very often at the root of things, madam,' said Hutchinson, 'I've seen it more times than I can tell you. Murder is hardly ever a damned thing to do with hate, if I might speak so plainly. Oh no. Love and money is what it comes down to. And drink. But this kind of murder that we're looking at here? Love and money, mark my words.'

Then, like the barrels of a lock holding the safe door closed, all the pieces fell in together with a click.

'I've got it,' I said. 'He married her. He married his ordinary Miss, when it looked as though there was no reason for him not to. His brother had heirs and successors coming out of his ears and Robin married his girlfriend without his brother's approval or consent. Then . . .'

'Then came the 'flu,' said Alec, taking up the tale, 'and down went the heirs, with Robin helping the last one on her way. Now everything was different. Now his brother's blessing was make-or-break and such a marriage would have broken it to bits but it was too late. The deed was done. Then what?'

'Then what?' cried Hutchinson, so sharply that Alec swerved off the lane and we bumped along in a soft verge for an exciting moment until his wheels found the ash again. 'Then his young wife, who saw him kill the niece, or maybe heard that he had, had a sensible think to herself and realised that she was next for the shove off the cliff top and she hooked it.'

'To the circus?'

'Maybe that's where he found her in the first place,' I said. 'That would explain why he'd be so sure his brother wouldn't accept the creature.'

'And he's been looking for her ever since?' said Alec. 'Scouring every show in the land?'

'Trying to find her and persuade her into a divorce—let's give him the benefit, eh?—or find her and do away with her before his brother hears about it. If his brother dies and she comes out of the woodwork there'd be an almighty scandal.'

'But would Robin care about a scandal?' I said.

'Maybe what's worrying him is that she would hold the drowned niece over his head and take him for his last penny,' said Alec.

'And you know what it does help us with, all of this?' said the inspector. 'It explains why he would sneak out right there and then and bash her head in on the ground. No time to lose, see? His brother was sinking. Hang the consequences if it all went wrong.'

'It wouldn't be the first time he'd leapt into action,' said Alec. 'I mean, we don't think he dragged his niece to the cliff top and threw her over, do we? We think she set out to kill herself and he helped. Or he happened to find her at the edge of the cliff and gave her a timely shove.'

'Oh, don't say it like that,' I begged him. 'Don't let's speculate at all. Nurse Currie is going to tell us the worst soon enough.'

*　　　*　　　*

It was dark before we reached Stirling, the three of us gaunt with exhaustion—Alec actually asleep—although Inspector Hutchinson was revelling in his turn at the wheel.

'I learned to drive in a Vauxhall,' he said, polishing a portion of the woodwork with his coat sleeve, and not for the first time. 'An old Prince Henry and I always say, if it was good enough for His Majesty it's good enough for me. Now, madam, what's that address you've got there?

348

What are we looking for?'

By the light of Alec's electric torch I could just make out Mrs Mallen's laborious pencilled printing, but we had to stop and ask for directions from a newspaperman on a street corner who came out of his kiosk to peer into the car at the lady and gentleman who some copper was taking to the baby hospital. What was the story here, then, his face seemed to say as he told us the way.

'No better than you should be,' said Hutchinson when he climbed back in and we set off again, 'that's what he's decided, madam. He'll be telling that tale till closing time.'

The practised eye of the nurse who answered the bell at Campsie Grange was not taken in for a second, though. Even in my bulky Persian lamb I presented an outline far too svelte for a customer and she was at a loss. When Inspector Hutchinson introduced himself and showed his card with his policeman's number, however, her look of fascination knocked that of the newspaper seller's for an effortless six.

'If you could fetch Nurse Currie then, miss?' said Hutchinson. 'And if you could just say she has a visitor, please? I don't want her alarmed. Now, is there a sitting room or some such where we could speak to her?'

There was rather a splendid nurses' sitting room, in fact, out of which three off-duty girls in curlpapers and knitted slippers were unceremoniously bundled to make way for us.

'Well, go and sit in the doctor's room,' hissed our guide. 'There's nobody in there tonight.' To further grumbling we heard an exasperated 'Well, *light* it then. It'll soon warm up. Or fill a bottle.

349

Now, let me go and get Susan for these . . . people.'

Feeling rather guilty, Alec and I tucked ourselves on to a sofa by the fire, which had been burning all day and was a pulsating heap of orange, delicious after the endless drive. The inspector strode about the room, whistling, flipping through picture papers lying on the desk and even, I was rather shocked to see, poking his pen into a pile of letters and reading the names on the envelopes. Then quickly, as the door opened, he turned.

Nurse Currie was a woman of forty, small and with a mass of dark curls which hugged her white cap and tumbled over her forehead, despite attempts at the back to tame them with pins and netting. She had the bloom that most girls have in their youth but only the very lucky or very healthy retain throughout their middle years, pink lips, pink cheeks, clear eyes and a softness of skin one usually associates with woodcutters' wives who live in clearings in the forest, rather than working nurses in the middle of their shift. Surely they should look either wan or ruddy from toil? For a moment, Alec's idea of Nurse Currie as Robin's abandoned Miss reared its head again.

'Can I help you?' she said, sitting down very neatly in a small chair just inside the door. I supposed nurses must need to work up a neat way of sitting, for what could be more unseemly than a birth-room, or indeed a deathbed, sprawl?

Inspector Hutchinson introduced himself and the two of us to her and she looked puzzled, as how could she not, but her wide eyes showed no scheming; there was no leap of guilt or flare of fear.

'We would like to talk to you about a young lady you nursed a few years ago,' Hutchinson began. 'A Miss Ambrosine Laurie.'

'Lady Ambrosine Buckie,' I corrected.

'Aye, right,' said the inspector. 'No one like the aristocracy for collecting names. Outside of the circus, anyway.'

'I'm sure, Nurse Currie,' I said, 'that even in the course of a long career, you will remember this case.'

She nodded, pursing her mouth slightly. 'Robert, Thomas, Charlotte, little Victoria, then Her Ladyship, until there was only Amber left. That's what the family called her, madam— Amber—and I did the same.'

'Yes, well, it's Lady Amber that we need to ask you about most particularly,' said Hutchinson. 'It's recently come to my attention that you might know more about her death than almost anyone.'

Now Nurse Currie's eyes did just cloud over slightly and she bowed her head before she spoke again.

'It's a thing I've never done before or since,' she said, 'and you'll just have to take my word for it. You've been speaking to that Mrs Wilson, haven't you?'

Inspector Hutchinson nodded.

'Well, there's proof of it,' she said. 'I knew it would be her you'd got it from because I've never told another living soul. The things I've heard in sickrooms and I've been twenty-two years nursing this Easter. That was the only time I talked and I had to, sir. Had to.' She spoke with great emphasis. 'Because I didn't know what to do for

351

the best and it would have pressed on me like a knife if I'd tried to ignore it.'

'You didn't know what to do for the best?' echoed the inspector. 'Where was the puzzle? If there's been a crime, you report it. That's what's best, every time.'

'But I'm not sure that it *was* a crime,' she said, the anguish beginning to sound in her voice. 'That's what I couldn't decide. And Mrs Wilson told me the best thing to do was just try to forget about it and not let it eat away at me.'

'I'll bet she did!' said Alec, grimly.

'But what was there to decide?' I said. 'Robin Laurie drowned his niece. Isn't that so? Whether he threw her into the water or held her under or even just stood on the cliff and did nothing. He killed her. Ina Wilson told us that.'

'No,' said Nurse Currie, 'that's not what happened at all and it's not what I said. Mrs Wilson is misremembering, or at least maybe she never understood properly in the first place. She was ill, weak, and she only let me say it once then she just insisted that we both forget it and never mention it again.'

'That sounds about right,' Alec said.

'So what did happen?' said Hutchinson.

'Amber didn't catch the 'flu that winter, not like all the others did,' Nurse Currie began. 'She was just her own same self, playing her games and telling her wild tales—she was a girl like no other one I've ever seen; her father used to say she was a changeling.' I nodded, encouraging. 'But when her little brothers and little sisters died and then her mother that she loved so much, for they were the closest of families, unusual for people of that station in life—' Here she stumbled over her words and coloured a little, realising her audience. 'Well, anyway. She crumpled up. The sorriest thing you could ever hope to see. And when her mother was gone, Amber left a note and then she went too. I saw the note, sitting against her bedroom mirror— I was done with nursing by then, because there were no children left to nurse and half the maids were sick so I was helping. I was putting pressed linens away and I saw it. "To the finest father I could ever have hoped for," it said on the envelope. I didn't know where to put myself, what to do. I must have stood there for ten minutes together, just saying "Think, Susan, think" to myself but unable to move. When I finally came to again, I went round the grounds, round the gardens, the park, down to the beach, to her favourite little place where she played at palaces and pirate ships and crusaders—even though it was only a little shack really—and that's where I saw him. He was looking for her too—her uncle was—and he had the letter in his hand. He came out of the shack and stood on the beach then he took a match from his pocket—I was hiding behind a tree watching him—he took a match from his pocket and he lit that letter on fire and dropped it on the sand.'

She stopped, her eyes straining at the effort of dragging the memory up and into the room for us. Inspector Hutchinson delved into an inside pocket and drew out a slim flask. He offered it to Nurse Currie but she only frowned at him, smoothed her uniform skirt over her knees and carried on.

'I thought maybe he had read it and had thought it best his brother never saw what she'd written

353

there. I just waited, scared to move in case he saw me, waited for him to leave the beach first, but then what did he do? He ran into the sea, clothes, boots and all, in he went. I was just going to run out and go after him, try to call to him, tell him not to do it, when he turned and came out on his own. Then off he went, up to the house, and that night they told the staff. Told all of us. Amber had drowned. Amber was gone and even her uncle hadn't managed to save her.'

She could not have asked for a more rapt audience than the three of us; we sat like stone, each of us thinking.

'I didn't know what to do,' Nurse Currie said. 'If her letter had told her poor daddy that she was running off and leaving him, then her uncle did a kind thing, didn't he? But would it be better for His Lordship to have hope and a reason to search for her?'

'But why are you so sure she ran off?' I said. 'Why don't you believe she really did jump into the sea? A note can just as easily mean suicide as it can a runaway and you say yourself you didn't read it.'

Nurse Currie nodded. 'But she just wouldn't, madam, you'd have to have known her. She was as lively as ten monkeys; she'd have rallied again and been back to all her daft ways. Joan of Arc with her sword, Marie Antoinette in her tower, Empress Anastasia hiding in the palace till the murdering rascals were gone. That was her favourite game of all.'

'Anastasia!' said the inspector, sitting back so suddenly that the word was forced out of him in a rush.

'See, that's how I knew she'd not kill herself just because her mother and all the little ones were gone. She had played that game with me, in the very sickroom, if you believe it. She told me that Anastasia was strong and she had fought for her life and not lain down and died with the others. "That's the kind of girl I want to be, Nurse Susan," she said to me. "I'm going to have adventures and be thrilling and people will clap and cheer when they see me." How could that girl have thrown herself into the sea?'

'But how did she get away?' said Alec. 'It's miles from Cullen to anywhere.'

Nurse Currie was going to answer, but I got in before her.

'She took her pony,' I said.

17

'How to convince the boss, though?' said Inspector Hutchinson. We had been silent for the first few miles of the road home, each turning the fantastical idea this way and that, viewing it from all angles.

'Could he doubt it?' Alec cried. 'You said yourself that Laurie had the opportunity and a history already—even if Mrs Wilson isn't much of a witness and I agree with you there—but now he has a motive too.'

I was at the wheel and was concentrating hard on the patch of yellow light in front of us on the black road—driving this after my little Cowley felt like steering a cargo ship—so I left the inspector to argue.

'It's all pretty footery though, sir,' he said. 'A girl's nonsense. A note that's gone. She *might* have recognised him. He *might* have gone round the back when he slipped out. Nothing to bang your fist on. We need more.'

'Well, all I can say is that your superintendent must be a man of very little imagination,' said Alec.

'If as much as that,' the inspector said.

We had entered a straight stretch and I relaxed a little, flexing my fingers, for I had been gripping the wheel so tightly that my gloves were squeaking.

'I've thought of something,' I said. 'Robin could have played the tricks. Was it after he first visited the circus that all the nonsense with the rope and swing came out or before? And he said he was going back down after dinner, Alec, didn't he? He could have done it then.'

'The rope and swing, perhaps,' said Alec. 'But what about the flour and balloons? No one who didn't know what he was doing would think of that.'

'And would he want to alert them with a lot of daft mischief?' said the inspector. 'Put them on their guard for more trouble to come?'

'I only thought it was something solid for the superintendent,' I said. 'What else would convince him?'

'A confession,' said the inspector. 'A confession is what he likes best, and not just him neither. A jury would have a rum old time with the Anastasia story and the uncle running into the sea. They like a bit of colour in the Sunday papers, but give them their due, you get fifteen men in a jury room and

356

they turn as cautious as a bunch of old biddies about any kind of fancy nonsense.'

'Robin Laurie is about as likely to confess to it as I am,' said Alec. 'He's kept the thing about his niece quiet this long so he's hardly going to pop his head up about Anastasia when all the hounds are baying.'

'I was thinking of flushing him out,' said the inspector, 'if I can join you, sir, and put it that way. I'm not a hunting man, but isn't that the term I'm after? We send one of the hounds in and flush him.'

'Which hound?' I said.

'Nurse Currie,' said Hutchinson. 'Who else? She can write him a letter, put her address on the top as innocent as can be and then we'll stick a man on her and wait for Laurie to show up.'

'It's a lot to ask of her,' I said. 'I mean, what if he gets to her when the man you've stuck on is looking the other way? Think of what happened to Ana—or do we call her Amber now?'

'I don't know about that one,' Alec said. 'Could it really have been her? Could Lady Ambrosine Buckie really have been living in a wagon at Cooke's Circus?'

'What a to-do that would have been, eh?' said Hutchinson. 'When His Lordship finally gave up the ghost and the brother moved in for the spoils only for Amber to pop up and scoop the lot! And after seven years too.'

I was distracted once more by trying to thread the long bonnet of Alec's motor car along the twists of the black, winding lane but something in what they said tugged at me, or not even as much as that, but something touched me the way a

357

cobweb will fall against one's face, or the way a stray lash will lie on one's cheek, almost imperceptible, just tickling.

'So it's Susan Currie to the rescue?' Alec said.

'We've not got much choice,' Hutchinson replied. 'Unless we try to drum up a story that someone saw him at the circus, that is.'

'Hang on!' I said and I pressed my foot very firmly against the brake. Alec and the inspector both sailed forward and jerked back again. Bunty and Milly woke up and yipped in surprise. 'Sorry about that,' I said. 'But I've had an idea and I can't think, talk and drive all at once. In fact—Alec, if you feel rested can you take over again? I'm either going to kill us all or I'm going to scratch the paint and then you'll kill me. You slide along, darling, and I'll go round.'

'Right then, let's hear it,' said Alec when we were rearranged and under way once more.

'Topsy,' I announced. 'She'll say she saw him, I'm sure she will. She could have seen him from her rope if she'd looked. Besides, we think Robin Laurie might have been the one who tampered with her props—I do, anyway. We can ask Topsy to send a blackmail letter, pure and simple, asking him to a definite rendezvous. Then ten burly policemen can jump out and grab him when he comes.'

'But as you said before,' said Alec, 'it's a lot to ask. We're asking her to face a man who killed a girl just like her.'

I smiled at him.

'That little monkey? Tumbling Topsy Turvy?' I said. 'She'll leap at the chance.'

Topsy, as I suspected, would cheerfully have asked Robin Laurie to meet her in a dark alley the very next night and set upon him with her own two bare little hands, and when the story spread around the circus she could have amassed a very healthy gang of helpers. For the ten burly policemen, however, even the four burly policemen that Hutchinson decided in the end would be plenty, the fabled 'super' had to be persuaded and so, after a week of organising, it was not until New Year's Eve that we all gathered at the winter ground once more.

I was thrilled and petrified in equal measure to be there, as well as bursting with pride at my welcome, for the circus folk had hailed me like a conquering hero when I first returned and had continued so to hail me every time during that suspenseful week that I came back again to view the progress of what Alec called (sounding like a gangster) our sting.

Topsy had sent to Robin Laurie's town address a letter which modesty prevents me from describing as a masterpiece of subtle menace since I was the chief architect in its composition. It simply invited him to a meeting in the performing tent at ten o'clock on the evening of the 31st to discuss a matter of mutual interest and then went on to say that Topsy would be rehearsing and Robin should feel free to enter either way since she had a clear view of both the front and the back doors from her position.

Two policemen were in props boxes just inside the ring doors and the other two were wedged under second row seats, lying stretched out, quite invisible in the dim lighting. I was to be safely tucked away from all the action behind one of the canvas wallings in the backstage with Alec and the inspector, and although Lally Wolf and Zoya Prebrezhensky were in their wagons with their little ones, doors locked and lamps snuffed, it was, I suppose, inevitable that the rest of them, Bill Wolf, Charlie, Ma and Pa, Tiny, Andrew and Kolya, were all there behind the wallings too, stock still but seething with a pent-up anger that we could feel thrumming through the ground under our feet as we waited there. Only Topsy was moving, swinging, spinning, coiling and climbing, her toes pointed and her hands wafting like petals. One could just make out the pale ovals all around as everyone looked up at her.

I could not tell what time it was there in the dark, though I fingered the face of my wristwatch, and it felt as though we had been standing still for hours when we heard the distant sound of a motor-car engine stopping far off in the trees. Then came another long wait. I imagined Robin Laurie creeping up to the edge of the clearing and standing there, hugging one of the pine trees, watching, watching. Would the very quietness warn him? Would he sense the trap and steal away again?

Even as I thought it, I heard the sound of a wagon door opening and boots descending the stairs. Tiny threw himself on to the grass and lifted the bottom of the canvas, peering out under it.

'It's Zoya,' he breathed.

After a minute came the sound of soft knocking and Zoya's voice.

'Is me, Lally,' she called. 'I come for cocoa. So

lonely tonight with them all go drinking.'

'Oh, what a brave girl!' I whispered to Alec. 'She must have seen him hesitating.'

'That's what comes of a Scotch rum-coll,' said Lally, and the ten generations of showmen were there in her voice, for she must be terrified and yet she spoke with a chuckle. 'Flaming Hogmanay!' she said. 'You'll get used to it, Zoya dear.' Then the wagon door closed on them and we were back to silence.

Only a moment of it, though. I flinched and felt Alec jump too when Topsy's voice suddenly sounded.

'I thought you'd come,' she said. Looking up we saw her gripping the rope with her legs and gazing downwards, smiling, her arms folded. 'Sure it's going to be a happy new year for me this year, isn't it?'

'You little vixen,' came Robin Laurie's voice. 'You filthy little sneak,' and the rope started to jolt and jerk around.

'He's trying to shake her off it,' I breathed to Alec.

'I saw everything, you know,' said Topsy, her voice as strong as ever although it was strained from the effort of holding on to the juddering rope. 'You're not going to—'

'Enough,' the inspector whispered beside me and I saw a faint gleam as he put his whistle to his lips and blew.

Then came chaos, shouts and curses, rushing feet and the sudden deafening crack of a pistol shot. I was knocked over by someone racing past me and I stayed down with my arms around my head, shaking. I could not get my trembling legs to lift me up again. There was the sound of bodies crashing together, slamming against the ground, and a shout of pain. My eyes were squeezed shut and the shout echoed on and on.

'We've got him,' said the inspector's voice eventually. 'We have him. Out you come, madam, sir.' Slowly, I lowered my arms and sat up. The circus folk were gone and only Alec and I remained in the backstage passageway. Only he and I had cowered here after the shot. So Alec was blushing to the tips of his ears when we emerged into the ring and saw them all. The policemen were standing ranged around the inspector, slightly kicking at the sawdust for something to do, and in the middle of the ring Robin Laurie lay, trussed in a rope like a swaddled infant, with one of Bill Wolf's boots planted on his middle and one of Andrew Merryman's long feet resting rather hard against his neck. Pa and Charlie held the ends of the rope and Ma, I was astonished to see, held a pistol. Only Tiny and Topsy seemed unaware of Robin; they sat with arms about one another on the floor of the ring, Tiny bawling like a bull calf and Topsy covering his face with kisses.

'All right, lads,' said the inspector, 'let him up and let us get the handcuffs on him. If you please, Mrs Cooke.' While Pa and Charlie unwound the rope, Ma cocked the pistol and aimed it at Robin Laurie's head.

'And don't you think I wun't there,' she said.

'Rather unorthodox, Inspector,' said Robin Laurie. 'I'm not sure what the Chief Constable will think of you treating me this way.'

'What way's that, sir?' said Hutchinson, opening his hangdog eyes very wide. One of the constables

'Mind you,' said Hugh, 'they're lucky to get her off at all, never mind to a title, and . . . I don't mean to be crude but . . . at least he's sure of the heir because she's already proved she has no trouble in that department.'

'I should hate to hear you when you do mean to be crude then.'

Hugh frowned. 'Why's he writing to tell you?'

'He's not. He mentioned it in passing in the covering letter he sent with my fee.' I picked up the banker's cheque and waved it tantalisingly in front of Hugh. He tried to look as though he were uninterested in reading the figures written upon it. 'I feel rather guilty accepting it, but he won't brook a refusal, he assures me. I shall send your congratulations, shall I, when I write to say thanks? Perhaps we can stop in on our way to the Brodies at Easter?'

'We certainly will not,' said Hugh. 'I'd like a line drawn under the whole affair if you don't mind, Dandy. And I haven't decided about Easter at Cairnbulg yet.'

'The boys will be pleased to hear that,' I said. 'It's a boring house for children and we'll need to pull out quite a few stops to live up to their last trip home.' This was enough to put Hugh back behind his newspaper again. I opened another letter and began to read.

'Hah!' said Hugh, after a while. 'Benachally is up for sale. Hah!'

'Really? They've really gone?'

'Fella like that trying to run an estate!' said Hugh. 'With his draper's daughter playing lady of the manor. I'm not surprised he didn't stick it out.'

'Her father was a don, not a draper,' I said.

'Perhaps that's where his daughter got all the advanced ideas from,' said Hugh. 'She turned out to be a bad egg in the end, didn't she, your friend?'

Poor Ina. Poor silly, spoiled Ina. It made me shiver whenever I thought of her now.

'Well, let's just hope for someone decent next time,' said Hugh. 'Miles of common boundary, you know, and it's most inconvenient when the owner is a man one cannot meet on any terms. I do not have your taste for unusual company.' He looked quite sickened as he said this. 'People like ourselves are perfectly sufficient for me.'

I nodded in agreement and waved the letter I was reading, which was from a person just like ourselves. Hugh gave me an approving look, almost a smile. He would not have done if he had known any more.

'Ma and Pa left for Chicago a week ago,' Andrew Merryman had written. 'But they left us the liberty horses and Lally Wolf is doing a grand job with them and has got little Tommy up on Harlequin too. (Thank you for sending him home in such good heart, Dandy. He was so bonny I wonder if all our horses should have a holiday every so often. If you decide to take up off-season livery in any organised way, do let me know!) Zoya and Kolya finally decided that they *would* stay, for which we are all very thankful, and Charlie, to my great surprise, has made enormous concessions to soothe their wounded pride. I know it must seem odd that we are all banded together under Charlie's leadership after what happened and even he would say it was not his finest hour, but Cooke's Circus has been Cooke's Circus since 1750 and so it's only fitting that there should be a Tam Cooke

376

at the helm. (He's Thos on the posters, but he'll always be Charlie at home.) Tiny and I have worked up some good stuff now that we're a double act and not a trio any more and Charlie is very happy just to manage the animals. Yes—animals! It's a considerable financial gamble, but we shall see. The tigers arrived on Tuesday and are magnificent, but Zoya and Lally are in constant hysterics trying to keep the children away from them. I can't see it myself, but Tiny reckons Akilina might have a feeling for them. Until she is big enough to see over their backs, however, we pick up a cat man—one of the Codonas and a distant relation, of course—in Glasgow on our way south to start the season. The elephants are coming into Glasgow too, up the Clyde by boat, and Charlie thinks we shall gather some good "press" when we go to collect them (perhaps even be filmed for the newsreel). Tiny and Topsy's wedding is to be in Glasgow too. They did not want to wait, but neither did they want to be married anywhere near the place where we have all been so very far from happy. It would have been an ill omen for the start of their life together. Besides, boatloads of Turvys are coming over the sea from Dublin to be there. (Tiny has reminded me several times now that Topsy has four sisters. Again, we shall see. I am determined to move at a more stately pace if anything of that nature ever befalls me again.) It is to be a quiet wedding, Turvys excepted, but you would be welcomed with open arms if you were to come. I feel I should give you fair warning that you are unlikely to meet any of us again if you wait for us at home, for no one at Cooke's Circus wants ever to get within a hundred miles of that winter ground again. You might feel the same, but if you could face it we should all like to think of there being flowers on her grave. The mason has finished the stone and erected it so you will have no trouble finding the spot. He was not best pleased with the inscription—a very conventional man—but she had no other name that we could ever discover and besides, I think it's the truth about her. It's who she was. We all have to decide in the end. So the stone reads "Anastasia, of the circus". If you can bring yourself to visit her we will all be very grateful to you. Yours sincerely, Andrew Merryman (of the circus).'

Poor Benachally, I thought. How everyone hates it. And none of what happened there was the fault of the castle or the park and hills.

'Why don't we buy it?' I said. Hugh looked up. His lip curled in preparation for a long rant about our penury, the government and the state of the nation, empire and world, but my expression stopped him. His eyes flicked to the cheque, lying by my bread plate, and then back to my face again. I gave him a beatific smile.

'Buy it and add it on?' he said.

'Buy it and keep it separate,' I corrected. 'For Teddy. Two brothers with only one inheritance is rather brutal on both in the end.'

'And how would we explain being able to?' he said. 'People will wonder. Even the boys will wonder.'

'Tell the truth,' I answered. 'I am a detective, Hugh, quite a successful one.'

'You,' said Hugh in a voice I had never heard before, 'are a wife and mother.'

I took time considering my reply to this.

'I am,' I agreed at last. 'I am Mrs Hugh Gilver and I never forget it. But I am Dandy Gilver, Detective, too.'

Hugh took even longer than I had to answer.

'It could be worse, I suppose,' he said in the end.

'But it's not worse,' I told him. 'Wife, mother and detective, nothing more. *Nothing* more.' I meant it as I spoke, Andrew Merryman's words still clear in my mind. In the end, we all have to decide who we are.

An Invitation to Gilverton

If you have enjoyed spending this time at the winter ground, why not visit Dandy at home at www.dandygilver.co.uk?

There you will find much more of her world than can be fitted into the books: illustrations and descriptions of the real places and people behind some of the make-believe; floor plans and estate maps of Gilverton; biographies of the characters; postcards from old friends and details of past cases.

Open the green baize door to hear Mr Pallister's thoughts on the smooth running of a household, look at Grant's selection of seasonal modes and read Mrs Tilling's recipes. (If there is too much suet in her Christmas menu perhaps Tiny Truman's all-day onion stew might tempt you.)

There is a Visitors' Book open on the hall table at all times, and you are warmly invited to leave comments, corrections, complaints, compliments and questions for any member of the household, or its creator. You can also email directly to cmcpherson@homecall.co.uk. It would be a pleasure to hear from you.

Catriona McPherson, 2006